He opened her eyes
to passion.
She opened his heart
to love....

W9-BSG-687

continued . . .

Blue Skies

Blue Skies

❀

Catherine Anderson

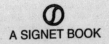

A SIGNET BOOK

SIGNET
Published by New American Library, a division of
Penguin Group (USA) Inc., 375 Hudson Street,
New York, New York 10014, U.S.A.
Penguin Books Ltd, 80 Strand,
London WC2R 0RL, England
Penguin Books Australia Ltd, 250 Camberwell Road,
Camberwell, Victoria 3124, Australia
Penguin Books Canada Ltd, 10 Alcorn Avenue,
Toronto, Ontario, Canada M4V 3B2
Penguin Books (N.Z.) Ltd, Cnr Rosedale and Airborne Roads,
Albany, Auckland 1310, New Zealand

Penguin Books Ltd, Registered Offices:
80 Strand, London WC2R 0RL, England

First published by Signet, an imprint of New American Library,
a division of Penguin Group (USA) Inc.

First Printing, January 2004
10 9 8 7 6 5 4 3 2 1

This book is dedicated to a wonderful young woman, Melissa J. Lopez, who not only inspired me to write this story but also devoted her time to interviews and proofreading so I got all the facts correct. I'd also like to thank her physician, William E. Whitson, for the times when he provided information behind the scenes. I'd also like to take this opportunity to thank the wonderful people at NAL, especially my editor, Ellen Edwards, for so enthusiastically supporting me in this endeavor. Their enthusiasm and unfailing belief in this story gave me the confidence I needed to write it.

Chapter One

A drumroll reverberated through the bar, punctuating the end of the last band number. The lead country singer hooted into the microphone, the sound of his voice seeming to bounce off the walls. After tipping his Stetson to a pretty lady in red on the dance floor, he smiled and lightly strummed his guitar, leading into the next song, "She'll Leave You with a Smile." The music throbbed in the air, bearing testimony to the state-of-the-art acoustics that made Chaps the most popular country-and-western nightclub in Crystal Falls, Oregon.

Tapping the toe of his boot in time to the base guitar, Hank Coulter balanced a quarter on his thumb, took careful aim at the empty beer mug at the center of the table, and let fly. Flashing in the spiraling lights, the coin flipped end over end in a high arc, struck the edge of the glass, and bounced away. The other men sitting with Hank laughed, and someone shoved a full mug of beer toward him.

"Chug it down, partner!"

Everyone at the table took up the chant, yelling, "Chug! Chug! Chug!"

Determined to shake off his bad mood, the result of a quarrel that afternoon with his older brother Jake,

Hank laughed and started to drink. The rule of the game was to consume the beer without coming up for a breath. Foam touched his nose as he gulped. When he slapped the empty mug back down on the table, his buddies cheered. Hank wiped his mouth with his shirtsleeve. Eric Stone, seated to his left, refilled the mug.

"Go again," he ordered, yelling to be heard over the loud music. "Pray for better aim this time, partner, or you'll be drunk on your ass before pumpkin hour. What's that make now, three?"

"Five," Hank corrected. "And getting drunk won't cut it. I've got plans for later tonight."

"Don't we all?" Eric nudged back his tan Stetson to survey the bar, his brown eyes dancing as he took inventory of the babes. "I've got dibs on that cute little brunette over there."

Hank had noticed the brunette and toyed with the thought of hitting on her later. She had a saucy smile and a way of swinging her hips that warmed a man's blood. "Go for it, son." Hank winked. "Maybe you'll get lucky."

Accepting the coin that Pete Witherspoon slid toward him, Hank took aim at the glass again. For the life of him, he couldn't recall how he'd gotten talked into tossing quarters. He came to Chaps on weekend nights to have a few laughs, toss back a few beers, and hopefully end the evening with an accommodating female. Getting drunk on his ass at so early an hour was not part of his plan, but now that the competition had commenced, he couldn't very well beg off.

Once again, the quarter missed its mark, this time ricocheting off the glass and rolling onto the dance floor. Joe Michaels guffawed and dug in his pocket for more change while Hank swilled the contents of his mug. With six sixteen-ounce beers under his belt, he was definitely starting to feel the effects of the alcohol.

Seated at a nearby table, Carly Adams watched the cowboy. His hair was the same rich color of the fudge her friend Bess had made the other night. As he leaned his head back to swallow, his throat worked, and his larynx bobbed. Watching the play of muscle drove home to Carly how differently men were made than women. Her own throat felt soft when she touched it, no muscles in evidence unless she strained to tighten them.

Carly had no idea how old he might be. In his late twenties or possibly older. Accurately judging someone's age took practice, and having had her sight restored only a week ago, she'd had precious little opportunity to hone that skill. No matter. Finally, at long last, she could actually *look* at a guy. Little wonder her friends in high school had spent so much time whispering and giggling about boys. Everywhere Carly was soft and full, he was hard and flat, and every place she was smooth, he had interesting bulges.

Carly wasn't sure why she found this particular man so fascinating. Unlike the other cowboys in the bar, most of whom were decked out in flashy, western-style clothing, he wore a plain, wash-worn shirt, a pair of old jeans, and sturdy, no-nonsense boots with badly scuffed toes. Maybe he stood out in the crowd because he wore no hat—or maybe he was just so handsome that he drew the female eye. She honestly couldn't say if he was attractive by societal standards. She only knew she found him intriguing.

Even at a distance of several feet, his deep, rumbling laughter was infectious, and he had a wonderful, lazy way of grinning that made her want to smile. Fortunately for him, the new coin changed his luck, and he got the quarter into the glass with his next toss. Looking relieved to be off the hook, he rocked back on his chair to watch as the next player took his turn.

Carly wanted to study everything about him, and she was glad of this time alone so she could do so without feeling embarrassed. Her friend Bess would tease her, she knew. *Hey, Carly, it's just a guy,* she would say. *Don't stare. People will think something's wrong with you.* News flash. It was difficult for Carly *not* to stare when she was seeing so many things for the first time. Bess tried to understand, but no one who'd been sighted since birth could really grasp what it was like to suddenly have the lights come on after twenty-eight years.

Carly decided that she especially liked the way the man's shoulders and chest filled out his shirt. Every time he moved, muscles rippled and bunched under the cloth. She even liked the way he held himself, his dark head cocked to one side, his attention fixed on the game. His posture was relaxed, his arms elbowed out, his thumbs tucked over a wide leather belt that rode low at his narrow hips. Each time his chair tipped back, a large silver belt buckle flashed at his waist.

He was gorgeous, she decided. In her opinion, anyway, and that was all that counted. A lovely tingling sensation spread through her as she watched him.

A woman with bright red hair approached his table. Her large green eyes were heavily lined with makeup. When she spoke, the cowboy glanced up, then grinned and pushed to his feet. Before escorting the woman onto the dance floor, he grabbed a dark-colored Stetson from the table and settled it on his head.

Carly couldn't take her eyes off him as he guided the redhead to the center of the dance floor. At a distance, she had trouble keeping him in focus. One moment, she could make out his features, the next he was a blur. When the music started, the pair began dancing, their feet executing the steps so quickly that Carly couldn't follow them. The cowboy swung the woman with an easy strength and polished precision, shifting his hold on her hand so she could duck under his arm. Occasionally, the redhead sidled away to cut circles around him, her boots tapping out a fast tattoo, her denim-sheathed hips and legs moving with seductive grace, her long hair cascading down her back.

A sharp pang of envy moved through Carly. It would take months of practice before she mastered the art of putting on eye makeup after her eyes healed, and she'd probably never get the hang of styling her curly blond hair. Tonight, Bess had helped her get ready, dispensing with her usual ponytail and lending her an outfit to wear, but Carly despaired that she'd ever be able to manage as nicely by herself.

The dance number suddenly ended. The cessation of noise jerked Carly back to the moment. The cowboy caught the redhead in the circle of his arm to lead her off the floor. At the edge of the jostling crowd of dancers, a short lady with dark hair clasped his arm and went up on her tiptoes to whisper something in his ear. He smiled, bent to kiss the redhead's cheek, and returned to the center of the floor with the other woman.

The man's popularity with the ladies answered one of Carly's questions: he must be very good-looking.

While waiting for the next number to begin, he chatted with his new partner, listening intently when she spoke, smiling or laughing when she said something amusing.

Suddenly, as though he sensed Carly watching him, he glanced up. Carly was so embarrassed to be caught staring that she wanted to die. Her face went prickly and hot. *Oh, God.* She anxiously scanned the dancers, looking for her friend, Bess, who had been line dancing for almost an hour. It was impossible to find her in the blurry throng of bodies.

Carly pushed to her feet and cut through the tables to go to the ladies' room. En route, she could have sworn she felt the cowboy's eyes boring a hole into her back. She cringed and hastened her pace, her one thought being to escape for a few minutes. Maybe by the time she returned to her table, he would have forgotten all about her.

When it came to attractive women, Hank had a memory like an elephant. After returning to his table, he kept one eye on the back wall of the bar, watching for a glint of golden hair. When the blonde emerged from the restroom, he spotted her immediately. And he wasn't disappointed. She was every bit as stunning as he'd judged her to be at first glance.

Trying not to be obvious, he observed her as she slowly worked her way through the crowd. He knew most of the women who frequented Chaps on weekend nights. He'd never seen this one. Long, curly hair framed her angelic face with wispy, rippling curtains of gold. He'd never seen more delicately molded features or bigger blue eyes. She also had a soft, lower lip that pouted and begged to be kissed. Her pink western blouse hugged small but perfectly shaped breasts and accentuated her slender waist. New jeans showcased a world-class ass and shapely legs that seemed to stretch forever.

Hank nudged Eric with his elbow, indicating the blonde with a slight nod of his head. "You know her?"

Eric gave the woman a long, careful study. "Not yet."

Hank laughed and pushed back his chair. "Forget it, partner. I saw her first."

"You always get first crack at the prime cuts," he complained.

"Hey, you've got dibs on the brunette, remember?"

"Maybe I just changed my mind."

"Bring in the new day alone then," Hank shot back. "She's taken."

Carly stiffened when she saw the dark-haired cowboy walking toward her. Heart pounding, she glanced quickly away, fixing her gaze on her glass of beer, which she'd been nursing all evening. He would move right past her, she assured herself. He probably knew someone at one of the tables behind her.

From the corner of her eye, she saw him stop beside her chair. At a distance, he hadn't seemed quite so tall. She looked up—and found herself staring into the most beautiful eyes imaginable. They were a deep, clear color that put her in mind of a picture she'd seen a few days ago of a tropical lagoon.

His wide, firm mouth tipped into a grin that deepened the creases in his lean cheeks and flashed strong, white teeth. The burnished cast of his skin emphasized his chiseled features. As straight and sharp as a knife blade, his nose jutted from between thick, dark eyebrows.

"Hi," he said.

Only that, just one simple word. *Hi*. But the deep timbre of his voice made Carly's pulse grow erratic. "Hi," she managed to reply.

A twinkle warmed his eyes. "May I have this dance?" he asked, extending an upturned palm to her.

Carly couldn't think what to say. Finally her brain clicked into gear. "Oh, no—I can't. Really. I'm sorry."

He hooked his thumbs over his belt and glanced over his shoulder. "You here with someone?"

"A friend. She's line dancing."

The corners of his mouth twitched. "Girlfriends don't count. I meant a guy."

"Oh." Carly felt stupid. "I, um—no, I'm not with a guy."

He extended his hand to her again. "Well, then? Come polish my belt buckle for a while."

Carly dropped her gaze to the silver oval at his waist. "Pardon me?"

He chuckled, turned a chair out from the table, and straddled it to sit down. Nudging back his hat, he gave her a slow once-over, ending with a long look at her white running shoes. "Is this, by any chance, your first time at a country-western bar?"

"Yes." Carly decided he was a little drunk. Considering the quantity of beer she'd seen him consume, she supposed that was to be expected. "My friend Bess loves to line dance. I came along to watch."

"That explains the language barrier, I guess. Sort of like visiting a foreign country, isn't it?"

Carly nodded. "It's interesting. I've always been told that men are supposed to remove their hats inside a building. Here, everyone wears them."

He feigned an expression of mock horror. "Take off our hats? Bite your tongue. Cowboys can't dance without their Stetsons. They'd feel half dressed and lose their balance. Most of us only take them off when we sleep, and even then, we hang them on the bedpost, in case of emergency."

Carly laughed. She liked this man, she decided. He wasn't afraid to poke fun at himself.

"When a cowboy asks you to polish his belt buckle, it's just another way of asking you to dance," he explained. "Same goes if he invites you to rub bellies with him for a while."

Carly's cheeks went warm. "I see."

He arched a dark eyebrow. "So, whad'ya say?"

"I can't." She threw a panicked glance at the dancers. All her life, she had prided herself on never being afraid to try new things, but she wasn't ready for the Texas two-step. So soon after surgery, walking on even ground was challenging enough. "I don't know how. It looks complicated, and I was born with two left feet."

"Country-western dancing isn't as complicated as it looks." He lifted his hands, the gesture implying that her lack of experience wasn't a stumbling block. "Not to worry. I know enough about boot scootin' for both of us."

Before Carly could guess what he meant to do, he grasped her wrist, swung off the chair, and drew her to her feet. Hooking an arm around her waist, he steered her through the dancers to the center of the floor. When he turned her to face him, he winked and grinned. "Don't be nervous. Everyone here had to learn how at some point. It's really not all that different from regular dancing."

Carly had never danced in her life, regular or otherwise. People were bouncing around everywhere she looked, ladies twirling under the arms of their partners and executing fancy footwork. Her body broke out in a clammy sweat.

"I really, *really* can't do this."

He took her right hand and slipped his other arm around her waist. "Sure you can. Stop watching everyone else and concentrate on me." He smiled when she looked up at him. "There's a girl." He started to move, a slow, swaying motion that wasn't difficult to follow. "We'll keep it simple."

"Simple's good," she agreed breathlessly.

He ran his gaze slowly over her face. "Damn, you're beautiful. I suppose you hear that from men all the time."

Carly stared up at him, feeling as if she'd somehow fallen asleep and slipped into a lovely dream. He thought she was beautiful? Even if he was lying, she wanted to believe him—just for this little while.

He swung her in a wide arc, and she stepped on his boot. "Oh, I'm *sorry*! Did I hurt your toes?"

He laughed and tightened his arm around her waist. "Don't worry about it, darlin'. I walk on 'em all the time. Let's try it again, the other direction this time." He dipped to the left, pressing his thigh against her right leg to make her step back. "There, you see? Easy as pie."

To Carly's delight, it actually was easy. By following his lead, she was spared the difficulty of navigating on her own.

He trailed his gaze over her face again. "Where have you been hiding all my life? When I spotted you a while ago, my heart damned near stopped beating. You looked like an angel, sitting there."

An angel? Carly knew better, but it was a lovely compliment, anyway. "I just moved to the area. I'll be starting grad school here in Crystal Falls this September."

"Ah. That explains why I haven't seen you before. Where you from?"

"Portland."

"Uh-oh, a city gal. No wonder we speak a different language. Right turn," he inserted, cuing her with his body before executing the swing. Then, "You've got the most gorgeous blue eyes I've ever seen. I swear, they were shining at me like beacons from clear across the room. Tinted contacts, right? No eyes that blue can be natural."

While pursuing her bachelor degree, Carly had heard men in college campus bars say things like this to her friends. Pick-up lines, nothing more. He was hitting on her. And, *oh, God,* it felt wonderful. All her adult life, she'd sat on the sidelines, listening to life happening all around her and wishing that someone would notice *her.* Now, at long last, someone finally had. Even better, he was handsome and charming. She felt like a princess in one of the fairy tales her mother had read to her years ago.

"Nope, no contacts," she assured him with a tinkling laugh. She fluttered her lashes. "These are the real McCoy."

"You're kidding. Damn. Is this my lucky night, or what? You're the most beautiful woman in the place."

Carly knew he was only telling her what he thought she wanted to hear. And he was right. It *was* what she wanted to hear. *My turn.* A reckless, dizzying excitement coursed through her. Just this once, she wouldn't analyze or question or worry about getting hurt. She had waited a lifetime for this moment, and she meant to enjoy every delicious millisecond.

"My name's Hank Coulter," he told her, his voice deep and raspy, yet oddly soft, like the sound of raw silk rubbed against the grain.

"Carly Adams."

He bent his head toward hers. "Come again?" After she repeated her name, he said, "Glad to meet you, Charlie. Boy, howdy, am I ever glad."

"Carly," she corrected.

He nodded and smiled. Carly let it go at that. When the song ended, he would escort her back to her table, and she'd probably never see him again.

He moved with an impressive grace for so large a man, lean muscle and bone working in a harmony of motion as he guided her through the steps, the tendons in his thighs bunching under the faded denim of his jeans, his lean hips shifting in time to the music. Before Carly knew quite how it happened, he had her twirling away from him, then shuffling back to spin on her toes under his arm.

"Hoo-yah!" he said with a laugh after she executed a perfect swing step. He winked, hooked an arm around her waist, and drew her snuggly against his hard thigh to circle at a dizzying speed in a two-step shuffle. "Cut a rug, darlin'."

The press of his leg against the apex of her own made Carly's heart leap, and her whole body felt as if it were humming. It was the strangest thing. Every part of her tingled, inside and out. When he suddenly moved away, sliding his big hand down her arm to grab her hand, he tipped his hat to her. Then he shuffled back, his intense blue eyes holding hers, his dark, chiseled features oddly taut.

Sensory overload. All the instincts Carly had honed to sharpness as a blind person were still in fine working order, making her aware of him in every pore of her skin, and her eyes added visual delights she'd never before experienced. Having a man make love to her with his eyes. Seeing his broad shoulders dip toward her. Feeling the firm yet gentle grip of his big hands. His scent—a blend of musky maleness, woodsy cologne, leather, and sun-dried cotton—working on her olfactory nerves like an intoxicant.

Much too soon to suit Carly, the music faded. She drew away from his embrace and smiled. "Thank you for asking me to dance. It was fun, after all."

He caught her hand, his fingers so long they curled over her wrist bone, his palm warm and slightly rough, yet another indication that the cowboy attire wasn't just for looks. At her questioning expression, he grinned and tightened his grip. "Don't go. Please. Spend the evening with me."

Before Carly could reply, the band broke into "Be My Baby Tonight." Hank threw back his dark head and laughed. "Is that perfect timing, or what?" He caught her in his arms again and started singing along. By the time he reached the "could ya, would ya, ain't-cha" part of the song and asked if she'd be his baby tonight, Carly was laughing too hard to feel self-conscious. He swung her in a wide arc that set her head to spinning. "Please, darlin', don't say no," he murmured near her ear. "You'll break my heart."

Carly leaned back to look up at him. She felt like a candle sitting on a sunny windowsill, her body warm and suddenly boneless. She knew she should end this before she waded in too deep. But somehow, knowing that and doing it were two different things. Would she ever get this chance again?

"I'm here with a friend," she reluctantly reminded him.

"Ditch her."

"I can't do that."

He wrapped both arms around her, pressed his face against her hair, and fell into a simple two-step. "Maybe she'll hook up with somebody and ditch you," he said with a hopeful note lacing his deep voice.

Carly knew Bess would never do that. "Maybe," she settled for saying.

"Meanwhile, stay with me," he urged softly.

Carly nodded her assent. She felt his lips curve in a smile. When the song ended, he led her from the floor. At the edge of the crowd, the redhead he'd danced with earlier stepped in front of them to ask Hank to dance.

Carly tried to pull her hand free. "I don't mind, Hank." It was easy to sound convincing. She'd been taking a second seat to other women all her life. "Really, I don't. Go and have fun."

He tightened his grip on her fingers. "Sorry," he told the redhead with an apologetic smile. "I'm bushed. We're going to sit this one out."

The woman shrugged and moved on. Carly glanced after her. "Really, Hank, I wouldn't mind. She's a good dancer, and I'm—well, not."

"You're fabulous, and there's no way I'm leaving you. All my buddies would be after you like bees for honey."

He fell into a walk, leading her to a back corner.

The blue haze of cigarette smoke that hung over the table burned her sensitive eyes, and the smell of beer was strong. "Maybe we can talk here," he said as he drew out a chair for her. "Normally, I don't mind the noise, but tonight, it's a pain in the neck. I want to know everything about you."

Carly was relieved to lower herself onto the chair and escape the smoke. He sat next to her, turning his seat so they were facing each other.

"Tell me about yourself, Charlie."

"Carly," she corrected again.

He nodded. "Gotcha. So tell me about yourself."

"There's nothing much to tell."

"Age?"

"I'll be twenty-eight in August."

"I'll turn thirty-two in December." He arched a dark eyebrow. "What are you going to grad school for?"

"I'm a teacher. I taught visually disabled elementary kids for two years. Now I want to get my master's in special education."

"No kidding?" Amusement warmed in his eyes. "I love teachers."

"You do?"

"Absolutely. They make a man do it until he gets it right."

Carly gave a startled laugh. The waitress appeared at their table just then. Hank ordered them each a beer. While they waited for their refreshments, he told Carly that he was a rancher. After their beers arrived, he explained that he was partners with his brother. They ran a few hundred head of cattle and bred and trained quarter horses for a living.

"So you're a real-life cowboy, not the dime store variety."

"Or a buckaroo. Not as romantic sounding, is it? Buckaroos work with horses, cowboys with cattle. Jake and I still run cows, so either term fits." He inclined his head at her mug. "I'm already on empty, and you've barely started." He signaled for the waitress. "You need to get busy over there."

Carly obediently took another sip of beer. He reached over to smooth away the foam mustache on her upper lip. His touch was gentle, his expression tender. "I am so glad I spotted you. Talk about a great cure for a gloomy mood."

"Why were you in a gloomy mood?"

The second round of beers came just then. He paid the barmaid and took several hearty slugs before answering the question. "I had words with my brother Jake right before I came to town. My sister's husband's brother's wife's birthday is today."

"Say that again?"

"Exactly, a shirttail relative. Maggie Kendrick's a sweetheart, but her birthday party isn't my idea of a great way to spend Friday night. Jake objects to my lifestyle. Says I'm on a one-way path to nowhere and that I'll never meet a nice woman in a bar." He lifted his mug to her and grinned. "Wrong."

Carly was flattered. "That's a lovely compliment. Thank you."

He finished off the second beer, gave her a thoughtful study, and said, "At this rate, you're never gonna get a buzz on, darlin'. How about a mixed drink?"

Carly almost declined. She was still on painkillers and the doctor had told her to have no more than two drinks. But she'd had only a few sips of beer, she reminded herself, and she was tired of always being cautious. Hank ordered them each a slammer. By the time the drinks arrived, Carly had skirted a dozen personal questions, telling Hank just enough to satisfy his curiosity. She hesitantly tasted the drink he'd ordered and asked what was in it.

"A love potion. After taking one sip, a woman falls madly in love with the first man she sees. I guess that means this is my lucky night."

Carly thought it was just the reverse, that it was her lucky night. She could scarcely believe she was sitting there with him—or that he seemed to have eyes only for her. "It's very good," she said after tasting the drink again.

He flashed another of those lazy grins that she had admired earlier. It was far more potent at close range. "Go easy, darlin'. A slammer is almost straight booze, cut with a little citrus juice. You used to the hard stuff?"

She was no teetotaler. "I'm as used to it as the next person, I guess."

"Good. My aim is to loosen you up, not knock you on your butt."

She eyed him over the rim of the glass. "Trying to ply me with liquor?"

"Damn straight."

She laughed and took another sip of the drink.

Hank tried to decide what it was about her that he found so appealing. He'd met a lot of gorgeous women in bars and never wanted any of them the way he wanted her. Maybe it was her sweet face. She had an innocent look in her eyes that he hadn't encountered in a good long while. *What an illusion.* No woman her age was still innocent, and if, by some weird chance, she were, she sure as hell wouldn't be hanging out in a place like Chaps.

Even so, there was a lack of artifice about her that he found attractive. As near as he could tell, she wore no cosmetics. Her hair fell to her shoulders in a rippling curtain of curls that made him yearn to run his hands through it.

Later. When she had a little more liquor under her belt, he'd herd her back onto the dance floor. Nothing like a cozy two-step to warm a lady up.

The seductive images that drifted through Hank's mind had him reaching for his drink. He took a hefty swallow. When he moved to put the glass back on the table, he lost his grip and almost dropped it. It occurred to him in that moment that he might be a little drunker than he thought.

"Are you okay?"

Hank dried his hand on his jeans. "Fine as a frog's hair. Just a little tipsy. But, hey, that's why we're here. Right? To have a good time."

"Right." She lifted her drink in a mock toast. "To having a good time." She took a dainty swallow. "Yum. The more I drink, the better this tastes."

Hank sat back to study her. It wasn't often he hit on a woman and actually meant it when he said she was beautiful. Usually his motto was, Whatever Works. Aside from telling a woman he loved her, he'd say almost anything to score. The gals who frequented places like Chaps normally came for the same reasons men did and understood the unspoken rules. They pretended that the tired old lines were fresh and clever—and possibly even true. It was fun, meaningless, and in the morning, no one looked back.

Hank liked it that way. He wasn't ready to get locked down. If he had been, he sure as hell wouldn't shop for a wife in a bar where all the prospects had been ridden hard and put away wet by countless other men.

"Have I told you how absolutely gorgeous you are?"

She dimpled a cheek at him. "Nope. *Gorgeous* is a word I'd remember."

"Forgive the oversight. You're gorgeous. I can't believe I'm the lucky fellow who spotted you first. Their loss, my gain."

She rolled the glass between her hands, then caught a drop of condensation with a fingertip. When she glanced back up, her eyes had a dreamy, unfocused look. "You're right. This slammer is strong."

Hank was feeling no pain himself. "Don't drink too much." He wanted to loosen her up, not make her sick. "It packs a punch." As he lifted his tumbler, he wondered if he shouldn't heed his own advice. Somehow, though, the glass reached his lips. *What the hell.* Alcohol had never affected his performance in bed. No sense in wasting perfectly good booze.

After a few more minutes of meaningless conversation—the usual prelude to sex, with both parties pretending they'd just stumbled upon the find of a lifetime—the band started a new number. It was a slow song. Hank drew Charlie up from her chair. She lost her balance and staggered into him. Clamping his hands over her shoulders, he somehow managed to catch her from falling even though he was none too steady on his feet himself. They both laughed, acknowledging without words that they'd had too much.

Curling an arm around her waist, he led her to the dance floor. When he drew her close, she melted sweetly against him. He imagined holding her like this in a horizontal position. Skin to skin, her slender limbs intertwined with his. He ran his hands lightly over her back. Then he dipped his head to nuzzle her curls and nibble below her ear. She moaned softly and made fists on his shirt, clearly as aroused as he was. *Oh, yeah*.

He glanced toward the front door and began dancing in that direction. *Sweet, beautiful Charlie*. She gave a startled squeak when they reached the exit and Hank pushed the door open. As he swirled her outside, a cool rush of May evening air enhanced the feeling of heat building between their bodies.

"My friend Bess," she murmured halfheartedly. "I can't—"

Hank cut her off with a deep, searing kiss. *Sweet Lord*. She tasted even better than he had imagined, her mouth soft and vulnerable. She met the searching thrust of his tongue with a hesitant flick of her own. Then she retreated. Hank thought he saw uncertainty reflected in her big blue eyes.

"Are you okay with this?" he asked in a voice gone husky with desire. "If it's a problem, just say so."

"No, no. I'm just—" She broke off and smiled. "I'm fine with it."

That was all Hank needed to hear. He grasped her wrists and drew up her arms to hug his neck. With a throaty sigh that inflamed his senses, she stepped onto his boots to lessen the difference in their heights and pressed her softness against him.

Hank's head swam. *Holy shit*. For a split second, he likened the feeling to touching a hot electrical wire. Then his brain blanked out, and he was riding on a current of pure need. He turned—smoothly, he thought, considering how drunk he was—to sandwich her slender body between his and the cement wall of the building. He ran his hands up from her waist to cup her breasts. Through the layers of her clothing, he felt her nipples harden to the passes of his thumbs. She jerked when he rolled the tips between his fingers.

Dimly, Hank registered her reaction, only he couldn't put his finger on what was bothering him. She felt so good. He couldn't remember the last time he'd been this turned on. His body was afire with needs he couldn't satisfy in a public parking lot, that was for damned sure.

Continuing to kiss her, he hooked an arm about her waist and hurried her across the asphalt to his new Ford pickup. When he opened the front passenger door, he came up for air long enough to say, "There's a motel two blocks away. Will you come with me?"

She cast a worried glance at the nightclub. "If Bess can't find me, she'll get worried."

Hank almost argued the point, but before he could articulate the thought, he was kissing her again, and he promptly forgot what he meant to say. He settled for opening the rear passenger door. The full-sized back seat wasn't the most romantic place to make love, but if she wouldn't go to the motel, he had no other choice. He grasped her at the waist and lifted her inside, then quickly joined her. He was kissing her again before he got the doors closed.

All his visions of holding her nude body against him went out the window. Some levels of intimacy couldn't be attained in a parking lot. Hank settled for touching her through her clothing. She sobbed into his mouth, heightening his own arousal. When they were both so hot and hungry that he could hold off no longer, he unsnapped her jeans and lowered the zipper. Her skin felt like sun-warmed velvet.

"Wh-what are you doing?" she asked in a tremulous voice.

Hank thought she was worried about protection. "Hold tight."

He angled his body over the front seat, fumbling for the glove box where he kept a carton of prophylactics. When he finally got the compartment opened and found the damned box, his fingers caught on the uplifted lid, and the entire container fell to the front floorboard. Hank cursed under his breath. He almost climbed over the seat to retrieve a foil packet. Only somehow, between thinking and doing, he found himself kissing Charlie again.

He felt like a randy teenager—long on urgent need and short on control. He'd never engaged in unsafe sex. At the back of his mind, alarm bells clanged even as he ran a hand inside her jeans to touch her moist, hot center. Then he thought, *"What can it hurt?"* Women who hung out in bars usually took the Pill. Barring an unwanted pregnancy, wherein lay the risk? She was too damned sweet to be carrying an STD, and he knew damned well that he wasn't.

She whimpered and jerked when he touched her clitoris. Honeyed wetness spilled over his fingertips. He thrust a finger inside her, and she cried out in pleasure. He pulled her jeans and panties down to her ankles, unfastened his pants, and positioned himself between her thighs. Holding himself with one hand and stabbing to find his target, he clamped her to his chest with one arm angled up her back so he could kiss the sensitive place just below her ear.

"Hank?"

"What, darlin'?" His body was knotted with arousal. He pressed his hardness against her, found the wet, welcoming center of her, and promptly lost it, semen pumping in uncontrolled spurts before he even gained entry. "Oh, *damn*. I'm sorry," he whispered raggedly when she made a soft sound of distress. "It's okay. It's all right. Just give me a second."

Hank grabbed for breath. *No problem.* Even sloppy drunk, he was always good for two rounds. He could still make it worth her time. He centered himself over her again. With one hard thrust of his hips, he plunged into her.

And she screamed.

Hank felt the fragile barrier of tissue tear. He froze, his breath coming in harsh, rasping pants. He cursed raggedly, the echo of his own words bouncing against his eardrums like a Ping-Pong ball. Lights went off inside his head like camera flashes. He blinked, trying to see her face in the dim light that filtered faintly through the window from the nightclub sign.

A *virgin?* That was his last thought. Between one breath and the next, he passed out.

Chapter Two

A damned bird chirped near Hank's ear. The sound made his head hurt. He lay there, trying to think how a bird had gotten in his bedroom and why his comfortable bed felt as lumpy as a sack of spuds. He cautiously opened his eyes. Sunlight stabbed his pupils like ice picks. He groaned and attempted to angle an arm over his face, but his shoulders were wedged into a tight space, and he couldn't move. *What the hell?*

Squinting against the brightness, he struggled to focus. At first, he had no clue where he was. Then, with mounting bewilderment, he determined that he was lying on the back floorboard of his truck, his torso sandwiched between the seats. He stared stupidly at the rear passenger window above him. The bird that had serenaded him awake was perched on the edge of the lowered glass. *Chirp-tweet, chirp-tweet.* The sounds exploded inside his head.

It felt as if blender blades were pureeing his gray matter. He rolled onto his side and rose up on one elbow. The inside of the truck slid into a sickening spin. He stared stupidly at the small gray bird, which had cocked its head to study him with beady little eyes.

"Shoo!"

Not smart. *Oh, God.* His head. Bracing an arm on the seat, he waited for the pain to pass and then pulled himself to a sitting position. Why had he slept in his truck? He dimly recalled driving to town last night, but the events of the evening grew foggy after that. He had obviously gotten drunk. When he drank too much, he usually locked his vehicle, called a cab, and slept it off at a motel.

Craning his neck to look out the window, he identified the deserted parking lot of Chaps. Slowly, in blurry disorder, the events of the previous night came back to him. He'd begun the evening by tossing quarters with his buddies and had been three sheets to the wind by ten o'clock. Shortly after that, he'd hooked up with a woman. Some blonde. Marly? No, Charlie, that was it. Big blue eyes, a face like an angel, and a tidy, curvaceous figure, showcased to best advantage in skintight Wranglers and a pink blouse. They'd danced, talked, and had a few beers. Then, in hopes of lightening the mood and loosening her up, he'd ordered them each a slammer.

What the hell had he been thinking? Slammers were Chaps's version of assisted suicide. All that beer and a stiff drink, to boot? Little wonder his head hurt. Both he and Charlie had been loop-legged when they left the bar.

Hank went still. A shivery sensation crawled up his spine. His memories of her were like scattered pieces of a jigsaw puzzle, the pictures coming to him in fragments. But he remembered one thing with harsh clarity. He'd brought her out to the truck and had sex with her on the back seat.

He dropped his gaze to the gray cushions, and in a

swirling flash, he could almost see her, lying there beneath him. There was a smear of dried blood on the light-colored leather. His already queasy stomach dropped with a sickening lurch. *Oh, God.* A virgin, she'd been a virgin.

The same feelings of shock and incredulity that he'd experienced last night coursed through him again. How many women were still virgins in their late twenties? And of that minuscule number, what percentage of them frequented places like Chaps? There had to be a mistake. Maybe she'd been having her period— and the fragile barrier he'd felt had been something other than a hymen.

Deep down, he knew better. He distinctly recalled how she'd cried out in pain. After that, he couldn't remember anything. Had he passed out? He'd been shit-faced more times than he cared to count, but he'd never lost consciousness. Only what other explanation was there?

Shit. A virgin. He hadn't tried to be gentle—hadn't realized there was a need. He twisted to sit on the seat and saw more dried blood on the fly of his boxers. With shaking hands, he zipped his jeans. Then he propped his elbows on his knees and cupped his face in his hands. What, in God's name, had he done? He couldn't remember the lady's last name and had no idea how to find her.

After staring blearily at the closed nightclub for several minutes, Hank concluded that sitting there and feeling rotten would serve no useful purpose. What did he expect, her last name to suddenly appear in large block letters on the side of the building?

Miserable, with a splitting headache, he crawled over the front seat to drive home. The sight that greeted him as he slid under the steering wheel made him mutter a curse. Foil packets littered the floor-board. He *always* wore protection. It was a hard-and-fast rule. What had he been thinking? That was the whole problem, he concluded. He'd been stupid drunk and not thinking, period.

When Hank parked his truck near the house a half hour later, his older brother Jake waved to him from the stable, a huge, rectangular metal building of forest green. Hank was in no mood for another lecture about his social life. He'd broken all the rules last night, just as Jake had warned him he eventually would. Hank wasn't about to give him an opportunity to gloat and say, "I told you so."

Hank kicked at a condom package under the brake pedal. One slip in thirty-one years wasn't such a bad average, he assured himself. Then a mocking voice at the back of his mind whispered, *Right, bucko. One slip is all it takes.*

He swung from the truck, waved to Jake, and loped toward the front steps of the two-story log house. Jake probably needed help with one of the horses and would be pissed that Hank had ignored him, but this was Hank's morning off. He needed some pills for his headache, followed by some peace and quiet. No lectures, no arguments, no judgmental scowls. Those could wait until he'd slept off this hangover.

Kid stuff littered the glossy hardwood floor of the entry hall. Hank toed a Mattel driving toy out of the way, accidentally touching the button that activated the voice mechanism. "Beep! Beep! Coming through!" blared behind him as he strode to the kitchen. Jake's wife, Molly, stood at the stove with

Hank's nephew Garrett perched on her hip. Sunlight from the flank of windows behind her glanced off her copper hair, which lay in a cap of silky curls around her head. She had a pencil thrust behind one ear, cluing Hank in to the fact that she'd been working in the downstairs' office, juggling her duties as a wife and mother with her demanding career as high-end stockbroker and investment consultant. Jake had hired a full-time housekeeper, but Molly insisted on caring for their child herself.

She turned and flashed a bright smile. "Well, well, look what the cat dragged in."

Hank winced at the sound of her voice. He walked in what he hoped was a reasonably straight line to the cupboard, popped the childproof cap from a bottle, and shook three ibuprofen onto his palm.

"You look like death warmed over," Molly observed softly.

Hank filled a glass with tap water. "G'morning to you, too."

"Your eyes are so bloodshot, I think you need a transfusion."

"Don't start."

Hank swallowed the pills and set the glass on the counter with a little more force than he intended. The sharp report made the baby jump. Garrett twisted in his mama's arms to fix big, suddenly wary blue eyes on his uncle. The next instant, his little chin started to tremble. A shriek soon followed. Hank's head felt as if it might blow off.

"Now just look!" Molly cuddled her son close and shot Hank an accusing glare. "You've frightened him."

The sound of the child's screams made Hank want

to run for cover, but he already had enough counts against him. "Hey, buddy." He rubbed a hand over Garrett's narrow back. "It's just me." He leaned around to tweak the child's nose, which resulted in a cessation of the noise and earned him a drooling grin that flashed four front teeth. "Come here, partner."

Mollified, Hank's sister-in-law relinquished the toddler. She smiled at the way her son hugged his uncle's neck.

Hank met her gaze over the top of Garrett's head. "Sorry. I didn't mean to be a grump. It's just that I have a splitting headache. You know?"

"That's what happens when you drink the well dry."

That wasn't all that could happen. A picture of Charlie flashed through Hank's mind.

Molly grabbed the glass and put it in the dishwasher. "I worry about you, Hank. It doesn't seem to me that you're making very wise choices."

"What's so wrong with a guy having a little fun?"

"Unless you want an honest answer to that question, don't ask."

Hank decided there was wisdom in that suggestion. He held the baby a moment longer, then handed him back to Molly.

"I think I'll take a walk."

"You sure you wouldn't like some breakfast? I was about to make eggs and toast. It's no trouble to fix extra."

Just the thought of food made Hank's stomach roll. "No, thanks." He brushed past mother and child to reach the back door. "Maybe later."

As he started outside, Molly called softly, "I love you, Hank. If that makes me an interfering pain in the neck, I apologize."

Hank stopped on the threshold to look back at her. Molly was one of the kindest people he'd ever met, a fact that was evidenced right then in her big brown eyes. "I love you, too, even if you are a pain in the neck."

She shrugged and smiled. "For a guy who's supposedly having so much fun, you don't laugh very often anymore."

"Observation noted. I'll work on it."

After letting himself out the back door, Hank stood for a moment on the porch. Despite the splashes of lemon-yellow sunlight that dotted the yard, the surrounding forest cast deep shadows that touched the May morning with coolness. The gusts of chill, pine-scented air soothed the pain in his temples.

He considered sitting on the steps but discarded the idea. The hired hands usually entered the house by the back door, and during the day, the foot traffic was heavy. Hank needed time to himself.

He headed toward the creek that meandered the length of the property. The ankle-high field grass licked his boots with morning dew, turning the scuffed leather uppers dark brown. An occasional grasshopper skittered from its hiding place to whir around his legs. A pungent odor rose from the soggy earth. Hank took a deep breath, the smells and sounds easing the tension from his shoulders.

He'd always gravitated to the creek when he was troubled. Upstream from the main house, there was a grassy place along the north bank. He couldn't recall the first time he'd sought privacy there. He only knew that the sound of the rushing water had always helped center him, even as a kid.

When he reached the water's edge, he sank down

on the damp, grassy bank to wallow in his misery, which was one part physical and three parts emotional, the emotional parts so tangled inside him, he couldn't separate the guilt from the regret. *Charlie.* Right at that moment, Hank would have given his right arm to turn back the clock and undo the events of the previous night. He remembered that innocent glow he'd glimpsed in Charlie's eyes and wanted to kick himself. He'd always had a knack for sizing people up. Why, the one time when it had been vitally important, had he ignored that little voice in his head?

Every warning his mother had ever issued came back to haunt him now. *Sooner or later, Hank, you'll do something you regret. You can't dance with the devil and never get burned.* Hank had always tuned his mother out, chalking off her lectures to the generation gap and too much Bible reading. Now he wished he'd paid more attention. Just a few months ago, he'd read an article about teen sex, and it had said that a large percentage of twelve-year-olds were sexually active. How in bloody hell had he managed to stumble upon a virgin in her late twenties?

For just a moment, Hank started to feel angry. Looking at it rationally, this whole mess was actually her fault, not his. She had been looking for trouble, hanging out in a rowdy honky-tonk, and she'd damned well found it. How was he supposed to know she'd never been with a guy? She'd been dressed to kill in those skintight jeans, just asking for someone to hit on her.

Hank's anger flagged the instant it began gathering steam. There was no law that said virgins had to wear signs, broadcasting their sexual inexperience. And there was damned sure no law against their going to a bar. It wasn't Charlie's fault that she was pretty, and as much as he might like to shift the blame, he couldn't hold her accountable for his own behavior. When he'd ordered her the slammer, his sole intent had been to get her drunk. She'd been staggering by the time they left Chaps, and he'd taken full advantage of it.

An awful thought suddenly occurred to him. Why would a virgin be taking the Pill? He groaned and fell back on the grass. What if he'd knocked her up? She could be out there somewhere, pregnant with his kid. He had to find out who she was in case a problem developed.

And if a problem developed, what did he intend to do about it?

The answer was there in Hank's head before he completed the thought. Coulter men didn't shirk their responsibilities, and a child was one of the biggest responsibilities of all. From age fourteen, Hank had had that drilled into his head by his father. *Get a girl pregnant, and there'll be no walking away. You'll shoulder the responsibility and make it right, or I'll know the reason why.*

No ifs, ands, or buts, Hank had to find Charlie. The question was, how?

At precisely ten o'clock that evening, Hank reentered Chaps. He'd timed his arrival for ten because it was normally the busiest time of night. The latecomers had usually trickled in by then, and the hardcore partiers still hadn't left. Somewhere around eleven, people would start pairing off, and not long after, couples would start ducking out. Hank wanted to speak with as many regulars as he could on the off chance that one of them might know Charlie.

Standing inside the doors, he scanned the crowd, hoping he'd see her. A blue-gray haze of smoke hovered in layers above the tables. The smell of beer, whiskey, and sweat drifted to his nostrils, the uneven cacophony of raised voices in constant competition with the blare of music. Occasionally, a decibel above the din, filthy language spewed from the rumble like backwash from a gutter grate.

Being at Chaps again brought Hank's memories of Charlie into clearer focus. Glancing at the table where she'd been sitting last night, he recalled her saying she didn't know how to dance. At the time, he'd believed she meant country-western dancing, but now he wondered if she'd ever danced at all. The same went for a score of other things. At one point, he'd worried that she wasn't accustomed to drinking hard liquor. He'd also noticed a shy hesitancy in her response when he kissed her. The memory made him cringe. Where the hell had she been all her life, in a convent?

Hank sorely regretted now that he'd had so much to drink. If he'd been sober, he would have realized something was off plumb and never would have touched her.

If wishes were horses, poor men would ride. He'd gotten sloppy drunk, and he *had* touched her. That was the bottom line.

Hank made the rounds, stopping at first one table, then another. At each, he launched into the same spiel, reminding people of the blonde he'd been with last night and asking if anyone knew her. Unfortunately, no one he spoke with, including Gary, the bartender, had ever seen Charlie before. Hoping she might return to the honky-tonk, Hank left his name and phone number so Gary could contact him.

As Hank left the bar, he paused just inside the door to look back at the room. For months now, this place had been like a second home to him. Now he wondered why he'd come there so much. It was strange how quickly a man's tastes could change.

As he stepped outside and moved past the light of the overhead sign into the darkness, he stopped to stare at the sky. Like diamonds on black velvet, thousands of stars twinkled down at him. As a boy, he'd liked to sit on the porch with his grandfather McBride to stargaze. The old man had often challenged Hank to choose the brightest star, look away, and then try to find it again. That endeavor had always ended in failure.

Hank feared that finding Charlie again might prove to be just as difficult. Crystal Falls and the outlying areas had a population of 150,000. Without a last name to go on, he had no idea how to even start searching for her. To complicate matters even more, Charlie might be a nickname.

Hank's only hope was that she would return to Chaps, and that was a long shot. It was up to Fate from this point forward, he guessed. He'd done everything he could to find her.

Chapter Three

That night, Hank dreamed he was an old man, still working on the Lazy J ranch. In the beginning, it was a nice dream. He was forking hay into a stall, and morning sunlight poured in from the adjoining paddock to warm his shoulders. The smell of horses was all around him. The shuffling of hooves and the soft blowing of the mares soothed him.

As is often the way in dreams, Hank had no recollection of his life, only a sense that he was old and that he'd lived it well, working with horses, as he'd been born to do. He had a wonderful sense of rightness and peace.

Then he heard a car pull up outside. Straightening from his work, he cocked an ear and listened. An awful sense of dread filled him. He didn't know why. He leaned the pitchfork against the wall and walked up the center aisle, his trepidation mounting. On some level, he knew he was dreaming, and he told himself to wake up, but his mind insisted on playing out the scene.

Outside the stable, Hank saw a tall, dark-haired young man standing by a dusty red car. At the sound of Hank's shuffling footsteps, he turned and blasted Hank with blazing blue eyes. *Coulter eyes*. Hank had never seen the younger man, but somehow he knew this was his son. Hank judged him to be in his mid-twenties. That was about right. Twenty-five years had passed since that fateful night at Chaps when Hank had deflowered a virgin and passed out before he could learn her last name.

"Can I help you?" Hank asked.

The younger man ran a searing gaze from Hank's soiled boots up to his face. "I'm looking for Hank Coulter."

Hank sensed the young man's anger and knew it would be unleashed the moment he identified himself. "You've found him."

The kid knotted his fists and stepped forward. "You son of a *bitch*!"

Hank saw the blow coming, but he wasn't fast enough to deflect it. When he hit the dirt, he lay there, blinking and trying to see, thinking stupidly that his son threw a hell of a punch. A regular chip off the old Coulter block, sure as hell.

"I thought I'd stop by and introduce myself. My name's Hank. My mother named me after the bastard who sired me and never gave me his last name."

Hank jerked awake and bolted upright. *A dream, only a dream.* But it had seemed so real. His body was drenched with sweat. He fought his way free of the clinging sheets and sprang from the bed. Gulping for breath, he stood at the center of the room, his heart pounding wildly.

Slowly reality closed in around him. He sank onto the edge of the bed and rested his head on his hands. Memories flashed in his mind like film clips. *Charlie, lying beneath him.* At the last second, when he'd realized she was a virgin, he'd pulled back, but he knew damned well his swimmers hadn't.

He had a horrible feeling that the dream had been prophetic, that he'd done the unthinkable last night and fathered an illegitimate child.

Still groggy from sleep, Carly sat in a living room easy chair, her legs tucked beneath her. In the predawn gloom, there were few sounds coming through the walls and ceiling from the surrounding apartments. Not even the wind chimes on the front porch of the ground floor unit were making any noise. Over the last three weeks since she and Bess had rented this place, Carly had grown accustomed to the musical tinkling. In a couple of hours, many of the neighbors would start stirring, some leaving for work, others emerging to walk their small dogs on the grassy center common. But for now, Carly felt like the only person in the world who was awake. She couldn't even hear any cars passing by on the street, which was usually busy during the day.

She'd lighted a candle to chase away the shadows and the bad dream that had awakened her. Somehow the flickering glow didn't make her feel much better. Visions of Hank Coulter's face kept slipping into her mind, and each time, a burn of humiliation mixed with shame pooled like acid in her belly.

She decided a glass of milk might soothe her stomach and her nerves. Not wishing to awaken Bess, who had always been a light sleeper, she tiptoed into the adjoining kitchen. She'd just gotten a glass from the cupboard and started pouring when Bess's voice startled her.

"What're you doing?"

Carly jerked and sloshed milk. "Bess, what are you doing up?"

Her friend flipped on the fluorescent ceiling lights. Carly winced and narrowed her eyes. "Do we have to have those on?"

Bess muttered something about living like vampires and plunged the kitchen back into semidarkness. "How long before your eyes heal enough for us to turn on the lights like normal people?"

"A few more days. I know it's the pits, but bright lights are still pure murder." Carly resumed pouring the milk. "I'm sorry I woke you. We need to ask the landlord to fix the refrigerator door. It creaks."

"Get your finger out of the glass. You aren't blind anymore."

Carly curled her offending finger around the outside of the tumbler.

"You can't train your visual cortex unless you use it, you know."

"You're cranky. Why don't you go back to bed?"

"Because I'm awake now, thanks to you." Bess stifled a yawn. "You never answered my question. Why are you up so early?"

Carly returned the milk to the refrigerator and mopped up the counter. "What time is it?"

Bess glanced at her watch. "Not quite five. This is the second night in a row that you've paced the floors. What's the matter, Carls? If you need to talk a little more about what happened the other night, I don't mind listening."

One hand pressed to her still tender abdomen, Carly grabbed her glass of milk. She circled her friend and returned to her chair in the living room. Trailing behind her, Bess headed for the adjacent sofa. After plopping on a cushion, she drew up her legs and hugged her ankles. In the candlelight, with faint streaks of dawn washing the window behind her, her dark hair looked like a drape of silk lying over her shoulders.

Normally, Carly could confide almost anything to Bess, but certain details about the incident with Hank Coulter were different somehow—intensely personal and, even worse, horribly humiliating. She set her glass aside and tugged at the hem of her nightshirt. "I'm a little worried," she confessed. "I don't think Hank used any protection."

Bess's eyes widened. "You're not sure?"

Carly shook her head. Bess already knew about the painkillers and alcohol not mixing well. There was no point in going over it again. "I wasn't tracking very well. I remember him leaning over the seat to get something, but I think he may have dropped it—or changed his mind."

A worried frown pleated Bess's brow. "Oh, Carls," she whispered. "What if he got you pregnant?"

That was Carly's worry as well. "The instant he realized I was a virgin, he stopped. I'm pretty sure he didn't ejaculate inside of me. That being the case, aren't I pretty safe?"

Bess said nothing for a moment. "Coitus interruptus isn't a fail proof means of birth control, Carly. He penetrated. Even if men don't ejaculate, they can have seepage. All it takes to get a woman pregnant is one sperm."

Carly's stomach turned a slow revolution. Deep

down, she'd already guessed as much. "In my case, there wasn't much coitus. Maybe, this one time, it worked."

"And if it didn't? What if you're pregnant? Do you even know how to contact this guy?"

With a stubborn lift of her chin, Carly said, "I'm not calling him, if that's what you're thinking. I never want to see him again."

"If you're pregnant, what choice will you have?"

"He cursed at me," Carly reminded her. "Afterward, I felt so dirty—the kind of dirt that never washes away. I owe him nothing, absolutely nothing."

"Maybe not. But he owes you. Besides, a man has a right to know when he's fathered a child, and every child has a right to know its father. You'll have to get in touch with him."

"I'm not pregnant. That just can't happen." Even as Carly uttered the words, she knew she was kidding herself. "Having a child would derail my education, possibly my whole life. It just can't happen."

Bess pushed her hair back from her eyes. "Let's just hope nothing comes of it. If you're pregnant, we'll cross that bridge when we come to it."

Carly hauled in a deep breath. "At least I accomplished one thing. I'm no longer the last twenty-eight-year-old virgin on earth."

Bess laughed, albeit worriedly. "True. Before we know it, you'll be a veteran giving *me* advice."

Carly shook her head. "Once was enough for me. In my opinion, the joys of sex are highly overrated."

"It gets better."

"If it's all the same to you, I'll just take your word for it." Frankly, she wouldn't care if she never had sex again.

Chapter Four

Six mornings later, Carly woke up feeling sick to her stomach. When Bess found her in the bathroom kneeling by the toilet, she bathed Carly's face with a cool cloth and started saying, "Oh no!" as if it were a mantra.

"It's only the flu," Carly managed to say between bouts of nausea. "Morning sickness doesn't start this early. Does it?"

"It depends." Bess lowered herself to the floor and rested her back against the vanity doors. "Some women get sick from the very start."

Carly's stomach finally settled enough for her to sit back on her heels.

"Just to be on the safe side," Bess said, "maybe we should call Dr. Merrick to make sure the meds you're taking won't hurt the baby."

"What baby?" Carly made tight fists on her knees and peered owlishly at her friend, whose face was a misty blur. "There *is* no baby, Bess. There can't be." Another wave of nausea struck. Carly leaned back over the toilet bowl and cradled her head on her arms. "Oh, God, what am I going to do? I'm not running a fever. Usually, with the flu, I run a fever."

Bess curled a hand over Carly's shoulder. "Well, first of all, we aren't going to panic."

"Right," Carly said thinly. "Probably just something I ate."

"Exactly," Bess replied in a calm, reassuring way. "Nausea can be caused by countless things. We'll just have to wait and see. If your period's late and you're still feeling puny, then you should take a home-pregnancy test."

Carly couldn't believe this was happening.

"Meanwhile," Bess went on, "it only seems wise to call the doctor and ask how a fetus might affect your eyes. Lattice dystrophy is such a rare disease, you just never know." She quickly tacked on, "Not saying there *is* a baby, mind you. You'll just be covering all the bases that way."

"Right." Carly cautiously straightened again. The flush lever on the toilet tank swam in her vision, its metallic glint creating a brilliant, dancing orb. "My focus is all out of whack."

Bess leaned over to push a hank of hair from Carly's eyes. "That help?"

"No." Carly pressed her fingers to the base of her throat, closed her eyes, and took several shallow breaths.

"I'm sure it's nothing to worry about," Bess said. "The doctor told you to expect bouts of blurry vision for several months."

Carly nodded, recalling the doctor's warnings that the visual aberrations would frequently incapacitate her for at least three months, making it almost impossible for her to hold down a job or function normally. That was why she'd scheduled the first surgery, called superficial keratectomy or SK, for late May, so the blurry vision and other visual problems would be mostly over before school started in September. Later, because the improvements brought about by SK didn't last forever, she would probably need another operation.

A few minutes later Bess led the way to the kitchen, dialed the number of the corneal specialist in Portland, and handed Carly the phone. When the doctor got on the line, he was not pleased to hear that Carly could be pregnant.

"If you were planning to have a baby, you never should have had the first SK," he said. "Pregnancy can adversely affect lattice dystrophy and shorten the effectiveness of the procedure."

Carly's eyes throbbed from the recent bout of vomiting, and all she could think to say was, "I see," which seemed stupid, given the circumstances.

Merrick sighed. "I should have stressed the dangers of pregnancy more strongly. During one of our talks, you gave me the impression that you weren't sexually active and pregnancy wasn't an immediate concern. I planned to go over the long-term instructions in more detail during your six-week checkup."

Carly remembered the conversation to which he referred, and he was right; she'd told him that she wanted to be able to see while she was attending grad school so she could have a more normal social life and possibly start dating.

"Circumstances change," was all she could think to say. "I didn't plan the encounter, Dr. Merrick. It just—sort of happened."

"I see." Papers rustled at his end. A brief silence ensued. "If you are pregnant and your condition shortens the life of the SK, I will strongly advise against your having a second procedure until after the child is born."

Carly's headache made it difficult to think. "Are you saying I might go blind again before the baby comes, and you won't be able to do anything?"

"If you are pregnant, and the first SK fails quickly, it'll be a strong indication that your lattice dystrophy will have an adverse effect on any follow-up procedures done during the pregnancy. You can only have so many superficial keratectomies and corneal transplants. Why waste an entire series at a time when your disease is running rampant? You'd be throwing away years of sightedness."

Carly understood his reasoning; she just found it difficult to accept. "I definitely don't want to have more surgeries done while I'm pregnant if they're just going to fail. That's why I waited so long to have the first operation, so I'd be sighted when I entered the workforce. I'll want to see as long as I possibly can."

The doctor cleared his throat. "At this point, you're not positive that you're pregnant. Correct?"

"Correct."

"It might be wise to go in for a blood test. They're accurate before a missed menses." She heard a thump at his end of the line and then the rustling of pages, indicating to her that he might be leafing through a book of some kind. "Here we go," he said. "St. Luke's is the hospital there. I'll fax them an order this afternoon so you can go in for a blood draw first thing Monday morning. That way, we'll know for certain straight away."

"Okay," Carly said hollowly.

"In the meantime, don't worry too much about losing your sight. No point in borrowing trouble. Pregnancy affects some lattice patients adversely at a very rapid rate, but others skate through with only minimal problems. If you are pregnant, maybe you'll be one of the lucky ones."

"I'm having trouble focusing right now. Things get clear, and then they go all fuzzy."

"Have you followed through and seen the doctor I recommended there in Crystal Falls for a postsurgical exam?" Papers rustled again. "Ah, yes, here's the report. According to him, everything looked fine. That was what—ten days ago?"

"About that."

"He's a topnotch eye surgeon and qualified to spot any problems arising from the surgery. The blurry vision you're experiencing right now is probably normal. Even if your vision has improved to twenty-twenty now that your corneas are healing, your visual cortex is still inadequately trained to process and assimilate all that your eyes take in. As a result, there'll be times when it plays tricks on you. It's not uncommon to look directly at something and not see it. Or to think you see something that isn't actually there. Think of it as a new memory bank over which you have little control—much like one experiences during dreams, with random images popping up. Only with you, it can occur when you're awake."

Carly knew all about seeing things that didn't exist, namely the tenderness she'd glimpsed in Hank Coulter's eyes.

"Incidents of blurry vision," the doctor continued, "will gradually become less frequent and go away in time. You'll still have trouble noticing details, such as background patterns, and your depth perception may always be poor, but your focus will sharpen. You just need to take it easy until your visual cortex has had time to adjust."

"If I'm pregnant and it adversely affects my lattice, how long do you think it will take for me to lose my sight?"

Alarmed by Carly's side of the conversation, Bess came to stand nearby.

Dr. Merrick took a moment to reply. "There's no pat answer to that question. It all depends on the patient, the severity of the lattice to begin with, and a host of other things. You may notice no change in your vision for months. Then again, your sight could go quickly."

"I've forfeited my legally blind status, Dr. Merrick. If I lose my sight again, how long will it take to get me reinstated so I can get special financial aid for school?"

"Once you've had corrective surgery and your sight is restored to twenty–two hundred or better, you become ineligible for legally blind status until all possible surgical procedures to correct the problem have been done. In short, you can't get reinstated unless you have another SK, then a transplant, and both procedures fail."

Carly leaned weakly against the counter. "That doesn't seem fair. If I go blind from the pregnancy and can't have a corrective procedure done until after the baby's born, how will I attend grad school? I won't have any special funding."

"I don't make the laws," he reminded her. "Before we start painting worst-case scenarios, let's be sure there's cause for concern. Erring on the side of caution, you should stop taking those pain pills I prescribed over the weekend. Hopefully, your corneas have healed enough by now that the analgesic drops will keep you comfortable."

Carly felt numb by the time she hung up the phone. "Well, that was an uplifting conversation." She quickly filled Bess in on everything the doctor had said. "If I'm pregnant and it messes up my SK, I'm sunk until after the baby's born."

Bess looped an arm around Carly's shoulders. They stood there, leaning against each other for some time. When Bess finally drew away, she said, "If you lose your sight again, you'll have to have special financial aid to stay in school. I can't believe they would make you have two more surgical procedures before you could be reinstated."

"Those are the breaks. I'll have to drop out and reapply for the master's program next year."

"Oh, Carly, you've worked so long for this. If you drop out, I'm afraid you'll never go back. With a child to support, getting that master's degree will be all the more important. Not only will it make you more marketable, but it'll substantially increase your income."

"I already have my bachelor's. At least I have that going for me." Carly's head was killing her. "I'll get my master's, Bess. One way or another. It may just take longer than I hoped." Carly sat at the table. "I can't believe this is happening to me."

The following morning, Carly felt sick again. The nausea abated in the afternoon and was gone entirely by early evening, which she took as a bad sign. She lay on her bed, one hand pressed to her lower abdomen. *A baby.* She couldn't believe that a life could begin in such a sordid way. Children should be wanted and loved by their parents, not looked upon as mistakes.

Until that instant, Carly hadn't thought of the baby

as a little person with feelings and needs, but now that she had, she couldn't banish the images from her mind. *A child.*

Now that she had come to think of the baby as an individual, it was difficult for her to wish it gone. As a very young girl, she'd always wanted to have kids someday. Later, when she reached her teens and began to realize boys weren't interested in her because of her blindness, she'd abandoned her dreams of motherhood and focused on becoming a teacher of the visually disabled instead.

Curling onto her side, she wrapped both arms around her waist, feeling suddenly protective of the life that might be growing inside her.

Bess came in and sat on the edge of the bed. "Penny for them."

Carly rolled onto her back. "I've just been coming to terms with the possibilities. Not knowing for sure if I'm pregnant yet, it's kind of hard to decide how I feel, but I think—well, if I am, Bess, I think I owe it to the baby to be happy about it. So what if it turns my life upside down? There are worse things."

Bess braced her arms on the mattress behind her. "I agree. Looking on the gloomy side doesn't seem productive. If you're going to keep this baby, we need to be upbeat about it."

Carly stared at the ceiling. A few days ago, she'd been able to make out some of the texture swirls in the plaster. Now she couldn't. She hoped that was due to the dim light. "I'll definitely keep the baby. Clinical abortion goes against everything I'm about, everything I believe in."

"We've never really discussed it, but I've always sensed you felt that way."

"It's the only way I can feel," Carly murmured. "When I was conceived, my mom was forty-three. I'm sure they must have considered ending the pregnancy because of her age. If they'd made that decision, I wouldn't be here."

"That's a pretty heavy thought to carry around all your life."

Carly ran her fingertips over the chenille. "It's kept things in perspective for me. There were times, particularly in my teens, when I felt bitter about being born blind. I always cheered myself up by considering the alternative, not being here at all. It hasn't always been easy, but I've enjoyed my life, and before it's all said and done, I hope to make it count for something by working with the visually disabled. When I think in terms of all or nothing, I'm really glad my folks had me."

"I'll second that. The world wouldn't be the same without you in it."

Carly smiled. "You just love me." She fell silent for a moment. "Looking back on my childhood, I know it must have been difficult for my parents sometimes. Having a disabled kid is no walk in the park. But they never once seemed to regret having me. I'll always be grateful for that."

"I didn't realize your mom was that old when you were born. Do you suppose her age was a contributing factor to your blindness?"

"Maybe." Carly had wondered the same thing herself. There was no history of congenital cataracts or lattice dystrophy on either side of her family. "It doesn't matter what caused it. What I look at is my quality of life. It's been hard sometimes, but I've had a lot of fun, too, and I'm excited about the future.

That being the case, how can I arbitrarily decide to deny my baby the chance my folks gave me?"

"I understand, Carly. You don't have to explain. Abortion would never be an option for me, either." Bess cast Carly a sideways glance rife with mischief. "I've always wanted to be an aunt. It'll be fun to spoil a baby rotten and leave you to deal with the backlash."

Carly laughed. "That's what you think. We'll probably still be living together."

"I hadn't thought of that. You're right. Maybe I should rethink my position."

"Definitely not. I want my child to have an aunt who'll spoil it. I never had that. My mom had no siblings, and my dad's only brother was killed in Vietnam. Being a midlife baby, I can barely even remember my grandparents."

"That must have been lonely."

"You don't really miss what you've never had."

"Your baby will have me and Cricket as aunts," Bess assured her.

Thinking of their friend Cricket made Carly smile again. She had grown up with Bess living on one side of her and Cricket on the other. All of them being the same age, they'd become inseparable in kindergarten and been like sisters ever since. "I sure wish we could call her more often. I'm thrilled that she got chosen to go to Colombia on the dig, but I miss hearing her voice."

"You can bet she's happy as a clam right now," Bess mused aloud. "Up to her elbows in dirt, dreaming that she'll make the greatest archeological discovery of the new millennium."

"What is it with her and dirt?" Carly shook her

head. "Even when we were little, she loved to dig. Remember the bones she found in Mrs. Kirkpatrick's flowerbed?"

"I'd nearly forgotten that! She thought she'd dug up a dinosaur. Come to find out, it was the grave of Mrs. Kirkpatrick's Great Dane, and we all got grounded." Bess chuckled. "When you think about it, we're a pretty unlikely trio, a business management major, a teacher, and an archeologist. What do the three of us find to talk about?"

"Beats me. But I bet I could run up a huge bill if we could get in touch with her. It's too bad her cell phone reception is so lousy down there."

"She'd just lecture you for thirty minutes, listing all the reasons you should never have left the bar with a stranger. Then she'd be all over you for drinking when you were taking painkillers. After that, she'd want to hear all about Hank."

Carly didn't even want to think about Hank. But if a child was on the way, she supposed she'd at least have to notify him. "Did you get a close look at him, Bess?"

"Close enough. Why?"

"Is he cute?"

Bess gave a startled laugh. "You're asking *me*?"

"You know very well I don't have a clue about looks. When you spend your whole life blind, physical beauty isn't a concept you can easily grasp. While you're gone on job interviews, I try to watch movies. It's a good way to see different topography, animals, and all kinds of people. At first I assumed that the actors with leading roles must be attractive, but they're all so different. I'm still not sure what beautiful is."

"Maybe that isn't a bad thing. We're all brain-washed. The entertainment industry creates the standard, and we buy into it like sheep. I think it'd be sort of nice not to have preconceived notions about physical beauty."

"From where I'm standing, it's just confusing. I liked the way Hank looked, and right then, that was all that seemed important. Now, with a baby possibly coming, I need to know if he's—you know—handsome or homely."

"And if I say he's a dog?"

"I'll be worried. I'd like my baby to have good genes."

"He's handsome," Bess assured her. "*Very* handsome. No worries on that front, sweetie. You chose a hunk."

The tension eased from Carly's body. "That's good to know. It means my baby will have a fifty-fifty chance of being attractive."

"Fifty-fifty? You aren't exactly chopped liver yourself. You and Hank will make a beautiful baby."

Carly smiled. "I hope so."

"Can't miss."

Carly pictured Hank's dark face, and a thickness gathered in her throat.

"You okay?" Bess drew up a foot and tucked it under her other leg. "If you need to talk about it, my offer to listen is still open."

Carly turned onto her side and cradled her head on the bend of her arm. "I guess what bugs me the most is that I was so incredibly naive."

"You weren't firing on all cylinders," Bess reminded her. "A guy at Chaps told me if you can finish a slammer, leave the bar on your own steam, and walk back inside, you can drink the rest of the night for free."

"Hank warned me that it was strong. I just didn't realize how strong. Dr. Merrick said the pain pills were mild and that I could safely have two drinks over the course of an evening. I'd only had a few sips of beer when he ordered the slammer. I thought it'd be okay if I went easy on it."

"I think slammers are made with high-proof alcohol, and lots of it. It's a wonder you could even navigate."

"I definitely wasn't thinking straight. I never should have gone outside with him, but somehow, I shelved my common sense and let myself believe—I don't know—that I'd found someone special, I guess."

"Oh, sweetie."

"I'm over feeling sad about it. Really." Carly flashed a strained smile. "Now I just feel humiliated."

"When we first start dating, we're all naive. I'm including guys in that statement. Before we wise up, we all get our hearts broken a few times."

"Maybe so." Personally, Carly found it hard to believe that Hank Coulter's heart had ever been broken. If what Bess said was true, he was one of the beautiful people and had probably traded on his looks all his life. "All I know is, I don't want to go through this again."

"We all feel that way right after a bad experience. You'll get over it."

Carly doubted that.

On Monday morning after doing her daily job search on the Internet, Bess drove Carly to St. Luke's to get a pregnancy test. After her blood was drawn,

Carly was told that someone would call to give her the results the following day.

The call came shortly before noon on Tuesday while Bess was gone on a job interview. By the time Carly hung up the phone, she was shaking. Facing the possibility that she was pregnant had been one thing. Knowing for certain was far more sobering.

For an hour, Carly wandered from room to room, searching for ways to keep busy and take her mind off her worries. In desperation, she dug out the books she had ordered before the surgery to train her visual cortex. After staring for thirty minutes at pictures in a visual encyclopedia, the captions for which she struggled to read, she wanted to scream. She was pregnant. Soon she'd be responsible for supporting a child, and here she sat, looking at a stupid book. She needed to do something. Only what? She wouldn't be able to hold down a job for at least three months.

She finally grabbed her sunglasses and left the apartment to take a walk and train her visual cortex in a more physically active way. While outdoors, she still flinched at sudden movements—cars whizzing by, birds swooping down from trees, branches swaying in the wind. As a blind person, she'd lived in a gray, motionless world, and it was extremely difficult to grow accustomed to all the activity that other people scarcely noticed. Just looking down as she walked was a challenge. The sidewalk seemed to move beneath her feet, and it made her feel dizzy.

Four blocks from the apartment, Carly passed the supermarket and strip mall where she and Bess now shopped. They'd made it a priority when they were looking for an apartment to find a location within walking distance of stores so Carly wouldn't be stranded when Bess wasn't available to drive her places. The supermarket faced a main thoroughfare. At the corner, Carly stopped and looked both ways at the heavy traffic, yearning to trust her eyes and step off the curb. Only what if there was a car she couldn't see or the vehicles were closer than they appeared to be? Recalling Dr. Merrick's warning that her visual cortex would often deceive her, she decided to err on the side of caution and turned left instead. The side streets that spilled onto the main drag weren't quite as hazardous to pedestrians.

Carly was so lost in thought that she had no idea how far she'd walked when she came to a large parcel of land encircled by a tall, iron fence. Inside the enclosure, blocks of cement and chiseled rock peppered large expanses of lawn. She'd never seen anything like it. But then, no big surprise. Everything was new to her.

Curious and determined not to turn away until she found out what this place was, Carly walked along the sidewalk until she reached a large gate. A sign affixed to the arched entrance read ROSE HILL CEMETERY. It took Carly a moment to decipher the letters. A graveyard? She hugged her waist as she gazed through the fence at what she now realized were headstones. So many dead people. She'd never imagined that there could be so many graves in one place.

The realization soothed Carly somehow. Yes, she had big problems. When she considered the ramifications of this pregnancy, she felt panicky. But it wasn't the end of the world. She was young and, aside from her vision problems, healthy. Even if she went blind again and couldn't go to grad school, she had her bachelor's degree to fall back on. If worse came to worst, she could return to the Portland area and try to land another teaching job. The money wouldn't be very good, and she'd have to live on a shoestring budget, but over time, she'd get raises. Until then, she'd manage somehow. She and the baby would be okay.

That evening, Bess came home in a gloomy mood because she still hadn't gotten a job. "It's not as if I'm looking for a career job in business management," she grumped as she got a glass of ice tea. "I'll take anything—a position as a receptionist, even as a bookkeeper. Some of them say I don't have enough experience. Others insist I'm overqualified. Go figure. I'm starting to worry I won't find a job."

"You'll find something," Carly assured her. "It may not be what you're hoping for, but it'll all work out."

Carly decided to save her news until Bess had had some time to unwind. Over dinner, she finally said, "They called with my test results this morning."

"Ohmigosh, I was so upset over the job situation that I totally forgot." Bess stopped chewing. "What did they say?"

"I'm pregnant."

The pronouncement hung in the air like a pall. Carly went back to pushing green beans around on her plate. Bess laid down her fork.

"They're sure?"

Carly tossed her napkin on the table and got up to get a drink of water. Her hands shook as she turned the faucet handle. "I think the blood test is pretty accurate, Bess, and it came out positive." Carly's heart did a funny little dance, and her stomach felt much like it had the first time she'd gone skydiving with Cricket. "Congratulations are in order."

Carly drank the water. Then she set the glass on the counter to dry her hands. Her meal forgotten, Bess crossed the room to give her a hug. "Ah, Carly," she whispered. "I don't know what to say."

Clutching the towel between them, Carly pressed her face against her friend's shoulder. "There's nothing much to say." She expelled a shaky breath. "I know this will sound really dumb. My mom's been gone for over two years. But, oh, God, I miss her right now. I want to call her so bad."

"You want to phone mine? After she goes into cardiac arrest, she'll probably handle the news fairly well."

Carly laughed weakly. She'd known Bess's mom, Norma Grayson, practically all her life, and the woman was nothing if not excitable. "I guess I could try to get through to Cricket. After the first shock, she'll make all the right noises."

Bess pulled back to look Carly in the eye. "Isn't there a certain cowboy you should call first? This is his baby, after all."

Chapter Five

The last person Carly wanted to speak with was Hank Coulter. As childish as she knew it was, she gave Bess a pleading look and asked, "Do I have to?"

Bess lightly tapped Carly's chin with her fist. "Yeah, you've got to. It's the right thing to do."

Carly clamped her palms to her waist. "What'll I say to him? Hello, and by the way, I'm pregnant? What if he doesn't believe it's his baby?"

Bess rolled her eyes. "Give me a break. You went from being a twenty-eight-year-old virgin to Lolita overnight? If he doesn't believe it's his, he's a jerk, and you and the baby are well rid of him. The important thing is for you to know he's been notified."

Finding Hank in the phonebook was more difficult than Carly anticipated. There were several Coulters, but none had the right first name.

"You'll just have to dial them all, I guess." Bess slowly read off the first number while Carly punched in the digits.

"Darn it!" Carly depressed the receiver to start over. "I never had trouble like this when I couldn't see the dratted phone!"

"Here, let me." Bess tried to take over.

"No. I need to do it myself. It's only a number pad,

for heaven's sake. I know the layout by heart, but now that I can see, it seems backward."

"It's a whole new ball game now," Bess reminded her. "If you need to, just close your eyes."

"What about training my visual cortex? You're always grumping at me about it."

"Yeah, well, under the circumstances, I think it's okay to make an exception."

Carly was in no hurry to get Hank on the phone. She persevered, staring at the number pad, trying to correlate the visual images with the number shapes she'd memorized by touch. The digits began to blur, and then the lot of them started jumping around. She closed her eyes and passed the phone to Bess. "Maybe you should do it, after all. I don't need this right now."

"Just calm down. If he gets nasty, it's no skin off your nose. Right?"

"Right."

Bess began the process of dialing each number and then handing Carly the phone. Midway down the list, Carly finally spoke to an older woman who claimed to be Hank's mother.

"I, um—well, I guess you could say I'm an acquaintance of Hank's," Carly explained after introducing herself. "And I really need to get in touch with him. Do you have a number where I can reach him?"

"Have you called the ranch?"

"I, um—no. Hank mentioned the ranch, but he never told me the name."

"That's strange," the older woman mused aloud.

"Yes, well. I guess he just never got around to it."

"Normally," Mrs. Coulter went on to say, "I don't like to give out contact information over the phone. But if you're a friend, I'll make an exception."

Carly wasn't sure she qualified as one of Hank's friends, but the thought of trying to explain the exact nature of their relationship kept her from correcting that impression. When Mrs. Coulter gave her the number, Carly signaled Bess to jot it down as she repeated the digits.

"He'll be outside working yet," Mrs. Coulter said. "At this time of year, he doesn't quit until almost dark. That's his cell phone number I gave you. If he has it turned on, which he generally does, you should be able to get through to him. If not, you can leave him a voice message or call the Lazy J."

"The Lazy J. Got it. Thank you, Mrs. Coulter."

After Carly broke the connection, Bess quickly dialed the cell phone number before Carly could lose her nerve. Carly groped for Bess's hand when the phone started to ring. A man with a deep voice answered. "Yo?"

Carly gulped and said, "Hank?"

"Yeah, this is Hank."

Carly threw Bess a desperate look. "I, um—this is, um, Carly Adams."

"Who?"

A chill moved through Carly. She shut her eyes, scarcely able to believe her ears. For a week and a half, this man's face had haunted her dreams, and for the last few days, she'd spent more time hugging the toilet than not because of him. Yet he didn't remember who she was?

For several awful seconds, she could do nothing but stand there. Then fury pulsed through her in searing waves. She slammed the receiver down in its cradle with such force that the jolt went clear to her elbow.

"What?" Bess asked. "Oh, God, Carly, what did he say?"

" 'Who?' "

Bess's expression remained uncomprehending. "What?"

A sob welled in Carly's chest. " 'Who!' " she repeated shrilly. "That's what he said. *Who*. He doesn't remember me."

All the color drained from Bess's face. "He *what*?"

Carly was seldom given to displays of temper, but the anger building within her demanded release. She picked up the phonebook and threw it across the small living room with all her strength. "He can go stick his head in a lake, for all I care, and I hope he drowns!"

"Carly, calm down. You're pregnant, remember. This isn't good for you or the baby."

"Calm. Right." Carly covered her face with her hands. When she looked at Bess again, she said, "I don't know why I'm upset. The truth is it suits me just fine." She took three paces, then whirled back around, jabbing her chest with a finger. "This is *my* baby, mine and only mine. He just forfeited all rights. I never want to speak to the creep again."

Bess followed Carly into the living room. "How could he *not* remember you, Carly? It's only been a week and a half."

"Because he's a conceited, self-serving *jerk*! He came on to me, and then he got me drunk, and then he—he—" Carly sent Bess a miserable look. "It didn't mean a thing to him, Bess. I wasn't even a blip on his radar screen."

"Oh, honey."

Carly held up a hand to ward off another hug.

"Don't. The last thing I need right now is sympathy. Just tell me I was an idiot and that he's a world-class creep."

"If he doesn't remember you, he's definitely a creep."

"Right." Carly exhaled in a rush. "I want to forget I ever met him. From this moment forward, my baby has no father. I never want to hear his name again."

Carly went to her bedroom, slammed the door, and threw herself down on the bed. *Who? Oh, God.* She *hated* him. How could he have sex with a woman and not remember her a little over a week later?

Hank turned on the overhead lights and stepped into the center aisle of the stable to stare at his cell phone. An awful suspicion slammed into his brain. *Carly, Charlie.* The two names were very similar, and he'd been pretty damned drunk that night. With all the noise, had he misunderstood her name? As he stood there, mulling it over, he dimly recalled her correcting him on her name at some point during the evening, but he'd been too drunk to care if he got it right. Charlie had worked for his purposes—a one-night stand, ending with a predawn "So long, baby."

Damn. Hank didn't like remembering his mindset that night. He wasn't sure when he'd come to think of sex as a form of recreation. His parents had raised him better. They would be so disappointed in him if they knew—almost as disappointed as he was in himself.

He called her number back up on the cell phone window. When the digits appeared, he memorized them, punched them in, and put the phone to his ear as it began to ring. His heart was pounding, and a cold sweat broke out on his body as he waited for Charlie—no, *Carly*—to answer. It had been almost two weeks since that night. He hadn't heard a peep out of her in all this time. Why would she suddenly call him?

Hank had a bad feeling he already knew the answer to that question. It was early on yet for her to know if she was pregnant, but given the unpleasant way their encounter had ended, he couldn't think of any other reason she might initiate contact.

She answered the phone almost immediately. He said, "Carly? This is Hank Coulter calling back." He meant to explain his confusion with the names, but she didn't give him a chance. "I'm sorry about—"

"*Who?*" she asked with biting sarcasm.

Hank knew he had that coming. "Listen. I know how it must have sounded but—"

A loud crashing noise cut him dead. Hank swore under his breath and hit redial. This time, her phone rang endlessly. She clearly knew who was calling and refused to answer.

"Okay, fine," he said, his voice gravelly with frustration. "You're pissed. Unless you've got Caller ID, I can wait you out and catch you by surprise later."

Hank realized he was talking to himself and glanced over his shoulder. One of the mares eyed him curiously as she munched her grain. He entered Carly's number into the cell phone memory, and then clipped the apparatus over his belt. In an hour or so, when Carly was no longer expecting him to call, he'd try her again.

"That was Hank calling back, wasn't it?" Hands at her hips, Bess stood over Carly's bed.

"Brilliant deduction. How did you guess?"

"Why else would you yell at me not to answer when the phone rang a second time? What did he say?"

"Nothing," Carly replied. "He didn't say anything."

"He must have said *something*."

"I didn't give him a chance." Carly sent her friend a mutinous glare. "I served him up some of his own medicine, hung up before he could say much of anything, and didn't answer when he tried again. I told you, I never want to speak to him again. And I *mean* it. I tried to let him know about the baby. I owe him nothing more, and no matter what you say, I won't change my mind."

Bess switched on the bedside lamp. Carly angled an arm over her eyes. "Would you please turn that off?"

"I want to see your face while we talk. Your eyes will adjust in a minute."

"It feels like knives stabbing my pupils."

"Don't look directly at it." Bess leaned against the wall. "Ah, Carly."

"Don't start lecturing me, Bess. I mean it. He's a slime ball."

"A slime ball that at least tried to return your call. I can understand how you're feeling, Carls, honestly, and I don't really blame you. But you know what I think?"

"No," Carly said wearily, "but I'm sure you're going to tell me."

"I think you should at least talk to the guy. You're pregnant with his baby. If he's willing to help you out financially, you'd be insane to pass on the offer."

"Help me out financially?" Carly couldn't believe Bess was suggesting such a thing. "I didn't call him hoping he'd offer me money. Is that why you were so bent on it—because you figured he'd cough up some cash?"

Bess lifted her hands. "It *is* his child. My answer to that isn't just yes, but hell, yes."

"I don't take handouts."

"You've taken special grants for school. How is this so different?"

Carly jackknifed to a sitting position. "How is it *different*? Grants are funded by governmental agencies and the private sector. There are grants for research, grants for the disadvantaged, grants for single mothers, and grants for the disabled, to name only a few. I qualified for the help. When I applied, my file was one of hundreds, probably thousands. There was nothing personal about it. It's not the same as begging for a handout—or holding a mistake over some guy's head and making him pay through the nose for the next twenty-one years."

"It's okay for you to suffer for the mistake, but he gets off scot-free? Is that how it goes? That doesn't strike me as being very equitable."

"You're not the one who's pregnant. It's not your call to make."

Bess crossed her arms. "So you'll accept my help, but not his."

"You're my friend. If you ever need me, I'll try to be there for you, too. This isn't the same. Surely you can see that. I don't want Hank Coulter's money. I'd feel like a charity case. Besides, say he offered and I accepted? That would give him rights I'd prefer he not have."

"Such as?"

"Such as—I don't know. I'd just feel beholden, that's all. I don't want to see him again, Bess. Can't you understand? Every time I think about that night, I want to die."

Bess scuffed the toe of her shoe over the carpet. "Carly, unless he has a below average IQ, don't you think he has some idea why you might have called? He's going to think about it and put two and two together. When he comes up with four, he'll try to find you if he's got a shred of decency."

"A shred of decency? You're crediting him with decency?" Carly flopped back on the bed. "He *cursed* at me when he realized I was a virgin. He didn't care that he'd hurt me. He just jerked away, cursed, and passed out. Now, a little over a week later, he didn't remember me? Don't talk to me about decency." Carly pulled the pillow over her face to block out the light. "I can't talk about this anymore. My head is killing me."

She heard Bess turn off the lamp. "You want your drops?"

"No, not yet. They're expensive. I'll wait to see if my eyes stop hurting on their own first."

"You need your drops, but they're expensive, so you're going to suffer instead of using them? Whether you accept Hank's money or not, he'll still have rights, Carly. Sooner or later, he may demand to see his child. What're you going to do then? Tell him no?"

Carly pulled the pillow tighter over her face. "I'd never do that. *If* he's smart enough to figure it out, and *if* he finds me, and *if* he gives a damn, I'll let him see his child. Just don't hold your breath waiting for it to happen. He's a jerk, I tell you. Jerks couldn't care less about exercising their visitation rights, and they don't particularly care if their children are provided for."

Carly listened as Bess left the room. When she was alone, she rolled onto her side and hugged her knees. *Who?* Every time she remembered Hank's saying that, she grew so furious she trembled. Even worse, it hurt more than she cared to admit, even to herself.

Hank kept his cell phone turned on all evening, wondering how Carly had gotten the number. He gave it out to very few people, and he knew damned well he'd never given it to her.

At ten, Hank said goodnight to Jake and Molly, then went up the log staircase to his bedroom to try calling Carly again. A woman with a deeper voice answered midway through the first ring, giving him the impression she'd been hovering near the phone. Hank knew it wasn't Carly. Earlier in the evening, her voice had been soft and tremulous. This gal sounded like a Marine Corps sergeant.

"I, um—" Taken off guard, Hank couldn't think of what to say. "This is Hank Coulter. Is Carly there?"

Long silence. Then the woman said, "She's asleep right now."

Hank figured this must be Carly's friend. She sounded like a ball buster. "Would you please tell her I called? It's extremely important that I speak to her."

Hank half expected the woman to hang up in his ear as Carly had done. Instead, she said, "This is Bess, Carly's roommate."

"Ah. Glad to make your acquaintance, Bess."

"Somehow I doubt that. And I *seriously* doubt that you've got any idea just how important it is that you speak to Carly."

Hank's stomach clenched, and icy foreboding moved through him again.

"Unfortunately," Bess went on, "you blew your chance. She'll never get in touch with you now. She only tried to begin with because she felt obligated to let you know. And then you didn't remember who she was. Tell me, Mr. Coulter, do you deflower so many virgins in the back of your truck you can't keep them straight?"

Hank sank onto the edge of the bed. He couldn't dredge up the indignation to defend himself.

"Carly is pregnant." Bess's whiskey voice quivered with anger. "That is your fault and, by extension, mine. I never should have taken her to that bar in the first place, and I sure as hell shouldn't have left her alone so some predatory creep could home in on her."

Hank wanted to say he wasn't a predatory creep, but the truth was that he'd come to see a lot of things differently since that night, and Bess was essentially correct. He'd gone to Chaps to have fun and end the evening with an accommodating female, no strings attached. For reasons beyond him, Carly had happened onto his hunting grounds.

"I didn't realize," he said. "If I'd known she was a virgin, I never would have touched her, I swear, but she didn't send out those kinds of signals."

"Maybe you were just so drunk, you weren't reading her signals very well."

Hank clutched the phone with such force his fist ached. Memories flashed through his mind—Carly, sipping the drink and wrinkling her nose; Carly, resisting momentarily when he waltzed her outside; Carly, uncertain where to put her hands when he kissed her. Bess was right. He hadn't been reading her signals very well.

Bess sighed as if the anger had drained her. In a

hollow, sad voice, she said, "To make matters worse, Mr. Coulter, Carly wasn't just any virgin. She was born blind with congenital cataracts and recurring lattice dystrophy. She had surgery to restore her sight only two and a half weeks ago, a mere week before you met her. Do you have any idea what that means?"

Hank felt as if the mattress had suddenly vanished from under him. "Blind, did you say? I'm sorry. You blew my mind clear off track. Cataracts and what kind of dystrophy?"

"Lattice. It hardens and cracks the surface of the corneas. In severe cases like Carly's, it causes blindness. The only solution is to scrape the surface of her corneas or do a corneal transplant. Carly had her first superficial keratectomy a week before you met her."

Hank didn't want to hear this. He really, really didn't want to hear this.

"Right now, her visual cortex is like that of a newborn baby," Bess continued. "That's the part of the brain where visual images are recorded as memories, for want of a more scientific explanation. When we're born, the visual cortex is blank. Because she was born blind, Carly's has remained blank. Now that she can finally see, she's struggling to learn her colors, to visually recognize numbers and letters, familiarize herself with the world around her, and getting terrific headaches from the ceaseless onslaught of stimulation. Now, thanks to you, she can't even take pain medication because she's pregnant."

Hank swallowed, hard. He felt sick to his stomach.

"The night you met Carly, she'd gone with me to Chaps to sit at a table and simply watch. She'd never seen people dance, and the few men she'd ever seen had been at a distance. When you started coming on

to her, she actually believed all your hokey lines."
Bess made a sound of frustration. "Oh, she says now
that she actually didn't, that she just went with the
moment, knowing deep down that it was all a bunch
of blarney. But I've known her all her life. On some
level, she believed every miserable lie you told her.
Otherwise, she never would have gotten in the truck
with you."

Hank's heart gave a painful twist. *Oh, God.* He remembered wondering if Carly were fresh out of a convent or something. He hadn't realized at the time how
close he was to guessing the truth. He'd been one of
the first men she'd ever seen at close range? His own
voice rang in his memory. *You're so damned beautiful.
When I first saw you, my heart damned near stopped
beating. Where have you been hiding all my life, darlin'?* He'd come on like a high wind.

Hank couldn't blame Bess for lighting into him, and
he listened in miserable silence as she went on to tell
him that this pregnancy could have an adverse affect
on Carly's lattice dystrophy. "Her first SK may not
last as long as it should now, and her specialist advises
against her getting a second one while she's pregnant.
Do you understand what that means, Hank? My
friend, who's waited twenty-eight years to finally see,
may go blind again during this pregnancy and remain
that way until the child's born. To make matters even
worse, she'll no longer be eligible for special grants to
help her finish school. In order to be reinstated as
legally blind and become eligible for the financial aid
again, she'll have to undergo another SK and a corneal
transplant, and both procedures must fail. How do you
think that's going to affect her studies, not to mention
her finances?"

Bracing an elbow on his knees, Hank pressed a knotted fist to his forehead. *Shit, shit, shit!*

"Having a baby will be expensive, too," Bess added.

"Doesn't she have insurance?"

"A major medical policy with a rider for eyes that her dad got right before she graduated from college, but it only covers eighty percent."

"She has private insurance? I thought she was a teacher."

"She was a teacher, but she knew from the start that she would leave the job in two years to attend grad school. Her group coverage stopped the moment she quit."

"Couldn't she get on Cobra until school convened and she could get student insurance?"

"Cobra is frightfully expensive, especially with eye coverage, and she could only stay on it for eighteen months."

That seemed like plenty of time to Hank until Bess added, "Carly had no guarantee that her first eye surgery would be successful. If it hadn't been, the specialist would have waited to let her eyes recover, and then he would have done a corneal transplant, lengthening the time before she could start attending classes and qualify for student insurance. Even if Cobra had extended her coverage on the preexisting condition, she couldn't have paid the huge premiums for any length of time."

"Ah."

"When you've got an ongoing condition like Carly's that will require numerous surgeries and you're not yet ready to settle into a permanent career job because you want to further your education, you have to look ahead and make sure you'll always have insurance, no matter what. Too many things can go wrong. If you let your private coverage lapse, your chances of finding another private insurer to take you on are slim. Most times, they won't even consider accepting someone with a serious preexisting condition. The only reason she was able to get the coverage she has is because she'd been covered for years under her father's policy. When she finished college and became ineligible as his dependent, his provider was obligated to give her coverage under her own policy."

Barely able to concentrate, Hank passed a hand over his eyes, trying to remember how they'd gotten off on a discussion about insurance. *Pregnant.* He needed a few minutes to regain his equilibrium and collect his thoughts.

"Just picture it, Hank. A blind college student, pregnant with your child, doing without her eye drops because they cost too much. Major medical doesn't offer prescription co-pays or help with office calls."

Bess fell silent for an interminably long while. Finally she said, "Well? Aren't you going to say something?"

Hank couldn't think what to say. This was far worse than he had imagined. What in God's name had he done? "Give me a minute. I'm trying to think."

"Think about what? Without your help, this pregnancy will screw up Carly's whole life."

"I understand that."

"Do you? It took her ten years to get where she is right now. This baby may make it impossible for her to go to grad school. It's hard anytime a single woman gets pregnant while she's trying to get through college. For a blind woman, magnify those problems a hundredfold."

Hank nodded, then realized she couldn't see him.

"Are you still there?"

"Yeah, I'm here," he replied.

"You're not saying much. Has any of this sunk into that boulder you call a brain?"

Normally, Hank wouldn't have taken that from anyone, but at the moment, he honestly felt he had it coming. No matter how many shots Bess took at him, it was Carly who'd taken the hardest hit. *Dance with the devil, and you're bound to get burned.* Oh, how he wished that were how it worked. But instead of ruining his own life, he'd destroyed someone else's.

"Right now, the boulder comment isn't far wrong. I'm still reeling at this end."

"And that's it? That's all you've got to say, that *you're* reeling?"

"You think I come up against a situation like this every day? Try to imagine my side in this. I didn't just hit on a virgin—which I'll point out to you is damned near impossible nowadays—but I hit on a blind virgin. Correction, a formerly blind virgin, who is now pregnant and may go blind again, thanks to me. I'm trying to absorb all this and figure out what the hell I should do."

"It seems pretty obvious to me."

Hank flopped back on the bed. He'd screwed up a few times, but never like this.

"No offers of money?" Bess asked shrilly. "No assurances that you'll try to make this right? All you can think about is yourself. Well, let me clue you in on a couple of things, buster. It hasn't been you puking your guts up every morning. And it isn't you whose future has just been blown to hell."

"Bess, I—"

"What can she do, sling hamburgers to cover the extra expenses? She can't even read yet. Toss in vision that blurs at the drop of a hat or conjures up things that aren't there, and maybe, just maybe, you can start to imagine how impossible it would be for her to work right now."

"Just give me a minute, Bess. I'm not bailing out here."

"When I see you, hat in hand, with your wallet extended, maybe I'll believe it."

"Don't hang up."

"Go screw yourself."

"I can't show up with my wallet extended if I don't know where she lives."

"I can't give you our address. She never wants to clap eyes on you again, and now that I've talked to you myself, I don't blame her. And, by the way, cowboy, you're a rotten lover. I don't know exactly what happened in your truck that night, but it definitely wasn't something Carly will remember with fondness for the rest of her life."

With that parting shot, Bess slammed the phone down in his ear. Hank lay there listening to the dead zone, still stunned by everything Bess had told him. That he would take care of Carly financially went without saying. But, somehow, that didn't seem like enough.

Puking every morning? And judging by other things Bess had said, the morning sickness might prove to be the least of her physical problems during the pregnancy. He couldn't just cut her a check to salve his conscience, arrange to support his child, get visitation, and then walk away.

Chapter Six

Hank needed to talk with someone. Somehow, he couldn't quite bring himself to confide in Jake, who was reclining on the sofa, his pretty wife tucked under one arm, his son asleep on his chest. He looked too damned respectable for words. Instead Hank drove out to see his brother Zeke, who was almost two years older than him, still single, and might understand how a guy could land himself in such a mess. Hank was relieved to see lights still on in his brother's newly purchased ranch rambler. He parked on the circular gravel drive.

The chill night air crawled down his collar as he walked up the stepping-stone path to the wide, country-style veranda. Two months ago, when Hank had helped his brother move, Zeke had meant to purchase some deck chairs so he could sit on the porch of an evening and gaze across his land, but so far, they hadn't appeared.

Once at the door, Hank leaned on the doorbell. An instant later, the sharp report of boot heels striking the entryway tile reached his ears.

"Hey, Hank," Zeke said as the door swung wide. "What are you doing out here so late?"

Trust a brother to bypass the pleasantries. The smell

of fish wafted through the open doorway. Hank guessed that Zeke had dined on one of his famous gourmet meals. As masculine and tough as his brother looked, he loved to cook. Their mother was fond of saying that he'd make some lucky woman a wonderful husband, but so far, Zeke had managed to ignore her hints.

"I need to bend your ear, Zeke. I hope I haven't caught you at a bad time."

Zeke glanced at his watch. "I've got to be up early tomorrow, but I can spare you a couple of minutes."

This was going to take a lot longer than that. Hank stepped inside. He heard the low drone of the TV, a newscast, judging by the sound, which reminded him that the world hadn't spun off its axis. He only felt as if it had.

"Got my tomato plants in today," Zeke said as he closed the door. "If you'd come earlier, you could see the garden."

The last thing Hank wanted to discuss was gardening.

"I've really messed up bad," he informed his brother.

"Yeah?" Zeke frowned, so closely resembling Hank's reflection in a mirror that it was uncanny. "Let me guess. You got in an argument at the bar, a fight broke out, and you smacked somebody."

"I haven't stepped foot in a bar for almost two weeks. I wish it were just a fight I had to worry about. If only it were that simple."

"Well, hell."

Zeke led the way to the family room, which stayed fairly tidy because there was no one but him to mess it up. After switching off the TV, he stepped over to the well-stocked wet bar. "Take a load off," he said, indicating the sofa with a nod of his head.

The mirrored wall behind the bar reflected the light, flashing into Hank's eyes as he lowered himself onto a cushion.

"Name your poison." Zeke set a bottle on the counter. "Whiskey, Scotch? If you prefer beer, I've got Black Butte and Fat Tire."

Hank shook his head. "Nothing for me, thanks. I've backed off on the drinking."

Zeke froze, one large hand curled over the whiskey bottle. "No more hanging out in bars, and you've backed off on your drinking?"

"That's right." The stunned expression on Zeke's face irritated Hank. "I'd think you'd be happy. You've bitched at me for almost a year to do both."

A long silence ensued. Finally, Zeke abandoned the bottle and stepped from behind the bar. "Jesus, Mary, and Joseph, what have you done?" He sounded like their Irish-Catholic grandfather on a rant. "It must be something really bad if it's convinced you to straighten up your act."

Hank sat forward on the sofa and propped his forehead on his fists. "I got a girl pregnant."

Zeke dropped down on the adjacent easy chair and sprawled his legs. From the corner of his eye, all Hank could see of his brother were long stretches of dusty blue denim and the well-worn soles of his boots.

"Okay," Zeke said. Another silence. "*Damn*. I'm not the oldest. Why dump this in my lap? Jake's the one to talk to."

"Jake's married. I felt more comfortable coming to you. I thought you might better understand how I got into a jam like this."

"Think again. Unless the condom broke, there's no excuse for knocking a woman up."

Hank rubbed a hand over his face. "I wasn't wearing any protection. Normally, I do. This one time, I—" He shrugged. "Like you say, there's no excuse. I was a little drunk." Hank glanced at his brother's dark face. "Okay, dammit, a lot drunk."

"So drunk you lost all common sense? Sorry, I'm not buying."

"I started to get the condoms out of the glove box. The carton slipped and spilled all over the floorboard. We were in back, and I was—" Hank swallowed to steady his voice. "The unvarnished truth is, I was too drunk to give a shit. Not thinking straight. You know? I figured just once wouldn't hurt."

"Famous last words. You did it in your *truck*?" Zeke looked appalled.

"She wouldn't go two blocks over to the motel." Hank swept off his hat to push at his hair. He tossed the Stetson onto the cushion beside him. "I don't blame you for coming down on me, but right now, I need advice, not an ass chewing. I messed up. I admit it. Now I've got to figure out a way to fix things."

Zeke sighed and pinched the bridge of his nose. "A pregnancy is kind of hard to fix."

"It gets worse, Zeke. She was a virgin."

"A *what*?"

"You heard me."

Zeke sat forward on the chair. Then he unfolded his considerable length to return to the bar. "God help us. How old is she?"

"Twenty-eight. At least give me credit for having a few standards. If a woman doesn't look well over twenty-one, I run the other way."

Zeke's blue eyes flashed with disapproval as he un-
capped the whiskey bottle. "I wasn't implying that you
have no standards." He poured bourbon into a glass,
not even bothering to add ice. As he retraced his steps
to the sitting area, he said, "You just took me off
guard. Where in the hell did you find a twenty-eight-
year-old virgin?"

"At Chaps."

"What was she doing there, living dangerously?"

The question started Hank to talking, and before he
knew it, he'd blurted out most of the details, including
everything about Carly's eye disease. Afterward, Zeke
just sat there, staring at the toes of his boots.

"Would you please say something?" Hank prodded,
his voice ragged with stress and embarrassment.

"I can't think of anything." Zeke downed the contents of his glass in three gulps. Whistling at the burn,
he said, "I can't believe I'm hearing this, Hank. A
blind girl? What in the hell are you gonna do?"

"That's why I'm here, for advice. It's not the usual
situation. I can't just help her out financially, arrange
to see the kid, and let her manage on her own."

Zeke leaned his head against the chair back. When
he looked at Hank again, he said, "You need a drink,
little brother. You're shaking like a leaf."

Hank glanced at his hands, saw that Zeke was right,
and said, "Maybe so. I'm still in shock, I think. When
her friend Bess started laying all this on me, I felt
numb. Now feeling numb would be an improvement.
I can't believe I did something so damned stupid. That
it was with someone like Carly only makes it worse."

"A drink or two can't hurt," Zeke assured him.
"Maybe it'll calm you down so you can get this sorted
out. The sofa's yours for the night."

"Thanks. I'm sure as hell not going to drink and drive. The way my luck's running, I'd have an accident."

Zeke paced back to the bar. "Pardon me for pointing it out, but it sounds to me as if you've broken that rule a few times." At Hank's questioning look, he added, "Driving two blocks over to a motel. Ring a bell?"

"There's a connecting alleyway," Hank explained, "and it's always late at night. I only have to cross one public street, and it's a side street with no traffic at that hour. Most of the time, though, I just lock my truck and call a cab."

"I'm glad to hear it. I'd hate to think you drove on a main thoroughfare in that condition."

"Never." Hank met his brother's gaze. "I know it may not sound it, but for the most part, I've been responsible. The situation with Carly was a deviation from the usual for me."

"How did you get that far into things without—you know, realizing she was a virgin? At some point, didn't you notice she wasn't practiced at all her moves?"

"Her moves seemed pretty damned good to me. She was—" Hank broke off and frowned. "You aging that whiskey or pouring it?"

Zeke finished filling the glasses and resumed his seat. After handing Hank a tumbler, he said, "If this Carly loses her sight again, how in the world will she stay in school without grants and financial aid? That aside, she'll have a lot of additional costs—doctor bills, hospital bills, and possible complications during the pregnancy. And how will a blind woman deal with the day-to-day burden of caring for an infant while she's trying to attend classes?"

Hank just shook his head, feeling heartsick.

"You're right," Zeke said. "Picking up the tab for everything won't be enough. I'm not even sure that's a practical solution. Just the cost of supporting two households for a couple of years would be a huge drain on your pocketbook. You may not be able to swing it, Hank."

Hank had thought the same thing.

"Do you like this young woman well enough to marry her?"

"I can't honestly say if I like her or not," Hank confessed hollowly. "That night, getting to know her wasn't on my agenda. She was pretty. I wanted to score. The chitchat was just window dressing—something a guy does to break the ice. As for marrying her?" Hank puffed a breath into his cheeks. "It's the only affordable solution I can think of, and my druthers don't really matter."

"Have you mentioned marriage to her as an option?"

"No. I never got around to discussing options with her. She won't talk to me. Every time I call, she hangs up."

Zeke arched his dark eyebrows. "You had sex with the woman, and now she won't speak to you?"

Giving his whiskey a slow swirl, Hank explained the confusion about Carly's name. "I wasn't exactly what you'd call a prince that night, either. I can't clearly remember what happened, only that she cried out. That was when I realized she was a virgin. Directly afterward—well, I think I must have passed out. I woke up the next morning on the back floorboard. She was long gone. I've been worried sick for a week and a half. I couldn't remember her last name to track her down, and she didn't get in touch with me until this evening."

"Well, little brother, it's definitely a complicated situation. Maybe you should go to her house and talk to her, face to face. It's been my experience that women find it more difficult to cut a guy off when he's there in the flesh."

"I'll have to track her down first. She won't give me her address." The dull ache behind Hank's eyes had sharpened and magnified. "Before I do that, I need to have all my ducks in a row. For obvious reasons, she's not going to be hot on the idea of marriage. But no matter how I circle it, I can't think of a better answer. With the eye problem, she can't possibly work and help out with any of the costs. And her friend Bess told me her health insurance is a bare-bones major medical policy that only covers eighty percent. Mine is more comprehensive, with eye and dental, plus prescription co-pay. Jake and I joined a rancher's association that offers great group insurance at reasonable rates. If Carly's my wife, she'll automatically be covered."

"Even for preexisting conditions?"

"I read the fine print before I left the house. For new spouses, there's only a three-month waiting period on all preexisting. Family rates will cost me more, but I could cover the dividends on both her policy and mine for three months. Then she'd be covered for everything, eye surgeries and childbirth included."

"That alone would save you a bundle."

"Yeah," Hank said, his voice gone hoarse with exhaustion. "Cohabiting would be cheaper, too. One household, one set of utility bills, and all that. I was thinking we might live in the cabin along the creek.

It's not the Ritz, but there's no rent, and I can fix the place up. I'm making pretty good money now, and I've got a nice nest egg tucked away, but I'm still not a rich man."

"It's a hell of a way to begin a marriage, Hank."

"I know. But what choice do I have?" Hank stared morosely into his whiskey. "Getting married isn't high on my list. Trust me on that. But it is my baby. Carly's whole future is riding on me and how I face up to my responsibilities."

Zeke's weathered face creased in a slight smile. After searching Hank's face, he said, "You keep on, little brother, and I might start thinking you've finally grown up."

Hank had a knot in his chest the size of a baseball. "I deserve that, I guess. I was a little late sowing my wild oats. Wasn't I?"

Zeke sank back in the chair and crossed his ankles. "You could say that. I got all of it out of my system in college."

"I was working two jobs and taking a full course load in college," Hank reminded him. "Dad was going bankrupt paying our sister's medical bills my first year, and he lost the ranch the next."

"Ah, that's right." Zeke frowned and his expression turned grim. Hank knew that his brother was thinking of their sister Bethany and remembering that sad time in their lives. Despite the many surgeries and all of their father's sacrifices, Bethany's accident at eighteen had left her a paraplegic, and she'd been confined to a wheelchair ever since. "I guess sowing your oats wasn't an option. Was it?"

"No, and after I graduated, I was too busy working and saving to go in partners with Jake to take any time out for foolishness. This last year, the tide turned. I started making better money, and I didn't have to work myself into the ground doing it. It was the first time I could enjoy myself. I went a little crazy for a while, I guess. Buying myself toys, drinking. Now Carly is paying for it." Hank sighed. "I never dreamed something like this might happen. I feel so—" Hank rubbed the back of his neck. "I can't describe how I feel. Like a shit, only worse."

"You know what Dad says. 'There's no better teacher than regret.'"

Hank turned his glass in his hand. "Enough about that. It's done, and beating up on myself won't change anything. I have to think about Carly and what's best for her and the baby. There'll be time enough later to kick myself in the ass."

"True. The child will be your responsibility for the next twenty-one years or until it graduates from college."

"Right now, I'm more concerned about the immediate future. The way I see it, if I can convince Carly to marry me, I can swing everything financially. My schedule is fairly flexible at the ranch, so I could watch the baby, too, eliminating the cost of childcare and freeing her up to study. The same applies if anything goes wrong during the pregnancy. I'll be able to take care of her. Her friend Bess seems to be very fond of her, but from what I gathered, she's a college student, too. She can't very well attend classes, work a job, study, and still find time to help with the baby or take care of Carly if she gets sick."

"How do you think Carly will greet this idea?" Zeke asked. "It's bound to take some convincing."

Just thinking about Carly's possible reaction made Hank's headache worse.

"Maybe you could go into it as a temporary arrangement," Zeke suggested. "Just for a couple of years, until she's had another surgery to restore her sight, gets her master's, lands a job, and can make it on her own if you help her out financially."

Hank quickly warmed to that idea. "Two years sounds a hell of a lot better than a life sentence. Go on."

Zeke nodded. "Locking down for a lifetime with someone you don't love is a frightening thought. This way, you could pay all her expenses, help her get through the pregnancy, and take care of the baby while she's going to school. When she gets her degree, you can give her some start-up cash, and then it's *adios*. She won't be devastated by the hardship, the kid will have your name, and you'll automatically be granted visitation privileges by the state. It's not an ideal solution, but in this day and age, a lot of kids have divorced parents. Afterward, you'll both be able to move on with your lives."

For the first time since his conversation with Bess, Hank felt a ray of hope. "She just might go for that. If I can get her to speak to me, that is."

"I've got no brilliant ideas on that front. You're the one with the charm, little brother. I was in the back row when charisma was handed out."

"You're charming enough."

Zeke laughed and threw Hank a sofa pillow. "Right. Horses love me. Women—well, they're another matter. I call a spade a spade. Women like a man to lie a little." He pushed to his feet. "One question. If

Carly refuses to give you her address, how are you going to find her?"

"I have her phone number. A good friend of mine at the police department should be able to get her address from a reverse directory. Finding her won't be a problem. Convincing her to talk to me will be the hard part."

Chapter Seven

Carly ran her fingers over the bottles on each shelf of the medicine cabinet in search of the sterile eyewash. Since her surgery three weeks ago, she often awakened of a morning with matted eyes.

After locating the squeeze bottle, she filled the plastic cup, pressed it over her eye, and leaned her head back to let the solution soften the crust that had matted her lashes. Even after she cleansed both eyes, the edges of everything still looked fuzzy.

Concerned, Carly went to the kitchen. After several aborted attempts, she finally managed to dial the office number of her corneal specialist in Portland. When he finally came to the phone, Carly was so upset she was trembling. Haltingly, she described her blurry vision and told him that washing her eyes hadn't helped.

"Has the pregnancy been confirmed?" he asked.

Her stomach squeezed with anxiety. "Yes. They called with the results yesterday."

"I'm not going to lie to you, Carly. As I explained during our last conversation, pregnancy weakens your resistance to lattice, diverting most of the nutrients and vitamins to the baby instead of to your eyes. In cases like yours, where an SK was done on already diseased corneas, the lattice already has a foothold and can escalate quickly. In short, if the blurriness is that pronounced, it may be due to the pregnancy. I really wish you hadn't gotten pregnant right now."

Not long ago, Carly had wished the same thing, but now she'd come to want this baby. Bracing herself for the worst, she asked, "With it starting this fast, how quickly do you think I may go blind again, Dr. Merrick?"

The doctor took a moment to reply. "It's impossible to predict." He paused again. "Let's think positively. All right? The blurry vision could be due to a number of other things. Your visual cortex may be acting up. Or you could be developing blepharitis, an inflammation of the eyelids. Yours are badly scarred from the lattice." He paused for a moment. "Just to be safe, I'd like you to be examined. Given the distance, it'd be silly for you to drive four hours to come here when the doctor in Crystal Falls is perfectly qualified to check your eyes. Can you arrange for transportation to his office today?"

Bess had left for another interview, but Carly expected her back in the early afternoon. "I could get there by two or three."

"Good. I'll call his office, have them work you in, and let you know what time to be there."

"Thanks, Dr. Merrick."

"Chances are it's only a mild case of blepharitis or something similar. He may just tell you to continue with your antibiotic drops, give your eyes frequent rests, and try not to worry too much. Getting upset isn't good for you or the baby."

Carly looped an arm around her waist. The doctor was right. How she felt about losing her sight again wasn't the primary concern anymore. She had a little person to think of now.

The specialist concluded the conversation by saying, "According to my records, your six-week checkup is on July seventh. I'll be able to tell you more then."

"If the blurry vision is from the lattice, should I come sooner?" she asked.

The doctor hesitated before replying. "If the lattice is to blame, Carly, there's virtually nothing I can do until the baby's born. We just need to make sure you don't have a postsurgical infection. If, by some chance, that's the problem, the doctor there can treat it as well as I could."

After hanging up the phone, Carly put a piece of bread in the toaster and then stood before the open refrigerator, trying to see what sat on the shelves. Nothing looked appetizing. Over the last week, she'd been craving sour foods. She plucked out an unopened quart of chocolate milk, and then turned to the cupboards. On the middle shelf, she found what she hoped was a jar of sauerkraut.

When she unscrewed the lid, the sour smell that wafted to her nostrils was heavenly. She grabbed a fork, took a tentative taste to identify the contents, and then began eating ravenously straight from the jar. *Wonderful*, she thought as she chased down a mouthful of fermented· cabbage with flavored milk. Rationally, she knew the combination should make her shudder, but oddly it didn't. Even better, it seemed to settle her queasy stomach.

After eating, Carly showered and dressed. Upon emerging from the bathroom, she felt more like her old self than she had in days, the nausea and wooziness nearly gone. *Sauerkraut and chocolate milk.* She made a mental note to stock up on both items so she would have plenty on hand for breakfast each morning. Brussels sprouts sounded good, too. She remembered hearing somewhere that food cravings during pregnancy were often caused by vitamin and mineral deficiencies.

She'd just finished brushing her hair when the doorbell rang. When she opened the door, she found a man standing on the porch. At a distance of five feet, with sunlight behind him to create a blinding nimbus of gold around his dark head, his features were indistinct. She stared blankly at him, the sudden brightness lancing into her eyes like needles.

"Hi, again," he said.

Carly would have recognized that deep, silken voice anywhere. Her stomach knotted and then felt as if it had dropped to the region of her knees. She clenched her hand over the doorknob, momentarily unsteady on her feet. She was too startled to speak, her mind circling dizzily around unanswerable questions. How had he found her? Why had he bothered? And how dare he say, "Hi, again," as if they'd parted under the best of circumstances?

"Don't you recognize me?" he asked with an incredulous laugh.

Carly wasn't about to explain that the sun was blinding her. He stepped closer, which brought his dark, chiseled features into better focus and made him seem to loom in the doorway, far taller and broader through the shoulders than she remembered. The brilliant blue of his eyes rivaled the sky behind him.

Carly's first urge was to slam the door in his face

and run to the bedroom. Instead, she stood there, clinging to the door for support. "Hello, Hank."

He shifted his weight, bending one knee and cocking a hip. Dressed in faded jeans and a blue shirt, he looked exactly as she remembered, the very epitome of rugged strength. When he grinned, flashing even, white teeth, her heart bumped against her ribs, and she couldn't help but stare at his mouth, remembering how she'd felt when he kissed her. The memory infuriated her and filled her with shame. How could she have been so witless? Their encounter had meant nothing to him. *She* had meant nothing to him. He probably slept with a different woman every weekend.

"Go away," she managed to squeeze out.

He braced a hand on the doorframe. "You know I can't do that, Carly. I spoke to Bess on the phone last night. I know about the baby."

"Bess told you?" Carly's sense of betrayal came hard and fast.

"Someone had to. It is my child. I had a right to know."

Bess knew how Carly felt about seeing Hank again. "And she gave you our address as well?"

"No, no." He held up a hand. "She wouldn't tell me where you lived. I had your phone number. A friend of mine ferreted out your address."

Carly pressed a protective hand over her stomach. She didn't like the determined glint in his eyes. As an undergraduate, she'd known girls who accidentally got pregnant, and she remembered very well how most of their boyfriends had reacted. *Get rid of it.* If Hank had come here, hoping to convince her to do something like that, he had another think coming.

"I'm sorry for not recognizing your name when you called last night. With all the noise at the bar, I thought you said your name was Charlie. It took me a second to make the connection, and by then, you'd hung up. It wasn't that I didn't remember you. I even went back to the bar and put out feelers, hoping to find you. If you don't believe me, call Chaps and ask Gary, the bartender."

"At this point, I don't really care if you remembered me or not." Even as Carly said the words, her heart panged. "I just want you to go away."

He dragged a boot heel over the doormat. "You're carrying my child." His voice dipped to a husky timbre. "I can't walk away from that."

"I'm not giving you an option."

He locked gazes with her, his blue eyes suddenly sharp and piercing. No smile softened his expression now. "I'd like to talk to you about how we should handle this."

Trembling, Carly said, "I'm having this baby. If you're here to offer me money for an abortion, you can forget the idea as quickly as you forgot me. My baby isn't a mistake to be rectified. Is that clear?"

"Crystal clear. I'm not here to suggest anything of the sort. Will you ask me in and hear what I do have to say?"

"You can say it on the porch."

Carly didn't care if she sounded hateful. She'd behaved so foolishly that night. Every cliche she'd ever heard seemed to apply—acting like a besotted idiot at the top of the list.

Frowning, he straightened and hooked his thumbs over his belt. "Do you really want everyone in this apartment complex to hear our business?"

"*Our* business? There is no *we* in this equation."

That glint crept into his eyes again. "Let me re-phrase that. Do you want everybody to know *your* business, namely that you're pregnant with my kid?"

"It's a baby, not a kid, and it's mine, not yours." Her stomach rolled, and the sauerkraut she'd so greedily gobbled for breakfast sent a rush of acid up the back of her throat. "I won't contact you in five years with my hand out, if that's your worry. You can walk away, never look back, and pretend this never happened."

"Is that what you think I want—to just walk away?"

"I don't really care what you want."

"No matter what your opinion of me, that doesn't negate the fact that I'm the father of that baby."

"Yes, biologically, you're the father. So is a sperm donor."

His jaw muscle started to tic. Carly felt an irrational rush of trepidation. Having been blind all her life, she'd developed a sixth sense with people, radar of sorts that helped her feel their auras. That night at Chaps, she'd sensed in Hank an underlying kindness that had made her trust him. Now she felt strength and determination emanating from him in overpower-ing waves, and she instinctively knew he didn't give up easily once he set his mind to something.

"Maybe I am only a sperm donor. But be that as it may, I feel obligated to make sure you and the baby want for nothing. Bess told me about your eye prob-lems, Carly, and how this pregnancy may affect you, both physically and financially. I want to lighten the burden on you in any way I can."

Carly stiffened as the implications of that sank in. "News flash. I don't want you to feel obligated, not to me or my baby. Is that what you think, that I called to tap you for money? I just felt you had a right to know that you'd soon be a father. Fleecing you for support was not my objective."

Hank could see this was getting him nowhere. While he stood there, trying to sort his thoughts, he couldn't help but congratulate himself on at least one thing: he'd chosen a beautiful woman to be the mother of his child. Even in the harsh light of day, Carly had delicately drawn features, complemented by flawless ivory skin and big, expressive blue eyes. Streaked with strands of honey brown, her hair looked naturally blond and lay over her slender shoulders in rippling drapes of gold. A white T-shirt and snug blue jeans showcased her figure, emphasizing small, perfectly shaped breasts, a narrow waist, nicely rounded hips, and shapely legs.

Seeing her like this brought memories rushing back to him that had eluded him until now—how right she'd felt in his arms, how heady her kisses had been, and how much he had wanted her. In his recollection, he'd never wanted a woman quite so much.

As lovely as she was, though, what struck Hank hardest was her look of angelic sweetness. He'd noticed it that night—and shrugged it off. The women who frequented bars usually had a hard look. Carly's heart shone in her eyes.

Those eyes. So beautiful he could scarcely believe they were flawed. Even worse was the realization that his careless use of her body had possibly condemned her to months of blindness. How would she attend grad school without his help?

A squeaking sound drew his attention. Her left forearm was shifting, the tendons from wrist to elbow distended as she turned her clenched hand on the doorknob. It was the unconscious gesture of someone rigid with tension. All his senses went on red alert. He slid his gaze slowly back to her face, noting the tautness of her facial muscles. Was that fear he saw in her expression?

The possibility gave Hank pause. It wasn't as if he'd forced himself on her. As he recalled, she'd melted into his arms when he kissed her, a consenting partner every step of the way.

Maybe, he decided, that was the problem. She'd surrendered to the moment, giving herself to him without reservation. Standing back from it now and trying to see it as she must, he supposed she had reason to feel wary. *She believed all your hokey lines.*

"I have things to do," she informed him. "If there's something more you want to say, get it said. I can't stand here all morning."

He scratched behind his ear and wished for his hat. In tense moments, a Stetson always came in handy.

"Will you go out to dinner with me?" Definitely not brilliant.

A tiny frown puckered the smooth skin between her brows. "How can you think, even for a moment, that I'd ever consider going out with you."

"I don't mean on a date. I was just thinking—well, you know—that you might feel more comfortable on neutral ground, someplace public, where we can discuss this and reach some decisions."

"We were on neutral ground the last time," she reminded him.

Hank could think of no immediate comeback to refute that point.

"And any decisions regarding this baby are mine

alone to make," she added. "I'll notify you when the child is born. If you want visitation privileges, I won't deny you that right. But I want nothing more to do with you."

This was not going the way Hank had hoped. "Carly, please, I—"

Those gorgeous eyes went bright with anger. "Do you know what you said to me right before you passed out?"

Hank hadn't a clue. Evidently, that showed on his face because she jutted her small chin and said, "It was an appropriate ejaculation, given the circumstances. Does that refresh your memory any?"

Before he could reply, she closed the door in his face. An appropriate ejaculation? He cringed at the implications. Normally, he never used obscene language around women or children. It was a hard-and-fast rule, drilled into him by his father. He closed his eyes, feeling ashamed. She'd given him a precious gift—her virginity—and he'd said a filthy word like that to her?

He stood there, torn between pounding on the door until she opened it again and walking away. He decided on the latter. He'd made initial contact. She was feeling hostile, and rightly so. In a couple of days, maybe she'd be more inclined to talk to him.

When Bess got home three hours later, Carly explained how she'd awakened that morning with blurry vision. "The eye doctor here in Crystal Falls can see me at a quarter of five. Would you mind driving me?"

"Of course not." Bess frowned in concern. "Does Dr. Merrick think you may be losing your sight?"

Carly avoided meeting her gaze. "He says that

chances are it's only a little inflammation. But, given the pregnancy, it could also be the lattice regaining a foothold."

Bess clasped Carly's shoulder. "This fast? How can that be?"

"He says most of the nutrients from my food are going to the baby now instead of to my eyes. Some women lose their sight rather quickly." Carly tried to smile. "There's no point in getting upset, Bess. If it happens, it happens. For now, I'm trying to think positively. Why worry when it may only be an infection? Chances are I'll be able to see for months yet, maybe even until the end of my pregnancy."

Later that same afternoon as Carly left the medical building with Bess, she recounted everything the eye doctor had told her. "He says the matted eye problem is caused by an inflammation in my eyelids," she said. "I need to use the antibiotic drops more often and give my eyes frequent breaks." Carly grinned. "Eat your heart out. Frequent naps, doctor's orders."

Bess unlocked the doors of her old Toyota. Over the roof of the car, she asked, "And your corneas? How are they looking?"

Carly climbed into the vehicle and fastened her seat belt. Her stomach fluttered with nerves as she said, "He could see some deterioration, but at this point, it's not that severe. He'll call and confer with Dr. Merrick. One of them will call me tomorrow with more information."

Bess said very little during the drive back to the apartment complex. Once they were home, she went to the kitchen to pour herself some ice tea and Carly some juice. En route back to the living room, she fixed

Carly with a worried look. "You think you're going blind again, don't you?"

"You're forgetting that I've been blind all my life. If it happens, I'll deal with it."

Bess still looked worried, but she let the subject drop. Carly was relieved. If she went blind again, chances were that it wouldn't be soon. She didn't want to think about it until it happened. Then she would deal with it somehow. She was good at dealing with things. When you are born blind, you have to be.

Bess canceled a job interview the following day so she could be at the apartment when Dr. Merrick phoned. When Carly ended the conversation with the physician, Bess sat rigidly on a kitchen chair, her brown eyes shadowed with concern, her mouth drawn taut with tension.

"What did he say?" she asked.

Carly pushed her hair back. "There's a definite deterioration of my corneas. The local doctor could detect cracks developing."

Bess closed her eyes.

"On a bright note," Carly went on, "it's not a sure indication that I'll go blind during the pregnancy. Lattice is weird stuff. It may progress rapidly for a while, and then go into remission. Or, on the flip side, it sometimes causes little damage at the beginning of a pregnancy, and then runs rampant a few months later, causing blindness in a matter of days or weeks. My eyes are clear of infection. The deterioration thus far is minimal." Carly shrugged. "It's a wait-and-see game. Since the damage so far is slight, I'm hoping I'll be able to see for several more months."

"How can you be so calm? It drives me crazy."

Carly rolled her eyes. "You think it might help if I screamed and pulled my hair? I have to take what comes. Just pray for me, Bess. If possible, I'd rather not go blind. It'll be a lot easier if I remain sighted so I can go to school as planned."

On Monday night, Hank gathered his courage and dialed Carly's phone number. She answered on the second ring.

"Hi, Carly, this is Hank."

His lines well rehearsed, Hank took a breath to continue, and in the interim, the phone clicked and went dead.

"Carly?"

No answer. Hank held the phone away and stared at it. How in the hell could he communicate with her if she refused to speak to him? She clearly expected him to just walk away and forget she existed, that his child existed. Well, he had news for her. No child of his was going to grow up never knowing its father. And he'd be damned if he would abandon its mother when she needed him.

Hank sat down at his desk and wrote Carly a long letter, apologizing profusely for his inexcusable behavior the night they met and once again offering her financial and moral support during the pregnancy. By Friday, when no reply was forthcoming, either by mail or phone, he had to accept that a passive-aggressive approach wasn't working. As a last resort, he tried the old standby, sending flowers. When all else failed, sometimes a dozen roses did the trick.

Lying on the floor in front of the television, Carly frowned as she tried to put a puzzle together, a pastime that bored her to tears but was necessary to help train her visual cortex to recognize and learn to match different shapes. What really rankled was that a child's puzzle was so difficult for her to master. It made her feel dumber than dirt.

The doorbell rang just then, providing a welcome distraction. Swallowing her last bite of pickle, she sprang to her feet. For just an instant after she came erect, the room spun and the beige carpet seemed to undulate. Carly stopped and waited for her visual cortex to stop acting up before she proceeded across the floor.

His ruddy face a swimming blur, a thin man stood on the porch. In his arms, he held a long box that Carly decided was light pink. The many different shades of pink confused her, and she was beginning to despair that she'd ever learn them all.

"Are you Carly Adams?" the man asked.

"Yes."

He stepped forward to thrust the box into her arms. As he did, his face came into clearer focus. Carly saw that he was young, with red hair and funny little brown spots all over his face. *Freckles*. Carly had heard of freckles but never actually seen any. He flashed a warm smile. "These are for you, Ms. Adams. A card from the sender is inside. Hope you enjoy."

Bewildered, Carly watched the man lope away until he was nothing but a distorted blob bouncing across the swimming green backdrop of lawn that was shared by all occupants of the apartment complex. A lovely scent wafted to her nostrils, drawing her gaze back to the box. Roses? The smell was unmistakable.

After closing the door, Carly went to the kitchen table, opened the box, and gasped with pleasure as she peeled back the waxed green tissue paper to reveal the brilliant red buds. *Roses.*

As she stared down at the flowers, a part of her wanted to lift them from the box and examine them. She'd always loved their scent, but she'd never had an opportunity to study them up close. They were far lovelier than she'd ever imagined, the furled petals velvet soft. Only who had sent them? Her dad, presently living in Arizona, was on a fixed income. He might send her a card to congratulate her about the baby, but roses were beyond his budget.

Suddenly, Carly knew who'd sent the flowers. *Hank.* Her first impulse was to dump them in the trash, just as she had his letter, but somehow she couldn't bring herself to do it. Anything so beautiful deserved to be enjoyed. She lifted the long-stemmed blossoms from the box and lightly touched her nose to the petals. She couldn't throw them away. She just couldn't.

She consoled herself with the thought that Hank had probably ordered the roses over the phone and paid by credit card. He'd never actually seen the flowers, which lessened her feeling of distaste about keeping them.

Bess came home just as Carly was sticking the last rose into an empty sauerkraut jar, the closest thing to a vase that she had.

"How did the job interview go?"

Bess tossed her purse on the couch. "I was one of over fifty people who applied. I didn't even get a maybe."

"Next week you'll find something," Carly assured her.

"Oh!" Bess cried when she saw the flowers. "How beautiful!"

"Aren't they, though?" Carly stood back to admire the arrangement. The jar wasn't quite tall enough, and the buds sprawled in all directions, magnifying their presence on the table.

"Who sent them?"

"Don't spoil it by asking. I almost threw them away."

"Hank." Bess picked up the little gold card that Carly had left lying unread in the folds of tissue. She scanned the message, her expression turning pensive. "Hmm."

Carly didn't like the sound of that. "What does it say?"

"Nothing much, only that he's very sorry and hopes you'll call him."

"Not likely."

"A dozen long-stemmed roses, hand delivered by a florist, are expensive, Carly. He's obviously doing everything he can to make peace with you."

"Poor Hank, is that it? Sorry. I'm not buying."

Bess went to the refrigerator for her afternoon glass of ice tea. "In my opinion, any guy who sends roses to apologize ought to be allowed to say it in person. What can it hurt to hear him out?"

Carly stepped back to the table to fiddle with the flowers. When she reached for a sagging bud, she misjudged her aim and knocked over the jar. Water went everywhere.

Bess sprang to the rescue with a towel. "Is your vision getting that bad?"

Carly just shrugged.

"Answer me, Carls. Has your vision become that much worse over the last week?"

Carly didn't want to lie, but at the same time, she

found it difficult to say the words aloud. "A little worse. I'm hoping it's due to the blepharitis."

"Have you called Merrick?"

"Why? I'm using the antibiotic drops. They'll either take care of the blurry vision or they won't. Merrick told me, straight out, that he can do nothing if it's from the lattice. The disease will just run its course."

Bess flopped on the sofa with her glass cradled in her hands. She gazed at the roses for a moment. "Oh, Carls, I really, really think you should at least talk with Hank. How can that hurt?"

"Funny you should use the word *hurt*. That's exactly what I thought a dozen times that night while I was throwing sanity to the wind. 'What can it hurt?' And you know what happened? He *hurt* me. Forget the emotional aspects. He did me physical injury. I could barely stand straight for two days."

"Only because he was drunk and didn't know he needed to be careful. He's sorry, Carly. We all make mistakes."

"Mine was trusting him in the first place. I don't want to see him again. I don't want to speak to him again. As far as I'm concerned, he doesn't exist."

Bess mulled that over. "You're still attracted to him."

Carly pretended to gag. "Spare me."

"It's true. I see it written all over you. That's why you're so dead set against seeing him again. You're afraid he'll sweet talk you, that you'll forget how awful it was the first time and end up in the same situation again."

"Never." When Bess started to say something more, Carly threw up her hands. "*Enough!* How can you even think I'm attracted to him? Just because I made one stupid mistake doesn't mean my bra size is higher than my IQ.''

"Isn't he entitled to make one mistake as well?"

"Do you *really* believe I was his first mistake? Give me a break. I wasn't his first barroom score. Our encounter just ended on a more sour note than most."

"Maybe so. But, just for the sake of argument, is there a law that says he can't have seen the error of his ways? I think he deserves the benefit of the doubt. There aren't many guys who'd go to such lengths to stand good on their responsibilities."

"I don't want to be one of Hank Coulter's responsibilities."

Carly ended the conversation with that and went to her bedroom. She sat on the edge of the mattress and buried her face in her hands. Deep down, she knew Bess was right. She was afraid of Hank Coulter. The last time she'd been alone with him, disaster had struck. She remembered how he'd looked the other morning, standing on the porch, bigger than life and exuding strength. There was something about the man that rattled her. That being the case, all her feminine instincts warned her to stay away from him.

Chapter Eight

Kicked back on the recliner, Hank was dozing his way through a Winnie the Pooh flick that Molly had put in the VCR to soothe Garrett back to sleep after a bad dream. When the phone rang, he vaguely registered the sound and Jake's voice saying, "Hello." An instant later, Hank was being shaken awake by his sister-in-law.

"For you," Molly whispered.

Taking the portable, Hank kicked down the footrest and stood up. "Hello," he said as he moved toward the kitchen to escape the noise.

"Hi, Hank. This is Bess. I tried you on your cell, but you didn't answer."

Hank patted his belt. "Sorry. I must have left it in my truck." He rubbed his eyes to bring himself awake. "What's up? Is Carly okay?"

"No, actually, I'm afraid she may not be."

That brought Hank fully alert. "What's wrong?"

"I think she's losing her eyesight." Bess quickly related instances when she'd noticed Carly knocking things over and squinting to see. "I think it's happening very fast. In addition to that and the morning sickness, she's getting terrific headaches."

"Has she called her doctor?"

"He told her there's nothing he can do. I got on the Internet tonight and got some info about lattice during pregnancy. The prognosis is pretty grim. Some women go blind very quickly, in as little as three weeks in some cases, and judging by things I've observed, I'm terrified Carls will be one of them."

Hank passed a hand over his eyes again. "Three weeks?"

"She's seeing on borrowed time, Hank. She's hoping the blurry vision and messed-up depth perception are due to the inflammation of her eyelids, but I think she's deluding herself."

Hank braced a hand on the edge of the counter. "This is all my fault. I am so sorry."

"I'm beginning to believe you really are," she said softly.

"She still won't talk to me. I've tried phoning. I even went to the apartment one morning. That ended with her closing the door in my face."

"I heard. The roses were beautiful, by the way. She's not usually so witchy. It's just—well, the entire situation is overwhelming for her, and I think you frighten her a little."

Hank could think of a number of words to describe Carly, but "witchy" wasn't one of them. "I sensed her wariness. I'm just not sure what's causing it. As badly as I screwed up that night, I didn't force her into the truck with me."

"I'm not sure what's troubling her. She hasn't talked a lot about it."

"Any guesses?"

"A painful first experience, and a fear that she may fall prey to your line of blarney again? There was a boy, way back when. I won't go into details, but he did her really dirty. She believed him, she believed you. Maybe she doesn't trust her judgment anymore." Bess sighed wearily. "Hurt pride may be part of it as well. I'm reaching. I honestly don't know. Maybe it's a combination of several things. We women are complicated creatures."

"The very least I'd like to do is help her out financially."

"Maybe you should stop taking no for an answer."

Hank arched an eyebrow. "What, exactly, does that mean?"

"My friend is pregnant and, whether she'll admit it or not, about to go blind again. She's had morning sickness practically every day. The headaches from the sudden stimulation to the visual cortex have been persistent as well. That isn't to mention the complications any woman may have during a pregnancy. Come September I'll be going to school to get my MBA, plus working full time. Who's going to take care of her if she gets sick or has unexpected problems with her eyes? And how on earth is she going to make ends meet when the additional bills start rolling in?"

Hank had no answers.

"She'll be strapped, Hank. Her college savings will be gone by spring, pissed away on living expenses and medical bills, leaving her without the money she'll need for a second eye surgery. What'll she do, stay blind until she can save enough to get another SK?"

Hank started to say something, but Bess barely took a breath before she continued. "As a rookie teacher, she pulled in twenty-nine thousand annually the last two years. After taxes, that isn't much. By living together, we both managed to save for college, but it was tough. Even if she returns to Portland and gets her old job back, she'll be lucky just to keep a roof over her head. In short, Hank, she's going to need help, and lots of it. If you're willing to step in, I think you should, and soon."

"How can I help if she refuses to even talk to me?"

"The question brings me full circle. Stop taking no for an answer. Sometimes—" She broke off and huffed into the receiver. "God, I can't believe I'm about to say this, but sometimes a woman lets her emotions cloud her judgment, and Carly tends to be worse about it than most. A lot of disabled people accept their limitations and settle for less. Carly isn't made that way. If our friend Cricket and I could do it, she was bound and determined to do it, too, with as little help as possible. Riding a bike, jumping on a skateboard. Cricket and I yelled directions, and away she went until she hit a parked car or sailed off a curb. As a kid, she always had scraped knees and elbows, but she never gave up. Doing things by herself has always been extremely important to her."

Hank couldn't see how that pertained.

"Now she's pregnant," Bess said unnecessarily. "You're offering to play the big, strong man and come to her rescue. Carly didn't get where she is today by letting other people do everything for her. Does that make any sense?"

"Not really." Hank couldn't imagine a blind girl on a bicycle. What in God's name had her parents been thinking? "We all need help sometimes."

"Carly has needed help all her life. It wasn't the exception for her, but the rule. She had a choice, giving in and letting the blindness control her life—or fighting with everything she had to be normal. She developed an attitude, sink or swim, do or die. Even when she was little, she refused special treatment. She found her own way to our first-grade classroom. She carried her own lunch tray. She climbed the rope in gym. In high school, she walked the track to count off the steps between hurdles, and the next afternoon, she jumped them. If she fell, she righted the hurdle and tried again."

"Good God," Hank whispered.

"When she realized people could tell she was blind because she hung her head, she started standing ram-rod straight. She refused to let blindness make her different."

"In other words, she's stubborn as hell."

"Stubborn. Difficult sometimes. But just look at her. Would you ever guess that she was totally blind a little over a month ago?"

Hank definitely hadn't guessed it the night he met her. "No," he admitted gruffly. "Where are you going with this, Bess?"

"Carly may not want anyone's help, but she needs it, regardless."

"You're a fabulous friend, Bess."

"Right now, I'm being a Judas," she said shakily. "You have no idea how rotten that makes me feel."

"You're only trying to help her."

"And, in the process, I'm revealing things to you that she may never forgive me for." She hesitated, and then she plunged onward. "I think this pregnancy has become another string of hurdles for Carly to jump. In addition to her wariness of you, getting through it by herself is all tied up with her sense of self-worth. Other women get pregnant and have their babies out of wedlock. Other women manage to make ends meet while raising a child. They don't usually marry a man they don't love to get a free ride."

Hank rubbed the back of his neck. "She needs to think about the welfare of our baby."

"I know. But for her, maybe that's easier said than done. She'll want her son or daughter to be proud of her one day. To Carly's way of thinking, she'll be admirable only if she stands on her own two feet."

"So what's the answer?" Hank glanced over his shoulder to make sure he was still alone in the kitchen. Then he told Bess about the discussion he'd had with his brother Zeke. "If I could convince her to marry me, I'd do it in a heartbeat. It's the only workable solution I can come up with. We could go into it as a temporary arrangement, a stopgap measure until she has her next surgery and gets her master's. If, at that time, she still wants out, I'll cut her a check for start-up capital and give her a divorce."

"*If* she still wants out? Can I take that to mean you'll remain in the marriage if she doesn't?"

Hank turned to rest his hips against the counter and watch the door. "I'd be open to the possibility. What's to say we won't hit it off and be happy as clams? It'd be a hell of a lot better for our child if we stayed together."

Long silence. Then Bess said, "Go for it."

Hank frowned. "Go for what?"

"Marry her. You and your brother are right. It's the best solution. With all the other expenses that'll be hitting you, trying to support two households would bankrupt you. If Carly believes it'll be a temporary situation, she'll eventually accept it. Trust me on that. Give the girl lemons, and she makes lemonade."

"Problem. How the hell can I marry her when she won't even talk to me?"

"You don't strike me as being a stupid man, Hank. Get creative."

"How? I can't force her to marry me. There are laws against that kind of thing."

"There are also laws that give fathers certain inalienable rights. Carly is in no position to provide for a child right now."

A tingle crept up Hank's spine. "What are you suggesting?"

"You've tried being Mr. Nice Guy. Has that worked?"

"No."

"Well, then? Maybe it's time to play dirty. She won't risk losing that baby. I know her."

Hank didn't like the turn this conversation had taken. "Doesn't she have some family to help her out?"

"Only her dad in Arizona. Carly was a midlife baby, so he's an older man. She could stay with him, but it's a seasonal retirement community that rolls up the carpet in April. No schools, and as far as I know, no public transportation, either, making it next to impossible for her to commute to a nearby town to hold down a teaching position. She'll be blind, remember. The blind can't drive. Her dad would do his best, but he hasn't been well. He definitely isn't up to caring for a child while she works—and she may not be able to count on him for daily transportation."

"She'll have to be able to work, both for the income and the health insurance benefits."

"Exactly."

"And there's no one else?" Coming from such a

large, close-knit family, Hank could barely conceive that. "No brothers or sisters?"

"She's an only child. Her dad's seventy-three. Her mom died of ovarian cancer two years ago. I'll be there for her, of course, but I'm going to be stretched pretty thin, working and going to class. I can drop out of school, I guess, but I'd still have to work eight to ten hours a day. Our friend, Cricket, is in Colombia right now, working on a dig. She can't come home to help out, not without jeopardizing her career."

"I understand," Hank said, and he honestly did. This was his problem. He couldn't expect other people to drop everything and rush to Carly's aid. He'd gotten her into this mess, and it was up to him to get her out of it.

Carly awakened the next morning to discover, much to her dismay, that all the sauerkraut and Brussels sprouts were gone. Bess had already left for an interview at a vet's office, so a chauffeur wasn't at Carly's disposal. Because the sauerkraut and Brussels sprouts seemed to settle her queasy stomach, she quickly threw on her clothes, brushed her hair, and set out walking to the supermarket, four blocks away.

Forty-five minutes later, she turned back onto her street. Her mouth was watering for the foods she carried in plastic bags, one in each hand. The heaviness of the groceries made the handles dig into her flesh, and her fingers had long since gone numb.

She was almost to the apartment complex when she noticed a blue pickup parked at the curb. As she turned to walk up the center pathway that bisected the grassy apartment common, a man swung out of the vehicle and slammed the door. Though he was little more than a blur of blue denim, Carly knew it was Hank by his loose-jointed stride and the sharp click of his boots on the pavement.

Her heart tumbled wildly in her chest. She'd told him in plain English that she didn't want to see him again. Why wouldn't he leave her alone?

Each decisive tap of his boot heels told her how quickly he was gaining on her. She almost broke into a run to escape him, but pride held her back. She wouldn't give him the satisfaction of seeing her bolt like a frightened rabbit.

Before she could reach her porch, he came abreast of her on the walkway. "Here, let me carry those for you."

Carly kept walking. "No thanks. Just go away."

"No can do."

He wrested the grocery bags from her fists, somehow managing to do it in one fluid swipe despite the tight clench of her fingers. She considered making a wild grab to reclaim possession, but one glance at his well-muscled shoulders told her a physical contest would be an exercise in futility.

As if he guessed her thoughts, he flashed a slow grin. "Hello to you, too."

She wasn't about to exchange pleasantries with him. He added insult to injury by gaining the porch just before she did. "We're going to talk this out, Carly." The teasing warmth had left his voice, replaced by steely determination. "If you'd feel safer chatting with me at a restaurant, that offer's still open, but talk we will, one way or another."

"Safer?" Carly managed to scale the steps without tripping, which was no easy feat. Advancing on the door, she said, "I'm not afraid of you."

"Wary, then."

"I'm not wary of you, either."

Hands trembling, she dug in her pocket for the house key. Refusing to look at him, she stabbed at the brass deadbolt, hoping she might get lucky and hit the hole. *Not.* Frustrated beyond measure, she stabbed several times and still didn't hit her mark.

He shifted the sacks to one hand and snatched the key from her. On the first try, he inserted it in the hole.

Carly stepped over the threshold and turned to slam the door in his face. He thrust a boot through the opening, held up the key and groceries, and flashed another grin. "Forget something?"

He was a cocky, pushy, conceited, overbearing *jerk,* and she wished she'd never met him. She flicked a look at the grocery sacks, which held her morning sickness cure. After walking eight blocks round-trip to get the groceries, she wasn't about to let him make off with them.

She shoved her arm through the crack. "Give me my bags."

He smiled. "And have you slam the door in my face? If possible, I prefer to avoid yelling what I want to say through the keyhole. Let's negotiate a deal. You invite me in, and then I'll give you the bags."

Through clenched teeth, she fairly snarled, "Give me those groceries, or else."

"Or else what?"

Carly knew it would be childish to make threats she couldn't deliver on, so instead she cried, "Or else I'll call the police!"

He lowered the bags to look inside. "Frozen Brussels sprouts and"—he tipped his head to read a label—"sauerkraut? I don't think that qualifies as grand theft. I'll take my chances."

Between one breath and the next, Carly went from merely angry to absolutely seething. "You are *impossible*."

Still blocking the doorway with one boot, he lowered the bags to his side and relaxed his shoulders, apparently prepared to stand there all day if necessary. "Would you do me the honor of going out with me for breakfast? There's an IHOP a couple of blocks over, fabulous pancakes, great coffee, and always packed with people. We could talk there without drawing attention."

Just the thought of trying to eat a pancake made her gorge rise. "No, I will not. I just want you to hand over my groceries and go away."

"I was afraid you were going to say that."

Before she could guess what he meant to do, he planted a shoulder against the wood and pushed his way inside. Staggering back, Carly stared stupidly up at him as he closed and locked the door.

"Get out!" she cried. "You can't barge in here like this."

He panned the room, as if looking for reinforcements. "You and what army is going to stop me?" He tucked the key back into her pocket and thrust the grocery bags into her arms. "I tried doing this the nice way, Carly. Now we'll do it the hard way. End result, we're going to talk."

"I'll say this only one more time. *Get out.*"

"Sorry, darlin', it just ain't happenin'. You haven't seen stubborn until you've gone a few rounds with me."

Carly had an unholy urge to bean him with the bag

of jarred sauerkraut. "What can you possibly hope to gain by forcing your way into my apartment? Do you honestly believe such behavior is going to make me feel more inclined to talk to you? What do you hope to prove, that you're bigger than I am?"

"If I have to prove I'm bigger than you are, we're both in trouble."

Carly could only wonder what that meant. He wasn't forthcoming with an explanation. He folded his muscular arms. "As for your inclinations, I don't much care at this point whether you talk or not. I have plenty to say."

She didn't like the sound of that.

"Go ahead and put away the food," he offered congenially. "Don't let me stop you. I can talk while you work."

Carly took a mental inventory of her alternatives and quickly determined there weren't any. A very large, determined male stood in her living room, blocking the only exit. There was no way she'd ever get around him. To make matters worse, she recalled with bitter clarity how easily he'd swept her up in his arms and deposited her on the back seat of his truck that night. Did she really, *really* want to initiate a physical struggle?

The answer was no, not if she could avoid it.

She spun around and marched into the kitchen, acutely aware of him following at her heels. The groceries went *plunk* on the counter when she set them down.

"So, start talking. You've got five minutes. If you're not out of here then, I'll call the police." She shot a burning look at the telephone. "Don't make the mistake of thinking I won't do it. My patience with you is wearing perilously thin."

Resting a shoulder against the end of the wall that divided the kitchen from the living room, he flicked a lazy glance at the wall phone, then removed his Stetson and tossed it the length of the living room onto the sofa. The absence of the hat shaved a few inches off his height, but that failed to make her feel better.

He raked his fingers through his hair to remove the hatband ring. "Is there any way we can back up a few paces and start over fresh?"

"No. Why bother? There's no improving on abysmally awful."

She pulled a box of frozen Brussels sprouts from the sack, emptied the square chunk of frozen vegetables into a bowl, partially thawed it under hot water, and stuck it in the microwave. Then she turned her attention to putting away the other food. She left a jar of sauerkraut and a carton of chocolate milk sitting on the counter.

"Is that your breakfast?"

"If you don't care for my eating habits, you can leave the same way you came in."

He sighed and shifted his weight against the wall to cross his ankles. Never more than in that moment had the apartment seemed so tiny. Carly had had little practice at guessing people's heights, but she guessed him to stand well over six feet. His well-packed but lean frame dwarfed her and everything else, even the old tank of a refrigerator.

After uncapping the sauerkraut, she grabbed a fork and started eating. She had no choice. If she didn't get something on her stomach soon, she'd be on her knees in the bathroom, worshiping the porcelain god all morning.

Between mouthfuls, she said, "So? Start talking. Seconds are wasting. Five minutes. That's it. Then you're out of here, one way or another."

He flicked another glance at the phone hanging inches from his arm. "We're in this together, you and I," he said softly. "It'd be so much nicer if we could work things out in a way that satisfies both of us."

Carly forked more sauerkraut into her mouth, glaring at him as she chewed. "I want no part of togetherness with you. I might catch something."

He had the audacity to smile. "No danger. I've always used protection." He winced when her glare made him realize what he'd said. "You were my one and only slip."

"So you say."

"If you're honestly concerned about the possibility of an STD, I'll go get tested and show you the results."

Carly had been concerned about the possibility, but she would never admit it to him. He'd know then that she'd spent countless hours obsessing about their encounter. Better for him to think that he'd never crossed her mind.

"An STD is the least of my worries at the moment." She punctuated that statement by shoving more sauerkraut in her mouth.

"I know. Which is why we're due for a nice, long talk."

The microwave timer pinged. Carly pulled out her Brussels sprouts and hungrily began devouring them, alternating each mouthful with a huge mound of sauerkraut. Every few chews, she grabbed the chocolate milk and took a swig. She didn't care if the milk left a smear on her upper lip. She sincerely hoped Hank grew disgusted and walked out.

No such luck. He only watched her, his expression a mixture of incredulity and appalled curiosity. "No wonder you're getting morning sickness."

"Actually, this helps a little," she said with a Brussels sprout puffing out her cheek. "And how do you know I've had morning sickness?"

He looked momentarily nonplussed by the question. Then he recovered and said, "Most pregnant women do."

Carly was tempted to question him further, but she decided the less she participated in this conversation, the better. Even so, she couldn't resist saying, "For a man so determined to talk to me, you seem to have precious little to say."

"I'm working my way up to it."

Carly stepped to the sink to moisten a paper towel. As she moved away from him, his face became a dark blur of bronze. After wiping her mouth, she returned to her meal and said, "Your five minutes is quickly going."

He nodded. His jaw muscle started to tic. Carly remembered listening to novels on tape and wondering how a ticcing jaw muscle looked. Now, at long last, she finally knew. It looked angry—and determined— and more than a little intimidating. She had a bad feeling that Hank Coulter was on a mission and wouldn't back off until he had accomplished it.

Finally, he said, "Carly, I've come here to make you a proposition."

"A proposition?" She slanted him a burning look and shoved more sauerkraut into her mouth.

"Not that kind of proposition." He pushed his fingers into the front pockets of his jeans, which had the unsettling effect of making his shoulders look broader. "Let's look at the situation rationally. All right?"

"Are you implying that I'm not being rational, Mr. Coulter?"

"No, I don't mean to imply that you're being irrational," he said evenly. "Bad choice of words. What I am saying is that we need to look at this situation from all angles, weigh the potential problems against our resources to resolve them, and try to make decisions in the best interest of you and our child."

"My child," she corrected.

His blue eyes began to glitter. "*Our* child. I am the father."

"So you claim."

"It can be easily verified with a simple blood test. Don't even go there. I will play an active role in my child's life, with or without your cooperation. Trust me when I say things will be more pleasant for you if you cooperate."

Carly struggled to swallow a Brussels sprout. For a horrible moment, she thought she might choke. "Are you threatening me?"

"Interpret it any way you like. I'm the father of that baby, and I have certain inalienable rights, not to mention responsibilities. The state will back me on both counts. It's in your best interest not to be at loggerheads with me."

Definitely a threat. Carly's craving for the vegetables abruptly diminished, and she dropped the fork into the jar with a resounding clink.

"Here are the facts."

He went on to list all the reasons why she needed his help, some of which he couldn't possibly know unless someone close to her had given him the information. Carly was trembling by the time he finished.

"How do you know all this?"

"I did some digging. Have I said anything so far that isn't true?"

Carly just stared at him.

"Now for my side of it." He pushed away from the wall. "I'm not a rich man, but I make damned good money now. I broke all my own rules the night I met you, and as a result, I've messed up your life in ways that may affect your whole future."

"My future is my concern."

"Ordinarily, I'd agree with you. But now that you're pregnant with my child, I have a vested interest. It's my responsibility to safeguard that child's welfare, both emotionally and financially, and your successes and failures will have a direct impact."

"For a barroom lothario, you seem to take fatherhood awfully seriously."

Carly wasn't sure, but she thought his lips went white. "I have that coming, I guess." His Adam's apple bobbed as if he were swallowing one of her Brussels sprouts whole. "For the moment, though, let's leave my checkered past out of it and concentrate on straightening out this mess."

Carly wanted to say it was her mess to straighten out, but they'd already covered that ground.

"Here are the facts on my side of the equation," he went on. "I can't afford to cover all your eye-surgery expenses, plus the costs of childbirth and child care, help you stay in school, and pay for your living expenses if we maintain separate households."

The last of what he said jangled in her brain. "Did you say 'separate households'?"

"Don't get upset until you hear me out."

"Are you—?" Carly gulped and took a calming breath. "Are you suggesting that we live together?" She had a hysterical urge to laugh. "Surely you're not *serious*."

"I'm dead serious, but I'm not suggesting that we live together. I'm suggesting that you marry me, the sooner, the better."

Carly couldn't believe her ears. *"What?"*

"You heard me. And before you start saying no, let me add that we can enter into the marriage on a temporary basis—a stopgap arrangement, so to speak, until you get your master's degree. Until that occurs, I'll put you on my insurance, which covers everything, pay all your other expenses, help care for the child to eliminate child care costs, and provide you with transportation to and from campus. I'll also foot the bill for any special assistance you may need to complete your coursework if you go blind."

Carly held up a hand to silence him, but he just kept talking.

"After you acquire your degree and have surgery to restore your sight, I'll give you some start-up cash, we'll dissolve the marriage and go our separate ways. I will, of course, expect to have visitation with my child, the schedule for which will be determined by state guidelines. I'll also pay monthly child support, the amount of which will be based upon my annual income."

An acidic burn moved into Carly's throat. "You're out of your mind. How can you think, even for a moment, that I'd consider marrying you?" She hugged her waist. "Bess had no right to tell you all this. No *right*."

"Don't go blaming Bess. I won't lie and say we haven't talked. We have. But I didn't get all this information from her. She's a loyal friend to you."

"If she's so loyal, how do you know my insurance only covers eighty percent? And that my dad lives in Arizona?"

"I'm a whiz on the Internet. With the right software, you can find out almost anything, even what kind of movies people rent."

Carly didn't buy it for a minute. He knew too many details that could have come only from Bess. And, oh, how that hurt.

As if he sensed her thoughts, he said, "Bess is your friend, Carly. She cares very deeply for you. Maybe she has let a few things slip, but only out of concern for you and the baby."

"Your five minutes are up," she said tautly.

His jaw muscle started to tic again. "I'm not leaving until we've settled this."

"Oh, yes, you are. My baby and I are none of your business."

"That's where you're wrong. From where I'm standing, it doesn't appear that you'll be able to provide properly for my child."

Carly grabbed the phone. "Get out. If you don't leave, I'm calling the police."

He didn't budge.

"I mean it, Hank." She squinted at the number pad. She needed to dial 911. Only where was the nine?

Before she could close her eyes and dial by touch, Hank depressed the receiver hook. "I really hoped we might be able to discuss this like two reasonable adults and agree on a solution."

Carly's fury mounted. "Have you any idea how

many women become pregnant annually and don't marry the fathers of their babies? No one calls them unreasonable."

"Those women aren't faced with the same set of circumstances. You may be losing your sight again, Carly."

And being blind somehow makes me less of a person? Even her best friend had turned against her. Tears stung Carly's eyes.

"All I want is to make things easier for you and better for our baby."

"I've said it once, I'll say it again, I don't need or want your help."

He kept his hand on the receiver cradle to prevent her from dialing out. "I wanted to avoid this, but you're leaving me no choice."

Carly threw him a wary look.

"Do you really think I'll just walk away, knowing my kid may be born into penury to a blind mother? You'll either marry me and remain in the marriage until you're over this rough patch that *I* caused, or I'll petition the court for custody of my baby."

All the blood drained from Carly's face. Her body suddenly felt like cold rubber. Her hand slid numbly from the phone. Her arms hung, heavy and lifeless, at her sides. "Surely you don't mean that."

"Try me."

Hank knew he had very little chance of actually getting custody. It was a bluff, nothing more. He could only hope Carly didn't realize it.

"I hate you," she whispered.

Hank had no doubt that she did. Her sudden pallor made him feel like a world-class bastard. It also told him the threat had frightened her. On the one hand, he regretted that, but on the other, he was relieved. Someone had to help her through this, and he was elected.

Her every emotion shone in her eyes as she stared up at him, incredulity, shock, and fear at war with swiftly diminishing anger. "Get out," she whispered raggedly.

Hank released his hold on the receiver cradle. As he crossed the living room to retrieve his Stetson, he said, "Don't make the mistake of thinking I won't go for custody. If you leave me no other choice, I'll do it in a heartbeat." Once at the door, he stopped and turned to look back at her. "I'll give you a couple of days to think it over. Then I'll be in touch. Bottom line, we either apply for a marriage license or I hire an attorney. Your choice."

"Go ahead and hire an attorney!" she flung at him. "See if I care. You can't take my baby away from me. You've got no grounds, and I'll fight you with my last breath."

Hank stepped out onto the porch. Before closing the door behind him, he said, "Maybe I have grounds, maybe I don't. That'll be up to a judge. If you want to take that gamble, go for it. While you're making up your mind, remember one thing. Hiring an attorney and going through a custody battle will be very expensive. I can afford it. Can you?"

Hank drew the door closed and stood on the welcome mat, battling with his conscience. Threatening to take her child was a purely rotten thing to do, and everything within him rebelled against it. He was sorely tempted to go back inside and tell her he hadn't meant it. But what was the alternative? To let her struggle to survive, by hook or by crook, while he went his merry way?

While he stood there, trapped in indecision, Hank heard a muffled sob come from inside the apartment. An instant later, an interior door slammed, the sharp sound followed quickly by yet more sobbing, which sounded as if it were coming from the bedroom to the right of the porch. He stared solemnly at the window, imagining Carly on the bed, her face pressed into her pillow.

Why was it, he wondered, that this woman made him feel guilty as hell, even when he was trying to do the right thing? He grasped the doorknob and almost turned it. Then, at the last second, he dropped his arm. Marriage was the best solution—the *only* solution. If he went inside and retracted all that he'd said, they'd be back at square one, with her refusing to accept a dime and hanging up every time he telephoned.

Hank couldn't let that happen. Whether she admitted it or not, she needed him, and he meant to be there for her, one way or another. If he made her despise him in the process, so be it.

Chapter Nine

Carly was in the bedroom when Bess came home for lunch three hours later. The sound of the front door opening and closing alerted Carly to her friend's arrival. Eyes swollen and nose stuffy from crying, she rolled onto her side and hugged her ribs, dreading the discussion to follow.

"Yoo-hoo! Carls? You'll never guess what! I think I may have a job! And at a dental office, no less! It'll be perfect for me!"

Bess flung open the door and burst into the bedroom. When she saw Carly's face, she reeled to a stop. "Oh, God, what's wrong?"

Carly put her legs over the side of the bed and sat up. At the sudden movement, the blood rushed to her head, and her temples felt as if they might explode. After staring silently at her friend for several long seconds, she said, "Hank stopped by."

Bess stepped closer. "Oh, Carly, your eyes. I can see just by looking that you've got another headache. I'll go get some ice."

"No, please, don't." Carly rose to a standing position. "I need to get this said."

"Get what said?"

"We've been best friends since we were five years

old," Carly told her. "I thought I could trust you with my life."

"You can."

"You went behind my back and told Hank everything—about the possibility that my eyesight may fail, how sick I've been, my insurance coverage, my finances, my dad—everything. What's more, I believe you encouraged him to use the information against me."

Bess went pale.

"To Hank's credit," Carly went on, "he did his best to cover for you, but too much of what he said had to have come directly from you." Carly felt tears welling again. She blinked them away. "He claims you're a loyal friend to me, and he's right. You have been a loyal friend." A tight sensation in Carly's throat forced her to swallow so she could go on. "Until now."

"Oh, Carly."

"At first I was angry. Now, I—" Carly gestured helplessly with her hands. "Why, Bess? How could you do this to me?"

Bess's eyes went bright. As if all the strength went out of her legs, she sat on the bed. "I did what I felt I had to. And just for the record, I didn't do it *to* you, I did it *for* you."

Carly leaned against the wall. "He's threatening to take my baby away from me. He says he'll sue for custody if I don't marry him."

A guilty look crossed Bess's face.

"You knew?" It wasn't really a question.

"We didn't discuss any particulars, but I did tell him to stop taking no for an answer. As for custody, I planted the idea. He apparently took it from there."

Carly felt as if her heart were breaking. "You told him to take my baby?"

"I hope it doesn't come to that. As for the suggestion, yes, I made it. What other leverage does he have? You need his help, Carls, but you're too damned stubborn to accept it. I've always admired that trait in you. You've mastered things most blind people would never even attempt, and I think you're an awesome lady. But you're carrying independence way too far this time."

"That isn't your call to make. It's *my* life."

"No, not anymore. You're making decisions for two now. And you haven't been making wise ones."

"You've no *right*—"

"Oh yes." Bess pushed to her feet. "I do have a right. I love you, Carly, and I'm going to love your baby. What's more, I know you better than you know yourself sometimes. I understand and sympathize with your need to do everything for yourself. But enough is enough. Stubbornness won't put food in the cupboards. It won't provide care for the baby if you get sick. It won't pay your grad school tuition. It won't pay the monthly premiums for your insurance coverage or the unpaid charges for medical services that'll soon start rolling in. What's more, it won't pay for an eye surgery next summer. Have you even considered that? What do you plan to do, remain blind for several more years while you scrimp and save for another operation?"

A sinking sensation attacked Carly's stomach.

"You haven't even made an appointment with a doctor for prenatal care yet," Bess accused.

"Wrong," Carly shot back. "I called and made an

appointment the same day that they called to confirm the pregnancy. I just couldn't get in right away, and I forgot to mention it."

"Good. I'm glad to hear it. But be that as it may, you still aren't thinking about that baby in many of the ways you should be," Bess went on relentlessly. "Not really. And what's more, you're not being realistic."

"Other pregnant women have their babies alone," Carly argued.

"Other pregnant women aren't faced with the same set of problems. Wake up, Carls. It's not about you standing at the finish line with your arms raised in victory anymore."

Bess turned to leave the room. Carly stared after her, stunned, hurt, and struggling not to cry. "This is my *child* we're talking about!"

Bess paused at the doorway. "Exactly, so start thinking like a mother."

Outrage drove Carly to follow Bess into the living room. "I won't prostitute myself in a loveless marriage."

Bess sat on the sofa, drew up her legs, and tucked her feet beneath her. "Is that what you think—that Hank will make physical demands?"

Carly wrapped her arms around her waist. "We'd be married. What if he decides all the cash expenditures entitle him to certain paybacks? I won't go through that again!"

Bess arched her eyebrows. "How do you know you won't enjoy it?"

"*Enjoy* it?" The very thought of enduring that pain again made her insides clench. "You're out of your mind. Never, do you hear? *Never.*"

"Not even if it means keeping your baby? There must have been some pretty powerful chemistry at work that night, or you never would have landed yourself in this mess."

"Oh, *please.* He was a total jerk this morning, muscling his way in here, refusing to leave, and making threats."

"And whose fault is that? He tried being nice. You threw it back in his teeth."

"I can't believe you're taking his side!"

"I'm on your side, Carly. And the baby's. The way I see it, Hank is your only lifeline. If you refuse to accept his help, what're you going to do, end up on welfare and borrow money from your dad to fight Hank in court?"

"You know I'd never dump this on my father. If he thought, even for a second, that I might lose my baby, he'd sell everything he owns and go into debt to prevent it. He's made too many sacrifices for me as it is."

"That's what parents do, make sacrifices," Bess said softly. "Maybe you should follow his example and consider making a few yourself."

Hank leaned over Zeke's pool table, drew careful aim, and started to take his shot just as his cell phone jangled. He jerked. Instead of hitting its target, the cue ball angled left, struck the eight ball, and followed it into the corner pocket.

"Well, *shit.*"

Zeke gave a choked laugh. "Saved by the bell. I thought you were going to whip my ass and take my ten bucks."

Hank pulled the cell phone from his belt. "Yeah, this is Hank."

"Hank?" a tremulous female voice said.

Hank shot his brother a meaningful look, then hunched his shoulders and turned his back to the table. "Carly?"

"Yes. I, um—need to talk to you."

There was only one reason Hank could think of that she might call; she'd decided to accept his proposal. A part of him wanted to whoop with relief, but another part of him was alarmed by the shakiness of her voice. This clearly wasn't an easy thing for her to do.

He stepped closer to the sliding glass door in an attempt to block out the TV and his brother's prying eyes. "Sure, we can talk. No problem. What's on your mind?"

"It sounds as if you're busy. I can call back later."

She sounded almost too eager to do that. Hank tightened his hold on the phone. The damned thing was too small for his hand, and he had to watch where he curled his fingers. "I'm not busy, honey." The instant the endearment passed his lips, he winced. The last thing he wanted was to scare her off. "I'm just hanging out at my brother Zeke's. You couldn't have chosen a better time to call, actually."

"Oh." Silence ensued. "It's awfully late."

Hank glanced at his watch. It was half past ten, not exactly the pumpkin hour. "What's on your mind?" he asked again.

"I, um—well, I don't know quite how to start."

He could tell that she didn't. "I haven't handled our conversations very well myself, so just spit it out, and we'll go from there."

Even over the phone line, he could feel her brittle tension.

"I've, uh, been doing a lot of thinking—about your proposition."

He'd figured as much. His whole body snapped taut. "And?"

"I'm toying with the thought—just toying, mind you—of taking you up on it."

All the starch went out of Hank's spine. If she was toying with the thought, it was only a matter of time before she agreed. "I see," he replied, struggling to let no note of satisfaction enter his voice.

He heard a rustle of paper. "I have two stipulations."

It sounded to him as if she'd made out a whole list. "Oh? What sort of stipulations?"

"First of all, I want it understood that I'll pay you back as soon as I can. I can't just take your money."

Hank doubted that she'd ever be financially able to reimburse him, and he sure as hell didn't expect her to, but that little wrinkle could be ironed out at a later date. If it made her feel better to think that she'd pay him back someday, he wouldn't argue the point. "All right. Sure. I'm okay with that."

"I want a tally kept of every cent you spend," she emphasized. "When we divorce, we'll deduct what you would have paid in child support during that time, and I'll owe you the remainder. We'll work out a monthly payment plan—something I can afford—and I'll eventually settle the debt."

She obviously had given this a great deal of thought. *No special favors.* As frustrating as her stubbornness was, he admired her for it. A lot of people went through life with their hands out, expecting a free ride. Carly had trouble accepting one even when it was shoved down her throat.

"Sure. That works for me." Hank waited a beat. Then he said, "And?"

"And, what?"

He smiled slightly. "You said two stipulations. What's the other one?"

In a muffled voice, she said something he didn't quite catch. He covered his opposite ear to block out the television noise. "Come again?"

"No *sex*," she repeated. The electricity that shot over the wire raised the hair on the back of his neck. "I don't want you approaching me three months down the road about the inequities of our arrangement. No sex, period, ever."

Hank rubbed beside his nose and cleared his throat. Until now, he hadn't thought about the specifics of the arrangement. He'd been so focused on getting her to agree that nothing else had seemed important.

"I see," he said.

If it was possible, her voice grew more tremulous. "You don't sound very happy about it."

Hank gazed bleakly out the window at the shadows that cloaked Zeke's patio. "Not unhappy, exactly. Concerned would be a better word." He shot a glance at his brother, who was carefully racking the billiard balls to avoid making noise. "I understand that this arrangement isn't one you'd normally consider. I also sympathize with your reservations. But, for the sake of our child, I was hoping we might at least enter into it with open minds."

"What's *that* mean?"

Hank glanced at his brother again. Zeke had finished racking the balls and was now making no attempt to hide his interest in Hank's side of the conversation.

"Just that I was hoping we might settle into the relationship and see our way clear to at least try to make it work," Hank explained. "You have to admit that it'll be a lot better for our child if we end up staying together."

"You said nothing about that this morning," she countered shrilly. "You said I'd be free to go my own way as soon as I get my degree and the eye surgery."

"You will be free to go your own way. That goes without saying, doesn't it? I'm just looking at the possibilities. Do you dislike me so much that it's inconceivable to you that we might somehow hit it off?"

"Yes."

Well, shit. Hank rested his forehead against the cool glass. Deep, slow breaths. He needed to stay calm and say the right things. Nevertheless, her ready response and the panic in her voice were grave causes for concern. "Carly, honest answer, okay? Was it so awful for you that night that you're afraid to have sex with me again?"

"Yes," she said faintly.

The TV suddenly went silent. Hank looked over his shoulder to see Zeke laying the remote control back down on the end table. Clearly, Hank's brother wanted to miss no part of this exchange. Hank thumped his forehead against the glass again.

"I'm sorry about how things went that night," he said, pitching his voice low. "You'll never know how sorry, Carly. I'd give my right arm to turn back the clock and treat you the way you deserved to be treated—to make it nice for you."

"Amen," Zeke intoned softly.

Hank wished his brother would keep his mouth shut or, better yet, disappear.

"I don't want to talk about that night," Carly said, her voice ringing with frustration. "As for the no-sex thing, I should have known you wouldn't agree."

"It's not that I disagree," Hank clarified. "If we can't put that night behind us and start over fresh, then of course we'll never have sex. I just hesitate to get locked down by promises that rule out any possibility of our making the marriage work. That's all."

"No sex?" Zeke spoke barely above a whisper. "Christ on crutches. Be careful what you promise, little brother. Two years is a hell of a long time."

"Well, understand something!" Carly cried in Hank's other ear. "I hesitate to enter into an arrangement that could, conceivably, turn ugly for me. I hoped we might set some ground rules."

Hank took a mental step back and tried to see her side of it. In all fairness, he supposed she had legitimate reasons to be wary. She knew very little about him. If he was a bastard to the core—and he'd given her little reason to believe otherwise—it went without saying that he had a physical advantage.

"Let's do that, then," he said softly.

"Do what?"

"Set some ground rules. I'm perfectly willing to promise you that nothing—absolutely nothing—will ever happen between us that you don't want to happen."

"Now you're talking," was Zeke's vote of approval.

"How do I know your word is good?" Carly asked.

Nerves frayed and tension building, Hank ran a hand over his face. "If my word isn't good, you've got no guarantee I'll keep any promise I've made so far."

"Like I'm not aware of that?" she cried.

Her admission drove home to Hank how precarious

this arrangement must seem to her. No wonder her voice was shaky.

Hank leaned his shoulder against the slider frame. To hell with what Zeke overheard. Getting this upset couldn't be good for her—or for his baby.

"Carly, sweetheart, listen to me. Okay?" Hank realized he'd just used another endearment and said to hell with that as well. He'd been hearing his father use terms of endearment all his life. Following suit came as naturally to Hank as opening doors for a woman or pulling out her chair. There was also the inescapable fact that Carly would never really get to know him if he continued to weigh his every word and pretended to be someone he wasn't. "You listening?"

"Yes," she said faintly.

"In my family, a man's word is his bond. I don't make promises lightly, especially not to a lady. If I did, my father and four brothers would stand in line to kick my ass."

"I get first dibs," Zeke inserted with a gravelly laugh.

"Oh," Carly murmured.

Hank doubted she believed him. Until she met his family and got to know him better, she was bound to feel uneasy about this entire situation. He wished he knew how to remedy that, but some things just couldn't happen overnight. Building trust in a relationship was one of them.

In the interim, he wasn't willing to strike bargains that would tie his hands. Maybe she was right, and their chances of making this marriage work were slim to nonexistent. All the same, he couldn't help but remember how sweetly she'd responded to his kisses that night outside the bar. There had definitely been passion between them. All he needed was a chance to rekindle it. In that event, what was to say they wouldn't decide that they wanted to stay together?

"I know I haven't given you much reason to believe this, but I'm really not such a bad guy."

Zeke chuckled. The proclamation was greeted with silence at Carly's end—a condemning silence.

Hank shifted to rest his hip against the doorframe. "I've given you my solemn oath that nothing will ever happen between us that you don't want to happen, Carly. If you think about it, isn't that as rock solid as your stipulation? Same results, different wording. No sex unless you say so."

"It doesn't seem as ironclad," she said faintly.

"If I'm a man who doesn't keep his word, nothing's ironclad. You can lock me down with promises 'til hell freezes over, and you'll still be going into this with no guarantees."

"I take it back," Zeke muttered. "You didn't get all the charm in the family, little brother. Even I could do better than that."

Hank cupped a hand over the mouthpiece. "Would you shut the hell up?"

"What?" Carly asked in a shocked little voice.

"Not you," Hank hastily assured her. "My brother's here, and he keeps adding his two cents."

"He's *listening*?"

Shit. Hank pressed a fist to his forehead. Speaking of stress headaches. "He's in the room. Not really listening, though." *Liar, liar.*

"Sorry." Zeke winced and shrugged.

"Where were we?" Hank asked Carly.

"You were saying there are no guarantees."

"Only if my word's no good. On the other hand, if

my word is my bond, you'll be as safe agreeing to my version as you would be if I agreed to yours."

Hank waited for her to respond. *Nothing*. He began to fear she might hang up. When push came to shove, the most important thing was that she agreed to marry him. Maybe, he decided, he should accept her dictate of no sex, and worry about changing her mind later.

He was about to tell her as much when she said, "I guess that's true," in a forlorn voice.

Hearing her hopelessness, Hank got a funny, achy sensation at the base of his throat. He wished he were there with her. Why, he didn't know. He doubted his presence would comfort her much. "Carly, you have to trust me," he said softly. "I swear to God, you won't regret it."

"I hope not."

"Does that mean we've got a deal?"

"I don't have much choice." He heard her swallow and grab for breath. "If you take me to court, how will it look to a judge? A pregnant woman, possibly going blind, who's on the dole with no hope of getting a job? I can't gamble with custody of my baby."

Hank sorely wished he hadn't been forced to play that card. The truth was, he'd never consider taking the child away from her. The very fact that she had chosen to carry the baby, regardless of the cost to herself, told him that she'd be a devoted and loving mother.

"I'm tired," she said, her voice trailing away on the last word. "Tired of fighting you, tired of fighting Bess. As long as I get to keep my baby, nothing else matters. I can survive anything for two years."

Hank wasn't sure how he felt about that statement. She could survive anything? What the hell did she think he meant to do, jump her bones the minute he got a ring on her finger?

"I'll want it in writing," she added.

He blinked and jerked his attention back to the conversation. "You'll want what in writing, that I won't press you for sex?"

"That you won't sue for custody after we divorce."

"Oh. Sure. I've got no problem with signing something like that."

"Am I to take that to mean you would have a problem signing a paper that says you won't press me for sex?"

For some insane reason, Hank nearly smiled. *Sex, a fate worse than death.* Only it wasn't really funny when he thought about it. It was his fault she felt this way. "No, of course not. You want it in writing, I'll give it to you in writing."

"Fine. I'd like that." Silence. Then, in a weary voice, she asked, "Will you draw it up?"

Hank considered the question. Somehow, he couldn't quite picture himself having an attorney draw up a document like that. "Yeah, I'll draw it up."

She sighed, the sound conveying exhaustion. Once they got all these messy details out of the way, he could take over and see to it that everything ran more smoothly for her. With some calm in her life, the headaches might disappear and the morning sickness might even abate.

"Now what?" she suddenly asked. "Are you, um, going to want to get married soon?"

"My insurance has a three-month waiting period for preexisting conditions. The quicker we get you signed up for coverage, the better. If anything goes wrong before that, a twenty percent co-pay will add up fast and your monthly premiums will be expensive as well." He struggled to organize his thoughts. "The first order of business is to apply for a marriage license. We'll have to go the courthouse to fill out the paperwork. I was thinking of a civil ceremony. Are you okay with that? I'm willing to do it in a church, if you'd prefer."

"No, not a spiritual ceremony. That would seem too final. It's only a temporary arrangement, after all. Besides, church weddings are more costly. If we don't keep the expenditures down, I'll be making payments to you for the rest of my life."

Red alert. Hank wasn't about to let her start pinching pennies and doing without because she didn't want to rack up a huge debt. He almost said as much, but remembering Bess's hurdle theory, he held his tongue. It was yet another issue that they could address later.

"Fine. We'll keep it low-key. We'll have to have witnesses, though."

"Do you have someone in mind?"

"I imagine my family will want to come. You okay with that?"

"I guess I'll have to meet them, sooner or later. I may as well get it over with."

Hank tried to imagine his parents and siblings formally shaking her hand after the wedding and then fading from the picture. It wasn't happening. The Coulters would make a big deal out of the marriage, even it was only a civil ceremony, and they'd consider Carly to be part of the fold the instant Hank put a ring on her finger. There'd be no such thing as getting it over with, not with them.

"Are you planning to invite Bess?" he asked.

"I, um—yes, if you don't mind." She still sounded

nervous and uncertain. Hank wished he could think of something to say that might ease her mind. "Bess is like a sister to me. Right now, I'm very upset with her, but I can't exclude her."

"How about your father?"

"My dad can't afford a plane ticket. The marriage will mean nothing. I see no reason to issue an invitation and make him feel obligated to come. I'll call and tell him after it's over."

A marriage that meant nothing? It went against everything Hank had been raised to believe. His problem, and one of his own making. He had concocted this crazy plan. "Right. He'll probably want to fly up when the baby comes. This way, he won't get stuck twice with the cost of airfare."

"Exactly. And I'll be more comfortable if there isn't a lot of fuss."

Hank just hoped he could convince his mother of that. Mary Coulter loved to give parties, and she'd probably insist on having a reception.

"I'll do some calling Monday morning to find out how we should proceed," he said. "I'll be in touch to let you know."

"I—okay. I'll be expecting you to call then. Monday, do you think?"

Hank had no idea how long it would take to get everything arranged, but he could certainly keep her posted. "Sure. Monday."

She ended the call without saying good-bye. Hank returned the phone to his belt. Zeke was behind the bar, mixing them each a drink.

"Well?"

Hank crossed over to sit on a barstool. "She's agreed to the marriage."

"You don't look very happy about it."

Hank took the tumbler his brother shoved toward him. He thumbed the condensation that beaded the glass. "I coerced her into it. I feel like a bastard."

"Sometimes, little brother, life doesn't offer a man any choices. If ever a lady needed help, I'd say it's her."

"She's worried that I'll go into Romeo mode the minute she says 'I do.'"

"You are only human."

Hank nearly choked on the Jack and Coke. "I've never forced myself on a woman in my life. I don't plan to start with her."

"I know you'd never force her, Hank. But sex is important to a man. What'll you do for two, maybe three years? Play around on the side?"

Hank snorted. "Not hardly. I'll be a married man."

Zeke nodded. "Exactly. It isn't in you. Which leaves you high and dry unless she comes around."

"I'm not going into this with a bunch of expectations riding drag. I've given her my word I won't press her for sex, and I'll damn well keep it."

"Of course you will. But a man has physical needs, like it or not. When those aren't met for a long period of time, even a mild-tempered fellow—which I'll point out that you're not—can get testy and hard to live with."

"I'm not bad-tempered," Hank retorted.

"You're no pussycat, either. Living with a woman—being close all the time—it can be a real bitch and put a strain on any relationship."

"I'll deal with it somehow." Hank rolled the glass between his hands. "If cold showers don't work, I'll mosey down to the stable and work until I drop before

I take it out on her. She's suffered enough because of me."

Zeke gave him a sharp look. "Are you developing feelings for this girl?"

"Feelings? Not hardly. She'd frustrate a saint."

"I see."

"I doubt it." Hank laughed humorlessly. "She's like no woman I've ever met—difficult and infuriating and—" Hank broke off, at a loss for words.

"And, what?"

"Sweet," Hank whispered. "So sweet that I need to be horsewhipped for ever touching her."

"Sweet?" Zeke grinned, his lean cheeks creasing into deep brackets at the corners of his mouth. "Oh, boy."

Seeing his brother's amusement, Hank took exception and said, "What's that mean?"

Lifting his glass, Zeke said, "Cheers, Romeo. You're a goner."

Chapter Ten

At a quarter to ten on Monday morning, Carly had just taken a sip of herbal tea when the phone rang. Knowing it was probably Hank, she leaped up from the kitchen table as if she'd been stuck with a pin. Then she stood there, rubbing her hands on her jeans, reluctant to answer.

On the fifth ring, she found her courage. "Hello?"

"Hi." His deep voice sounded warm, and she could almost see his slow grin. The image rankled. Without even bothering to identify himself, he asked, "How's the tummy this morning?"

Ordinarily, Carly wouldn't have been disturbed by an inquiry about her health, but coming from Hank, the question seemed intrusive and personal, not to mention proprietary. It was *her* digestive track, thanks very much. "Fine," she lied.

"No nausea? That's good news. How's the head?"

Having a headache had come to seem almost normal. It was only when the ache became a pounding pain that she was forced to lie down. "The head's fine, too."

"Good, good." A rapping sound came over the wire. She envisioned him striking a pen on a hard surface. "I just got off the phone with the courthouse.

No blood tests or physicals are required in Oregon now. It's a simple matter of going in to get a marriage license today or tomorrow and making an appointment with a JP for the ceremony. How does Friday afternoon strike you?"

"For the wedding, you mean?" Carly hadn't expected it to happen so fast. "Oh my." What was his big hurry? "That's, um, only four days away."

"I know, but there's no real reason to wait. We may as well get it done."

Done? Carly got the laundry done. She got the housework done. Legally binding herself to a man she barely knew didn't fall into the same category.

"You okay?" he asked.

"I'm fine," she insisted, even though she wasn't. In truth, she was horribly nervous, the kind of nervous that made her heart pound and her skin feel as if it were turning inside out. *Friday?* She remembered the urgent way he'd jerked at her clothes and spurted semen on her thighs, so eager to possess her that he hadn't even managed to aim straight. Now he was racing for the finish line again. What assurance did she have that he'd keep his promises after the wedding? "I'm just—dandy."

He said nothing for a moment. "Try not to get too wound up about this marriage business. All right? I don't want you getting a stress headache. Think of it as a technicality."

How did he know about her headaches, let alone that they might be caused by stress? *Bess.* And who did he think he was kidding, saying the ceremony would be nothing but a technicality? She'd be married to him, wouldn't she? Stuck out on some ranch, heaven only knew how far from town, and unable to drive. She'd be totally dependent upon Hank Coulter for everything. The thought set her teeth on edge. She was accustomed to doing for herself. Now she'd be relinquishing all control. There'd be no public transportation out at his ranch, no stores within walking distance. She'd be cut off from the world. She didn't even know if he'd provide her with a phone.

"I drew up that paper, by the way."

Her attention snapped back to the conversation.

"My brother Zeke witnessed my signature. No sex unless you say so. No filing for custody after a divorce. I also added a clause about the start-up cash I've promised to give you. If there's anything else you want included, just let me know. On a computer, it's easy enough to make changes, and it's no big deal to have my signature witnessed again."

The very fact that he was so willing to add other stipulations made Carly suspicious. If he truly believed the document was binding, wouldn't he be reluctant to include anything more than what they'd already agreed on?

"Speaking of our agreement, what will be your solution to that problem?"

"My solution to what problem?"

She ground her teeth, wondering if he were being deliberately obtuse. "To being celibate for two or three years." Tension had her stomach doing roller coaster dips. "Is it your plan to—well, you know— continue as you have?"

"Going out on weekends, you mean?"

That was a polite way of putting it. "Yes. Is that your plan?"

"I'll be married," he retorted, as if that said it all. "I won't step out. I'd be breaking my wedding vows."

Wonderful. He'd be all hers, sexual deprivation and all. "What do you intend to do, then?"

Another silence, followed by a weary sigh. "That's my problem, Carly. Trust me to handle it."

No, it was *her* problem. And she didn't trust him any farther than she could throw him. In her experience, people who used underhanded tactics in one situation were inclined to play dirty whenever an opportunity presented itself.

As though he sensed her thoughts, he said, "Carly, I've promised you that it'll be a marriage in name only unless you say otherwise. I've drawn up a document, guaranteeing that in writing. What else can I do to make you feel better? You name it, you got it."

"Forget I mentioned it," she said hollowly. "I was just—never mind. Forget I said anything."

Friday. What if he had a vile temper? What if he was an alcoholic? What if he was a wife beater? The list of possibilities was endless. That night at Chaps, he'd seemed like a nice guy, and Bess now seemed to trust him. But what did either of them really know about Hank Coulter? Nothing. If he got staggering drunk every night of the week, she wouldn't find out until she was married to him.

He interrupted her musings by asking, "Are you free this afternoon, by any chance?"

Her heart stuttered another beat. "Free to do what?"

"There's a waiting period after getting a marriage license. Three days, I think. We need to get the paperwork taken care of today or tomorrow to have the ceremony on Friday."

"Oh." Carly tugged on her ragged T-shirt and

touched her hair, which was still tousled from sleep. "What time this afternoon?"

"Will two work?"

That gave her nearly four hours. "If you're absolutely bent on doing this, I guess two will be fine."

"I'm bent on it," he said firmly. "Would it help if I sat down with you and went over my financial situation?"

"That won't be necessary."

"You sure? You might feel better about all this if you could see the entire picture and know in your own mind that we've got no other choice."

Carly doubted anything would make her feel better. She wasn't even sure she was thinking rationally. Bess didn't seem to think so. Maybe her hormones were in a state of flux, and she was being unreasonably difficult.

"I'm sure," she managed to assure him.

"Two it is, then. Before you hang up, can we try something?"

"What?"

"I just thought we might try saying good-bye this time, like normal people. So far, all our phone conversations have ended with you hanging up on me."

The teasing note in his voice caught her by surprise, and she almost smiled. Then she caught herself and firmed her lips. She wasn't going to be charmed by him again. Letting her guard down with Hank Coulter was dangerous. "I enjoy hanging up on you. It gives me a perverse satisfaction."

Brief silence. There was another smile in his voice when he said, "I always like to satisfy a lady. Go for broke."

Carly grinned in spite of herself as she dropped the receiver into the cradle without telling him good-bye.

Hank arrived on Carly's doorstep promptly at two. He knocked, three spaced raps with the back of his knuckles, and then cooled his heels on the welcome mat, waiting for her to answer. He heard rattling sounds coming from inside, then what sounded like bare feet pounding across the carpet.

When the door finally swung open, Carly stood at the threshold, holding three blouses on hangers in one tightly fisted hand. She wore an overlarge white T-shirt over a gathered blue skirt that sported a red-and-pink floral pattern. Hank took in her fine-boned bare feet and dainty little toes, her gracefully turned ankles, and a brief expanse of shapely calf before jerking his gaze back to her face. A guy could do worse in a shotgun wedding, he decided. A hell of a lot worse.

"I'm sorry," she said. "I meant to be ready." She pushed at her beautiful hair. "I have this embarrassing problem, and since Bess isn't here, I thought you might help me."

"What kind of problem?"

"I'm still lousy at matching colors." She held the blouses higher for his inspection. "Can you tell me which of these goes best with my skirt?"

One of the tops was hunter's orange with purple and green starbursts. Hank could scarcely believe she might consider wearing it with a floral print. Pointing to his choice, he said, "I'm no fashion expert, but if I were you, I'd go with the white one."

She spun away. "I'll be ready in two seconds."

He stepped inside and closed the door. "Don't rush on my account."

As she rounded the corner, she began tugging off the T-shirt. Hank got a tantalizing glimpse of bare back and slender arm. Then the bedroom door slammed shut, depriving him of the view. He sat on the sofa to wait.

Two minutes later, she emerged from the bedroom. Hank glanced up and barely suppressed an appreciative grin. She rubbed the end of her nose, making it turn a pretty pink. "Thanks for the help. Do I look all right?"

She looked fabulous. And so sweet and uncertain of herself that he yearned to lavish her with compliments. Not a good idea.

"You look great." He pushed to his feet. "If I'd known this was going to be a dress-up affair, I'd have changed my shirt."

She pressed a slender hand to her chest. Then she retreated a step. "You're right. A skirt is too dressy. Slacks would be better. Excuse me for a minute while I go—"

Hank snaked out a hand to catch her by the wrist. "You look perfect the way you are," he assured her. "I was only joking."

She stiffened at his touch. Hank quickly released her. Silence. He tried to think of something else to say. Nothing brilliant came to mind, so he settled for, "Well? You about ready to go?"

She rubbed the wrist that he'd just touched as though to remove contaminants. "As ready as I'll ever be."

"You'll need your purse."

"Oh, of course. I'll need ID. Will I need my birth certificate, too?"

"They don't require them here. Just a picture ID."

She went into the kitchen and returned a moment later with a small black clutch bag barely large enough to hold a wallet. Hank was accustomed to women carrying much bigger purses. As near as he could tell, Carly wore no makeup. Maybe that explained it.

"You travel light."

"What?"

He shook his head. "Nothing. Let's go get this done."

Once outside, she struggled to lock the door. Hank remembered Bess's hurdle theory and refrained from offering assistance. While he stood there watching, he couldn't help but notice how badly her hands were shaking. Nerves, he guessed. The realization bothered him because he knew he was the cause. He tried to remember that night—more specifically its ending. The images that circled through his head were vague and impossibly jumbled, culminating in blackness. Unfortunately, the proof was in the pudding, as his father was fond of saying. Whether he could remember it or not, he'd definitely done something to make this girl scared to death of him.

The thought jerked Hank up short. *Girl?* She was twenty-eight years old, damn it, and he was going soft in the head. Even so, as he stood there fidgeting while she tried to get the door locked, he couldn't chase away the thought that she was as shy and uncertain as a young teenager.

After three tries, she finally got the key in the hole. Seconds later when he tried to help her into the truck, she avoided his hands and managed by herself. After she got settled on the seat, Hank closed the door and left her to handle the seat belt. When he swung in on the driver's side, she was sitting straight enough to rule paper with her spine. For a second, Hank couldn't think what might have kicked her anxiety level up another notch. Then he recalled what had transpired between them the last time she'd been inside this vehicle.

As he pulled out into traffic, his palms sweat bullets on the steering wheel, making the plastic slick. He sneaked a glance her way, wishing she'd say something.

She finally broke the silence with, "What a beautiful day!"

Grateful for anything they might talk about, Hank leaped at the conversational opening with absurd relief. "That's one of the nice things about Crystal Falls. Lots of sunshine. Over three hundred days a year on average."

"*Really?* How *interesting*. In Portland, it rains almost that much."

Hank almost said, *"Really?"* He caught himself before the exchange went from absurd to ridiculous. "You know what they say about Oregonians. We don't tan, we rust."

She laughed shrilly. "Not over here, though."

"Nope. Over here, we get honest-to-goodness tans and skin cancer like other folks."

Hank drew to a stop at a red light. Still brittle with tension, but trying to pretend she wasn't, she stared out the passenger window.

"I love the sky here," she said. "It's such a gorgeous blue. That was one of the first beautiful things I ever saw, you know, the Central Oregon sky."

"You were already living over here when you had your first eye surgery?"

"We moved into the apartment the week before and

then drove back to Portland for the operation. It made things a little hectic, but Bess had to be settled in over here so she could start interviewing for jobs as soon as possible. She hopes to work full time the rest of the summer and then go part time after classes begin."

Hank was glad that their friendship was still intact. He'd worried that Bess's defection might cause a permanent rift. The fact that Carly had forgiven her friend for the betrayal told him more about her than she could possibly know.

A few minutes later after Hank found a parking spot on Main for his overlong truck, Carly took off walking toward the courthouse without him. He hurried to catch up, then grasped her by the shoulders and circled to her left, putting her between him and the storefronts.

At her questioning look, he said, "Sorry. A man should always walk on the outside. The rules of gentlemanly behavior, according to my father."

"Hasn't he heard of the feminist movement?"

"The what?"

She rolled her eyes and rewarded him with a smile that rivaled the sunlight. "I realize this is a rural community compared to Portland, but it can't be that far out of the mainstream."

"Depends on the company you keep. My dad was a third generation rancher. We ranchers have our own way of thinking, especially about women."

"Oh?"

Hank verbally scrambled to clarify that statement. "It's a little known fact, but female ranchers claim to have *started* the feminist movement."

"Really?" Her eyes twinkled with amusement. "How do they figure?"

"They never needed to demonstrate with picket signs to get equal rights. They earned them by the sweat of their brows over a century ago. Take my mom, for instance. You'll never meet any woman who's more ladylike, but she held her own as a rancher's wife, taking care of the house and us kids, plus bailing Dad out whenever he needed her help. I've seen her butt heads with bulls, buck hay alongside men, take care of us kids while she was doing it, and still feed twenty hired hands at the end of the day. My father says she's a hell of a woman, and he's right. She saved his ass so many times you'll never hear him say that it was *his* ranch or *his* money. They each had their own roles, of course, but Dad would come in from the fields, throw on an apron, and do kitchen duty just as quickly as she'd throw on jeans and boots to work outdoors with him. 'Needs Must' was their motto, and they shared the workload."

"They sound wonderful."

"Yeah. My mom's a sweetheart, and my dad—well, you'll meet him soon enough. He's a curious blend of modern thinking and old-fashioned courtesy. He's all for a woman shattering the glass ceiling, but no man better treat her with disrespect while she's climbing the corporate ladder."

When they reached the courthouse steps, she said, "I'm so nervous my stomach has butterflies."

"About getting a marriage license?"

She shifted her small purse from one hand to the other. "I really, *really* wish there were another solution."

Hank nudged up the brim of his Stetson to better see her face. When she looked up at him again, he smiled gently. "It's going to be okay. I promise."

She nodded and straightened her shoulders. "Right. It's the most practical way to do things. I know that."

He just wished she could be marginally relaxed about it. He gestured toward the broad steps.

She turned and began the climb. Hank noticed her scowling in concentration, which told him the rises were difficult for her to see.

"It's my visual cortex," she explained when she caught him watching her. "I have trouble with depth perception and can't see depressions and edges."

"Ah."

Once at the landing, he pushed open the double doors and stood back for her to enter first. Then he grasped her elbow again to guide her to the elevator.

"We can use the stairs," she protested.

"I put in a hard morning," he lied.

As the metal doors of the elevator slid closed behind them, Hank pressed the button for the third floor. Then he settled against the handrail with his arms folded at his waist. Carly stood center front for the duration of the ride, fidgeting with her purse and hair. Hank noticed that her hands were trembling.

"It's not that big a deal, you know. In five minutes, we'll be finished."

She nodded. Then she graced him with a hesitant smile. Hank felt as if the sun had just peeked out at him from behind a cloud again. Her mouth was one of the loveliest he had ever seen, the upper lip a perfect bow, the lower one full and soft. "It just seems so strange," she said. "I've never gotten married before."

He chuckled in spite of himself. "Me, neither, come to think of it."

The elevator bumped to a stop and the doors

opened. He led the way to the clerk's office, opened the door, and ushered Carly inside. Moments later they were trying to fill out the required form. To see the fine print, Carly held the paper a few inches from her nose. Why, Hank didn't know. She had to study each letter to make out a word.

"Why are there so *many* different fonts?" she grumped. "One time, A's have curlicues, the next they don't. It drives me nuts."

Hank studied the words, and in the doing, he began to get a glimmer of understanding. Carly was seeing letters for the first time and trying to correlate them with the unchanging shapes she'd memorized by touch.

To save her unnecessary frustration, he began reading the lines aloud to her, which earned him a scolding frown from the clerk. He didn't care. He didn't want to be there for three hours.

"It's just a standard application," he whispered. "Is it absolutely necessary to read all the fine print?"

"I like to know what I'm signing."

Hank didn't know what possessed him, but as he began to read the next line, he altered the wording. "I hereby swear on this blank day of blank," he softly intoned, "that I'll be my lawfully wedded husband's sex slave, no questions asked, and will obey him in all things, even when he's criminally abusive and unreasonable."

Her eyes went wide. *"What?"* She snatched the paper away from him. For an awful moment, Hank feared he might have made a mistake by teasing her. But then she gulped back a giggle and rolled her eyes. "You're *impossible*. It doesn't say that."

"My point, exactly. It's just a standard form."

She sighed. "Oh, all right. Just show me where to sign."

He pointed and then made the mistake of glancing away. When he looked back, he saw that she'd put her John Hancock on the witness line. *Oops.* Hank signaled for the clerk. "I'm sorry. Could we get a fresh form?"

Carly squinted at her signature. "What? Did I mess up?"

"No big deal." Hank shoved the new application under her nose, pressed his finger to the correct line, and said, "Sign right there."

Sticking out the tip of her tongue, she pursed her lips in concentration and squeezed the pen hard enough to snap the plastic as she scrawled her signature. Hank forgot all about the form. *That mouth.* He would have happily forfeited his share of the Lazy J to kiss her again.

When she finished, she whispered, "Did I stay on the line?"

Not precisely. "You did great," he said and quickly added his signature. *Done.* He had his pretty little sex slave all wrapped up and tied with a bow.

Moments later, they showed the clerk their picture IDs and were finished. Carly puffed air into her cheeks as they walked to the elevator. "I'm glad that part's over."

Hank felt relieved, too. Why, he didn't know. It had only been paperwork. Carly fell silent as they walked back to his truck. Hank didn't try to help her in this time. Before he started the engine, he looked over at her.

"Would you like to go out for lunch or something?"

She looked surprised by the suggestion. "I've already eaten."

"Coffee, then?" He felt it was important that they spend some time together before the wedding, his hope being that she'd feel a little less nervous if she came to know him better.

"No thanks," she said with a smile to take the sting out of her refusal. "Coffee isn't allowed now. It may harm the baby."

Hank thought of all the drinks served in restaurants that wouldn't harm the baby, but he decided to let the subject drop. She clearly didn't care to go.

The drive back to the apartment complex passed in silence. When Hank had parked at the curb, he switched off the ignition. "Well, I guess I'll see you Friday?"

She nodded. Her fingers fiddled nervously with a button on her blouse. "Would it be possible for you to pick me up on the way to the courthouse? Bess got called back for a second interview at a dentist office today. That's a positive sign. If she gets the job, she may have to work that afternoon."

"Sure, I can pick you up," Hank assured her. "Will three thirty work?"

"That'll be fine." She sat there for a moment, clearly searching for something to say. Then she sighed. "Well, I'd better go. Until Friday, then?"

"Right."

It bothered Hank to just sit there while she exited the vehicle. He was accustomed to performing the gentlemanly courtesies. But he resisted the urge.

Before shutting the passenger door, she flashed him a brittle smile and said, " 'Bye."

Hank gazed after her as she moved along the walkway that led to her apartment. *Friday*. In four short days, he'd be a married man. As unnerving as that realization was, he knew it was even more unsettling for Carly. He wished he could do something to make her feel better about it.

But for the life of him, he couldn't think what.

Chapter Eleven

That night, Hank went to see his parents. Despite his familiarity with their suburban home, he had a surreal feeling as he sat down at the oval kitchen table. His mother sat across from him. His father took a chair to his right.

"Are you sure I can't get you something?" Mary asked. "Tea only takes a minute, and the coffee's still fresh."

Hank's nerves were already raw. He didn't need a jolt of caffeine to stretch them tighter. He settled back on the oak chair. "No thanks. I'm fine."

Mary took a sip of tea from a dainty little cup with gold at the fluted edge. "It's lovely that you stopped by. We haven't seen much of you lately."

"It's a busy time of year. Jake and I are still imprinting the spring foals, and we had four new horses brought to us this week for behavior modification." Hank's gaze shifted to the section of wall next to the window where six handprints were encased in aged plaster, one belonging to each of the Coulter brood. Looking at his own, Hank found it difficult to believe that he'd ever been that small. It occurred to him that one day soon, he might have his child's handprint hanging in the kitchen. "Things will slow down here shortly."

"I hope so. You and Jake work too hard."

Hank tried to think of a gentle way to tell his parents his news. While he discarded one idea after another, the old teapot clock on the wall behind him seemed to tick more loudly with each passing second.

"I have something I need to tell you. Prepare yourselves for a shock."

Mary sat more erect. Harv scowled, staring at Hank with those all-seeing, laser-blue eyes that had always unnerved him as a kid.

"I don't know how to work my way up to this, so I'll say it straight out." Hank waited a beat, and then he dropped it on them. "I'm getting married Friday."

Hank's parents stared at him incredulously. His mother, a small, plump woman with dark hair barely touched with gray, carefully set her teacup on its saucer, glanced at her husband, and smiled uncertainly.

"I'm sorry," she said with a laugh. "My ears are getting so bad these days. I could have sworn you said you're getting married."

Hank nodded. "You heard me right."

"I didn't know you were even dating anyone exclusively."

Hank hadn't lied to his folks since childhood, and he didn't want to now. "These things happen quickly sometimes."

"On Friday, did you say?" Mary touched a hand to her throat, and her eyes went soft and shiny. "This is so sudden."

"I know it must seem that way. I'm sorry for not giving you more warning."

Harv patted his shirt pocket for the cigarettes he'd

discarded four years ago. "How long have you known this woman, son?"

"Long enough," Hank replied evasively.

"Do you love her?" his mother asked. Then she laughed. "Silly question. You wouldn't be marrying her if you didn't."

If only they knew. Hank was grateful that his mother had answered her own question. If he could avoid it, he preferred not to get into the particulars of his relationship with Carly.

A frown pleated Mary's brow. "Friday, did you say? *This* Friday?" At Hank's nod, she said, "My goodness, that only gives us three days."

"We're keeping it simple, Mom. She has no family here. Just a civil ceremony with no frills."

Mary looked crestfallen. "Surely you won't mind if I give a reception. We can do it here. What kind of wedding will it be with no celebration afterward?"

"Carly and I don't really want a reception. We're, um—well, it's sort of sudden, and we want to avoid a bunch of fuss and—"

Hank's father broke in with, "Weddings aren't solely for the bride and groom. They're for the family as well. If your mother wants to have a small reception, I see no reason why she shouldn't."

Determined to be the winner of this debate, Hank tried to think of an argument that would satisfy both his parents. *Nada.* Then he made the mistake of glancing at his mother. Her eyes were filling with tears.

"You'll only get married once," she said shakily.

Not necessarily. But Hank preferred not to get into that, either.

"I want to do something special to mark the occasion. You're our *son*."

How was a guy supposed to stand firm when his mother was about to cry? Hank took off his hat and set it on the chair next to him. *Damn*. He could hold his own with men. Somehow, it was never so easy with women, and now he had two of them to please.

"It's bad enough that it'll be a civil ceremony," Mary went on, her voice growing more taut with each word. "But to not even celebrate with a reception afterward? We'll have no pictures, no wonderful memories to share as a family."

Under the table, Hank's dad gave him a nudge with his boot. Hank knew when he was licked and held up a hand. "Mom?" Mary just kept talking. "*Mother? Whoa!* Will you give me a chance to say something?"

Mary fell silent, her expression accusing. He had clearly just earned the honor of being the only son who'd ever broken her heart.

"If I say yes to a reception, will you give me your solemn oath to keep it very, *very* simple?"

Mary nodded. "Simple will be fine. I can do simple."

"All right, then," Hank conceded. "But it has to be small with only family members in attendance. Agreed?"

Mary immediately brightened. "Small is good. I can do that." She blinked her tears away and wiped one cheek. "It'll be more intimate that way." She sniffed and rubbed under her other eye. "I'm sorry. It's not every day our son gets married! I can't imagine treating it like any other day."

Hank had already read that, loud and clear. As long as his mom kept it simple, he guessed a reception wouldn't be so bad.

"Carly, did you say? That's a darling name." Mary sniffed again. "When will we get to meet her?"

Hank rubbed his jaw. "She'll be pretty busy all this week, packing and getting ready for the ceremony. You'll probably have to wait to meet her the day of the wedding."

"That's a shame."

Hank agreed, but he didn't want to throw too much at Carly all at once. There'd be plenty of time after the nuptials for his family to get to know her.

Hank fiddled with the bean mosaic that graced the center of the table. He'd made it for Mother's Day eons ago. His dad had coated it with a fiberglass resin to protect the design, an off-center, cross-eyed rooster with a spiky comb made of brown rice. The poor bird looked as if it had just been knocked silly with a tack hammer.

"What does she look like?" Mary asked.

Hank thought for a moment. "Blond, pretty." He felt his father's gaze sharpen. "Not the flashy type. Her hair is naturally blond, honey gold with darker streaks. She wears no makeup, near as I can tell. If I were to describe her in just a few words, I'd say she's more the church angel type—like the ones you see painted on chapel ceilings."

Harv relaxed. Mary beamed. "She sounds lovely."

She grabbed a pen and paper from the telephone stand and began jotting down notes. Glancing up at Hank, she said, "We'll have to invite the Kendricks."

Hank imagined the living room of his parents' home crammed with people. "Except for Ryan, the Kendricks aren't really family, Mom."

"Close enough. Your sister, Bethany, is a Kendrick

now. They'll be sure to hear about the wedding from Ryan." She began drawing up a list, which grew to alarming proportions even as Hank watched. "And we *can't* exclude Molly's parents."

Hank threw a pleading look at his dad. Harv's mouth twitched. "Molly's mom and stepfather might not make it down, sweetheart. They'll have to drive clear from Portland, and we aren't givin' 'em much notice."

Hank prayed his father was right. If fifty people showed up for the ceremony, how would he explain it to Carly? "I really think it'd be better if we include only immediate family. I've got four brothers and a sister, two of them married with kids. The JP's office won't hold all of us, let alone all our in-laws and shirt-tail relatives."

"Don't worry about a thing," Mary said. "Just leave the details to me."

That was what worried Hank, the details. Why did women have to complicate everything?

Mary glanced up at her husband. "We can't exclude Sly and Helen."

Harv angled a look at Hank. "Nope, I don't guess we can."

Mary dimpled a cheek. "Our Hank, getting married. Can you believe it, Harv? When he said he had to tell us something, that was the last thing I expected him to say."

"It came as a surprise, all right." Harv pushed up from the kitchen table. "Hank, while your mother works up an invite list, can you step out to the garage with me for a minute? I want to show you something."

Hank knew what that meant and braced for an interrogation as he followed his father outside. Harv didn't disappoint him. Once the fire door swung shut behind them, he pitched his voice low and asked, "What the hell is goin' on?"

"Nothing's going on, Dad. I'm just getting hitched is all."

"Far as I know, you haven't been dating one woman steady. Now you walk in here, big as you please, and announce that you're gettin' married?"

"Well, Dad—"

"Save the bullshit for your mother. She buys it. I want it straight."

Hank gave it to him straight, telling his father the entire story, including how he'd coerced Carly into marrying him. About halfway through the recounting, Harv sank onto a milk can, one of Bethany's tole painting projects in progress. Toward the end of the story, the older man's jaw muscle had started to ripple, a sure sign that he was clenching his teeth. His blue eyes flashed with anger.

"I'm sorry, Dad," Hank said when he'd told his father everything. "I know I've disappointed you."

"It's not my proudest moment as a father. I raised you better."

"If it's any comfort, I've learned a hard lesson. Mom kept warning me that sooner or later, someone would get hurt. She was right, only it wasn't me. No matter how it turns out between me and Carly, I'll never do the bar scene again."

"Is that what they call it now?" His father sat erect. "The bar scene? Seems to me a mighty polite term for drinking, carousing, and popping cherries in the back seat of pickup trucks."

Hank couldn't think of a single word to say in his own defense. His eyes burned as he met his father's sharp gaze. "You know the worst part?"

"No, what?" Harv asked.

Hank's throat went tight. "She's everything I would have chosen in a wife if I'd had the brains to go looking. She's sweet and beautiful and kind with just enough sass and vinegar tossed in to keep me guessing." He sighed and kicked at a dry leaf that had blown in from the yard last fall. "Every time I look at her, I wonder how I could have thought she was a run-of-the-mill barfly. Not knowing she was a virgin, I wasn't concerned about being extra careful. I hurt her, I'm sure. She's wary of me now."

"As slick as you are with nervous fillies, I'm not too worried on that count. You'll find a way to settle her down."

Hank wasn't so sure about that. "Maybe."

Harv pushed wearily to his feet. Hank kept waiting for him to say, "I told you so," or to rant and rave for a while. Instead Harv clasped Hank's shoulders, looked him directly in the eye, and smiled, albeit sadly.

"I wish you'd never put the poor girl in a position like this. I won't pretend otherwise. But, given the fact that you have, I'm proud of you for facing up to your responsibilities."

It was the last thing Hank expected him to say. "It's my baby, Dad. No question about it. This pregnancy will ruin her life if I don't step up to the plate."

"A lot of men would still run like hell."

"I was taught better."

Harv nodded. "Ordinarily, I'd never approve of you coercing her into marriage, but nothing about her situation sounds ordinary."

That was an understatement if ever Hank had heard one.

Harv sighed. Then he patted Hank's arm. "She'll have plenty of family to support her from now on."

Hank glanced at the door that opened onto the kitchen. "Yeah, plenty of family."

In the not so distant past, Hank had resented the large, close-knit Coulter clan. But now he was glad of it. His mom would take Carly under her wing and be wonderful to her. He could also count on Jake and Molly to make her feel welcome at the ranch. Carly might feel a little overwhelmed at first, but Hank was convinced that she'd soon love his family almost as much as he did.

"She'll also have a good man at her side," Harv said softly.

The comment surprised Hank. He gave his father a questioning look.

Harv bent his head and took a turn at kicking the leaf. "Raisin' sons, a man's got a tendency to paint himself better than he is, tryin' his damnedest to set a good example. I made my mistakes, things I never talked about in front of you boys." He glanced up, looking sheepish. "Tossed a number of skirts, sowed my wild oats. Didn't want to get married. Couldn't picture myself with a passel of kids to support. No way, not me. Then I met your mama." He winked. "Fell in love with her at first glance and spent the next few months takin' cold showers. She was a *nice* girl, not the kind to get her skirt tossed without a ring on her finger. Wasn't nothin' for it but to marry her. Her daddy had conniption fits. Said I was a good-for-nothin' scalawag who'd do her wrong. Wouldn't give us his blessing. He was mad as hops when we ran off and got married anyway."

"Grandpa McBride didn't like you?" Hank asked incredulously.

Harv chuckled. "Wasn't nothing to like. He was right; I was a good-for-nothin' scalawag." He jabbed Hank's chest with a rigid finger. "Took lovin' a good woman to straighten me up, and she's kept me dancin' to her tune ever since. Your grandpa McBride grew to respect me. By the time Jake came along, he and I got along fine. Did until the day he died." Harv's mouth twitched. "His last words to me were, 'You treat my Mary right, or I swear, boy, I'll come back from the grave and kick your ass.'"

Hank laughed, still finding it difficult to believe that his father had ever been a skirt chaser.

Harv narrowed his eyes. "Seeing as how Carly's daddy isn't here to say it, I will. Treat her right. If you don't, I'll kick your ass."

"No worries, Dad. My scalawag days are over. Soon, I'll be raising a child and painting myself better than I am, too."

"I know you will," Harv said with a nod. "I raised you, didn't I?"

When Harv turned to reenter the house, Hank stopped him with, "Dad? There's one more thing."

Harv swung back around. "If it's bad news, save it. I've heard enough for one night."

"Nothing bad." Hank rubbed the back of his neck, thinking carefully before speaking. "I hate to ask this. I know you don't like to keep secrets from Mom. But in this instance, would you mind keeping Carly's pregnancy to yourself for a few days?"

Harv frowned. "I'd rather not."

"I know, and I understand. Honestly. It's just—well, if you tell Mom, she'll turn right around and tell Bethany. Before I know it, the whole family will be in on the secret. I don't want someone to slip up and say something to humiliate Carly on her wedding day."

Harv finally nodded. "All right, son, I'll keep it to myself. You'll need to tell your mother soon, though. I'll give you a week, and that's it. She and I don't keep things from each other."

"I won't even wait a week," Hank promised. "Just a few days. For Carly's sake, not mine. She might take it in stride. Lots of women get pregnant before marriage these days. But, then again, she might not. Her life experience hasn't been ordinary."

Harv rubbed his chin, his fingertips rasping on a five-o'clock shadow that was now more silver than dark. "Your mother will be delighted about the baby, you know. She doesn't have it in her to be judgmental about things like that."

Hank puffed air into his cheeks. "I'm not worried about that, not for a minute. It's just that Carly's never met any of you. She needs a little time to settle in before Mom starts gushing and presenting her with baby gifts."

Harv chuckled and gave Hank a push toward the door. "You'd better get back in there before she invites half the town to your wedding."

Hank wanted to think his father was joking, but when he reentered the kitchen, Mary was already on the phone with his sister Bethany, chattering a mile a minute. "Yes," Mary chortled. "Friday at four! No warning, nothing. He says her name is Carly. Yes, well, you know your brother. He never crawled. Just up and started walking at seven months. Nothing's ever changed."

Hank heard the faint sound of Bethany's voice coming over the line. He pictured his sister, sitting by the phone stand in the high-tech wheelchair that her husband Ryan had special ordered, her brown eyes dancing with delight.

Mary laughed at something her daughter said and thrust the phone at Hank. "She wants to hear all the details, straight from the horse's mouth."

On Friday at precisely three thirty, Hank rang Carly's doorbell. While he waited for her to answer, he checked his bolo tie, shrugged his shoulders to straighten his western-cut tweed jacket, and then fiddled with his belt buckle to make sure it was centered. He was nervous. A fine layer of sweat filmed his body, intensifying the scent of his cologne. It wasn't every day a guy got married.

When the doorknob rattled, he snapped to attention, tucked the bridal bouquet behind his back, and pasted on what he hoped was a friendly grin. When the door swung open, the grin froze on his lips and all he could do was stare. His church angel had undergone an astounding transformation that could only be described as *Debbie Does Dallas*.

Carly was wearing a slinky white metallic sheath with a neckline that totally redefined the word plunging. The shimmering knit hugged every delightful curve of her body, and the skirt sported a slit that shot clear to midthigh, revealing one shapely leg almost in its entirety. Her makeup looked as if it had been slathered onto her face with a palette knife. And her hair stood out at either side of her head in a wildly untamed cloud of blond curls that looked stiff enough to support Christmas tree ornaments.

"Hi," she said, sounding agitated.

Hank was shocked speechless.

She smoothed a hand over her hip. "Bess laid out a dress for me, but a button came off. I tried to sew it back on, but I stuck myself and bled on the bodice." Her voice went shrill. "It's the only white dress I own. This one is hers. I found it at the back of her closet. I'm lousy at choosing clothes. Does it look okay?"

It would have been every man's wet dream if she'd been wearing spike heels. Instead she wore the simple white sandals again, which were anticlimactic, to say the least.

Still stunned, Hank stepped inside the apartment and closed the door. He couldn't look away from the inverted, green half moons above her beautiful eyes— or the thick layers of black mascara on her eyelashes.

"You're wearing makeup," was all he could say.

She touched her cheek. "It's safe to wear it now. I called Dr. Merrick and checked." She fixed him with uncertain eyes that were almost eclipsed by the eye shadow. "I've never put on makeup. I had to start over three times."

She had obviously spent a great deal of time applying the cosmetics. For a first effort, there were precious few smears or globs. Taking in the lipstick that defined her soft mouth in glaring red, Hank decided that she must have borrowed Bess's stuff. The shades were far more suitable for a brunette.

In that moment, he was swept back through time to the night of his sister's senior prom. Their mother had been called to the stable on an emergency while Bethany was getting ready for the dance. Hank had been the only member of the family who'd remained at the house, waiting for a return call from the vet. Bethany had emerged from the bathroom, looking pretty much like Carly did now, her face smeared with garish color, her hair a nightmarish mess of inexpert curling and too much hairspray, the only difference being that Bethany had realized how awful she looked.

Carly obviously didn't.

Hank thought about taking the coward's way out. He hated to hurt her feelings. On the other hand, he couldn't very well say nothing and allow her to show up for her wedding, looking like this. Later, when she realized how inappropriate the dress and makeup were for the occasion, she'd be humiliated every time she remembered her wedding day.

Evidently his thoughts showed on his face. She splayed a hand over her heart and said, "I look awful, don't I?"

"You could never look awful." He laid the small bouquet on the sofa and turned to study her. "It's just that the dress is too flashy for a wedding, your hair looks much nicer natural, and you've put on way too much makeup."

She looked stricken. "Oh, God." She turned as if to do something, then whipped back around to fix him with imploring eyes. "Can you help me pick a better dress?"

Hank intended to do more than that. He jerked off his jacket and rolled up his shirtsleeves as he followed her to the bedroom. Boxes were piled all over her bed, telling him that she'd already packed to move to the cabin. Fortunately, she'd left some of her garments on hangers. When she opened the closet, his gaze immediately fell on a simple light blue dress.

"This is perfect," he said, pulling it out.

"What about my hair and makeup?"

"It just so happens that I'm something of an expert

on hair and makeup. I used to help my sister Bethany get ready for dates." He glanced at his watch, resigning himself to the fact that they would be late for their wedding. There was no way around it. "Can you lose that dress, throw on a robe, and meet me in the bathroom?"

Moments later when Carly appeared in the doorway of the bath, Hank had already turned on the sink faucet and was adjusting the water temp. She flicked him a nervous look when he advanced on her with a wet washcloth. With the aid of some cold cream he'd found, he quickly managed to remove all the makeup. She emitted a startled squeak when he drew her to the vanity, gently pushed her head down, and started dousing her hair.

"This is one of the most humiliating experiences of my life," she muttered.

"It's not your fault that you haven't developed an eye for hair and makeup—or that you can't see the spangles on a dress."

He soaped her hair, being careful not to get any suds in her eyes. Then he did the quickest rinse job in history. Her soft bottom pressed against his fly. The contact reminded him of their "no sex" agreement and rekindled his determination to change her mind about that stipulation.

"There," he said as he wrapped her head in a towel. "Where's the makeup?"

She gestured at a small bag sitting on the vanity. Hank opened it and quickly rifled through the contents, choosing only three items, some mascara, a blusher, and a light pink lipstick. Carly stood before him, wide-eyed and tense as he went to work on her face. In his opinion, hers was such a perfect countenance that she didn't really need cosmetics, but he understood her desire to be at her best when she met his family. A little makeup wouldn't hurt, and it might bolster her confidence.

"General rule of thumb with makeup, less is always better," he explained as he applied a touch of mascara to her long, silky eyelashes. "The idea is to look natural."

"I'm sorry for making us late," she whispered.

The front of her robe hung open slightly, revealing the lacy cups of her bra and the upper swells of her breasts. Hank looked only once, then riveted his gaze to her face, a feat that tested his self-control to its limits.

"It's not your fault. I should have come earlier."

"Will your parents be angry?"

He dabbed some color on her lips. "I don't think so." He winked at her. "If they're slightly put out by the wait, they'll get over it the second they see their pretty new daughter-in-law."

When he drew the towel from her head, her fine hair fell to her shoulders in damp ringlets. Hank combed them a little with his fingers, marveling at how absolutely lovely she was. "All finished," he said. "Run, throw the dress on, and we'll be ready to go."

She glanced worriedly in the mirror. "I need to dry my hair. I can't go like this."

"It'll be almost dry by the time we get there," he assured her. "And it'll look fabulous." At her dubious look, he added, "I'm the barroom lothario, remember. Trust me to know what looks good."

She pushed past him to return to the bedroom. By the time she emerged a few minutes later, looking beautiful in the simple dress and white sandals, Hank had retrieved the bouquet.

"You look absolutely perfect," he said, and as the words left his mouth, he knew he meant them with all his heart. She *was* perfect, sweet and nervous, trembling and uncertain. "I'll be the proudest man in six counties to walk into that courthouse with you on my arm."

He presented the flowers to her. "I know you wanted to keep this simple, but I thought you should at least have a bouquet."

Her eyes shone as she accepted the small cluster of blossoms. "Oh, Hank, you shouldn't have. They're *gorgeous.*" She buried her nose in the blossoms and breathed deeply of their perfume. "Carnations? They're my absolute favorite."

Hank realized she had to identify the flowers by smell. When she gently touched a fingertip to another blossom, he said, "That's a daisy." He'd asked the florist for an arrangement of wildflowers, and she'd done her best on such short notice, using what she had on hand. He touched a delicate, lavender petal. "These are wild orchids." Moving on to a tiny violet flute, he said, "And these are bluebells. The purple ones with the yellow and black centers are just garden-variety pansies."

"Just? Thank you so much. I've only ever gotten flowers once—the time you sent me roses." Even with the blusher to camouflage her natural skin tone, he saw her cheeks turn pink with pleasure. "Flowers have always been my favorite things on earth—I guess because they smell so wonderful. Even when I couldn't see them, I could enjoy them."

Hank made a mental note to make sure she got

flowers frequently from now on. He reached into his pocket. "I, um—also picked up some rings."

She flashed him a startled look.

"We'll have to have rings for the ceremony. When I went to the jewelry store, I meant to get plain gold bands and nothing else. But when I saw all the wedding sets, I couldn't resist."

He flipped open the blue velvet box on his palm.

"I wasn't sure what you might like, so I chose something that reminded me of you." He lifted out the engagement ring, which sported a dainty swirl of diamond chips around a small sparkling center stone. As he slipped it onto her slender finger, he congratulated himself on the choice. It looked perfect on her fine-boned hand, not too gaudy, not too small, and the delicate design suited her. "I had to guess at the size. I'm glad it fits."

Carly lifted her hand, her expression troubled. "You shouldn't have, Hank. This must have cost a fortune."

"It wasn't that much." Watching her, Hank found himself wishing . . . hell, he wasn't sure what he wished. That things were different between them? That he could propose in a more conventional way, and that she might accept? "If we're going to do this, we may as well do it right. If worse comes to worst, you can give it to our son or daughter someday."

She flashed him a wary look. "If worse comes to worst?"

Bad choice of words. He glanced at his watch. "We're already running way late. We'd better make tracks."

"It's a lovely ring, Hank. Thank you."

She looked none too happy about wearing it. Hank supposed it was the symbolic meaning that bothered her. Traditionally, an engagement ring was a promise of forever, and a wedding band sealed the bargain. A man was also staking his claim when he put a ring on a woman's finger.

That worked for Hank. He didn't know what it was about her, but she touched him in ways no other woman ever had.

Chapter Twelve

Hank and Carly were late for their own wedding. Only by thirty-five minutes, but for those who had shown up on schedule, that was a long time to wait. It resulted in lots of family—*his* family—standing elbow to elbow in the overly small room, sweating in their Sunday best, fidgeting and growing impatient. It also meant that the JP was growing irritable. He stood beside a small table along the back wall, his eyes as searing and censorial as Judge Roy Bean's.

As Hank pushed open the door, Carly pressed close to him, one hand knotted on his jacket, the other clutching her bouquet. He considered assuring her that there was no need to be so nervous, but the moment he saw his parents, he decided to let them convey that message to her themselves. If there was anything Hank had always been able to count on, it was his mother and father's kindness.

Carly moved beside him like a robot with faulty wiring. Hank instinctively slipped his arm around her shoulders and drew her close to his side as he led her into the room and closed the door. Rubbing her shoulder, he tried to convey without words that these were friendly people who'd welcome her with open arms.

The JP's glare made it clear that he was anxious to get this show on the road, but Hank refused to rush Carly into saying "I do" until she had at least been introduced to the individuals who'd come to witness the nuptials. He'd make it up to the JP later with a generous tip.

"Mom, Dad, this is Carly. Carly, I'd like you to meet my parents, Mary and Harv Coulter."

Hank had never been more proud to be a Coulter than in that moment. His mom flashed a delighted smile and stepped forward with her arms spread wide. "My name is Mary, dear heart, but I hope you'll call me Mom. It's so lovely to finally meet you!"

Despite her nervousness, Carly's natural poise seemed to kick in. She flashed one of those radiant smiles that had sideswiped Hank that fateful night at Chaps. "I'm equally pleased to meet you! Hank's told me so many nice things about you."

Mary beamed with pleasure. Hank glanced past his mother to see Bess emerge from the press of bodies. She beamed a smile but hung back, clearly not wishing to interrupt. Harv grinned broadly as he gathered Carly into his arms for a hug. Over the top of her blond head, he caught Hank's gaze, his expression conveying that he wholeheartedly commended his son on his good taste.

"You look so much like Hank!" Carly marveled as Harv released her from his embrace.

Harv chuckled. "The Coulter stamp. My sons are all cursed."

Mary came over to give Hank a hug. "She's beautiful, sweetheart. Absolutely beautiful."

"Thank you, Mom. She's a really special lady."

By now, everyone in the Coulter clan knew about

Carly's eye disease and consequent vision problems. True to his word, Harv had kept silent about the pregnancy, but he'd felt no such compunction about sharing the other information that Hank had given him.

"She's amazing," Mary whispered. "Just by looking, you'd never guess she couldn't see such a short time ago."

Hank was about to move back to Carly's side when his father handed her off to Zeke, who gave her a hug, kissed her cheek, and passed her on to his twin brothers Isaiah and Tucker. Hank quickly shouldered his way through the milling bodies to reach Carly's side in time to make the introductions. When he slipped an arm around her waist, she jumped as if he'd touched her with a hot coal.

Hank firmed his hold, met Tucker's twinkling gaze, and said, "Sweetheart, I'd like you to meet my brother Tucker. Tucker, this is Carly Adams."

Carly squinted and leaned closer to peer at the twins. "Oh, my God," she whispered in genuine dismay. "I've started seeing double."

Tucker threw back his dark head and barked with laughter. Isaiah, the quieter and more reserved of the two, merely grinned.

"You're not seeing double, honey. Isaiah and Tucker are identical twins," Hank explained. "It's even hard for me to tell them apart sometimes."

"Really?" Carly studied each of them with amazed curiosity. "I've heard of identical twins, of course, but I've never actually seen any." She glanced up at Hank. "They look a lot like you."

"Like Dad says, we all kind of look alike."

Tucker sent Hank an amused glance. "So, tell us about yourself, Carly," he said, his gaze warming when he shifted it back to her upturned face. "Mom said something about your being a teacher?"

"Oh yes. I'm on a sabbatical right now to attend grad school."

That was a subject dear enough to Isaiah's heart to prompt him to engage in the conversation. "Really?" he said. "What will you be getting your master's in?"

Unaware that everyone in Hank's family already knew about her blindness, Carly explained about her lattice dystrophy. "Growing up blind and knowing firsthand how difficult it can be for blind kids in public school, I want to focus on special ed and work with visually disabled students."

"That's great," Tucker inserted. "I'll bet there's a shortage of teachers in that field."

"A shortage of good ones, anyway," Carly agreed. "All the better for me. It'll be much easier for me to find a position after I've finished grad school. With only my bachelor's, it was difficult to find a steady job. I subbed for a year and finally got lucky, but only because a teacher grew ill and had to retire. The ease of finding a job wasn't my reason for wanting to attend grad school and focus on special ed, though. Having been blind myself, I honestly feel I have something special to offer."

The conversation continued for a couple of minutes, and then Tucker steered Carly away to meet their sister Bethany, who had recently opened a riding academy for disabled kids. That gave the two young women something in common. Gazing after his future bride and twin brothers, Hank breathed a sigh of relief that everything was going so smoothly. Before this day was over, Carly would probably love every member of his overlarge family whether she wanted to or not.

Confident that she would be okay with Tucker to look after her, Hank took the opportunity to take care of last minute details with the JP.

Contrary to Hank's belief, Carly was not okay. She had been expecting only a few people to show up for the ceremony. Instead there were at least twenty, possibly more, and the sea of unfamiliar faces was making her dizzy. She would never remember all their names. Even worse, Hank's relatives and friends clearly believed this was to be a real wedding, with forever as part of the package. Knowing otherwise, Carly felt horribly guilty.

She didn't believe in lying, and this was the biggest lie of her life, pretending to love a man she barely knew. The only thing she and Hank had in common was their baby. In two or three years, they would get a divorce and go their separate ways. How was she supposed to look these people in the eye, smile, and pretend this was the happiest day of her life?

She couldn't *do* this. It was one thing to sign papers and get married for financial reasons. It was quite another to pass this off as a real wedding and let people welcome her into their family with such sincerity. Bethany was so friendly and interesting that Carly loved her on sight. Ryan Kendrick, her husband, looked enough like Hank to be part of the Coulter family—a tall, dark cowboy with twinkling blue eyes and a friendly grin. Indeed, they were all so nice that Carly found herself pulling back, not wanting to like them too much or encourage them to like her because she knew this marriage was nothing but a farce.

After visiting long enough with Bethany to be polite, Carly turned away to look frantically for Hank, who was nowhere to be seen. As though sensing her change of heart, Zeke suddenly appeared at her side and slipped a hard arm around her waist. "Getting cold feet?"

Carly cast him a miserable look. "Very cold feet."

"Hank's over this way," he said as he led her through the crowd. "Everyone gets nervous, you know. It's normal. In five minutes, it'll all be over."

The way Carly saw it, in five minutes it would only just begin. Because she knew Zeke had been present last Friday night when she'd spoken with Hank over the phone and agreed to this crazy idea, she felt safe in saying, "I can't deceive everyone like this. They think this is a real wedding." She clutched his hand. "Would you get me out of here, Zeke? Please? I can't go through with it."

He stared down at her in appalled alarm. Then, tightening his hold on her hand, he yelled, "Hank? Yo, Hank!" He waved to get his younger brother's attention. "Conference time. Your bride needs you."

Carly wanted to die. Now everyone in the room was staring at her.

Zeke gave her fingers a comforting squeeze. "Don't worry about it. No one knows what you need to talk to him about."

Carly realized she was clinging to his hand like a lost child, but when she tried to slip her fingers free, he tightened his grip. "Don't take off," Zeke murmured, his deep voice so much like Hank's that it was uncanny. "Hank's coming. At least talk to him before you make like a runaway bride."

A tweed jacket suddenly swam before Carly's eyes. "What's wrong, sweetheart?"

Hank's voice. Carly leaned toward him, relieved when Zeke relinquished his hold on her hand. "I've decided I can't do this," she said weakly. "It's all a lie. A big, horrible lie. I just can't do this."

Hank slipped an arm around her shoulders and bent closer. Feeling him, being held by him, worked on Carly's nerves like a soothing balm, which struck her as the greatest insanity of all.

"Hey," he said. "Nothing's changed. This is just a technicality."

"Not to your mother. She asked me to call her Mom."

He rubbed her shoulder. "She's maternal by nature. Even the neighborhood kids call her Mom or Grandma. Calm down, sweetheart. Remember our reasons for doing this?"

Carly nodded numbly.

"We have to think of our baby. Right?"

She nodded again, wondering why it seemed so sensible when he talked about it and always seemed so insane when she was left with only her thoughts bumping around inside her brain.

"In a few days," Hank assured her, "we'll come clean and tell my folks our plans. All right?"

"Then they'll despise me for using you."

"No, they won't. They'll think you're a wonderful, brave young woman who's doing the very best she can for their grandchild."

Bess joined them just then. Hank quickly explained that Carly was having second thoughts.

"You can't back out now," Bess insisted. "You've come this far, Carls. Just do it. Forget everything else and just think about the baby."

The JP called for silence just then and asked who was going to give away the bride. Bess raised her hand. "I am!" she hollered.

Every head in the room swiveled toward her.

"Carly's father isn't here," Bess explained with a shrug. "We've been best friends all our lives. It only seems right that I should be the one to give her away."

Laughter followed that pronouncement. Bess ignored it and straightened the flowers in Carly's bouquet, talking softly as she gently fluffed each blossom. "You *have* to do this, Carls. Don't think. Just stand up there with Hank and say the words. They don't mean anything."

"Since when?"

"Since you and Hank agreed they don't."

The crowd parted. Hank went to stand to the JP's left. He straightened his shoulders, looking like Zeke at a distance. Carly's stomach tumbled, and she was afraid she might get sick. That was all this awful gathering needed, the bride puking in the trashcan. From a distance, she couldn't tell one brother from another. Not that it mattered. Zeke, Hank. She couldn't honestly say she had a preference. She didn't care who married her, just so long as she got a husband who'd pay the bills. It was ugly. It was a sacrilege and a mockery of everything holy. She couldn't believe she'd sunk this low.

"It's not right to deceive his family and friends like this." Carly's heart bumped wildly against her ribs. "They're all so nice, and they've been so kind."

Bess patted another flower and smiled. "And aren't you lucky that they are? People like these will understand why you did this, and they'll be glad of it."

A dark head leaned down to their eye level just then. Carly almost jumped out of her skin. *Zeke.* He touched a hand to her shoulder. "Your friend is absolutely right. My niece or nephew is the primary concern at this moment. Don't worry about anyone else.

If they can't understand the necessity of this marriage, I'll personally set them straight."

Bess smiled and said, "Oops. I didn't realize we had an eavesdropper."

Zeke grinned. "I have a talent for listening in when I shouldn't." He turned a friendly gaze back to Carly, and his expression softened. "In all seriousness, honey, you have no choice but to do this. And don't think of it as a big deception. When it comes to the welfare of a child, who the hell cares?"

Carly took that thought with her to the front of the room, where she stood beside a man she barely knew to become his lawfully wedded wife.

Hank said his vows first. He turned her hands palm up as instructed, supporting them with his own, and repeated his lines after the justice of the peace. "These hands will be yours, from this moment forward, yours in times of sorrow to comfort you, yours in times of hardship to sustain you, yours in time of danger to protect you. With your help, they will work to make your dreams come true. They will give you strength when your own falters. They will give you courage when you're afraid. And I swear to you before God and all these witnesses that they will never be lifted in anger against you."

Tears blurred Carly's vision, which was a bad thing because then she couldn't even see him. His hands were there, though, holding fast to hers, already fulfilling two of the promises he'd just made, lending her strength when her own was flagging and courage when she was afraid. The rest of his vows entered her brain and resounded to create a jumble of disjointed words.

Then the JP said, "Carly Jane Adams, please repeat after me." He went on, cueing her with short lines, which she parroted, word for word, promising to love and honor Hank Coulter until death did they part. She didn't hear the word *obey* in the vows she was asked to repeat, but she was so upset and nervous that, for all she knew, she'd just recited the Gettysburg Address.

Somehow, she got through the ceremony, allowing Hank to slip the rings onto her finger, then managing, with his assistance, to slip a ring onto his. When the justice of the peace pronounced them man and wife, Carly's legs turned watery, but Hank's arm was there, strong and hard around her waist, to hold her up. When he was told that he could kiss his bride, he kept the kiss light and impersonal, a feathery touch of his lips on hers that was more dream than reality.

It was done. Carly turned with him to face their guests. The JP introduced them as Mr. and Mrs. Hank Coulter. Everyone rushed forward to congratulate them.

Afterward, Carly went through the motions, signing her name to a paper she could barely see, then hanging onto Hank's arm to leave the courthouse. The drive to his parents' house passed in a swimming blur, and once they arrived, Carly once again went through the motions, feeling as if she'd become trapped in a nightmare. Voices erupted around her—white noise that penetrated her eardrums, filled her head, and didn't register. She would get through this. She *had* to get through this.

Hank never left Carly's side. Though she tensed every time he touched her, he frequently slipped an arm around her, feeling a need to reassure her.

After circling the room to chat with everyone, Bess joined Hank and Carly by the fireplace. "This is a lovely reception," she said. "I can't believe Mary pulled it off on such short notice."

"My mom is pretty amazing," Hank replied. "And she loves to entertain, probably because she has such a knack for it."

"Everything's perfect," Carly inserted. "When I think of all the trouble she's gone to, it makes me feel awful. It wasn't supposed to be like this."

Hank had already apologized for the size of the gathering and the fact that his mom had insisted on a reception. Mary started circling the room just then with a platter of hors d'oeuvres. When she reached Hank and Carly, Carly politely took a small plate and dutifully selected several of the offerings.

"Yum!" Bess said after sampling a stuffed mushroom. "How delicious!"

After filling a plate for himself, Hank complimented his mother on the preparations and thanked her yet again for all her hard work.

"It was nothing!" Mary protested. "You know me. I love doing things like this." She beamed a smile at Carly. "It's a very special day."

After Mary moved away, she frequently glanced around the room to make sure all of her guests were attended to, which prompted her to look back at Hank and Carly each time she scanned the room.

"If the hors d'oeuvres aren't to your taste, you don't have to eat them," Hank whispered to his bride. "I know your stomach is easily upset right now."

Carly smiled and shook her head. "I was so nervous about getting ready today that I forgot to eat lunch. It's good to get something in my stomach. I tend to get queasy if I don't eat."

She managed to get down three small crackers,

spread with specialty cheeses and garnished with green olives. Then Hank noticed her picking at the food.

"Too rich?" he asked.

She nodded almost imperceptibly. Hank hurriedly cleaned his own plate and switched with her. She flashed him a grateful look.

"Thank you, Hank. I wouldn't want to hurt your mom's feelings by not eating the food."

Hank had already determined that—and it only drove home to him what a sweet, caring individual Carly was. A few minutes later, she cemented that opinion by exclaiming appreciatively over the cake Mary had baked and decorated.

"Everything's so lovely," Carly said, touching the pretty wedding napkins with reverent fingertips. "No one's ever had a nicer reception, Mary. Thank you so much for going to all this trouble."

"It's Mom to you," Mary reminded her, "and it wasn't a lick of trouble. I was happy to be able to do it."

When Hank and Carly went to the table to cut the cake and toast each other with champagne, Hank had a bad moment. Pregnant women weren't supposed to drink alcohol.

"It's safe," Zeke whispered in Hank's ear. "I emptied a bottle and filled it with sparkling cider."

Hank wanted to hug his brother. "Thanks, Zeke. I owe you one."

Zeke glanced at Carly. "How are you holding up?" he asked with a teasing grin. "We're a rambunctious group. Are you overwhelmed yet?"

Carly laughed. "You do have a large family. But you're all so nice that I'm not feeling the least bit overwhelmed."

That was true, up to a point. Carly did like Hank's family. How could she not? But that didn't mean she felt at ease. Since the wedding ceremony, Hank had taken to touching her frequently and in a manner that she perceived as being possessive. Each time he curled an arm around her, her heart bumped wildly against her ribs, and it was all she could do to breathe normally when he splayed a hand over her ribs, his fingertips coming perilously close to the underside of her breast. What if he'd changed his mind about their prenuptial agreement? So far, he hadn't given her anything in writing as he'd promised.

Carly had little time to dwell on that concern as the reception festivities got under way, but the worry was there at the back of her mind, ready to leap to the foreground each time her husband touched her in a proprietary way.

Hank filled the champagne flutes, which were bedecked with ribbon at the stems, then linked wrists with Carly and joined her in drinking to their future. As he swallowed the sparkling cider, he couldn't help but look at his bride with burgeoning pride. As difficult a situation as this undoubtedly was for her, she'd comported herself with charming grace the entire afternoon. Hank couldn't count the times that relatives and friends had told him what a lucky devil he was to have landed such a catch, and he totally agreed with them. How he'd managed to single out someone like Carly in a rowdy honky-tonk, he'd never know.

He held her hand to cut the cake. Everyone applauded. He served up a piece onto a little paper plate decorated with silver ribbons and flowers. Carly gamely gave him the first bite, taking care not to smear frosting on his mouth. Afterward, he put a small amount on his own fork and tipped it into her mouth.

Everyone cheered and toasted to their happy future. Hank kept an arm around his wife's shoulders as the toasts to their happiness began. Harv started them off, saying that he and Mary were delighted to welcome Carly into the family, and that they wished the newlyweds nothing but happiness.

After refilling everyone's glasses, Jake, the eldest Coulter son, took over. "It seems really strange to be standing here," he said. "I've watched my little brother grow up, wiping his nose, putting Band-Aids on his scraped knees, and guarding his back as a teenager when he got into fights. Along the way, I guess I got to thinking he would always be my little brother, that nothing would ever change." Eyes shining, Jake raised his flute. "Welcome to our family, Carly. Congratulations, little brother. The best to both of you."

Zeke came forward then. "I can scarcely believe that my baby brother has gone and gotten married. As I watched him tie the knot today, I thanked God throughout the ceremony that it wasn't me." Everyone laughed. Zeke settled his gaze on Carly. "Mostly, anyway. I have to say that there were moments, while looking at my brother's bride, that I felt envious. He's definitely landed a keeper. A more beautiful bride I've never seen."

The women cooed, "Oh, how sweet." The men said, "Here, here!"

Zeke took a sip of champagne, then turned his attention back to the newlyweds. "Now I'm just wondering why you're still hanging around, little brother. If I had a bride that beautiful, I'd be champing at the bit to hustle her out to my truck and begin my honeymoon. What's keeping you?"

Mary cried, "We haven't even had cake yet, and they still haven't opened their gifts!"

Hank sorely wished that it were possible for him and Carly to duck out early. He didn't know how much more of this Carly could gracefully take. On the one hand, he appreciated the fact that both his father and Zeke, who knew the marriage was only temporary, hadn't let the cat out of the bag. On the other hand, he also understood that it must be trying for Carly to endure all the best wishes for a happy future, not to mention the hints that Hank might be eager to leave so he could consummate their union.

He was glad to see Carly eat an entire piece of cake. After the refreshment portion of the reception was over, everyone gravitated back to the living room to watch the newlyweds open their gifts. Hank had never seen so many small appliances in one place, and he quickly lost track of who had given them what. He was relieved to see that his sister-in-law Molly was keeping a list and made a mental note to thank her later.

When the gifts had all been opened, Hank drew his wife into the curve of his arm to make the rounds and thank all their guests for coming. Carly graciously shook hands with the men and returned the women's hugs. She was especially sweet and appreciative when she thanked Hank's mother.

Hank could have done without the rice and bouquet tossing, but Mary Coulter was a stickler for details. In a shower of rice, he hurried his bride toward his truck, which was parked on the street. At the curb, Carly turned to throw her bouquet.

"Right here!" Bess yelled. "If I catch it, maybe I'll get lucky!"

Carly laughed. "Here it comes!" she called.

The bouquet went flying, only not toward Bess as Carly intended. Instead the cluster of flowers veered left and hit Zeke dead center in the chest. He reacted instinctively, grabbing the bouquet to prevent it from dropping to the ground. Then he grimaced, which made everyone burst out laughing.

"No way," Zeke said. "I'm not next. I'm staying a bachelor."

He tried to hand the flowers off to Bess, but she shook her head. "Nope. You caught it. You're stuck."

Everybody was still laughing as Hank helped his wife into the truck. Without thinking, he reached across Carly's lap to fasten her seat belt and then adjusted the shoulder strap to angle across her chest. In the process, the backs of his knuckles grazed her breast. She sucked in a sharp breath. He froze. For a tension-packed instant, they stared at each other, Hank acutely conscious of how her nipple had hardened at the slight touch.

He quickly collected himself and closed the passenger door. By the time he circled the front bumper and climbed in on the driver's side, Carly was huddling as close to the door as possible, her arms wrapped tightly around her slender waist. Her posture screamed, "Don't touch me!"

It was a hell of a way to begin a marriage, Hank thought as he tromped on the accelerator to get away.

Chapter Thirteen

As Hank drove across Lazy J land to the cabin by the creek, the truck lights cut a golden swath through thick stands of pine, the bouncing beams creating a shadow play of black shapes that danced among the trunks like madcap ballerinas. Beyond the illumination, the woods were eerily dark.

Carly leaned against the passenger door. She felt mildly nauseated and could only hope she didn't get sick. She stared at the blurry world beyond the glass, wishing she were going to the apartment so she could sleep in her own bed. The day's events had drained her. Her face ached from smiling so much.

"You okay?" Hank asked.

Just ducky. She was married to a man she barely knew, and this was their wedding night. She wanted to believe that Hank would stand good on his promise to her, but given the fact that he'd never given her the signed agreement as promised, she couldn't help but worry that he'd changed his mind. She wished now that she'd thought to ask him for the document, but it had been such a crazy, fast-paced day that she'd forgotten about it until it was too late.

"I'm fine," she replied. "Just tired."

"Me too. It's been a trying afternoon."

She seriously doubted the evening would be much better. *Married.* Every time she thought about it, she found it difficult to breathe.

He stopped by a squat, shadowy structure, shifted into park, and turned off the lights and engine. "Home sweet home," he said. "It's just a small log house, two bedrooms, nothing fancy. But we can fix it up. I figured you'd feel more comfortable here than at the main house. This way, you'll have more privacy."

At the moment, Carly didn't care what the place looked like. All she wanted was to lie on a reasonably clean surface, preferably alone, and sleep.

"Sit tight," he instructed. "I'll come around. It's black as pitch out there, and the ground's uneven."

He leaned over the seat to grab her overnight case. When he opened his door, the dome light flashed on, the brightness lacerating her aching eyes. Cool night air rushed into the cab, raising goose flesh on her bare arms. She was relieved when he slammed the door, swamping her in darkness again.

Seconds later, he tapped her window. At the warning, Carly pushed erect and unfastened her seat belt as he opened the door. When he touched her elbow, she turned, thinking he'd offer her a steadying hand as she exited the vehicle. Instead he caught her around the waist and swung her easily to the ground. During those brief seconds of contact, Carly felt the strength in his shoulders and arms—pads of vibrant muscle that bunched under the wool jacket . . .

He slipped an arm around her waist, his big hand splaying over her side. "Sorry about the holes. Most times the cabin sits empty, and we haven't kept up the yard. Careful." He tightened his hold on her as he leaned around to retrieve the overnight case that he'd left sitting on the front bumper. "Some of these chuck holes are pretty deep."

Carly was relieved when they reached the porch. He released her to open the door, then stood back to let her enter. As she stepped into the interior darkness, she shivered, despite the warmth that curled around her. Hank flipped on a floor lamp to bathe the room in dim, golden light.

"Bess mentioned that light hurts your eyes," he said, "so I put forty-watt bulbs in all the lamps. I hope it helps."

It helped immensely, the glow dim and golden rather than glaring. She could scarcely believe he'd been so thoughtful. "It's great, Hank. Thank you for thinking of it."

"I left the kitchen and bath fixtures as they were. If they're too bright, just say so, and I'll take care of it."

He pushed the door closed, then drew off his jacket and tossed it over a comfortable-looking brown leather chair. Still shivering, Carly rubbed her arms as she took in the small living room. A river rock–faced fireplace graced a wall to her right. A leather sofa and chairs sat at angles in front of the hearth, conjuring visions in her mind of cold winter evenings spent before a cheery fire. Beyond the sofa, she saw an old wooden table and chairs.

"I've got a fire laid," he assured her. "Would you like my jacket until it warms up in here?"

The room didn't actually feel that cold. Carly suspected that her chills were due more to nervousness. "I'm fine."

He moved to the hearth. At a distance, the features of his dark face were fuzzy, the outline of his tall frame indistinct, but that did little to diminish his size. He stood head and shoulders over the floor lamp beside her, and his white shirt swam in her vision, making him look even broader through the chest and shoulders.

He crouched to light the fire. Amber flames leaped and sputtered, casting his lean body in gold. Her heart pattered. Her breathing became quick and shallow. It was madness to think of the night they met, but she couldn't stop herself. Kisses that had made her bones melt, the tingling warmth that radiated from his big hands, and the sweet things he'd said. As always, a cold knot bunched in her stomach when she remembered the pain that came later.

Recalling the power she'd felt in his arms and shoulders when he'd lifted her from the truck, she knew she'd be helpless to stop him if he chose to exercise his marital privileges. The possibility made her nerves leap, which in turn made her nausea worse.

"It should warm up in here soon," he told her.

He pushed erect and turned toward her. Even at a distance, the blue of his eyes was intense and unsettling. Carly tried to make her mind go blank—but the traitorous thoughts clung tight. Now, for better or worse, she was about to discover if Hank Coulter was a man of his word.

Resting his hands at his waist, he slowly crossed the room, his movements a purely masculine undulation of lean hips and long, powerfully muscled legs. When he came to stand in front of her, he smiled, looking almost as tense as she felt. His expression gave nothing away.

"Would you like a quick tour of the house?"

"Oh, sure. That would be nice."

He led the way around the wall that divided the kitchen off from the small living room. "Here we have the kitchen." Laughter lighted his eyes as he met her gaze. With a wave of his hand, he indicated the table. "Complete with a not-too-fancy dining area that has the added feature of doubling as a game room, breakfast nook, and office." He indicated a door beyond the dining set. "That's the back bedroom. I've got all my stuff stowed in there." Inclining his head, he added, "The front bedroom is—well, in front."

Carly laughed nervously as he preceded her to the open doorway and leaned in to switch on the overhead light. The mellow illumination told her that he'd stepped down the wattage of the bulbs in the ceiling fixture. She hesitated before following him into the room. Then she chided herself for being a goose. If he reneged on his promise to her and pressed her for sex, she would survive. So far, he didn't strike her as being a cruel man, only a somewhat thoughtless and self-centered one.

"Like I said, it's nothing fancy, and it's not very big," he apologized as she took in the small bedroom.

"What a beautiful bed. Is it brass?"

He nodded. "Molly says it's worth a lot because it's an antique. It's been in the family for years. Small, though—people used to be a lot shorter than we are now. My feet hang over the end."

Carly tried to imagine him sleeping there, his long legs dangling over the end of the mattress, his feet thrust through the brass footboard. The breadth of his shoulders alone would take up more than half the mattress.

"Will this be my room?"

"Yep. I had the housekeeper come in and do a deep clean. She washed out the drawers and all the shelves. There isn't a lot of storage, but hopefully, you'll have room to put all your things away."

"I haven't all that many clothes." She leaned over to pat the mattress. "Being blind, I never got into fashions and all that."

He rubbed his jaw. "If you're apologizing for not being a clotheshorse, don't. I'll be paying the shopping bills for a while, so you won't hear me complain." He winced. "Not that I'll mind if you buy clothes."

It bothered Carly to be so dependent on him for everything. "No, of course not. I didn't think you were implying that."

"The bathroom is directly to the left as you leave the bedroom. If you'd like to take a shower, you'll find fresh towels and washcloths in the linen cupboard across from the sink."

"A shower sounds good."

He stepped into the living room to retrieve her one piece of luggage. "Are you hungry?" he asked as he handed her the case.

Carly's stomach rolled at the very thought of food. "No, no. I couldn't eat a thing."

He ran a hand through his hair. Then he cleared his throat. "Well." He smiled slightly. "Deep word with a hollow ending. I think I'll fry up some bacon and eggs. You sure you won't join me? Mom's hors d'oeuvres and cake didn't last me long."

Carly shook her head. "No, thanks. You go ahead. I think I'll just freshen up and get ready for bed."

She was relieved when he finally left her. Quickly grabbing her overnight case, she made for the bathroom, hoping to hurry through her shower and be in bed, pretending to be asleep, by the time he finished cooking.

When she switched on the bathroom light, the glare of the ceiling fixture momentarily blinded her. She blinked away the black spots as she closed the door. *Problem.* There was no lock. She felt uneasy about showering without a way to make sure Hank didn't walk in on her. But there was no helping it. She couldn't very well live there without sometimes bathing when he was around.

The bathroom's white porcelain glared in the bright light. She set her case on the back of the toilet and squinted to protect her sensitive eyes as she turned on the overhead fan and peeled off her clothes.

Only minutes after she turned on the shower and stepped into the tub, a sickening smell wafted strongly to Carly's nostrils. *Bacon.* Ever conscious of cholesterol, Bess avoided eating pork, and since becoming pregnant, Carly breakfasted on unconventional fare. She hadn't been exposed to the smell of frying bacon in weeks.

That was a blessing, she decided, as the odor grew more pronounced. The air itself felt saturated with grease, coating her tongue and throat every time she took a breath. The exhaust fan in the bathroom ceiling seemed to be sucking the smell of the frying meat in under the door. She'd heard of pregnant women getting horribly sick when they smelled grease, but never had she imagined it would be as awful as this. Her stomach rolled. She gulped frantically, trying to swallow her gorge. Her feeling of nausea went from mild to pronounced in seconds. Sick, she was going to be sick.

Carly barely managed to get her hair rinsed before the nausea hit her in punishing waves. She shoved back the shower curtain, stumbled from the bathtub, and barely had time to grab a towel before her stomach started turning inside out.

Hank had quickly changed out of his monkey suit while the bacon fried. His work shirt not yet buttoned, he was about to crack an egg into the skillet when he heard an odd sound. He cocked his head to listen. It sounded as if Carly was gagging. He turned off the gas burner and raced to the living room. As he approached the bathroom, he called out, "Carly, are you okay in there?"

"Don't—come—in. Fine. I'm f-fine."

She didn't sound fine. He curled his hand over the doorknob. He heard her retching again. When he could stand it no longer, he cracked open the door. Wrapped in a towel, she was on her knees by the commode, her slender hands clenched over the rim of the bowl to support her upper body. He took one look and pushed inside. She saw him from the corner of her eye and released her hold on the porcelain to hug the terrycloth to her breasts.

"Go *away*. I'm not dressed." A violent spasm racked her body. When it subsided, she sobbed and said, "Get *out* of here. Please. I need some privacy."

No way. Hank grabbed a clean washcloth from the bowl by the sink and wet it with cold water. Then he went down on one knee behind her.

"Here, sweetheart," he said as he slipped an arm around her waist.

Her hands closed over his wrist and forearm. The towel started to slip, and she mewled in distress.

"Easy, easy." Hank discarded the washcloth and grabbed the nightgown she'd pulled from the overnight case and left on the vanity. "It's all right, sweetheart. I'll get you covered."

Beneath his wrist, he felt her stomach muscles knot. The next second her body jerked as another wave of nausea struck. She got nothing up. After drinking binges, he'd experienced the dry heaves a few times and knew how they hurt. He also recalled how utterly exhausted he'd been afterward.

After the spasms abated, he supported her weight with one arm while he worked the nightgown over her head. When he grasped one of her hands to poke it down a sleeve, she resisted, clinging frantically to the towel.

"I won't let the towel slip. There's my girl. Give me your hand." Working in increments, he finally got the nightgown on her. "See there?" The roomy folds of cotton encompassed both woman and towel. "You're completely covered."

His heart caught when she let her head fall back against his shoulder. Her wet hair felt cold where the strands dangled against his bare chest. He tugged the towel from under her gown and dried her hair with one hand to keep her nightclothes from getting soaked. She leaned weakly against him as he worked.

"Sick, so sick," she whispered. "The bacon. The smell."

"Oh, God, I'm sorry." Hank remembered his mother telling him how sick she'd always gotten if anyone fried bacon around her when she was pregnant. "I never even thought."

"Me either," she said weakly. "I didn't know it'd make me sick."

Hank wished he could trade places with her. The bout of vomiting had left her looking totally exhausted. He could feel her body quivering. "I'm here, sweetheart. I don't have much practice caring for pregnant ladies, but I'll learn as I go."

He tossed aside the towel and grabbed the washcloth again. He cranked on the faucet, freshened the terry with cold water, and bathed her upturned face. As he dabbed under her eyes, she wrinkled her nose and frowned. Her small face was a roadmap of black streaks, compliments of the mascara that he'd applied to her lashes earlier that day. After rubbing her cheeks clean, he tucked in his chin to regard her pale features. *Perfect.* Even with her hair hanging in damp ropes over her shoulders, she was beautiful—a church angel, just as he'd described her to his father. Only she was wonderfully real and all the sweeter for it—an impossibly pretty lady who'd lived in a bubble all her life, until he'd come along to burst it.

"I'm hoping the coolness will help. It always makes me feel better."

"Mm," she murmured and rested more of her weight against him.

Hank moved the cloth to her arched throat. She sighed, her soft bottom coming to rest high on his thigh. A certain part of his body hardened, and he clenched his teeth, hating himself for responding to the contact. She might not realize that a man had no control over things like that. He didn't want to alarm her.

"When this passes, I'll get you to bed. Maybe you can fall asleep."

With no warning, she began retching again. Hank gripped her shoulders until the nausea ran its course.

The violence of the heaves worried him. He feared that she might injure herself or the baby. Afterward, he pressed the wet cloth to her convulsing throat again. The coldness seemed to help, and she sighed shakily.

"This is so humiliating. I could just *die*."

Hank's heart caught at the hopeless resignation in her voice. He rested his jaw atop her head. "Don't be silly. Everyone gets sick now and then."

She shuddered and gulped. He simply held her for a while. Then he gathered her into his arms, struggled to his feet, and carried her to the bedroom. The backs of her bare thighs felt damp and warm against the inside of his right forearm. In order to lay her down, he circled to the far side of the bed.

She moaned when her head touched the pillow. Then she pushed weakly at the hem of the gown, trying to cover her legs. Hank lent assistance, tugging at the cotton where it was trapped under her bottom. His knuckles connected with soft flesh, and memory blips flashed through his head of that night, how silken and smooth her skin had felt when he'd pulled down her jeans.

"I need to stay in the bathroom," she protested. "Sick. I'll get sick again."

Hank hurried back to the bathroom for a freshly lined wastebasket. When he took it to her, she rolled onto her side, hugged it with one arm, and hooked her chin over the edge. He sat beside her and smoothed her hair back from her face, wishing to God he knew what to do.

"Aside from that little bit at Mom's, you haven't eaten anything since breakfast. Right?"

She nodded almost imperceptibly.

Hank glanced at his watch. It was nine o'clock. If she'd eaten at eight that morning, she'd put nothing substantial in her stomach for thirteen hours. Going on an empty stomach made him feel slightly nauseated sometimes, and he wasn't pregnant. He tugged the sheet up over her legs.

A moment later, her body convulsed, her knees jerking up to bump his hip. Her delicate features contorted. In the light from the bathroom, he could see tiny red spots appearing on her eyelids. She was straining so hard that capillaries were bursting. That couldn't be good for her or the baby.

He wet a fresh washcloth and pressed it to her throat. Then he went to the kitchen to phone his mother. If anyone on earth knew what to do, it had to be Mary Coulter. She'd borne six children.

Mary was laughing when she answered the phone. By that Hank knew the wedding celebration was still in full swing. "Mom, this is Hank. Carly's really sick. Dry heaves. I'm a little worried."

Mary clucked her tongue. "That flu is nasty stuff. Do you have anything for an upset stomach?"

Hank released a weary breath. "It's not the flu, Mom. She's pregnant. I can't give her just anything for fear it may hurt the baby."

Long silence. Then Mary said, "Oh. I see."

Hank wished he'd been able to break the news to her a little more gently. *The best laid plans.* He heard Carly retching again and ran a shaky hand over his hair. "This is bad, really bad. I have no idea what to do."

"Saltines and Seven-Up always settled my stomach when I was expecting."

"I doubt she could hold it down." He glanced

toward the bedroom again. Carly had quieted now. "I'm afraid all the straining will make her miscarry or something."

"I used to get so sick I thought I'd die, but I didn't, and neither did my babies. You need to get something in her stomach if she's got the dry heaves. Do you have any saltines?"

"No, but I can check at the main house or run get some."

"And Seven-Up," Mary added. "Room temperature's best. Let the carbonation dissipate a bit. Tiny nibbles of saltines and sips of the soda. Too much, too fast will only make her sick again. If that doesn't work, you should call the ER and see if you should take her in. I'm certainly no doctor."

"Thanks, Mom."

Mary sighed. "You're welcome, Hank. I'll expect a call in the morning to let me know how she and my grandchild are doing."

Hank knew that tone. "I'm sorry for dropping the news on you like this. I intended to tell you soon. I just didn't want to say anything before the wedding."

"A baby, Hank? How on earth did that happen?"

Hank started to answer, but then, for the life of him, he couldn't think what to say. For years, his mother's naiveté had been a family joke. She'd told all her children the stork had left them beside the bed in their father's boot. None of them had ever believed it, of course, but Mary had seemed so certain of her facts that they'd been pretty sure she did. Now that he was grown, Hank knew better, but he still found it difficult to discuss things of that nature with her.

"It just happened, Mom," he settled for saying.

Mary clucked her tongue. "Well, it's a lovely sur-prise. And here we are, running low on champagne. This is definitely reason to celebrate. A new little Coulter is on the way."

Hank pinched the bridge of his nose. His mother would announce the news to everyone the moment she got off the phone unless his father managed to gag her. *Ah, well.* It wasn't as if the secret could be kept for long. She'd save him the trouble of telling everyone. It'd be less embarrassing for Carly that way.

"Love you, Mom."

"I love you, too." She paused. "Should we have a mother-and-son talk?"

"About what?" he asked cautiously.

"I don't want to see that lovely young woman hav-ing one baby after another, with barely a break in between. You need to plan these things."

This woman had popped out six kids like a Gatling gun run amok, and she was lecturing him? "I know."

"Yes, well. After this, try doing it to music with a nice beat. I've heard it helps."

Music? The tips of Hank's ears burned. "That's a new one."

"Not really. Been around for years. It's called the rhythm method."

An airless pounding began in his temples. He was holding his breath, trying not to laugh. Great joke— if she was kidding. Dangerous ground if she wasn't. "Hmm."

"If that doesn't work, try using your socks."

The image that leaped to mind made him wince. "My socks?"

"Yes, sweetie." Mary giggled. "When you take off

your boots, stuff your socks in them. That way, the stork can't make his delivery, and he moves next door to the neighbor's house."

Hank was still standing there, grinning like a fool, when his mother broke the connection.

Seconds later when he reentered Carly's room, she was resting. He hated to disturb her, but he didn't want her to waken and not know where he was.

He touched her shoulder. "I'm going to get some stuff that may settle your stomach." When she stirred, he added, "I hate to leave you like this. If I have to go clear to the store, will you be okay for about thirty minutes?"

She made an unintelligible sound. Hank drew up the covers so she wouldn't get chilled. "I'll hurry. Okay?"

She nodded.

Hank didn't want to leave her, but he had no choice. On Friday night, the hired hands went to town. Molly and Jake were at his parents' house. If there were no saltines or Seven-Up at the main house, he'd have to drive to the market for some. Remembering how light hurt her eyes, he turned off the overhead fixture as he left the room.

Carly yearned for sleep, but the bouts of nausea came so frequently that dozing was impossible. She tried lying on her back. No help. Her stomach churned no matter what she did. *Oh, God.* She was so sick she thought she might die. When another wave of nausea struck, she almost wished she would.

Afterward, she lay with her head resting on the edge of the wastebasket, her eyes unfocused on the white plastic liner forming a cocoon around her face. She wondered what Hank had gone to get. She hoped it helped, whatever it was, and would be safe for the baby. She had no idea what time it was, only that it had grown late. She couldn't believe he'd dressed and left the house just to get something for her stomach. It was sweet of him. Maybe, she decided dimly, he wasn't as self-centered as she believed.

As if her thoughts had summoned him, she heard the rumble of his truck. Moments later, headlights bathed the room. She heard the engine die. Then a door slammed, and boots thumped across the porch. He had a distinct walk, a decisive but relaxed stride, one heel shuffling with every other step. An expert at identifying people by their walks, she filed that information away. If her eyesight failed completely, she might need to know the sound of his walk someday.

He entered the house with exaggerated care, barely making any sound. Carly realized he hoped she was sleeping. Oh, how she wished she were. Eyes closed, she listened as he approached the bed.

"I'm awake," she told him, her voice so hoarse it didn't sound like her own.

"How's the tummy?" Gentle concern thickened his voice.

"Same."

"I was afraid of that. I'll be right back. Okay?"

He left the room, making no attempt to be quiet now. She heard the rustle of paper sacks, then the sound of his footsteps going to the kitchen. When he returned to the bedroom a minute later, he said, "Here it is, the Coulter cure for morning sickness, saltine crackers and Seven-Up."

She clung to the wastebasket. "I can't. It'll make me sick."

The glass clicked as he set it on the table. A gentle glow of amber bathed the room when he flipped on the bedside lamp. The mattress sank as he sat beside her. The soft light bathed his chiseled features so she could see him clearly.

"There's nothing in your stomach. That's why you've got the dry heaves." Paper crinkled as he opened a sleeve of crackers. "Tiny nibbles and sips." He tugged the wastebasket from her limp embrace and set it on the floor. "Let's try the pop first. Your mouth is probably too dry to swallow."

"I can't," Carly insisted.

He slipped an arm under her shoulders to cup the back of her head in a big hand. Bringing the glass to her lips, he said, "Just a little, sweetheart."

Carly was too weak to argue with him. She took a tiny sip. To her surprise, it tasted good. He tipped the glass higher to give her a bit more. Then he lowered her head back to the pillow, handed her a single saltine, and urged her to take one bite.

"Just hold it on your tongue until it starts to dissolve," he advised. "We'll sneak some food down you. How's that? Maybe your tummy won't notice."

The rationale eluded her, but he was determined. She nipped off a corner of the cracker and held it on her tongue until it grew mushy. Then she finally swallowed. She expected her stomach to turn inside out, but instead it growled.

Hank chuckled. "There, you see?" He glanced at his watch. "Three minutes. Then we'll do it again."

Silence settled over them. Carly had no idea how much time passed. She only knew he gave her five sips of the pop, presumably at three-minute intervals, and she was starting to feel a bit better when he suddenly said, "What we need is conversation. I doubt you feel like talking, so I guess it falls to me." He rested his arms on his knees. "This is a first. I can't think what to say." He slanted her a sidelong glance rife with mischief. "Could be the surroundings. Most times when I get a lady into bed, talking is the last thing on my mind."

Carly wasn't sure how to take that. He distracted her with a snap of his fingers. "That reminds me." He reached in his pocket and drew something out. "Our agreement," he explained. "The no-custody-suit, no-fun-for-Hank paper."

He laid it on the table, safely away from the glass of pop. "I'm sorry I didn't remember to give it to you at the apartment. I intended to, along with the bouquet and ring, but then you answered the door, and—" He broke off, tugged on his earlobe, and smiled. "We kind of got sidetracked." He let that hang there for a moment. "In all the rush, I hope I didn't hurt your feelings by insisting that you change dresses and all that. You looked beautiful. Honestly. It was just a little much for an afternoon wedding."

Carly stared at the moon-washed window. Receiving compliments from him was embarrassing, a brutal reminder of how foolishly she'd behaved the night they met. He didn't think she was pretty, had never thought so, and she'd been an idiot to climb in that truck with him.

He startled her by touching her hair. She flicked him a wary look to find him studying her with a wondering frown. "Okay, out with it. I just said something that upset you."

"It's nothing." *Nothing important, anyway.* She wouldn't allow it to be.

He arched a dark eyebrow. "Do I have to go back over everything I just said, point by point, and figure it out myself?"

"It's not important."

"Uh-huh." His tone conveyed he wasn't convinced. He lifted her head from the pillow to give her another sip of pop. Then he handed her another cracker. While she lay there, moistening a piece of saltine on her tongue, he began repeating everything he'd just told her. "I said I was sorry for not giving you the paper this afternoon." He paused to study her face. "Nope, that wasn't it." He grinned and tried again. "Then I mentioned the bouquet and ring." He regarded her closely as he spoke. "I'm batting a terrible average. One more strike, and I'm out. After that, I said—"

She swallowed the bit of cracker. "Would you stop? This is silly."

His eyebrow went up again. "Bull's-eye. You're upset because I said you looked beautiful."

Carly trailed nervous fingers over the chenille spread. She wished he wouldn't stare at her that way. "I don't like it when you pay me compliments. That's all."

"I see." Another silence settled over them, which he finally broke by asking, "Would you care to tell me why?" When she didn't answer, he fired a second question. "Does it make you nervous, knowing I think you're beautiful?"

She didn't want to discuss this, but she could see he wouldn't let it drop. "I just feel uncomfortable when you say things I know you don't mean."

"What makes you think I don't mean it?"

The air in the room suddenly seemed too thin to

breathe. How could she answer that question? She preferred not to tell him that before he'd come along, no other man had ever given her a second look. Carly sat up, feeling an urgent need to get away from him. Her head went dizzy.

"Whoa." Hank caught her by the shoulders. "If you don't lie still, you're liable to wind up with your pretty little head poked in the wastebasket again."

"Would you stop?" she cried, even as he pressed her back against the pillow.

"What'd I say now?"

"My 'pretty little head.' It's not little, for starters, and it's definitely not pretty. *I'm* not pretty. I've never been pretty. I don't, therefore, want to be told I'm pretty. Is that clear?"

He kept his hands at her shoulders, preventing her from sitting up again. "Just calm down. I don't want you getting sick." His grip gentled, and he lightly massaged her skin through the long-sleeved gown. "That's obviously a sore spot. I'm sorry I said it. We'll discuss it later. Okay?"

"I don't want to discuss it later. Just don't say it." Looking up at his dark face, she remembered him asking, *Have I mentioned that you're gorgeous?* And, oh, God, she'd believed him. She didn't know why that hurt so much, only that it did—like dull knives, slicing at her heart. "Just don't say it."

He released her and drew back, running a hand over his hair, which had been mussed by his hat and lay in tousled waves over his forehead. She expected him to argue, making heartfelt avowals that she was the most beautiful woman he'd ever met, which she would have known was a lie. Instead, he grinned and asked, "Are we having our first scrap?"

The question caught her by surprise. "What?"

"Language barrier again? 'Scrap.' In city English, that translates to spat, quarrel, wrangle, fight, skirmish, tiff. You ever call it a 'set-to' up in Portland?"

He made her want to smile, which only irritated her more. "*Set-to* isn't a term we use often in Portland, but I'm perfectly aware of what *scrap* means."

"Good. If you're gonna do it, you ought to have the definition down pat."

"I have no intention of scrapping with you."

"You start trying to tell me what I can say, and we're going to scrap, darlin'. No two ways around it."

"I'm not trying to tell you what you can say."

"You aren't?"

"No. I just don't appreciate your saying things I know you don't mean, and I'm sure you don't really think I'm beautiful."

"Well, hell." He rubbed beside his nose. "Now you're telling me what I can think? I've married a bossy woman."

Carly flung an arm over her eyes. Her heart hurt when she looked at him. How was it possible to feel that way and want to laugh at the same time? "Just go away. I want to sleep now."

"I'm your official pop and cracker dispenser. I'm not going anywhere until five of these crackers are down the hatch."

She held out her hand for the remaining crackers. "Fine. Give them to me, and I'll eat them. I don't need you sitting in attendance."

"My mom says you have to eat them slowly. I'll stay if it's all the same to you."

"It isn't all the same to me. I want you to go away."

"That's not in our contract."

She lowered her arm to stare at him. "In our what?"

He gestured at the folded paper on the nightstand. "Our contract. It says I won't press you for sex, and it says I won't change my mind and sue for custody of our child. But there's not one damned word in there about you being able to tell me where to go." He flashed her a slow grin. "Trust me to know. If that had been one of your stipulations, I never would've signed it. I know exactly where you'd send me." He paused. "Not saying I'd blame you."

Carly smiled in spite of herself. Then she jumped half out of her skin when he touched a fingertip to the corner of her mouth. "There it is, that fabulous smile. Notice I didn't say beautiful. I'm nothing if not cooperative."

"I want to sleep now."

"We covered that. You've only had one bite of the third cracker."

"You're impossible."

"We've covered that, too. I think we need some new subject matter. How's about if I tell you about the ranch?"

He didn't wait for her assent before he launched into a soothing monologue, describing the Lazy J. He began by telling her about the fire that had destroyed the main house shortly after Jake's marriage to Molly. Then he went on to describe the reconstruction process, how he and Jake had used timber from their own property for the two-story log home that Jake and Molly lived in now.

"I thought logs had to be dried before you could use them," she said drowsily.

"They should be. We hired an outfit to kiln dry ours."

He broke off to give her another sip of soda, urged her to take a bite of cracker, and then began talking again, telling her about the vast expanses of land that comprised the Lazy J.

Carly grew drowsier while he talked, soothed by the deep, silky timbre of his voice. He told her about their hired hand, Shorty, a squat, sandy-haired little man whose best friend in the world was an ugly mongrel dog named Bart who'd bite the hand that fed him. Then he told her about Levi, a wiry fellow with twinkling green eyes, a thick southern drawl, and a battered old pickup dubbed Mandy, which he held together with coat hangers and baling wire.

In between descriptions, he lifted her head to give her sips of soda and push crackers at her face. Soon five crackers were gone, and she felt so sleepy she could barely hold her eyes open.

"You love them, don't you?" she asked groggily.

"Crackers?"

Struggling to keep her eyes open, she laughed softly and said, "No. Shorty and Levi."

"Oh, them." He shrugged and massaged the back of his neck. "Love's a strong word. Shorty's a little cantankerous, and Levi, well, he's so set in his ways he's flat irritating, but they're both loyal to a fault."

He went on to tell her about Danno, a lanky young fellow with a mop of red hair and more freckles than brains, whose appetite was so voracious that he could eat the south end of a northbound jackass.

"The south end of a what?" she asked, slurring the words.

He grinned. "Sorry. I need to clean up my language now that I've got a wife. A male donkey." At her bewildered look, his grin widened. "If a donkey's heading north and you eat its south end, which part will you sink your teeth into?"

Carly shook her head. "Its rump, I imagine. You'll have to forgive me for being slow on the uptake. That's a visual. I've never seen a jackass, never mind the south end of one."

"You *haven't*?" A twinkle lit up his eyes. "Seems to me, darlin', that you've had plenty of truck with one jackass." His smile faded, and he fussed with the covers. Then he changed the subject by asking, "How's the belly?"

Carly was still stuck on the "jackass" part of the exchange. He was clearly referring to himself, leading her to believe he regretted his behavior that night at Chaps. Yet, to her recollection, he'd never really apologized except to say that he wished he could do it all over again, getting it right the next time.

"I'm feeling better," she finally replied.

"That's good. The Coulter remedy must be working."

He handed her another cracker and launched into stories about everyday life on a ranch. As interested as Carly was, she found it increasingly difficult to keep her eyes open. At some point, the deep, husky drone of his voice moved away from her, and she slipped off into an exhausted sleep.

Hank fell quiet and studied his sleeping wife. Her hair had dried in a fan across the pillow. In the dim light, the rippling strands gleamed like molten gold touched with silver. Her long eyelashes cast spider etchings on her pale cheeks. Her soft mouth looked temptingly kissable.

Not beautiful? Dear God, when had he ever said or done anything to make her believe that? Getting her pregnant had been a shooting offense. Failing to comfort her afterward should have earned him a flogging before the bullet was lodged in his brain. But to make her believe she was somehow less than perfect?

That was unforgivable.

She was a puzzle. Definitely like no other woman he'd ever met, not that he was complaining. He just didn't know how to handle her. He spent half his time watching every word he said, afraid of offending or frightening her. The other half of the time, he was trying to take his foot out of his mouth.

He sighed and flexed his shoulders, weary enough to drift off to sleep himself. He thought longingly of the bed that awaited him in the back bedroom. Never mind that it was also too short and his feet hung over the end. Anything would feel good right now. He just hesitated to leave Carly for fear she might need him. The cabin's interior walls were made of logs, which absorbed sound. Sleeping in the back room, he might not hear if she called out.

He decided to lie beside her on top of the covers. The heat from the fire would keep him warm, and he'd be close at hand if she woke up. *Just for a while,* he assured himself, turning off the lamp. As he stretched out beside her, he stuck his boots through openings in the brass footboard to straighten his legs. *No matter.* He'd slept in horse stalls too many times to be fussy.

He fell asleep almost as soon as his head touched the pillow.

Sometime later, Carly awakened to discover Hank beside her. The room was cold, and he'd gravitated toward her. In a shaft of moonlight coming through the window, his dark face looked almost boyish in sleep, his firm mouth gone lax, the ridge of muscle that always delineated his cheek no longer in evidence.

Carly wasn't sure how she felt about sharing a bed with him. What if he got friendly in his sleep? She considered jabbing him. But it was late and she hated to wake him. With a sigh, she flipped her side of the bedspread over him. As she tucked the chenille under his chin, he muttered something and stirred. Then he stared blankly at her for several seconds.

When recognition came, he grinned sleepily and said, "Hey, Charlie." Then he fell asleep again.

Carly hugged her pillow, staring at his face. *Charlie.* He hadn't been lying to her, she realized. That night at the bar, he actually hadn't gotten her name right, despite the fact that she'd corrected him twice. When he'd told her about putting out feelers to find her, she hadn't really believed him. Now she had reason to wonder if he hadn't been telling the truth.

It changed nothing. She'd still been one in a long line of conquests—just another woman he'd scored with on a Friday night. But in an odd way, it made her feel better, knowing he hadn't forgotten her immediately afterward.

As she drifted back to sleep, Carly hugged that realization to her heart.

Chapter Fourteen

The next morning Hank slipped from bed at the first light of dawn, grabbed a shower, and quietly exited the bathroom. Finger-combing his damp hair, he stood by the bed to gaze down at Carly. She slept deeply, her face still pale from the ravages of last night's nausea. Even so, she was beautiful, one hand daintily unfurled on the pillow. He wanted to lean down and wake her with a kiss.

Madness. She wasn't ready for that, and until she was, he'd sworn to abide by a strict, hands-off policy. After creeping from the bedroom, he went to the kitchen to make coffee. Minutes later, he left the house with a steaming mug, taking his first sip after he cleared the porch. *Ah*. He gazed across the ranch, enjoying the pinkish hue that bathed the landscape. Soon the sun would be up, and golden shafts of light would gild the towering trees that bordered the fields.

Hank set off for the stables. After morning chores, he'd drive into town to get Carly's things. Before the wedding, she'd packed, and the boxes at the apartment awaited transport. Because she'd been so sick last night, he hated to make her go with him. He'd just drive over by himself. If Bess had left for work when he got there, he had Carly's key. He hoped to be back before Carly awakened for breakfast

Hank got home at twenty of eight. He had just put the first box in the living room when Carly emerged from the bathroom, wrapped in a white towel.

"Oh!" she squeaked, and promptly ducked back into the bathroom, slamming the door with a loud *thunk*.

"I'm going back out for another box. You can dash for cover while I'm gone."

The door cracked open, and one blue eye peered out at him. Still grinning, Hank exited the house. When he returned with another load, he decided to leave off carrying in boxes to get her breakfast on the table.

When she emerged minutes later, looking pretty as a picture in blue jeans and a pink top, Hank was sitting at the table, enjoying his mug of coffee.

"Breakfast's ready."

"Oh. I, um—mostly I don't eat regular food this early in the day."

He inclined his head at the table. "Trust me, darlin', nothing about this breakfast is regular. Sauerkraut straight from the jar, Brussels sprouts, and chocolate milk. How's that for memory."

She peered at the bowls, smiling hesitantly. "You didn't need to do this."

Hank thrust out a boot to nudge a chair. "Yeah, well, I did do it, so sit down and eat."

As she took a seat, he noticed that she'd slicked her hair back into a ponytail. He liked it better down. Seemed a shame to hide all those pretty curls. He settled back to study her. All his life, he'd heard the phrase, "flawless ivory complexion," but had never actually seen one. Except for the broken capillaries on her eyelids, Carly's oval countenance was without blemish, her skin as pale and smooth as newly risen cream.

He'd never tire of looking at her. Her nose was small and straight, her cheekbones fragile, her honey-gold brows gently arched over wide, expressive eyes. *Not beautiful?* Every time he recalled her saying that, his heart hurt. Normally, he'd take such a comment with a grain of salt, figuring the woman was fishing for a compliment. Most women knew if they were beautiful. But Carly was different. When she looked in the mirror, she might not see what everyone else did—an exquisitely lovely young woman with eyes a man could get lost in.

He expected her to devour the food. Instead she laid the paper napkin over her lap, then fussed and fiddled, looking so self-conscious that he almost left the table. But, no, he decided. The sooner she relaxed around him, the better. He'd be doing her no favor if he walked wide circles around her.

"I didn't add butter or salt to the sprouts," he warned.

She pushed at them with a fork. "Good. I don't put anything on them."

When she first began eating, she took dainty bites, frequently touching the napkin to her lips. After a minute, though, the cravings got the best of her, and she began shoving huge mounds of sauerkraut into her mouth, making soft sounds of ecstasy as she chewed.

Hank found himself wishing she'd go after him like

that. Then he remembered she had once—and he'd blown it.

She stopped chewing suddenly and fixed him with huge, luminous blue eyes. "What?" she asked.

He nudged his hat back. "Nothing. You just make that look good."

She speared a Brussels sprout with her fork and offered it to him.

"No thanks. Of a mornin', I stick to offerings from Over Easy and Scrambled."

"Pardon?"

"Our hens. We named 'em after egg dishes. Scrambled, Sunny-Side-Up, Meringue." He shrugged. "Dumb, huh? Molly's a bleeding heart. When the hens stop laying, they get put out to pasture like horses. The only time I get fried chicken is if one drops over dead from a coronary."

She eyed him bewilderedly. "You don't wring their necks?"

"Not without getting on her shit list. Every once in a while, I flap my arms and wave my hat, trying to scare one to death. Never works."

She popped the sprout into her mouth. A blissful expression moved over her face as she chewed and swallowed. Gulps of chocolate milk followed. She dabbed the mustache from her upper lip and said, "This is fabulous. Thank you for thinking of it. It's my morning sickness cure."

"Your cure?" Hank rocked back on the chair and propped a boot on one knee. "You sure it's not the cause?"

Her cheek was already puffed out with another Brussels sprout. "Mm."

He chuckled and took another sip of black coffee. Normally he breakfasted at the main house on more conventional foods. Molly had fits about the way the new cook fed the crew, convinced that everyone's cholesterol would shoot off the chart. If that proved true, Hank figured he'd die a happy man.

"You aren't a health-food nut, are you, Carly?" he couldn't resist asking.

She shot him a shy glance. "I like to eat healthful foods, but I'm not fanatical about it."

Regarding her breakfast, Hank had cause to wonder if her definition of "fanatical" was the same as his. Jake's wife Molly was a health nut, and she'd nearly starved everyone to death when Jake had first hired her as the ranch cook. Hank had never craved meat so badly in his life. "You a vegetarian?"

"Heavens, no."

"Now we're talkin'." Hank almost let the subject drop, but then another worry occurred to him. When he'd last visited Portland, he'd dined in restaurants and been appalled by some of the dishes that city people paid good money for. "You like field-green salad?"

"Mm. I love it."

Uh-oh. "You eat dandelions?"

"Not the flowers, although I've heard they make excellent wine."

Hank guessed he'd count himself fortunate that the lady ate meat.

"So tell me," he said when her feeding frenzy abated. "What is it about that particular combination of foods that settles your stomach? Any idea?"

She took another sip of milk. "No, not really. I just crave it."

"Were those your favorite foods before you got pregnant?" *Please say no.*

She wrinkled her nose. "I enjoyed frankfurters and sauerkraut occasionally, and sometimes I ate Brussels sprouts. Not very often, though."

Hank was relieved to hear it. And intrigued. "So one morning, you just up and knew sauerkraut, Brussels sprouts, and chocolate milk were what you needed?"

"Not exactly. I ate a gallon of dill pickles first."

A *gallon*? Hank suppressed a shudder. "All in one sitting?"

"Oh no. It took me a couple of days."

Even at that, she'd eaten a hell of a lot of pickles at a fast clip.

"If it settles your stomach, it works for me." As she sat back in her chair, looking replete, he asked, "How you feeling now?"

"Good." She stifled a dainty belch and blushed. "Excuse me."

Hank couldn't help but grin. "Don't hold back on my account, honey. Let her rip."

The pink in her cheeks deepened. She began gathering the dishes. "Thank you again. It was very sweet of you to remember."

Sweet. He'd chalk that one up in his favor. Only there was a troubled edge to her voice that worried him. She paused before going into the kitchen. "Thank you for the crackers and Seven Up last night as well. I didn't expect you to get dressed and drive somewhere that late at night."

"It helped. That's all that matters."

She smiled hesitantly. "Yes, well. It was still very kind of you."

Two points in his favor. Hank watched her for a
moment as she washed the dishes. Jake had recently
helped him install regular kitchen faucets, but the old
hand pump at the edge of the sink was still operational. When Carly touched the handle, he said,
"That's an antique. Draws straight from a spring. Water's colder than a witch's tit." She threw him a startled look. Hank realized what he'd said and wanted
to bite his tongue. "Colder than a well digger's ass.
How's that?"

She gave the handle a few tries and jumped back
when water came gushing from the spout. "I've never
seen a water pump."

It occurred to him there was a wealth of things she'd
never seen. The realization saddened him. She'd probably looked forward to experiencing so many things
after her surgery. Now she was about to go blind
again. She didn't know how quickly it might happen
yet, of course. He wasn't sure if that was a good thing.
He'd want to know so he could make the most of
every moment.

While she finished tidying the kitchen, he went outside for more boxes. When he came in with the last
load, she glanced up from a cardboard container she'd
just opened. "Where should I put my things?"

Hank lowered his burden to the floor. "Wherever
you want. This is your home now." He watched her
lift a small pillow and trail her fingers lovingly over
the surface with her eyes closed. The smile that
touched her mouth made him want to smile, too.
"Special?" he asked.

She nodded. "My mother made it when I was small.
She embroidered 'I Love You' on the face with
scratchy thread so I could trace the letters."

Hank tried to imagine a little girl reading those words with her fingertips. Until now, he'd never thought of how different life was for the blind. He bent to open another box. "How about if I lay stuff out on the sofa and let you put it away?" he suggested. "That way, you'll know where everything is."

She nodded, and they both set to work. In no time at all, Hank had the boxes unloaded. After that, he helped her put things away, always asking where she wanted them first. As they worked, the refrain of an old song continually moved through his mind: "Getting to know you."

He was conscious of her every movement and expression—the way she caressed the embroidered pillow more than once; the way she lingered over a small, stuffed bear with tattered ears that her father had given her years ago. Her treasures, the things that were truly precious to her, were all things a person could touch or hold close.

"You've got no pictures," he observed.

"I don't, do I?" She glanced around at the jumble of clothing and possessions. "Maybe I can get Daddy to send me a few. I'd love to see what my mother looked like. And him, too, of course."

She'd never seen her parents? Hank stopped what he was doing to stare at her. Of course she'd never seen them, he realized. She'd been blind until a little over a month ago.

"That strikes you as odd. My not knowing what my folks look like, I mean."

Crouched by the sofa, Hank sat back on his boot heel. "Not odd, exactly. Beyond my comprehension, I guess. Intellectually, I know blind people can't see. I just never thought much about what that means on a day-to-day basis. Never seeing your mom's face. I can't imagine that."

Her eyes went shiny and she glanced quickly away. "I saw her. Just not the way other people do. She used to hold me on her lap and let me touch her face." Her mouth curved up at the corners. "She was beautiful."

By the quaver in her voice, Hank knew how sorely she missed her mother. Uncertain what to say, he went back to sorting through her things. A moment later, he came across a tattered old ribbon that sported three knots and was tied in a circle. "You want this, or should I just toss it?"

Bewildered, she perused the bedraggled strand of silk. Then a radiant smile moved over her face. "Oh, that's my friendship ring. Lay it there by my clothes. I'll find a special place for it later."

"What, exactly, is a friendship ring?" Hank couldn't resist asking.

"The circle is symbolic of forever. The knots represent Cricket, Bess, and me, a reminder that we'll always be friends. Cricket made it for me right before I left for college. That first year, I had to attend a special school. It was the first time I'd been away from my family and friends." She pushed to her feet and came to take the ribbon from him. She closed her eyes and ran her fingertips over the knots. Then she held the frayed satin to her cheek. "When I got homesick those first few months, I always felt better when I touched this."

"They've been really good friends to you, haven't they?"

She nodded and gently laid the ribbon atop a stack of clothing. "They're like sisters. We were an indomitable trio. Cricket and Bess were my seeing-eye guides growing up."

He chuckled. "Your seeing-eye guides?"

"Without them, I never would have survived childhood." Her cheek dimpled. "I was dynamite on a skateboard with them yelling directions."

Hank's guts knotted just at the thought. "Bess mentioned that you rode a bicycle and stuff. What were your parents thinking?"

"That I was a normal kid in every way, except I couldn't see."

"You actually *skateboarded*? Weren't you afraid?"

"Of what?"

"Running into things. Sailing off an embankment. Hell, I don't know. Of everything, I guess."

She laughed. "That's a sighted person's perspective. I was born blind, remember. I had never seen an embankment. I couldn't see the things in front of me. I might be afraid now, but I wasn't then." She let her head fall back and closed her eyes. "I loved the sensation of speed, to feel the wind in my face. It was wonderful." When she looked at him again, she added, "The only other thing that ever came close was skydiving with Cricket right before I left for college."

"Skydiving? You jumped from an airplane?"

"I had no concept of height. It wasn't frightening at all to me."

Hank felt chilled just thinking about it. "It can be windy up there."

She sent him a questioning look. "You've jumped?"

"I have, and you either had a death wish or you were crazier than a loon. What if the wind carried her voice away, and you didn't pull the cord in time?"

"I didn't go alone. I buddy jumped with an instructor."

He was relieved to hear it. Just not so relieved that he could think about it without wanting to give her a shake. "It's a dangerous sport."

"So is bungee cord jumping, but people still do it."

"You didn't."

"No. It was from a bridge. I was afraid the cord might break, and I'd hit the water."

Hank saw the tense expression that stole over her face. "You were afraid of hitting the water but not hitting the ground when you jumped from a plane?"

She bent her head and pretended interest in the socks she was rolling. "Water is terrifying to me. It gets in my ears, making it difficult to hear, and I lose all sense of direction. If I go under, I'm not sure which way is up. And when I surface, I can't tell where the bank is. I swam with Bess and Cricket a few times, but I never really enjoyed myself."

She went into the bedroom to put a pile of socks away. A few moments later, Hank glanced up and saw her gazing out the window toward the corrals. When he went to stand behind her, she rubbed her arms and said, "Horses are so much bigger than I thought they'd be."

"You've never seen a horse?"

"I've seen pictures. On the western channel, they don't look so huge."

He couldn't conceive living one's entire life without ever seeing a horse. Every so often, during the course of their conversation, he'd think he was beginning to understand what it was like to be blind. Then she'd say something to make him realize he hadn't a clue.

To live in constant darkness, to never see the dawn, to never watch the sun go down.

Gazing down at her, he tried his best to grasp what it must be like for her. Only it was impossible. The whole world and everything in it was new to her.

Resting his shoulder against the window frame, Hank turned toward her. "What's it like, seeing for the first time in your life?"

She danced nervous fingertips over the glass. He didn't miss the way she moved slightly to put distance between their bodies. "Confusing." She tapped the glass with a fingernail. "I know the glass is there, but I can't see it. Bess says sunlight and images reflect off the surface if you really look, but I don't notice things like that."

Hank studied the glass. Once, as a kid, he'd walked into a patio door and damned near broken his nose. "Windows can be tricky for anybody."

"I suppose." She sighed and frowned thoughtfully. "Some things seem backward. That's worrisome because it isn't a difficulty my doctor told me about."

"What things seem backward?"

"Silly things." She shrugged. "Things I memorized by touch years ago—they seem all wrong somehow."

"Such as?"

"The dialing pad on a telephone, hot and cold water faucets, letters and numbers. It's like—" She shook her head. "In my mind, I had a picture of things, but I saw them on my side of the darkness. Does that make any sense?"

It didn't, but he nodded anyway, wanting her to go on.

"Now that I can see, things are outside, staring back at me."

Hank still wasn't getting it, but he smiled to encourage her.

Her scowl deepened. "When I dial a phone, for instance. If I close my eyes, I'm fine. But if I open my eyes, I get all confused, hitting the three when I want to hit the one. It's the same with letters." She trailed her fingertips lightly over the glass. "When you read braille, you trace the little bumps. Imagine the letter, traveling up your arm and into your brain, where you store it inside the darkness with you. You don't see it. You have it *in* you. Then, suddenly, it's outside, and for me, it's as if it got flipped over, wrong side up. I don't know if other people experience the same thing or not. Maybe I'm just weird."

"That sounds like dyslexia. You're having trouble interpreting spatial relationships."

"It does sound like dyslexia, doesn't it? Just what I need, a learning disorder on top of everything else."

Hank chuckled. "I doubt you're dyslexic, honey. Listening to you, you know what comes to mind? The way letters look in a mirror. They're always backward. When you consider how the eye works, it kind of makes sense that you might have trouble for a while. The retina has reflective layers, sort of like a mirror, conducting image impulses to the brain. Maybe your impulses are jumbled right now, and the images are getting flipped in transit."

"You think?" she asked hopefully.

Hank knew he shouldn't touch her, but he couldn't resist. He gently tweaked the end of that cute little nose. "I do," he assured her. "Stop worrying. Even if you are dyslexic, which I seriously doubt, it's no big deal anymore."

She looked none too sure about that.

* * *

That evening while their supper simmered on the stove, Hank suggested that Carly should call her father. She responded by saying, "I hate to run up long distance charges on your bill."

He unclipped the cell phone from his belt and handed it to her. "I've got a long distance package. Something like three-hundred minutes a month, and I use only about half of them. You can talk without it costing me a cent."

She squinted at the phone, then handed it back to him. "It's too small and confusing. Can you dial for me?"

She recited the number, and Hank punched it in. Then he went to the living room and flipped on the television, pretending to be watching the news while she talked to her dad, a conversation that began with a tremulous, "Daddy?" Then she settled down to talk, explaining to Art Adams about her temporary marriage to Hank. "He wanted to help me through this," she said haltingly. "In the end, he was so convincing I couldn't say no. I would have invited you, but it seemed senseless for you to spend the money on air fare when it was only a formality."

Convincing? He'd blackmailed her into saying yes.

"I know," Carly said softly. "I'm very lucky that he's here for me." A long pause. "No, Daddy. It's not like that. We, um, have an agreement. He seems okay with it." Another pause. "I won't get my heart broken, Daddy. It's just a convenient arrangement, something he offered to do for me and the baby. Neither of us has any expectations, and once I'm able to get out on my own, we'll dissolve the marriage."

When the conversation moved on from that topic

to life in general, Carly was soon laughing. "You did the jitterbug? She must be quite a lady if she convinced you to dance." A sigh. "What is the jitterbug, by the way?" His answer sent her into a fit of giggles. "I'm so happy for you. It's good to know you're having so much fun down there."

Hank was equally glad to know that she was so close to her dad. It was more in keeping with his idea of family. Too soon to suit him, Carly told her father she should say good-bye. "I shouldn't use up too many of Hank's minutes," she explained. "I'm using his cell phone."

Hank almost interrupted to tell her she could use all the minutes she liked, but then he'd be revealing that he'd been eavesdropping. He decided that she'd covered all the important stuff. He could work on her usage of his long distance allotment later.

"Thank you, Hank," she said softly as she returned the phone to him. "It was good to talk to him."

He could tell that she'd enjoyed the conversation by the glow of her smile and the pleased light in her lovely eyes. "What's he like?"

"Funny." She shrugged. "Wonderful. He's always been my rock."

Hank felt an unwarranted pang of resentment. He wanted to be the person she counted on. And where had that thought come from? He had to keep it firmly in mind that Carly had no intention of remaining in this marriage. If he started thinking in terms of forever, he'd be setting himself up for heartbreak.

As a distraction, he escorted Carly to the stables to meet his horses. The entire way there, she kept saying, "I'm not sure I'm ready for this."

Hank laughed. "You climbed on a skateboard. Trust me, my horses are a lot safer."

"So you say."

At the entrance to the stable, she put on her brakes and stared at a mare just inside the enclosure that stood with her head poked out over a stall door. "It's all right," Hank assured her.

She reluctantly allowed him to draw her closer. In that moment, Hank wasn't sure which made her warier, him or the horse.

"It's *huge*."

"*It* is a she." Hank reached out to scratch behind the horse's ears. "Her name's Sugar. She's a sorrel."

"I thought you raised quarter horses."

"Sorrel is a color, not a breed." He pointed further up the aisle to a gray-muzzled gelding. "That old fellow is a buckskin. Took to biting recently, and his mama brought him here for an attitude adjustment. In the next stall, the reddish brown mare with the black mane is a bay."

She shook her head. "I'm still struggling to learn all the different shades of pink. I'll never get horse colors straight."

"The horses won't give a hoot." He tugged on her hand to bring her closer. "Sugar's safe." *And so am I.* "It's all right. She won't hurt you."

She reached out a hand, then snatched it back at the last second. "Doesn't she have teeth?"

"Of course. She doesn't bite, though."

"Are you sure?"

He put his hand to the mare's muzzle. Sugar expected a treat and chuffed, wiggling her lips over his palm. "See? I've still got my hand." He grasped Carly's wrist and shoved her slender fingers under the mare's nose. "Don't be afraid."

"Oh, *God*." Rigid with tension, she squeezed her eyes closed, clearly expecting to lose half her arm. After a moment, she lifted her lashes and giggled at the ticklish sensation of the horse's lips on her skin. Hank wished he could nibble on her for a while. "She's so *soft*," she whispered.

"Like velvet," he agreed, remembering how soft her legs had felt last night. He released his hold on her. "Go ahead and pet her. She's a big sweetheart." When Carly hesitated, he laughed. "I'd never tell you to do something if you might get hurt. This horse is so gentle I could lay a newborn at her feet."

Carly stepped closer. Soon she was touching Sugar's ears and running her slender hand over the mare's mane. "Oh," she kept saying. "You're so *sweet*."

The sentiment seemed to be mutual. As if Sugar recognized a gentle soul, she began nickering and nudging Carly for more petting.

"I think she likes me," Carly said with a laugh.

What wasn't to like? Hank liked her, too. Perhaps more than was wise. Uncertain what to do with the emotions she evoked within him, he turned away.

"This is Sonora Sunset, Molly's stallion," he said at the next stall. "Poor fellow was whipped within an inch of his life. Molly showed up here one day in a Toyota, pulling a huge two-horse trailer. Sunset was inside, raising sand and shrieking to wake snakes in six counties. That's how Molly met Jake."

Carly came to stand by the gate, her stricken gaze moving over the stallion's scarred black coat. "How *awful*," she said softly. "Who did that to him?"

"Molly's ex, Rodney Wells. He's a sick son of a

bitch." Hank realized what he'd said and rubbed his jaw. "Sorry. I need to watch my language."

Carly suppressed a smile. "Your language doesn't offend me, Hank. I've heard much worse."

"From who? He needs to learn some manners."

"I went to college, remember—a special school for the blind my first year, but then I mainstreamed at Portland University. On a campus, people use all kinds of expletives." She fixed her attention on the horse again. "Why did Molly bring a wounded stallion to Jake? Tucker's the vet."

"So's Isaiah. They've started a practice together." He hooked an arm around the stallion's sturdy neck. "Molly wasn't looking for a vet. She needed a horse psychologist. Sunset was loco from all the abuse."

"Jake is a horse psychologist?"

"He and I have a way with horses. A lot of people think we're horse whisperers. Molly heard about Jake through a trainer, and she brought Sunset here in hopes that Jake could save him from being put down."

Watching Hank with the stallion, Carly could see that he had a way with the animals. "Are you?" she asked.

He flicked her a quizzical look. "Am I what?"

"A whisperer."

His white teeth flashed in a teasing grin. "I'll whisper in your ear any old time you want."

Carly could well remember the shivers that had run down her spine when he had. She hugged her waist. "I'll pass, thanks."

"I was afraid you'd say that." His grin broadened, and he winked. "In answer to your question, no, I'm not a horse whisperer. Is there such a thing?"

"I don't know. Is there?"

"I doubt it. I'm good with horses, is all. No big mystery. They're just like people, with fears and phobias, likes and dislikes. Some trainers are old school. They use harsh methods to get the job done. Others take a more gentle approach, but they've got a set way of doing things, regardless of the animal. Jake and I follow our instincts and take our time, always bearing in mind that each horse is different and may need different handling." A teasing twinkle warmed his sky-blue eyes. "They're sort of like women that way."

Carly chafed her arms.

"You cold?"

"No." She was, actually, but she hesitated to say so. He wore no jacket and might offer to share his body heat. She gingerly touched the stallion's nose.

"He's a big old love, just like Sugar," Hank assured her. "Didn't used to be, but Molly brought him out of it. He's gentle as can be now—for a stallion."

Carly jerked her hand away. "What's that mean?"

Hank grinned and turned to lead the way deeper into the stable. Trailing behind him, Carly admired the graceful harmony of his movements. His long legs bowed out slightly at the knee, a trait she'd noticed in his father and all his brothers as well. She assumed it came from sitting in a saddle so much of the time. Whatever the cause, it was attractive, giving him a rugged air that went well with his broad-shouldered, tapered torso.

He stopped at each open stall to introduce her to the occupant. Carly knew she'd promptly forget the horses' names.

"Are the closed stalls vacant?" she couldn't resist asking.

"Nope. Mamas and babies, down for the night." At

the end of the aisle, he gestured at two stalls that were larger than all the others. "Our version of birthing chambers," he explained. "They're bigger so the mare can comfortably lie down and stretch out her legs. We do imprinting in here as well."

"You brand your horses?" Carly had always felt that the practice was cruel, and she couldn't conceal her disapproval.

"Imprinting isn't branding. Most folks don't do that anymore." He studied her indignant expression for a moment, then chuckled and scratched under his hat. "Instead of branding, a lot of people tag the ears— kind of like a lady getting her ear pierced. The more expensive horses get ID chips, little information crystals inserted under the skin, or we tattoo the inside of an ear. It doesn't hurt."

"Oh." She was relieved. "What's imprinting, then?"

"Baby training, essentially. I'll bring you down to watch sometime—or better yet, to help. It's fun. Imprinting is basically situational conditioning begun directly after birth and continued over the first several months of life. You get a foal used to all the things that might frighten it as an adult. Imprinting is a lot of work, but in the end, the horse is better off. We seldom have to hobble an imprinted horse, and we hardly ever have to use a twitch. In short, imprinted horses are better adjusted, happier animals, and they're a joy to work with."

"What's a twitch?"

He rubbed his jaw. "It's a contraption that pinches the nose, one of the most sensitive spots on a horse's body. You anchor the twitch with just enough tension to make it hurt like hell. If the horse moves, it hurts a whole lot worse."

"That's *horrible*."

"It's necessary with a horse that refuses to stand while you give it shots or treat a wound. They're big, strong critters. You can't muscle them around. Try, and they'll show you how the cow ate the cabbage." His mouth tipped in a slight smile. "Now you can understand why we imprint our foals. We don't enjoy inflicting pain on a horse. Our imprinted animals seldom have to be subdued. We subject the foals to every conceivable experience, over and over again, until they think nothing of it. As adults, they do a horse version of a yawn while they're shoed or vaccinated or doctored. Not much throws them."

"Anything that saves them from a twitch has my vote."

He glanced at his watch. "We should head back to the house. The stew should be about done."

As Hank led the way from the stable, he couldn't help but remember all the girlfriends he'd brought out to the ranch over the years. Most of them had mixed with horses like oil with water. Carly didn't even seem to notice the horse shit, a fact that was driven home to Hank when she stepped in a fresh pile.

"Uh-oh." She shook her leg, trying to dislodge the smelly gook. "Oh, *yuck*. Is that what I think it is?" She peered myopically at her foot.

"If you're thinking it's horse shit, go to the head of the class," he said, going back to grasp her elbow.

Hank expected her to be pissed about her shoe. Instead she laughed and glanced around, looking like someone who'd just wandered into a minefield.

He guided her around the bombs as they left the building, smiling at the way she shook her foot every few steps. Once outside, she stopped to rub her shoe clean on the grass. She got all but a couple of blobs. Hunkering down, Hank grasped her ankle to turn her foot. She jumped at the contact and almost toppled over backward.

"Whoa." He grabbed her by the waistband of her jeans to steady her. When she caught her balance, he returned his attention to guiding her foot. "Now swipe," he instructed.

When her sneaker was clean, he pushed erect. She wrinkled her nose and smiled at him. "One of the dangers of an untrained visual cortex. I can't detect irregularities on a ground surface. I never knew the manure was there until it went squish under my foot."

The way she said "squish" set Hank to laughing again.

Hank lay on his back, arms folded beneath his head, feet dangling over the end of the mattress. Moonlight spangled the cedar ceiling of the back bedroom, the shadowy patterns shifting as the night wind swayed the trees outside the window. He couldn't sleep for thoughts of Carly—how she'd timidly petted the horses at first and then warmed to them; how she'd laughed over the manure on her shoe; how startled she'd been by the touch of his hand on her ankle; and how painfully nervous she'd been later when they returned to the house.

She was so beautiful he ached when he looked at her. He wished he could tell her that, but if he tried, she'd just think it was another hokey come-on line. She'd made that blatantly clear last night.

No question about it, he was swimming upstream against a strong current with her, and the best he could probably hope for was friendship. That frustrated him. He'd hoped, perhaps foolishly, that they might make this marriage work. But the more he was around her, the more convinced he became that he'd burned his bridges with her. Some screw-ups couldn't be fixed, plain and simple, and he'd screwed up big time. She had it in her mind that a second go-round with him would be awful, and he had no idea how to disabuse her of the notion.

So . . . friendship, it would be. All and all, that would be better than nothing. When she filed for divorce and moved out, they'd be able to keep in contact and work together at parenting, making things easier on their child.

Hank sighed and closed his eyes. *Friendship.* He could think of far more satisfying ways to spend two years with a beautiful woman, but a man didn't always get his druthers.

Chapter Fifteen

Over the next couple of days, making friends with Carly became Hank's goal. In order to accomplish that, the first order of business was to make her feel at ease with him. To that end, he began calling her at different times during the day, just to say hi. He invariably caught her busily at work, trying to train her visual cortex. One afternoon, she was going through all the kitchen drawers, identifying utensils by touch.

"There's this thing," she informed him. "It has handles you squeeze, with a little box at the end that has a bunch of small holes. I have no idea what it is."

Hank thought for a moment. "A garlic press?"

"Excuse me," she said with mock seriousness. "I'm asking *you*."

He laughed. "It has to be a garlic press." He explained how the peeled cloves are pushed through the holes. "It works, slick as greased owl shit."

"What a nauseating comparison. A garlic press. Hmm. That goes on my list of new things to try. When can we press garlic?"

Hank hung up smiling. Most people would feel silly not recognizing a garlic press, but Carly took it in stride, determined to learn all that she could as quickly as possible.

At other times when Hank phoned, he interrupted her daily eye-exercise regime. The specialist had given her charts to tack to a wall. One was headed by the basic colors, and below was a diagram, showing many of the possible shades that could be created by blending the basics. Another was a chart of shapes and symbols—shapes, squares, triangles, figure eights, and the like. Carly spent hours working to train her visual cortex to recognize them on sight. One morning, Hank walked in to catch her trying to work what looked like a child's puzzle. She quickly dumped the pieces back into the box and shoved it under the sofa, clearly embarrassed to have him know that she was struggling to master an activity that a five-year-old could easily do. The discovery enabled Hank to better understand the battle she was waging. It was horribly difficult for her to fit certain shapes together, something that most people had been doing all their lives.

In order to spend more time with her, Hank began taking all his meals at the cabin. He ate poached eggs on toast for breakfast because the smell of fried food made her sick, settled for sandwiches at lunch, and donned an apron at night to help prepare dinner.

After the kitchen was tidied, he used the hours before bedtime to take her to the main house to visit with Jake and Molly or to recline with her in the living room to watch TV or chat. Their time alone together was always tense. While walking, she kept an arm's length between their bodies and didn't say a whole lot. At the house, she sat across the room from him and fidgeted, toying with her clothes or plucking at the fringe of a sofa pillow. She frequently said good-night early, claiming exhaustion.

All Hank's life, he'd been told that he had more charm than all his brothers combined. He tried using it to best advantage with Carly. But in the end, Hank was the one to be charmed.

If there was a character trait he most admired, it was courage, and Carly proved to be the most determined, courageous individual he knew. Though he suspected her eyesight was growing worse, she never so much as hinted that she was worried or experiencing any difficulty.

When he returned to the cabin to check on her at various times throughout the day, he often found her poring over books she'd brought with her from the apartment. Sometimes she studied a tome titled *What's What*, a visual glossary of everyday objects. Other times, she worked on recognizing the letters of the alphabet. The print in her books was small, forcing her to lean close with her nose mere inches from the page, and more times than not she propped an elbow on the table, absently rubbing her temple as if she had a headache.

Hank wanted to ask why she tortured herself. She wouldn't be able to see a damned letter soon, let alone recognize one. Why get headaches for no good reason? Her determination to train her visual cortex worried him as well. Was she ignoring the obvious and clinging to the false hope that she wouldn't lose her sight during her pregnancy?

On Wednesday afternoon, five days after their marriage, Hank returned to the house unexpectedly to change his shirt. When he found Carly with her nose in a book again, he could keep quiet no longer.

"Honey, couldn't you put your time to better use?"

She cast him a bewildered look. "Why do you say that?"

Careful, Hank. "According to your doctor, it's possible that your eyesight may go before the baby comes. If that happens, what good will it do to recognize your letters on sight?"

Hank half expected her to get upset. If he were faced with going blind again, he sure as hell wouldn't appreciate a reminder. But Carly only smiled.

"Some lattice patients skate through pregnancy without a problem."

"So your sight seems to be holding steady?"

"Not holding steady, exactly."

Hello? If her sight was growing worse, she obviously wasn't going to skate through. "That's not a good indication, is it?" he asked cautiously.

"No." Her smile dimmed. But then she brightened again. "Lattice is unpredictable. Every patient is different, and every pregnancy is different. The disease may do damage swiftly, leaving me blind as a bat in only a few months—or it may go like wildfire and then slow down. I prefer to think positively."

Hank believed in positive thinking. He just didn't want her to be disappointed. A few months? Even though she'd noticed the deterioration of her vision, she obviously hadn't faced the truth yet, that she might go blind in a very short while.

"I've known people with lattice who've never gone completely blind," she said. "They're legally blind, of course, but they can still see to some degree for years and years. Who can say how severe my lattice actually is?"

She'd been totally blind, hadn't she? How much worse could it get?

"In addition to the lattice, I was born with congenital cataracts," she explained. "Which condition initially caused my blindness? Everyone assumes it was due to both conditions, but what if it wasn't? Maybe the lattice wasn't that bad when I was born, but worsened over time, and the initial blindness was caused by the cataracts."

Uncertain what to say, Hank sank onto a chair to study her small face. On the one hand, he could understand her reasoning—and her frantic hope that the lattice by itself wouldn't rob her of sight that quickly. On the other hand, he'd seen evidence that her vision was deteriorating at a rapid rate. If it hadn't escaped his notice, how had it escaped hers?

Maybe, he decided, she had noticed—and she was simply choosing to be optimistic until life kicked her in the teeth again. Taking measure of her determinedly cheerful grin, he wanted to weep for her.

"Well, I guess we'll wait and see. Maybe you'll be one of the lucky ones."

She nodded. "Please don't think I have my head buried in the sand. I know the odds are stacked against me." She rested her chin on her hand and narrowed her lovely eyes slightly to search his expression. "You look worried. There's no reason to be."

Hank rubbed beside his nose. Worried? He was heartsick.

"I'm a big girl, Hank. If the worst happens, I'll deal with it."

How could she sit there and look so calm? No tears, no outrage, no shaking her fist at God. He'd never even seen her act mildly depressed. Instead, she seemed at peace about it. Searching her expression, he knew she really was aware of the odds and that she would accept whatever came. The thought of being trapped in darkness for months on end terrified him. Carly might not be happy about the possibility, but she wasn't quailing in fear, either.

"I can tell it bothers your eyes to stare at those books so much."

"I'm used to eye pain."

He didn't want her to experience pain of any kind. "Why not enjoy this time some other way and train your visual cortex after your next surgery? You'll be able to see more clearly then, and it'll be a lot easier for you."

She closed the book and went into the kitchen for a glass of water. "I could wait, but then I'd be wasting today."

"You have lots of days ahead of you. This is only a temporary setback. Next summer, you'll have surgery and be able to see for years and years."

"Will I?" She turned, holding the glass midway to her mouth. "If all my surgeries are successful and each procedure lasts as long as it should, I'll be able to see for twenty, maybe thirty years before I begin to reject my transplants. But what if each procedure doesn't go well?"

His belly clenched with dread. "What do you mean?"

She trailed her fingertips over the glass, catching beads of water. Then she rubbed her hand on her jeans. "There are no guarantees. Dr. Merrick can promise me nothing. Dozens of things can—and do—go wrong. Something as simple as a flu shot—or a virus—or any number of other variables can escalate

the lattice or cause rejection. And, for a few, the surgeries don't work at all."

He swallowed hard, and suddenly he was the one
who wanted to shake his fist. What in heaven's name
was she saying, that things could go wrong and she
might never be able to see at all?

"Even if everything goes perfectly, my days of sightedness will be numbered. If things go wrong—" Her
eyes went dark with shadows. "There's just no telling.
I may have as many as fifteen years or as few as five
or maybe no time at all. Knowing that, if you were
me, would you waste a single day?"

Hank thanked God he was sitting down. No time
at all? "No," he admitted. "I don't guess so."

"Exactly. Each and every minute I can see is a precious gift." She took a long drink of water, then set
the empty glass on the counter. "The visual cortex
is a memory bank of sorts. Everything I see today,
everything I master visually, will remain in my memory. If my surgery next summer goes nicely, it may
take me a few days to orient myself, but then everything I learn now will come in very handy. I'll be one
step closer to reading proficiently, and it'll be easier
for me to do things, like dial a phone or balance my
checkbook. I'll have made headway if I use this time
wisely, and I'll be better prepared to make the most
of my life as a sighted blind person after the next
surgery."

The walls of Hank's throat felt as if he'd swallowed
Elmer's glue. A fierce protectiveness welled inside
him. He wanted to hold her in his arms and shield
her. Unfortunately, lattice dystrophy was a villain he
couldn't fight.

He looked out the window at the sunlight filtering

down through the pines. She had today. It was something he hadn't really understood until now. *Today.* Faced with those odds, he would have been outdoors, feasting his eyes on everything—flowers, blades of grass, and the way the wind swayed the trees. He sure as hell wouldn't stay in the house with his nose stuck in a book.

"It seems like a piss poor way to make the days count."

She gave a startled laugh. "What would you suggest?"

"Aren't there other things you'd like to do?"

She dimpled her cheek and sighed, her eyes going dreamy soft. "*Oodles* of things. But why dream and wish when it's not possible to do them?"

"If you could do whatever you wanted right now, what would you do?"

"One thing I always wanted to do was learn to drive." She shrugged. "Even now, my long distance vision isn't good enough to try. Maybe someday."

"And?" He waited a beat. "What else?"

"If I were rich, which I'm not, I'd travel."

"Where to?"

"*Everywhere.*" The dreamy look in her eyes became more pronounced. "I'd see everything I possibly could before my eyesight goes—the Eiffel Tower, the Egyptian pyramids, the Sahara desert, Mount Everest." She laughed lightly, the sound drifting musically on the air. "I'd *love* to see a camel."

"A camel?" They were the ugliest critters Hank had ever clapped eyes on.

"Oh, *yes.* And a zebra. Maybe even a tiger if I could manage it without getting eaten. I guess that seems silly to you."

In that moment, he thought she was the most amazing individual he'd ever known. He loved the way her face glowed when she dreamed. A searing sensation washed over his eyes. "If I had the money, I'd take you to all those places. We'd just pack our clothes and take off."

Her expression clouded. "I didn't mean to make you feel that way. You're already doing so much, more than you should, actually, and I'm very grateful."

He didn't want her to be grateful, damn it. All he wanted was to make her happy. If only he had the money, he would lay the entire world at her feet.

A sudden thought occurred to him. Maybe he couldn't give her Egypt and Paris, but he could come through with driving lessons and exotic critters. "When's your checkup with the corneal specialist?"

"It was on July seventh, but last week, I rescheduled for the following Monday."

"Why? I could have driven you up on the seventh."

"I wasn't sure what plans you might have for the holiday weekend."

Hank had forgotten the Fourth of July was on Friday. "Just a family gathering here. That evening, we may take the kids to watch the fireworks."

"Fireworks?" Her eyes sparkled with interest.

Hank realized that she'd never seen a firework display. "Wanna go?"

"I'd love to. If it won't be a big bore for you, that is."

"I *love* fireworks," he assured her. "I wouldn't miss them for anything."

There was so very much she'd never seen—and so much she might never see. It didn't matter how many times he'd done things. He'd enjoy the same-old, same-old because it would all be new to her.

He just hoped her vision held fast until her appointment with Merrick on the fourteenth. Mentally crossing his fingers, he smiled and said, "When we drive up for your checkup, plan on staying overnight in the city."

"Why? It's only three, maybe four hours to Portland. My appointment's at two. We can easily come back the same day."

"Nope. We're going to take a day trip when you're done that afternoon to take in some sights. The Columbia Gorge, for starters, and if we've got time, maybe Mount St. Helen's."

"We can't afford to—"

"Don't argue with your husband. When we get back to Portland that evening, we'll do the town—go out to eat at a five-star restaurant, stay in a fancy hotel. I'll order you a whole mixing bowl of dandelions." He winked at her. "You can have that strawberry shit on top that folks with sophisticated palates love."

"Strawberry vinaigrette?"

"There you go. And all day Tuesday, we're going to play."

"That isn't necessary. Fancy dinners and hotels cost a lot, especially when we'll need two rooms."

The lady was always thinking. Hank bit back a grin. "Let me worry about the finances. All right? I want to take you to the Portland Zoo on Tuesday, and I don't want to be in a hurry when we go."

Her eyes widened. "The *zoo*?"

Hank chuckled and pushed to his feet. "Now I'm talking your language. Camels, zebras, giraffes, elephants, maybe even a tiger. I haven't been there in years. I'm not sure what all they have."

A delighted smile spread slowly over her face. "The *zoo*?" He wouldn't have been surprised if she'd started jumping up and down, she looked so excited. Instead she raced across the room to clutch his shirtsleeves, her eyes fairly dancing. "Oh, Hank, that'll be so much *fun*! A zebra? I'll get to see a real, live *zebra*."

"Maybe a zebra." God, how he wished she'd followed through on the urge and thrown her arms around his neck. He had to settle for knowing that she'd come very close. "They may not have one."

As if she hadn't heard, she said, "And a camel!"

She twirled away from him, flinging her arms wide and laughing. Her balance wasn't the best, and Hank tucked his thumbs over his belt to keep from grabbing for her.

"The *zoo*. What a fabulous idea. I can barely *wait*."

When Hank left a few minutes later, she was still naming off all the critters she might see. Given his profession, the last way Hank wanted to spend a day was with a bunch of mangy animals, but he was grinning like a fool as he stepped from the porch. He stopped to gaze back at the house. Give the girl diamonds, and he got a hesitant smile and polite thank you. Offer her camels and zebras, and she almost launched herself into his arms.

Damn. Maybe he'd been baiting his hook with all the wrong lures.

Late that same afternoon, Carly was working on her letters again when she heard a vehicle pull up out front. She closed her book, wondering who was there. Hank's Ford diesel made a sound like rocks rattling in a bucket.

She stepped to the front window and peered out. An old gray pickup was parked near the porch. Carly couldn't make out the driver until he threw open the door and swung out. It was Hank, after all.

He cleared the steps with one long-legged leap, waved at her through the glass, and threw open the front door to poke his head inside. "You busy, angel face?"

"I, um—no, not really."

He flashed a broad grin. "Good. Let's go."

"Where?"

"For a ride." He narrowed an eye at her. "Come on. Don't look so suspicious. This barroom lothario has seen the error of his ways."

Carly pushed at her hair. "Will anyone see me? I'm a mess."

"Only me, and I think you look great."

Bewildered, Carly followed him to the truck. Her confusion increased when he circled around to climb in on the passenger side. She stepped closer to the vehicle and peered in the open driver's window. "Why are you over there?"

He plucked a beer bottle from a six-pack on the seat beside him. " 'Cause you're gonna drive. Climb in."

Carly's heart skittered. "*What?*"

He winked, twisted off the bottle cap, and gave it a flip out the other window. "Driving lessons. Remember? One of the things you'd love to do while you can still see. Stop gaping at me and get in."

"I can't drive! My long distance vision is terrible."

"Trust me, darlin'." He took a long pull from the

bottle and whistled as he came up for breath. "Let's go."

Carly had trusted him once when he was drinking, and just look where that had gotten her. "You're drinking."

"I worked in the hot sun all day. I'm wetting my whistle, not drinking."

"There's a difference?"

"There is. Trust me to know. Would you get in?"

"I can't *drive*. Have you taken leave of your senses?"

"Where's the fearless daredevil who skateboarded blind and jumped out of airplanes?"

"She developed common sense."

He gave her a twinkling look. "You chicken?" He tucked his free hand in his armpit and flapped his elbow like a wing. "*Bruck-bruck-bruck-br-rr-uck!*"

Carly had never been called a chicken in her life. She opened the driver's door, stepped up, and slid under the steering wheel. "If I kill us both, it'll be on your head."

"Won't happen." He motioned with the beer bottle. "Dirt roads, wide open fields. Not much out here to hit. It'll be fun. I learned to drive in this same old rattletrap when I was ten. Dad handed me the keys and turned me loose. I was so short, I could barely see over the wheel."

Carly dragged in a calming breath and stared at the dusty dash. It was nothing like the one in his Ford—hardly any gadgets or knobs. "What'll I do?"

He told her to depress the clutch, then spent a moment showing her how to operate the floor shift. "You'll probably never get out of second on this rough terrain, but once you get the hang of the first two gears, you'll have them all licked. Now, keep the clutch pressed down to the floor and start her up."

"How do you know this truck isn't a he?" she asked, stalling for time.

His mouth twitched. "Because it's high maintenance and totally unpredictable."

"That isn't nice."

He grinned. "Actually, I kept it polite and left out the satisfying ride. You gonna go, or are we going to sit here, talking it to death all night?"

Carly did as he said and bleated in terror when the engine roared to life. "Oh, *God!*"

"Just relax. As long as you hold the clutch in, you're in complete control. There's a girl. Now tromp the gas to get the feel of acceleration."

Moments later when Hank deemed her ready, Carly let out on the clutch. The truck lurched violently forward, then the engine coughed and died.

"What'd I do wrong?" Carly was so nervous she could barely breathe. Her legs started to jerk each time she pressed on the pedals. "This isn't a good idea. I appreciate the thought, Hank. Really I do, but—"

"Would you stop? You're doing great. Everyone kills the engine at first. You have to synchronize the pedals, letting off the clutch as you press on the gas. It takes a little practice."

A little? Carly started the truck again. On her second try, the vehicle lurched forward, but the engine didn't die. She clamped her hands over the steering wheel. "We're moving!" she cried in a voice gone thin with panic. "Now what? Tell me what to do!" She saw a tree up ahead. "Oh, *God! A tree,* Hank! What'll I do?"

"Steer." He grabbed the wheel, helped her veer around the tree, and then patted her arm. "There, you see? Easy as pie." He pointed to a rutted road off to their right. "Go that way. It circles around to an upper pasture and a nice, wide turnaround."

Carly turned too sharply and then overcorrected, but she finally got the truck on the road. The old pickup bumped over the ruts at a slow crawl, allowing her plenty of reaction time while she got the hang of steering. After a few minutes, she began to relax.

"I'm driving," she said. "I'm actually *driving.*"

Hank grinned and settled back to drink his beer. "You sure are, and doing a damned fine job of it. How's it feel?"

"Like I own the whole world." Carly laid on the horn. "It's even better than skydiving! Thank you, Hank. I can't believe you trusted me with your truck."

"Sweetheart, this old bucket is indestructible. Vintage Ford, 1949, and made for punishment. It's our ranch truck. We use it for all the heavy work. Been butted by bulls, kicked by horses, and battered at both ends by more trees and boulders than I can count. If you add a new dent, no harm done."

Minutes later, they reached the turnaround. Hank inclined his head at the windshield. "Watch out for the fence."

Sunlight slanted across the dusty windshield just then. Carly squinted, trying to see. "What fence?"

Hank sat straighter on the seat. "*That* fence. Stop. Hit the brake."

Carly slammed down her foot. Only somehow, she hit the gas pedal. At the sudden acceleration, the truck engine roared, the vehicle surged forward, and she finally saw the fence—just as she crashed through it.

"Holy *shit*!" Hank shouted. "Watch out for the cows!"

"Cows?"

Before Carly could see them, let alone avoid them, the pickup hit a mound of earth at the edge of an irrigation ditch and went airborne. An instant later, they landed smack-dab in the middle of the pasture, cows fleeing in all directions with loud and raucous bawls of complaint.

After the bovines escaped, a sudden silence descended. The truck engine had died. Carly sat frozen, her hands locked over the steering wheel. Hank still held his beer bottle, the contents of which now decorated the front of his shirt.

"Christ on crutches," he whispered. "I should've said, 'exciting ride.' "

Carly couldn't breathe and she wanted to cry.

"You okay?" he asked.

She nodded. Then, after struggling to find her voice, she managed to say, "Oh, Hank, I'm sorry. Sunlight hit the windshield, and I couldn't see. Are the cows all right, do you think?"

"You curdled their milk, that's for sure." There was an odd, tight sound in his voice. "Did you see the looks on their faces?"

"No. All I saw was their butts."

He snorted. Then he burst out laughing—not just chuckles, but great, huge, body-shaking guffaws. He laughed until the empty bottle slipped from his hand and dropped to the floorboard. He laughed until he was holding his sides. He laughed until tears streamed from his eyes.

When he finally fell quiet, Carly said, "I fail to see the humor."

For reasons beyond her, that only made him start laughing again.

"You're out of your mind. This isn't funny. I destroyed your fence, I scratched your truck, and I almost *killed* your cows!"

His mirth finally abating, he said, "I can fix the fence, the truck doesn't matter, and the cows are just a little shaken up. They haven't seen a woman driver since Bethany." He sighed and rubbed his belly. "Oh, man, I haven't laughed so hard in a coon's age." He gave her a weak grin. "I take it back. You can go fast enough to have a wreck out here. It just takes rare talent."

He straightened, drew in a deep breath, and slowly exhaled. "Well," he said, inclining his head at the ignition, "see if this baby will start."

"Oh no. I'm not driving back."

"Sure you are. You got us here in one piece, didn't you?"

He plucked another longneck from the pack. The instant he twisted off the cap, beer spewed from the mouth of the bottle, hitting him directly in the face. Foam dripped from his dark eyebrows. Rivulets ran down his cheeks.

"Well, hell."

Carly snickered. "I guess it wasn't only cows I shook up."

He shot her a burning look. "I fail to see the humor."

She clamped a hand over her mouth to stifle a giggle. This time, it was Carly who laughed until she was weak.

*　　*　　*

After dinner that night, Hank got out the checkers game that he'd sneaked into the house when he came in from evening chores.

"You ever played?" he asked Carly.

She approached the table, staring curiously at the box. "Played what?"

Hank hadn't stopped to think that she'd never seen a checkerboard. "It's checkers—a board game."

"Checkers?" She jerked out a chair to sit down, planted her pointy elbows on the table, and watched in fascination as he opened the board and began setting out the chips. "Bess and Cricket used to play. All I could do was listen."

"Well, tonight, darlin', you get to play."

"Is it complicated?"

It was so easy it bored Hank to tears, but he didn't tell her that. "Not too complicated." He held up two chips. "What color do you want, red or black?"

"Red." She wiggled on the chair and sat straighter. "What are the rules?"

Hank explained the game. Minutes later, Carly was playing in earnest, growing so excited at times that she'd come clear off her chair. "I nailed you that time!" she'd cry. "I'm good at this, aren't I?"

As skilled as she became at the game over the course of the evening, she frequently got her colors confused and jumped Hank with his own pieces. The first time it happened, he was about to call her on it when he looked up and saw the proud smile on her face. Damned if he could bring himself to say a single word.

All his life, Hank had played everything to win. He'd been told, more than once by family members, that he was far too competitive. Winning wasn't everything, they said. What truly counted was how well you played the game. He'd never understood that philosophy. Why bother to play if you weren't out to win?

That was a question no one had ever answered to his satisfaction. Now Carly had without even trying. Watching her, hearing her laughter, he understood that winning really wasn't the important thing. Sometimes, it was far more rewarding to get trounced and be warmed by the victor's radiant smile.

At evening's end, Hank waited to grab a shower and brush his teeth until he heard Carly emerge from the shower. Then, wearing only his jeans, he padded barefoot through the house. Just as he reached the bathroom, the door flew wide open and Carly, wrapped in only a towel, came barreling out.

"Oh!" she squeaked, colliding with his chest.

"Oops." Hank grasped her bare shoulders to catch her from falling. "Sorry. I thought you were all finished."

"No, I—"

She broke off and looked up. Their gazes locked. Hank tried to release his hold on her, but somehow his hands didn't seem connected to his brain. She looked adorable with her hair caught up in a tousled knot at the crown of her head, and she felt even better—all soft and clean and moist from her shower. A faint scent of roses clung to her that made him want to bend closer to get a better whiff. And, *oh, God,* how badly he wanted to kiss her.

She stared for a seemingly endless moment at his chest. When she finally drew her gaze to his face, Hank saw the flutter of her pulse at the base of her throat, a telltale sign that she was as attracted to him as he was to her. Her thick, honey-tipped lashes swept low to veil her eyes, and whether she meant it so or not, her soft lips parted in invitation.

It seemed to him the very air went thick and electrical. He was aware of her in every pore of his skin. The towel provided precious little barrier between their bodies. He imagined it slipping to the floor, imagined running his hands over her silken flesh.

Perhaps he bent closer. Or maybe she read his intent in his eyes. Hank only knew she tried to twist away, her eyes sparking with recrimination. "Don't," she whispered. "Please, don't."

Beneath his hands, he felt her trembling. That was all the impetus he needed to release her. "Carly, I—"

She clutched the towel to her breasts and backed from the doorway. "Never again. You made a fool of me once. Wasn't that enough?"

She ducked into her room and slammed the door. Hank's heart was pounding. He went limp against the doorframe, not caring that the sharp edge of wood dug into his spine. He'd made a fool of her? Where in blue blazes had she come up with that?

Hank went to the closed bedroom door and curled his hand over the knob. There was no lock. He steeled himself against the urge to barge in.

"Carly, can we discuss this?" he asked.

"No! There's nothing to discuss. And if you ever start to kiss me again, I'm moving out."

He splayed a hand on the thick panel of wood that separated them. "As I recall, you enjoyed kissing me that night. I may be foggy on what followed, but I remember that, clear as rain." No response. "Am I wrong? Did you or did you not enjoy that part?"

"I enjoyed it. Satisfied? Stupid me. Just go away! Leave me alone."

He rested his forehead against the door. "If you enjoyed it, Carly, why does the thought of kissing me again upset you so?"

"Because!"

Because? That was an evasive reply if ever he'd heard one. "That doesn't tell me much."

"Too bad. It's all you're getting."

"Honey, please, can't we—?"

"No, we cannot! If you want a convenient body, go find one in town. Been there, done that. I told you up front, no sex. I meant it."

He'd gotten that message, loud and clear. He was also starting to suspect that her abhorrence of him stemmed from a hell of a lot more than the physical pain she'd endured at his hands. A convenient body? Hank started to argue the point—to tell her their encounter had meant more to him than that—but the words just wouldn't come. If he hadn't hooked up with Carly, he would have found someone else. Meaningless intimacy had been his weekend entertainment.

Don't tell me I'm beautiful, she'd pleaded on their wedding night. *You don't mean it.* He'd been bewildered then. Now he understood too well. She knew that their encounter had meant nothing to him and, by extension, that she'd meant nothing. The knowledge had wounded her in ways that might never heal.

Hank turned from the door to stand with his back against the wall. Now what? He was losing his heart to that girl in there—falling Stetson over boot heels in love with her. And she shuddered at the thought of letting him touch her.

He carried that knowledge with him to bed, and it remained at the forefront of his mind for a good part of the night, making him toss, turn, and get little if any rest. Along toward dawn, he finally went still to watch the first streaks of daylight touch the sky. *A new beginning,* he thought, wishing he and Carly could start over in much the same way, the darkness behind them, only blue skies ahead.

Only how? He couldn't undo what had happened that night. Life wasn't a blackboard. Mistakes couldn't be erased. All he could do was say he was sorry and beg her forgiveness.

As that thought slipped into Hank's mind, he stiffened. In the letter he'd written to Carly, he had expressed his heartfelt regret and asked her to forgive him. But what if she hadn't read the damned thing?

He sat bolt upright in bed. Even if she'd tried to read it, his handwriting wasn't the best. She had trouble enough deciphering printed letters, let alone sloppy cursive. *Of course* she hadn't read it. He was an idiot for thinking she had.

Hank swung out of bed and grabbed his pants. No apology. *Oh, God.* He remembered telling her he was sorry over the phone one night, but not at length or from the bottom of his heart. The only time since then that he'd even come close had been on their wedding night when he'd teasingly referred to himself as a jackass.

Truer words had never been spoken. He *was* a jackass.

Chapter Sixteen

"Wake up, sunshine. I've got a surprise for you." Carly fought her way up from sleep and tried to focus on the dark face hovering over hers—sky-blue eyes, a chiseled jaw line, a firm yet mobile mouth that tipped slowly into a grin that flashed strong, white teeth. *Hank.* She stiffened and came fully awake in a rush, recalling their encounter the previous night with an unpleasant rush of resentment.

Pushing up on one elbow, she said, "Is it lunchtime already?"

"Not quite." His grin broadening, he held up a plastic shopping bag with red lettering emblazoned on the front. "I hit every office supply store in town this morning and found a present for you."

She tried to see through the semitransparent sack. "What is it?"

"A surprise." He plopped the bag on the old coffee table. "You feelin' puny this morning, sweetheart?"

"Better now. I overslept, ate late, and felt sick when I first woke up."

"Did you have your morning sickness cure?"

She nodded.

"I'll get you some Seven-Up and crackers," he told her as he moved toward the kitchen.

Carly was sitting up by the time he returned. After what had happened last night, she felt self-conscious in only her nightgown.

As if he guessed her thoughts, he said, "You're fine." His lips thinned with derisive humor. "If ever I've seen modest sleeping apparel, that's it. You're covered from chin to toe."

He lowered himself onto a cushion beside her, set the glass of soda down, handed her the sleeve of crackers, and reached for the sack. "It's not a very exciting present, I'm afraid. But I thought it might help with your letter recognition." He drew two boxes from the folds of plastic. "I got two different styles, one a modified script of sorts, the other a more standard font." He winked at her. "Flashcards, darlin', one set with curlicues, the other without."

When he opened the first box, Carly was amazed. Without leaning close, she could see the bold black letter on top.

"Oh." A stinging sensation washed over her eyes. "What a thoughtful gift."

He glanced over, saw her tears, and said, "Damn, honey, don't cry. It's flashcards, not a diamond necklace."

It was the thought behind them that touched her—knowing he'd come up with the idea and spent half his day driving from store to store.

He dumped the stack of cards onto a large, tanned palm. Holding one up, he said, "Cool, huh? No more squinting. We'll have you recognizing letters in no time."

Carly nodded, her throat suddenly so tight that she doubted she could speak. Last night, she'd wanted to slug him for almost kissing her. Now she wanted to hug him for being so sweet. Her yo-yoing emotions worried her. When Hank set his mind to it, he could be a difficult man to resist.

She laid aside the crackers and reached for the Seven-Up.

"We'll keep them in alphabetical order at first," he told her as he held up the first card. "That'll give you a reference point as you learn to recognize the letters." He arched his thick, dark brows. "And the first one is?"

"I can study with them on my own, Hank." She had a four-year degree, and he meant to teach her the alphabet? "This is humiliating. I feel like a five-year-old."

He laughed. "Your visual cortex isn't very old, and flashcards work best when someone else does the flashing. I'll make the lesson X-rated for a grown-up lady. How's that?"

Flashing the A, he pushed to his feet, jerked his shirttails loose, and exposed his belly. "A, for abs," he said, tightening his stomach muscles to make ridges appear. Carly was fascinated. His dark chest hair began narrowing just below his ribs, becoming a thin line at the waistband of his jeans.

When he held up the next card, he winked and said, "B, for biceps."

He promptly stripped off the shirt to display his arms. Carly had felt the strength in them. She wasn't surprised to see bulges and ripples. She'd been so focused on his chest last night that she'd barely noticed his arms.

"You okay with this?"

Afraid that he might stop, she nodded stupidly.

"C, for chest."

He tensed and made his chest muscles flex. She yearned to lay a hand over a mound and feel it move under her fingers. His skin was as burnished as the old oak kitchen table—a deep, brown color, much darker than hers. Her stomach felt funny. She wondered if she was going to get sick after all.

He soon had her laughing at his Popeye imitation, but despite the hilarity, Carly still found herself staring. His upper body was beautifully sculpted. Until now, she'd never seen a well-muscled chest or arms that rippled with strength. It was an unsettling experience, to say the least.

All too soon to suit Carly, he held up one of the last cards. "X, for X-rated," he said with a lazy smile. "Not exactly beefcake, but I'm all that's available."

Hank Coulter was X-rated without even trying. Carly's gaze fell to his silver belt buckle. Then she realized where she was looking and blushed to the roots of her hair. His blue eyes darkened, the twinkle of laughter becoming a smoldering heat. For what seemed an endless moment, their gazes locked. Then he quickly flashed the remaining cards, laid them on the coffee table, and put his shirt back on.

Carly stifled a sigh. "Thank you, Hank. Your version of the alphabet is a lot more fun than mine."

"Don't take off," he said as he resumed his seat. "I'm not done with you yet. We'll go through them a second time."

Carly wasn't sure her heart could take the excitement. His smile faded as he readied the cards for another round. When he held up the A, his expression went utterly solemn. His beautiful eyes turned a dark gray blue, reminding her of how the sky had looked one evening a few weeks ago right before a storm.

In a low, husky voice, he said, "A, for ass. Would you like to brand it on my forehead? It occurred to me last night that I've never told you how ashamed I am of my behavior toward you that night at Chaps. No two ways around it, I was a world-class jerk."

Caught off guard, Carly didn't know what to say.

He held up another card. "B, for bastard. I'll have it engraved on my belt buckle if you'd like, and I'll wear the damned thing every day for the rest of my life. I've cheated you out of an entire year or more of sightedness." The shine in his eyes became a swimming wetness. His voice dipped even lower, the tendons in his lean cheeks bunching with each clench of his teeth. "I can't undo that—or even start to make up for it. When you go blind, it'll be my fault. I'd give my right arm to make amends, but there's no going back, no fixing it."

Carly had once believed this man was a self-centered playboy in a Stetson and Wranglers who cared about no one but himself. Now he had tears in his eyes.

She didn't want this. In his own way, he *had* made amends, and over the next couple of years, he would continue to do so. "Oh, Hank, don't. Please."

"C is for Casanova, creep, carouser," he went on relentlessly. "My weekend pastime, chasing women. You happened onto my hunting grounds, and I sighted in on you without a thought." He flashed the next card. "D, for dickhead, if you'll pardon my French. And it can stand for a number of other things as well, a dirty, rotten, lowdown skunk at the top of the list."

He tossed the cards on the table. When he looked at her, his expression conveyed far more than he seemed able to articulate with words. Finally he said,

"I told you how sorry I was in that letter I wrote. It occurred to me last night that you probably never read it."

Carly wished now that she had at least tried.

"I won't say I'm sorry about the baby," he went on. "It doesn't seem right for any father to ever say that. But I am sorrier than you'll ever know about how it happened." He touched her hair, the weight of his hand so light and careful that she knew he truly did ache with regret. "You deserved better, and if I'd been sober, I would have made damned sure you got it."

"Oh, Hank, what point is there in this?"

"Just let me get this said." His throat worked as he swallowed. "I've hurt you in ways I never realized until last night. Now you're afraid to be intimate with a man again." He pressed his hand more firmly to her hair, his long fingers sifting through the strands to feather over her scalp. "I wouldn't mind quite so much if it were only me you wanted to avoid, but I've got a bad feeling that isn't the case. Knowing I've ruined it for you with anyone else makes me heartsick."

Carly squeezed her eyes closed.

"It's not always awful, sweetheart. When you're with the right person, sex can be beautiful. Magical, glorious, and sweet beyond your wildest imaginings."

Carly lifted her lashes. She still couldn't think what to say. She only knew she couldn't bear to see that awful look in his eyes.

"I also need you to know that you *are* beautiful. I was drunk that night, I admit. But I still know beautiful when I see it. I was on the dance floor with another woman when I spotted you. That was it for me. I didn't see anyone else in the whole damned bar from that moment on."

She'd never really expected him to apologize, and certainly never this way. No excuses, no attempts to cast himself in a better light. These words came from his heart—and they came hard for him. Even she could tell that.

"Someday, some guy's going to take one look at you and fall crazy in love." He cupped her chin in his hand, trailing his thumb over the hollow of her cheek. "When it happens, don't let your memories of what I did ruin that for you. Take a leap of faith. Trust him. Grab hold of the magic with both fists. If you don't, I'll be standing at the pearly gates someday with the blame on my head."

"Hank, I—"

"Just listen. Please." He released her chin and passed a hand over his eyes. "I can't remember all of what I did. I only know I screwed up and hurt you, and I'm sorrier than I can say." He took a ragged breath. "Don't take every man's measure by me. If you make that mistake, you'll miss out on all the best things life has to offer."

Carly nodded. Words were beyond her.

He pushed to his feet. "Just one more thing."

She glanced up, wondering what else he could possibly say.

"After last night, I understand a little better how uneasy you are about living here with me. I know you may not feel inclined to believe anything I say on that count, but I've got to say it, anyway. You don't need to worry. I refused to lock myself down with promises when you asked me to before. I'll do that now. No sex, period, *ever*. If that's what it takes to make this next two years easier for you, honey, you've got my oath on it."

He grabbed his hat and left the house. Carly gazed after him, still reeling, not quite able to believe he'd apologized in such a heartfelt way, yet convinced he'd been absolutely sincere. It changed nothing, yet, oddly, for Carly it changed everything.

She covered her face with her hands. For the first time since that night, she allowed her thoughts to drift back, remembering little details she had refused to think about since. At first, she recalled things as she wished to recall them, casting herself as the hapless victim. But Hank's apology, tendered only minutes before, shamed her into taking a closer look at the sequence of events, not as she wanted to remember it, but as it had actually happened. How her whole body had tingled when he drew her up to dance. How they'd laughed together as he tried to teach her the steps. How he'd made light of her clumsiness and put her at ease, even when she stumbled over her own feet. How much she'd enjoyed talking with him at the table, how intently he'd listened.

All this time, she'd been blaming Hank for everything, accepting none of the responsibility herself. But in truth, as drunk as he'd been, he'd also been a gentleman. Maybe, if she were brutally honest with herself, she was even more to blame for what had happened than he was.

More than once during the evening, she'd thought about mentioning her blindness, but at the last second, she'd chickened out, afraid it would spoil things, that he'd drop her like spoiled fish. And she hadn't protested when he ordered her a mixed drink. She'd

known, deep down, that it was unwise to drink anything more when she'd taken pain pills. But she'd
thrown caution to the wind and consumed the alcohol anyway.

Her turn. Meeting him, spending time with him. It
had all seemed so magical. Was it really Hank's fault
that she'd been walking on clouds? Was it really his
fault that she'd been spinning dreams and wishing for
a fairy-tale ending? He hadn't forced her to stay outside with him. She'd willingly kissed him back, and
she hadn't protested when he led her to his truck.

From that moment on, who was really responsible
for what happened? Hank hadn't forced her to do
anything. Once again, she'd thrown caution to the
wind, wanting to grab hold of the experience and
enjoy every delightful second. At any point, she could
have told him that she'd never been with a man.
Knowing Hank as she did now, Carly believed he
would have stopped. He'd certainly stopped quickly
enough when she cried out in pain.

She stared at the flashcards where he had dropped
them on the table. B, for bastard? She couldn't leave
it at that. He shouldn't be made to feel guilty for the
rest of his life over a mistake that had been as much
her doing as his.

Hank had just wrapped a gelding's foreleg and was
exiting the stall when a faint, feminine voice rang out.
He glanced over his shoulder to see Carly silhouetted
in the wide doorway, surrounded by a nimbus of
golden sunlight.

"Hey," he said, setting the roll of tape on a shelf.
"What brings you to the spider's parlor?"

She laughed and stepped inside. She wasn't quite as

jumpy as she'd been during her first visit, but he saw
her cast a nervous glance at the horse to her right.
Touching the buttons of her blue blouse with nervous
fingertips, she said, "I, um, need to talk to you. Can
you spare me a few minutes?"

"Sure."

Levi emerged from the stable office just then. He
bade Carly a friendly hello. She smiled and exchanged
brief pleasantries. Then she fixed Hank with a pleading look. "I promise not to keep you long. But I'd
like to talk in private."

Hank grabbed his Stetson from a peg near the office
entrance. "No problem. I'm never so busy I can't
spare a few minutes for a pretty lady. Let's take a
turn down by the creek."

She fell into step beside him as they left the building. Hank couldn't fail to note the tense way she
hugged her waist. After working with troubled horses
for so long, he'd grown adept at reading body language. Hers signaled uneasiness.

Hank was worried about what she needed to talk
to him about. When they reached the stream, he led
her to a grassy knoll and gestured for her to have a
seat. Still hugging her waist, she declined and stood
instead, her gaze riveted to the ground. Taking his cue
from her, he shifted his weight to one leg, folded his
arms, and waited for her to spit it out.

"I, um, don't know how to start," she said shakily.

Hank's heart caught. He had a bad feeling she was
about to tell him she no longer wanted to live with
him. "Just start at the beginning, honey. If your take-
off's rough, you can back up and have another go."

She nodded. Then she glanced up. Tears glistened

in her eyes, and her mouth quivered at the corners. "It's really different being a blind teenager."

Where that had come from, he didn't know. But he sensed this was something she needed to say.

"In high school, I used to dream that a boy would call and ask me to the prom." With a humorless little laugh, she quickly added, "The most popular boy in school, of course. If you're going to dream, why not dream big? It wasn't about having a crush on someone. I was pretty much bewildered by that sort of thing. While Bess and Cricket were whispering and giggling about how cute boys were, I was struggling just to form an image in my mind of what boys looked like."

Hank swung his foot in a wide arc, smoothing the grass with his boot.

"What were biceps, I wondered," she went on tremulously. "And *where* were they? I could see only by touching, and no boys volunteered their bodies for exploration. Verbal descriptions pretty much left me confused. My only point of reference about relationships were stories, and those mostly fairy tales my mom read to me, thus my dream that the school prince would fall madly in love with me. I was the ugly duckling—the blind girl all the boys avoided."

Hank still didn't know where this was going, but he listened quietly, his heart catching at the pain he saw flit across her face.

"I remained apathetic about sex into adulthood. While studying to become a teacher, specializing in visually disabled students, I learned that that's normal for blind people. When most kids are becoming sexually aware, blind kids—well, they aren't. There are no visuals to stimulate them that way, and they don't mature sexually the same way other people do."

"I understand," he finally inserted.

She looked relieved. "Do you? It must be so difficult for a sighted person to imagine. I could touch my own body and get a general idea of how I looked, but boys were a mystery. I was so startled that night at Chaps when you came to my table. Aside from all the other physical differences that I'd already noticed while I studied you, I could scarcely believe how tall you were. Much taller than me—and bigger as well."

Hank grinned in spite of himself. "You studied me?"

"I watched you, yes. I, um—" Her cheeks flushed with embarrassment. "I don't know why you caught my attention, only that you did. I barely noticed the other men." She took a huge breath and exhaled with a self-derisive laugh. "Anyway, as you've probably guessed, my prince never came along in high school."

She stared off at nothing for an interminably long while, giving Hank the impression that there'd been at least one frog in her past. He couldn't erase his impression that she was leaving something very important out. Her eyes reflected a wealth of pain, but he forgot about that when she began talking again.

"In college, it was the same. No prince came along. I stopped hoping that he ever would."

When she looked at Hank again, her eyes were shining. "Then I went to Chaps with Bess," she said softly, "and suddenly there he was, smiling down at me and asking me to dance. It was just like I had always dreamed, only better, because I could finally see what all the giggling and whispering had been about. He said all the things I always dreamed he might—that I was beautiful, that he'd been waiting all his life for me. He made me feel as if I were the only woman in the room."

"Ah, Carly, I'm so sorry. I'd give anything to turn back the clock and be the prince you deserved."

She shook her head. "No, you don't understand. I knew you'd said all those things to countless other women, that they were only pick-up lines. Blind doesn't equate to stupid, after all, and a woman doesn't live to be twenty-eight without gaining some insight into the ways of the world. I *chose* to believe you, Hank. Do you understand? It was my moment— after so many years of waiting, it was finally happening to *me*. I didn't want to spoil it by mentioning my blindness. I was afraid you'd look at me differently or possibly walk away. I didn't want you to know that I'd never been with anyone, either. For that little bit of time, just for that one evening, I wanted to be like everyone else.

"I got my wish," she whispered. "You treated me no differently than you would have any other woman you met in a bar. You laid on the charm. You said all the things I wanted to hear. You danced with me. You bought me a drink. One thing led to another, and before the evening ended, we got in your truck. At any point, I could have said something. You've assumed all the blame for what happened that night, and until now, I've been content to let you. But the truth is, I waded in with my eyes wide open, both figuratively and literally. It isn't your fault that I pretended to be someone I wasn't—or that I got in over my head."

"Like everyone else?" he repeated.

For some reason, her saying that disturbed Hank

more deeply than anything. Momentarily forgetting
the hands-off policy, he drew her into his arms. For
an instant, she stiffened. But then she relaxed
against him.

Burying his face in her hair, he stood there, ab-
sorbing the feel of her softness and sorting through
the implications of what she'd said. When he thought
of all the women he'd met in bars, their faces blurred
in his mind. But he would never forget Carly's—the
look of wonder in her eyes, the sweet curve of her
mouth when she smiled, or the way she seemed to
glow with goodness.

God forbid that she should become like everyone
else. She was a very special person. The more Hank
came to know her, the more special he realized she
was.

That she would tell him this—he couldn't think
what to say to her. What bothered him most was that
he probably would have made polite excuses and
walked away if he'd known about her blindness. He'd
never preyed on virgins in his life. Yep, sure as rain,
he would have walked away. And if he had? Carly
might have returned to her table and gone home with
Bess, none the worse for the experience. Or some
other man might have come along to take up where
he had left off.

At that thought, Hank ran his hand through her
hair, a fierce surge of possessiveness making him want
to lock her in his arms and never let go. Just the
thought of someone else touching her made him
shake.

As badly as he'd messed up—and as much as he
regretted his mistakes—he couldn't regret that she was
there with him now. Maybe, just maybe, she would

come to care for him over time—as he had come to care for her—and she'd find it in her heart to give him another chance.

In that moment, Hank knew he'd fallen completely and irrevocably in love with her. What he'd initially decided to do out of a sense of obligation had turned into something far more. He just hadn't had the sense to recognize his heart's desire until it had been shoved right under his nose.

Now he couldn't bear to lose her. He knew it hadn't been easy for her to reveal her deepest feelings to him—or to admit that she'd deliberately pretended to be something she wasn't that night at the bar. Her sense of fairness was yet another thing about her to love.

He finally dredged up the will to release her from his embrace. Catching hold of her hand, he gestured at the grassy knoll. "Sit with me for a while," he urged, his voice so raspy he sounded like a toad.

She glanced at the stable. "I've already kept you from your work."

"Please. I need you to understand a few things, Carly, and it'll take a few minutes to explain."

She searched his gaze. Hank had no idea what she read in his eyes, but in hers, he saw nothing but her heart shining. And what a gentle heart it was. They stood there for several seconds, lost in the mire of their emotions, fingers interlaced, palms joined.

Finally she nodded her assent, and Hank led her to the knoll. They sat side by side, she with her arms looped around her knees, he with one leg bent, the other extended.

"My childhood wasn't as difficult as yours, but it was hard in other ways," he told her, his vision blurring as his mind traveled back through the years. "Not in the usual sense, with my folks fighting or my dad knocking me around. It was just hard being the son of a rancher. The bottom fell out of the beef market back in the seventies. We were small-time cattle producers compared to the huge conglomerates. When I was knee-high to a grasshopper, my dad was hard hit financially and had to lay off all his help. It fell on his shoulders and by extension his family's to keep this place in the black. I got up with my brothers at dawn and worked until it was time for school, and when I came home, I was back in the fields, busting my ass again.

"Things picked up as I grew older, but Dad had gone into debt to stay afloat, so the surplus income didn't go for luxuries. It went to pay off loans. Being the youngest boy, I was also the last to leave home, and as my brothers left for college, more and more work fell to me."

Hank rubbed a hand over his face and sighed. He could feel Carly watching him, but he couldn't quite bring himself to look at her.

"I was so damned excited when I graduated from high school. One more summer of busting my ass, that was all I could think, and then I'd be free." He smiled humorlessly. "Looking back on it, I feel ashamed for those feelings now. My dad needed me, and I couldn't wait to jump ship. Right after my graduation, he asked me to postpone college for a year. I remember being so pissed. The folks had put all my brothers through college with the help of financial aid. I'd always figured it'd be the same for me, and there he was, telling me money was tight. I didn't look at it rationally, from an adult perspective. I just felt put upon. Nevertheless,

I stayed on another year, working my ass off for nothing. At least that's how I saw it. He sure as hell couldn't afford to pay me, and I didn't see room and board as fair compensation."

"If you managed to get a degree, you must have eventually gone to school."

"Yeah, just a year late. When the following summer rolled around, I was champing at the bit. Couldn't wait to pack my shit and take off. I thought it'd be so much fun, living on campus—studying just hard enough to get passing grades, but mostly dating pretty girls and going to parties. That isn't how it went."

"What happened?"

Hank took off his hat and reshaped the crown. "You met my sister, Bethany. Just three months before I was finally due to leave for college, she was injured in a barrel-racing accident that June and became paralyzed from the waist down. My folks had insurance, but like yours, it didn't cover everything. And the doctors believed surgery might enable her to walk. My father would have given everything he owned and gone bankrupt to make that happen, and over the next year and a half, that's exactly what he did. Borrowed money, left the ranch unmanned to be at her bedside in Portland. That June, right after it happened, I was young, focused on what *I* wanted. I could have said to hell with college and stayed home to help out, but it was finally my turn to leave the nest, and I'd already given him an extra year. I figured one of my brothers could come home and man the fort for a while if it needed manning."

He smiled sadly. "It was *my* turn. You aren't the only one who's ever felt that way, Carly. I loved my folks, and I adored my sister, but I burned to leave, all the same. Being a kid, still wet behind the ears, I didn't have a mature grasp of the financial problems. All I knew was that it was my turn, and I was a year late getting to go. Fair was fair." He shrugged and smoothed a hand over his hair. "This ranch was a chain around my neck—a burned out piece of land that had sucked my father dry. I was going to set the world on fire, get a better place, be somebody. At that time, I didn't think much of my father. Just a poor, struggling rancher with old nags in the barn, worn-out equipment, and bills up his ass."

Carly could understand how he must have felt. At eighteen, most kids were pretty self-centered.

"After Bethany's accident, my father slowly got himself into such a bind he had to file bankruptcy." Hank stared across the pastureland at the forests. "He lost this ranch, lost everything. I had to work two full-time jobs to stay in college. Campus life wasn't a big party like I thought it'd be, needless to say. And when I finally got my pigskin, there was nothing to come back to. The Lazy J belonged to someone else. My folks didn't have a pot to piss in."

Carly followed his gaze, squinting to see into the distance. "If this place belonged to someone else, how on earth did you get it back?"

"Long story, happy ending. I grew up some during college. Had my head on straight. Or at least I thought I did. Jake and I wanted to go in partners and buy our own spread. The minute I graduated from OSU, I came back and went to work on any ranch that'd have me, saving every cent I earned to help kick in on a place. Work, work, and more work. I never had much time for fun. As it happened, the guy who'd bought the Lazy J couldn't make a go of it, and Jake and I were able to buy the place back for a song."

Hank smiled, remembering. "We'd both seen our father try to make it as a cattleman. We knew we needed an edge. Both of us were really good with horses, and we decided to raise our own line, plus start a training program for an additional source of income. We originally thought it'd be a secondary enterprise that would make us a little money on the side to stay afloat. As it turned out, the training program took off, and about a year ago, we were making more at that, by far, than we ever could have grossed just raising beef."

"Where are you going with this, Hank?"

"Bear with me. I'm getting there." He plucked a blade of grass and stuck it between his teeth. "When we started making really good money, things changed for me. For the first time in my memory, I had time to play—and I had money to buy myself a few toys, a fancy truck, a hand-tooled saddle, and other things I'd never been able to afford. I could also kick up my heels when the mood struck, and I went a little crazy for a while."

He forced himself to look at her.

"I was raised with a sterling set of values, but for a while there, I forgot everything my parents ever taught me." He tossed the grass away. "Instead of toeing the mark and walking the straight and narrow, I chose to break all the rules. I told myself I wasn't hurting anyone, certainly not myself. I honestly believed I was the same old Hank, that I was only having a little fun for a change. Where was the harm in that?

"Only I wasn't the same old Hank. Slowly, insidiously, the lifestyle and the people I called friends began to change me." A tight feeling moved into Hank's chest. "I just didn't realize how much I'd changed until I woke up in my truck one morning outside Chaps with a monster headache and dim recollections of a hot little blonde I'd met in the bar the night before."

He interlaced his fingers and popped his knuckles.

"When I first came around, I could barely remember her face. But as my brain started to track again, I remembered more and more in bits and snatches—how I'd spotted her and moved in for the kill, never once wondering or even caring about her feelings. She'd been something I wanted, plain and simple, and I was hell bent to have every damned thing I wanted. In my mind, she wasn't a person, just a body. And I set out to have her, feeding her all the standard lines, buying her a stiff drink to relax her and dull her inhibitions."

Hank stopped and grabbed for breath, finding it difficult to go on. But he forced out the words, telling Carly how sick he'd felt when he saw the blood on the seat of his truck. "It drove home to me, like a light exploding in my brain, that I'd changed more than I could begin to comprehend, and that I didn't like or respect the man I had become. I didn't even bother to get your last name. It wasn't important to me. Come morning, I never meant to see you again."

She glanced quickly away. "I already know it meant nothing to you."

"You're wrong, Carly. The next morning, it meant more to me than I can tell you. When had I stepped over that line, becoming a man who no longer respected the feelings of others? At what point did I stop caring if I knew anything at all about the women I had sex with? All I cared about was making sure it was safe sex, and with you, I didn't even bother with that."

She rested her chin on her upraised knees. "It no longer matters. You've apologized. I've apologized. We can't go back and change what happened. We can only go forward from here."

He shook his head. "If we don't learn from our mistakes, we don't grow. What I did that night was a harsh wake-up call. I was desperate to find you and couldn't. I had nightmares and woke up in a sweat, wondering if you were all right, if you were pregnant. I kept remembering your sweet face and big blue eyes. I've never felt so ashamed in my life. You may believe you did nothing to let me know that the bar scene and everything else was new to you, but the truth is, you gave me plenty of signals. I was just too drunk to pick up on them.

"My choice. People can blame their behavior on the alcohol, but the bottom line is, I was in full possession of my faculties when I took the first drink, I knew exactly how I wanted the evening to end, and what happened later was my fault, not yours. You say you waded in over your head? In my opinion, a lady, sexually experienced or otherwise, shouldn't have to worry about how deep the water is, not if she's with a man worth his salt."

His voice shook with the intensity of his emotions, and his eyes pleaded with her for understanding. Carly couldn't think what to say, so she settled for touching his hand.

Smiling sadly, he studied her face. "I've learned my lesson. I'll never play by those rules again, telling a woman anything she wants to hear just to seduce her. That said, I'd like to set the record straight on a couple of things."

"What's that?" she asked in a choked voice.

"You really were the most beautiful woman in the bar that night. Drunk or sober, I know beautiful when I see it. And when I saw you, I honestly did wonder where you'd been hiding all my life. Not everything I said that night was a line."

Heat pooled in Carly's cheeks. The emotions she read in Hank's eyes alarmed her, making her yearn for things that could never be. *Her turn.* She knew Hank was thinking they might start over fresh, getting it right this time. But she was a long-term lady, wrapped up in a short-term package. If she allowed herself to believe what she saw in his eyes, it could only end in heartbreak for both of them. This ranch was no place for a blind woman, and eventually she would be exactly that, a blind woman with no hope of ever seeing again.

In the city, blindness was easier to deal with. There were sidewalks and crosswalk lights and public transportation. She could have the house organized by professionals so she could easily find everything she needed. More important, she could come and go freely without help, holding down a job and taking care of the everyday things, like shopping and doctor appointments.

Hank lived on a huge ranch, miles from town, which would be rife with dangers for a blind woman. She'd be totally dependent on him every time she ventured from the house, and he had no inkling of how difficult it would be for him to keep the inside of that house organized just for her.

Carly was also very much afraid that his fledgling feelings for her stemmed from emotions other than love. She was pregnant with his baby, and, being an honorable man, he felt a strong sense of obligation. She also feared that he might pity her. She wanted no part of anyone's pity, least of all his. When and if she allowed herself to love a man, it would be for all the right reasons, not the wrong ones.

"Thank you, Hank," she finally replied. "It helps to know it wasn't all just a meaningless game."

He reached to push her hair from her eyes, his smile so tender that her heart caught. "Is there a possibility—even a remote one—that you'll give me another chance? You won't regret it, I swear. I don't make the same mistakes twice. Next time, I promise you, Carly, it'll be as perfect as I can make it."

Oh, how she wished she might say yes. "I think it would be better if we just work at becoming friends," she forced herself to say. Gesturing at their surroundings, she said, "I'm not cut out for ranch life. If we forge emotional ties, it'll only make it that much harder when it's time for me to go."

He fell quiet for a long while. Then he nodded. "All right. Friends, it'll be. Just know that the offer is always open if you should change your mind."

The way Carly saw it, she had no options. She pushed hurriedly to her feet. Brushing at the back of her jeans, she flashed what she hoped was a carefree smile. "Back to the salt mines. I need to study, and you've got work that needs doing."

Chapter Seventeen

As recently as a month ago, Hank would have laughed his ass off if anyone had told him he'd soon be married and glad of it. But every time he looked at Carly, that was how he felt. *Perfect for him.* The thought went through his mind, again and again.

On the Fourth, the entire Coulter clan and all those connected to the family, by marriage or by employment, gathered in the backyard of the main ranch house of the Lazy J for a picnic. Hank was provided with an opportunity to see his wife interact with members of his family, several friends, and all the ranch hands. All his brothers loved her, and she got along well with everyone else, even Shorty's cantankerous dog, Bart.

Running thirty minutes late, Hank's mother arrived bearing gifts for the baby—a sweater set, crocheted in variegated yellow, blue, and pink, and a pair of baby rattles, festively beribboned with pink and blue at the handles. When Carly saw the presents, her face flushed an alarming shade of scarlet.

Hank didn't blame her a bit for being embarrassed. They'd been married for exactly one week, she had no idea anyone knew about the baby yet, and the yard was teeming with people she barely knew. He stalked across the lawn, furious with his mother for being so insensitive. Fortunately, Carly recovered her composure by the time Hank reached her, and she defused both the situation and him by hugging Mary and thanking her.

"My mother crocheted," she said. "I felt so sad when I learned about the baby because I knew there'd be no pretty little sweaters and booties from Grandma. Now just look! Grandma is making things for my baby, after all."

Given the fact that Carly had probably never seen a baby sweater, Hank seriously doubted that she'd been wishing for one. But, true or not, the response was exactly what his mother needed to hear. Mary's eyes filled with tears, she beamed a huge smile, and promptly tugged a half-finished afghan from her bag.

"I'll have this finished soon to complete the ensemble."

Again, Carly made all the right noises, somehow managing to look pleased as punch.

A few minutes later, Hank drew her aside. "I'm sorry my mother did that. She just doesn't think sometimes."

"I was embarrassed at first, but then I decided it was silly. Things like this happen, and everyone would have found out soon, anyway. This way, we got it over with fast."

"I could wring Mom's neck." Hank looked out over the yard. In addition to his family, all the Kendrick clan had come, along with their Rocking K ranch foreman Sly Glass, who was married to Helen, Rafe Kendrick's mother-in-law. "She didn't mean to embarrass you. She's just happy about the baby and didn't stop to think."

"She's wonderful. And it's nice that she's so happy about the baby. Ever since I found out, I've been missing my mom so much. She was the first person I wanted to call when I tested positive. Now I've got your mom. She's a lovely substitute."

Hank was relieved to know she felt that way.

A few minutes later, his father drew him away from the gathering on the pretext that he wanted to see this year's crop of foals. En route to the pastures, Harv clamped a hand over Hank's shoulder and said, "Talk about the luck of the Irish. That girl's pretty as a picture and sweet to boot."

Hank nodded.

"You're coming to care for her, aren't you?"

"I'm in love with her, Dad." Hank reached the fence. After hooking a boot heel over the bottom rung and resting his arms on the top rail, he stared off at nothing. "I know it happened fast. I'm in so deep it scares the hell out of me."

"Do I take that to mean she doesn't return your feelings?"

Hank shook his head. "Just wants to be friends. That's a step forward, but it's nowhere close to where I want us to be."

Harv settled in beside him. "Friendship works. You'll get her there."

Hank wasn't so sure. "We had a long talk yesterday, and she's more relaxed with me now. But that's the only encouraging sign."

"Time's on your side."

"That's true. She's still bent on eventually dissolving the marriage, though. Says she isn't cut out for ranch life."

"Not everyone is," Harv conceded. "But there's

nothin' that says she has to be. Take Molly, for instance. She's a finance wizard. On the surface, her and Jake don't seem to have much in common. Couldn't be more different if they tried, in fact. But I can't recollect ever seeing a happier couple."

"Carly's a teacher. She wants to work with blind kids."

"She works with kids, you work with horses. You've got common ground."

"I never realized what an optimist you are. She's big city, I'm a country boy. She never even saw a horse 'til a week ago."

Harv mulled that over. "When it comes to love, I reckon I am an optimist. Look at your mama. Fell in love with her the minute I first clapped eyes on her. Couldn't have found a woman more different from me."

"You seem perfect for each other to me."

"We were like night and day at the beginning. I was a drinker and partier. She went to church three times a week, read her Bible atwixt and between, and swore lips that touched liquor would never touch hers. I think the girl starched her drawers."

Hank chuckled.

"I cussed like a sailor," Harv went on. "She wouldn't say 'shit' if she had a mouthful. For damned near the first six months of our marriage, I never saw her naked. Every time I got a twinkle in my eye, she turned off the lights and hid under the covers."

"Enough, Dad. I'm convinced my mother's still a virgin. Don't disillusion me."

Harv rubbed his jaw. "Yep. Pure as new snow, that's your mama." His mouth twitched at the corners. "My point is this. Different isn't always bad. Your

mother brought fine things into my life—added some
'pretty,' if you know what I mean—and straightened
me up in the process. Left me once, early on. For nigh
on a week, as I recall. I had it in my head I could still
drink and carry on like I always had, married or not.
I didn't trifle on her. Never that. But she wasn't sure
I hadn't."

"I never knew Mama left you."

"Oh yeah. Pregnant with Jake at the time. Had a
tummy out to here." He gestured with his hand.
"Wasn't easy, packin' her out of her daddy's house, I
can tell you that. Didn't weigh much over a hundred
pounds, fully clothed and soakin' wet, but it was
damned hard to get a good hold without hurtin' her,
especially with her hissin' and spittin', bound and determined not to go."

Hank stared incredulously at his father. "You force-
fully removed my mother from Grandpa McBride's
house?"

"She wasn't about to come home otherwise." Harv
cocked an eyebrow. "Your mama's stubborn, in case
you haven't noticed. Wouldn't listen to nothin' I said.
When she first left me, I got my mad up and told
myself I didn't care, but once my anger burned out, I
missed her like blue blazes. That brought me nose to
nose with reality. I couldn't live without her. What
choice did I have but to go after her? Little hellcat
blacked my eye before I got her settled down."

"Mom hit you?"

"Made me see stars. Her fist is a perfect fit for my
eye socket."

"I never would've thought it. Mom's not the physically violent type."

"She's not so inclined as a general rule. But she was

flat pissed that afternoon. I think she would've stomped me flat if she'd been packin' a little more ballast."

"No wonder Grandpa had a problem with you."

Harv laughed. "By then, your grandpa knew how much I loved her, son. When I showed up, ready to fight buzz saws and win, he already had her bags sittin' on the porch. While he helped me load 'em in the truck, he said all newlyweds went through an adjustment period, and if I wanted to keep my Mary, I'd best start doin' a heap of adjustin'."

"In other words, you were the one who had some changing to do."

Harv nodded. "Even with all the changin', though, your mother and I are still mighty different. She came my way a little. I went her way a lot. We met somewhere in between. To this day, I can't really say I understand how her mind works more'n half the time, and she'd probably say the same of me. Life is full of surprises. I like it that way, and so does she."

Hank sighed. "It's weird, hearing stories like that. I can't remember you and Mama having a single fight."

"If you'd been me, would you have fought with her again?"

Hank thought about it. His father outweighed his mother by a fair hundred pounds and could have knocked her flat with one blow of his fist. "No, I don't guess I would. Doesn't sound like she fought fair."

They fell quiet for a time, both of them grinning sheepishly. Finally, Harv asked, "Where was I? I've flat forgot."

"I think you were trying to tell me that a few changes might swing the vote in my favor. Ordinarily, that might work, but Carly has a problem with my being a rancher. A man can't change the basic package."

"Nope. But he can sure as hell wrap it up in prettier paper." Harv patted Hank's shoulder and straightened away from the fence. "You'll coax her around to your way of thinkin', son. You're a Coulter, aren't you?"

As much as Carly enjoyed the Fourth of July picnic, she was weary by early evening and more than ready for a relaxing drive into town to see the fireworks. An hour after the picnic mess was cleared away, practically everyone who had attended the party was parked along the lakeshore, the pickups backed in toward the water for optimal viewing.

"The Kendrick/Coulter version of a tailgate party," Hank said.

Carly sat with Hank in the bed of his truck, their backs braced against the cab. He'd brought along two army blankets, one folded beneath them for padding, the other draped over their outstretched legs to ward off the chill that always descended after dark at such a high altitude. To their right, Rafe and Maggie Kendrick, Bethany's brother-in-law and his wife, were awaiting the display in much the same fashion, except that they were snuggling like newlyweds while their two children napped inside their vehicle. To Carly and Hank's left, Bethany and her husband Ryan were perched on the open tailgate of their Dodge, their son Sly asleep in the cradle of Ryan's arm.

"How come Ryan and Bethany named their son after a ranch foreman?" Carly asked.

Hank smiled. "Sylvester Glass is a great old fellow. Ryan thinks of him as a second father, and Bethany fell in love with the old fart shortly after she married Ryan. I guess they wanted to honor him."

"Ah." Carly liked the fact that the wealthy Kendricks weren't so high on themselves that they looked down on their employees. "That's nice." She sighed and added, "It's fun, knowing everyone who's parked around us."

Hank narrowed his gaze on his brother Jake and sister-in-law Molly, who'd spread a blanket on the ground down by the water, their son Garret soundly asleep beside them. "If that situation warms up, you may change your tune."

Carly squinted to see. Then she giggled. As blurry as her vision was at a distance, she could see that Hank's older brother was passionately kissing his wife. "Uh-oh."

Hank grinned. Then he yelled, "Jake! None of that in public."

Jake merely cocked the brim of his Stetson to impede Hank's view. Not wishing to infringe on the couple's privacy, Carly averted her gaze, only to discover that Rafe and Maggie were also sharing an intimate kiss.

"My goodness."

Hank chuckled. "You get embarrassed about being seen with 'em, just holler. I'll loan you my hat."

She glanced up at his Stetson. "What earthly good would that do?"

"You can tip it down over your face so nobody sees it."

"No way. The fireworks might start."

"Seems to me they already have." He drew up a knee. "You comfy?"

She shifted. "Except for the metal ridge poking my shoulder blades."

He glanced behind her. "Damn. It is jabbing your shoulder blades. I'm taller. Doesn't bother me." He drew away the blanket and bent both knees. "Sit between my legs. I make a great backrest."

Carly glanced at the fly of his jeans. "I'm fine right here."

"Don't be silly. Come on."

She didn't think it was a good idea. But he kept insisting, and she didn't want him to think she was afraid to be close to him. As she settled between his spread knees, he slipped a hard arm around her waist, which made her leap with a start. She felt his chest jerk with laughter.

"Relax. We're surrounded by people." He splayed his hand over her ribs. "If I'm gonna make a move on you, do you really think I'd do it here?"

As she recalled, he hadn't let the presence of others stop him once before. Her trepidation mounted slightly when he flipped the blanket back over them, hiding both her and his hand from view.

"No funny stuff. I promise," he assured her.

Just to be sure, Carly curled a hand over his broad wrist, which made him laugh again. "You don't trust me any farther than you can throw me."

"It's not a question of trusting you," she replied.

The instant the words left Carly's mouth, she knew they were true. She had come to trust Hank. She just wasn't at all sure she could trust herself. That night outside the bar, she'd responded to him with heedless abandon, her inhibitions swept away by the feelings he evoked within her. Now that they'd talked and resolved so many of the issues between them, what was to say she wouldn't respond to him that way again?

He removed his hat and rested his cheek against her hair. His breath sifted through the strands, tickling her ear. Carly's lashes swept low, and a delicious languor stole over her. It was lovely, being held by him. Even as darkness fell and closed around them, she felt absolutely safe.

She heard Bethany giggling. Then the deep timbre of Ryan's voice carried to them through the night. Bethany giggled again. "Ryan, *stop* it. What if Sly wakes up?"

"We should have parked by my folks," Hank said with a disgruntled sigh. "Strike that. They're probably fooling around, too."

Carly thought it was lovely to see married people still so deeply in love. They all seemed so happy, which had the perverse effect of making Carly feel sad. Would she ever experience love like that—or anything even close?

"You okay?" Hank asked.

"I'm fine," she said brightly.

"Now that it's dark, it shouldn't be long before the show starts."

His voice rumbled in his chest, treating her shoulder blades to tingling little shocks of sensation. Under the blanket, he tightened his arm around her. Then, using his free hand, he trailed his fingertips over her arm, seeking out sensitive spots she hadn't realized she had. When he reached the bend of her elbow and began circling lightly over the sensitive skin there, she shivered and nearly moaned in delight. Dangerous thoughts slipped into her mind—thoughts of his hands touching her like that everywhere.

She was about to ask him to stop when she heard a distant boom, like the discharge of a cannon. Hank's breath stirred her hair as he said, "Ah-hah. Here it comes, sweetheart. Feast your eyes on your first fireworks display."

The sky lit up with colorful bursts of light, the patriotic spray of red, white, and blue so brilliant that Carly forgot all about the way he'd been touching her. "Oh, my goodness! Our flag! Oh, how *beautiful*! What a perfect way to begin. Sometimes I forget the Fourth is Independence Day. We should all be thinking of the sacrifices that made our freedom possible." Another burst of patriotic color lit the sky. "Oh, *Hank*! Just *look* at that."

"You like it, do you?" Against her hair, she felt his lips curve in a smile. "It is beautiful. Isn't it? I'm always amazed at what they can do."

"Another flag. I can't believe it," she whispered as the design began to disintegrate.

He drew her more snugly against him, his hand shifting slightly on her ribs but not actually moving. Carly relaxed, her gaze fixed on the sky until the last bursts of light faded away.

A booming sound came again. "Here comes another one."

Carly rested her head in the hollow of his shoulder. When the third display filled the sky, she marveled at the colors and brilliance that streamed through the darkness. It wasn't just her first fireworks display, she decided, but the very first time she'd ever really experienced the Fourth of July in the same way other people did.

"I'm going to remember this night for the rest of my life," she told Hank softly.

"Me too," he whispered. "Me too."

*   *   *

Over the holiday weekend, Hank began to fear that Carly's sight was growing worse at a faster rate than she was willing to admit. On Saturday at lunch, she reached for her glass and knocked it over. Later that day, he caught her peering at things as though trying to make them out. On Sunday evening as he passed the open doorway of her bedroom, he saw her holding her hand at arm's length, staring at her splayed fingers. He couldn't imagine how horrible it must be for her, knowing that darkness might soon return.

Troubled by the thought, Hank got on the computer up at the main house the next morning to surf the Net, then visited the Crystal Falls library that afternoon. After doing some research on lattice dystrophy and the sighted blind, he was better able to understand Carly's disease, the surgical procedures that would hopefully restore her sight, and the problems she was having with her visual cortex.

The fact he discovered that most amazed him was that lattice dystrophy could be extremely painful, making the eyes hurt nearly all the time, especially when exposed to bright light. Bess had told him about that, and he'd tried at first to be considerate, but with Carly never mentioning the eye pain, he'd forgotten over time. Hank remembered how raptly she'd watched the fireworks at the lake, barely taking her eyes from the sky for fear she'd miss something. He suspected that the bright bursts of light had caused her pain, but she hadn't let on or closed her eyes to spare herself discomfort. *I'll never forget this night,* she'd whispered.

No guarantees. That was another fact Hank verified as he researched her disease. The second surgery might restore her sight, but then again, it might not.

Dozens of different things could go wrong, and it was entirely possible that Carly might never see another fireworks display. That was why she'd endured the bright flares of light and stared unblinkingly at the sky. Each day of sight truly was a precious gift.

Hank intended to take her to the Portland Zoo on Tuesday, the fifteenth, but that was a week away. In the meantime, he didn't want her to be cooped up in the cabin with her nose stuck in a book. She needed to be going places, seeing things, and making memories, not wasting this precious time trying to train a visual cortex she had no guarantee she'd ever be able to use.

Hank cornered Jake in the stable on Tuesday morning. "I need to take some time off," he told his brother.

Jake left off working with a colt. After closing the stall door, he said, "It's our busiest time of year, Hank. I don't need to tell you that."

Hank swept off his hat and slapped it against his leg. "I know it's a hell of a time to leave you in the lurch, but I don't have a choice. I'll do as much as I can around here, Jake, but for the most part, I need to be freed up."

As briefly as possible, Hank explained his reasons. "Except for Portland and a tour of the Crater Lake area, we'll do mostly day trips. I'd like her to see as much as she possibly can before the lights go out. You know? Even a few day hikes would be better than nothing. She's probably never clapped eyes on a waterfall or watched the sun go down over the Cascades. I want her to have those memories."

His expression solemn, Jake finally nodded. "I'll cover for you."

"I appreciate it. I know I'm putting you in a hell of a spot. But it's something I've got to do. By this time next week, she could be blind. I have no way of knowing."

"Go. I'll call Dad and ask him to help out. He'll enjoy working with the horses. We'll handle it."

Hank retreated a step. "Thanks, big brother. I owe you one."

Carly was getting a drink of water when she heard the front door open. By now, she recognized the distinctive rhythm of Hank's stride as he crossed the living room.

"Carly?" he called. "Where are you, honey?"

"Right here." She stepped out from the kitchen. "Is something wrong?"

He flashed that slow, lazy grin that never failed to make her insides tingle. "No, Mrs. Coulter, everything's absolutely right." He gestured at her sandals. "Get your sneakers on. We're going for a drive."

"Where to?"

"I don't know yet. Someplace special."

The mischievous expression on his face made her smile. "You don't know, but it's someplace special? How does that make sense?"

"Doesn't have to make sense. I'm taking some time off so we can go see some sights."

Carly understood then, and knowing what he had in mind made her heart pang. "You can't take off work. We have so many expenses coming."

"How many times do I have to tell you I'll worry about the finances? Go get your shoes on. Grab a sweater, too, just in case we get back late. I don't want you taking a chill."

Carly hurried into the bedroom, excited to be going somewhere. They were going to see some sights! *Yes*. She doubted there were that many things to see around Crystal Falls, but just visiting a few places would be fun.

That afternoon, Hank took her to the high desert. After he parked the truck on an old dirt road, Carly stared across the barren expanse of flatland, wondering why he had stopped. All she saw were clumps of sage and dirt.

"Isn't that beautiful?" he asked softly.

Carly realized he was staring off at the horizon. She followed his gaze and saw nothing but an indistinct red blur. *Oh, God*. He'd taken off from work, driven for miles, and wasted gasoline, all so she could see something pretty, and now she couldn't.

Carly almost told him. Only she couldn't bring herself to do it. This was his gift to her. It didn't matter if she could enjoy it. What counted was the thought behind it.

"Oh yes," she said. "That's *gorgeous,* Hank."

"The country's not much, but the rock formations out here are fantastic."

"They sure are."

"That one's called Old Man."

"Ah. I can see why," she said.

She felt him studying her. "Can you see clearly enough to make out his face and—stuff?"

"Hmm." She forced a smile and nodded. "Yes, I do see his face."

Watching her, Hank knew she was lying, not because she failed to pull it off with aplomb, but because she wasn't blushing to the roots of her hair. Old Man, the formation before them, truly did look like an old man lying on his back. One could see the clear outline of his facial profile at one end, his toes poking up at the other, and midway in between, a certain part of his anatomy was prominently displayed.

Just to be certain he wasn't misreading the situation, he said, "Mother Nature is really something. You'd swear it was a man standing there. I can even see his belt buckle."

When she nodded and beamed another smile, Hank's heart sank. "You're right!" she exclaimed. "I do see his belt buckle."

"Carly?"

"Hmm?"

She turned those beautiful blue eyes on him. Looking into them, Hank could scarcely believe that they were diseased. They were as clear as deep pools of blue water.

"You can't see the rock at all, can you?" he asked.

A stricken expression crossed her face. She caught her lower lip in her teeth and slowly shook her head, her eyes going bright with tears. "I'm sorry. You drove all this way and took off work. I'm so sorry."

She was sorry? She was the one going blind, damn it, not him. *Why?* It just wasn't fair. He doubted she'd ever done a wrong thing to anyone in her life.

"We need to talk," he said firmly. "You haven't been leveling with me about your eyes. If your sight has gotten that bad, why haven't you said something?"

She stared blankly out the windshield, her face taut and pale. Hank wondered how far into the distance she could see.

"I've been—I don't know—kidding myself, I guess." She placed her hands on her thighs and bunched them into tight fists. "Hoping it might stop, telling myself it

wasn't that bad yet. As for why I didn't say anything—"
She broke off and swallowed convulsively. "When you
say things out loud, they seem more real, not just secret fears anymore. I didn't want it to be true, so I
just kept quiet, hoping it might get better."

Hank ached to gather her into his arms.

She bent her head, brushed at her jeans, and then
plucked at the denim as though removing specks of
lint. "And I feel so guilty."

"Guilty? For what?"

She went back to staring out the window. "I knew
from the start that I might go blind during my pregnancy, but I never dreamed it'd happen this fast. In a
few months, maybe, and I hoped I wouldn't go totally
blind, even then. Some pregnant women get lucky,
and I so wanted to be one of them."

Hank could completely understand her having that
hope. Who wouldn't? But he still wasn't clear on why
that made her feel guilty.

"It doesn't appear that I will be," she said. "All
indications are that I may go blind very quickly. Sad-
dling you with a blind wife for a few months was one
thing, but now it looks as if you'll be saddled with one
for a year or longer. I told you once how difficult it
would be, that blind people have all kinds of special
needs. You said everything would be okay. But I don't
think you comprehend what you've gotten yourself
into."

"You feel guilty because you're afraid you'll be a
burden on me?" he asked incredulously.

She nodded. "If I'd known it would happen this
fast, I never would have—"

"Hold it." Hank reached out to grasp her chin and

make her look at him. "Don't even go there, sweet-heart. I went into this with my eyes wide open."

"How could you possibly? You had no idea it would happen this fast, and you've got no clue what you're in for." She twisted her face from his grasp. "The kitchen cupboards, for instance. Right now, they're arranged any old which way, and you can put things back wherever there's space. When I go blind, nothing can be out of place. *Nothing.* And that's just for start-ers. You throw your clothes on the floor. You kick off your boots and leave them lay. You pull chairs out and don't put them back. When my sight goes, I won't be able to live like that."

Hank had never considered just how much he would have to change in order to make this arrangement work. "You won't have to live like that," he assured her. "I'll become a neat freak."

She laughed shakily, which told him she was peril-ously close to tears. "You, a neat freak?"

"I'm not that old a dog. I can still learn a few new tricks. It'll be a simple matter of organizing everything so you can find it and changing my habits."

"I never meant to make you live that way for months on end."

"What was the alternative? As I recall, I didn't offer you a choice."

"I should have stood firm and refused to marry you. You never would have taken my baby away from me, Hank. Now that I've gotten to know you better, I feel silly for ever having believed you might."

Hank smiled sadly. "So you've got my number now, do you?"

"Yep, just like those silly chickens that won't go

into cardiac arrest when you chase them. You're a big love, just like Sugar and Sonora Sunset. And knowing you are makes me feel even worse. It's one thing to make a not-very-nice person miserable. It's quite another when he turns out to be one of the most wonderful people you've ever known."

That she'd come to think so highly of him meant more to Hank than he could say. "Thank you for that," he said huskily. "That's one of the nicest things anyone's ever said to me."

"I'm just so sorry for doing this to you," she whispered.

"Shit happens. I'd give anything for you to be able to see all through this pregnancy, but it doesn't look like it's going to happen."

"No," she agreed, the word trembling from her lips on a weary sigh.

"That being the case, let's get a few things straight. No matter how difficult it may be to live with a blind person"—he smiled and winked to soften those words—"I won't think of it as a burden. I knew from the start that you might lose your sight very quickly. I pray to God you aren't blind for a year, but if you are, we'll deal with it."

"It's not going to be easy."

Nothing worth having came easy. "Does that mean it won't be boring? I hate boring."

She laughed wetly. "Nope. It definitely won't be boring."

"Good."

They fell silent and simply looked at each other for a long moment. Then she said, "I think it's important to keep a positive attitude. Mind over matter, and all that."

Hank was all for her keeping a positive attitude. If anyone had the strength of will to beat the odds, it had to be her. "Damn straight. If the lattice suddenly backs off, you may still be able to see when you're nine months along." He winked at her again. "Except for your toes, of course. I have it from a credible source, my sister-in-law Molly, that pregnant ladies can't see their toes the last three months."

She laughed. "Being able to see my toes is the least of my concerns."

"I know." He gave her hand a final squeeze. "No more worrying. If your sight goes, we'll organize the house. It shouldn't take but a few days."

"Shouldn't we start on that now?"

"Hell, no. We've got sightseeing to do."

She gestured at the horizon. "I can't see the sights, Hank."

He cranked the ignition. "That only means I need to get closer."

When he took off across open country, Carly grabbed the dash. "There's no road!" she said with a laugh.

"That's the beauty of a four-wheel drive, darlin'. We don't need a road." He smiled over at her. "I'll take it slow. If it gets too bumpy for comfort, holler."

Carly was bouncing from her seat, but the cushioned upholstery provided her with a soft landing. Even if it hadn't, she wouldn't have asked him to stop. She was going to see the rock formation, after all.

A few minutes later, she could finally make out the craggy red rock, cast against a clear, powder-blue sky. "Oh!" she cried, her awe heartfelt this time. "How pretty! And it *does* look like an old man. He's lying on his back."

Hank chuckled. "That's right."

She fixed her gaze on the formation again. "I can see his toes poking up. And his knees." Her voice trailed away, and her cheeks went pink. "It really does look like a man lying there. Doesn't it?"

"Yep, all parts of one. Now I know you can see him. You're blushing."

From there, Hank headed east. Carly got to see a herd of deer along the road, which was exciting. Later they passed a group of antelope, which were close enough for her to make out. Then, just when she thought she'd seen it all, Hank slammed on the brakes and pointed to the top of a power pole.

"Bald eagle," he said.

Carly leaned forward to see. "Ohmigosh! Isn't he beautiful?" She cast Hank a bewildered look. "He's not bald. I thought they were featherless on top."

He burst out laughing.

At dusk, Hank stopped at a roadside café and got them sandwiches. A few minutes later, they ate while watching the sun go down over the desert. Carly had seen few things so spectacular. As the sun dipped low, it sent shafts of brilliant white light through the fluffy white clouds that were gathering on the horizon. Moments later, the entire sky turned a beautiful shade of dusty rose.

Pocketing a bite of food in her cheek, she said, "Thank you for bringing me here, Hank. This is magnificent."

"Enjoy," he said softly. "It won't last long."

He was right; the sunset didn't last long. But she knew she'd have a memory of it for the rest of her life.

As full darkness descended, Hank settled back and asked, "What's it like?"

His voice was so husky and thick with sadness that Carly immediately knew what he was asking about. "It's not real bad yet—sort of like looking through lightly steamed glass or a thin fog."

He said nothing, just sat there, a black shape in the darkness.

"I'm going to be all right, Hank. I'm used to being blind."

"I know you'll be all right, honey. I just wish God would give us a miracle."

"Maybe he will. If not, I think it'll be easier this time. Before, I had never seen the sky or the stars. When people spoke of a beautiful sunset, I couldn't picture it. What did pink look like? What did blue look like? I had no idea. Now I've seen a lot of things, and I'll have all those images in my mind."

Hank meant to make sure she saw a lot more things before her sight went. *Images in my mind.* Those words whispered inside his head all the way home. He had no idea how much longer she'd be able to see. He only knew they were going to make every second count.

Chapter Eighteen

For the remainder of that week and through the weekend, Carly came to feel like a vacationer with only a few days left to play. Hank took her for long drives to see everything in the area—rivers, snow-capped mountain peaks, forested high lake areas, and quaint lake resorts. They picnicked in grassy meadows dotted with dandelions and clumps of clover, napping afterward on the wool army blanket he kept in the truck. At other times, they dined in unique restaurants overlooking streams and lakes so she could enjoy the views even while she ate. When the vistas were too far away for her to see them clearly, Hank went to incredible lengths to get her closer.

For Carly, it was a magical interlude before darkness fell—a time for mischief and laughter and harmless flirtations with an incredibly handsome man who never pressed her for more. Holding hands. Wrestling and playing tag. Walking through the forest when the earth was dappled with sunlight. Dancing with only the wind to provide them with music.

Sometimes, at particularly pretty viewpoints, they'd find a comfortable place to sit and remain there for an hour or more, drinking in the panoramic vistas. During those stops, Hank pointed out things that

Carly might have missed—the spots on a fawn, a squirrel clinging to a branch, or clouds shaped like animals. During those lulls, he sometimes held her hand and toyed with her fingers. At other times, he'd casually drape an arm over her shoulders, his hand lightly caressing her skin through her blouse.

In those first three days, Carly cataloged countless memories of the world around her. She saw one of the largest obsidian flows in the world, a lava bed that stretched forever, and a spectacular view of Central Oregon from the top of Shoshone Peak. She couldn't see as far into the distance as she would have liked, but all that she could see was beautiful. She had to be content with that.

After touring the immediate area, they ventured farther afield, traveling the scenic Highway 101 into northern California to see the Redwood National Park. From there, they went to Crater Lake, where they spent a day hiking the trails to incredible viewpoints and taking a boat tour so Carly could clearly see Wizard Island.

With the passing of each idyllic moment, Carly became more achingly aware of Hank physically—of his height and breadth, of the way the muscles in his back and arms stretched his shirt taut when he moved, of the lazy, powerfully fluid shift of his lean hips as he walked. She found herself recalling that morning when he'd stripped off his shirt and posed for her—and she yearned to see him that way just one more time.

After Crater Lake, they cut across to Lake Lemolo, rented a small chalet by the water, and spent the evening in the quaint little resort bar, enjoying hamburgers for supper, drinking Seven-Up, and dancing to jukebox music long into the evening.

Carly had almost forgotten how charming Hank could be on a dance floor with music thrumming to titillate her senses. During his favorite ballads, he sang along, his voice so honey-rich and deep it seemed to move clear through her. She loved being held close in his strong arms—feeling the heat of him all around her. She enjoyed his large hand at her waist or back as they swayed with the music. Slow melodies, fast beats. She loved it all.

As the hour grew late, she found herself wishing she could capture the evening in a bubble and make it last forever—that she could do as Hank had once advised and grab hold of the magic with both fists.

"Penny for them," he whispered, his blue eyes delving into hers.

"What makes you think I'd ever sell out so cheap?"

"A nickel, then. Why so solemn? You must be thinking some pretty heavy thoughts."

She was thinking dangerous thoughts—things she didn't dare share with him. Over the last few days, she'd let down her guard, and the unthinkable had happened. She'd fallen wildly in love with him.

"I'm just tired."

He spun her in a slow circle. "Well, we can't have that, little mama. Let's call it an evening and get you home to bed."

When the music ended, he paid their tab, draped her sweater over her shoulders, and led her from the building. A cool night wind blew in off the lake, the air carrying with it the scent of water and pine. As they passed under a pine with low-hanging bows, Carly tugged on his hand to make him stop.

Just this once, she wanted to share a passionate kiss

in the moonlight—and she wanted to see the handsome man who kissed her.

"What?" he asked.

The request was there, hovering on her tongue. *Would you kiss me, Hank? Just this once? A deep, passionate, mind-boggling kiss. Think of it as one for the road.* Only when she looked up at him, she knew it could never end with only a kiss. She wanted so much more, *needed* so much more—and if she opened that door, she might never be able to close it.

So instead of asking him to kiss her, she said, "Listen. Isn't that a beautiful sound?"

He cocked his head. "The night wind, whispering in the trees," he said, his firm lips shimmering in the moonlight. "I've always loved it."

She nodded, staring hungrily at his mouth, remembering the feelings he'd evoked within her the last time they kissed.

"You okay?" he asked.

"I'm fine," she said with a sigh. She tipped her head back to gaze at the sky. "Uh-oh. I hope it's not going to rain. No stars."

Hank joined her in perusing the zenith of dark blue above them. The heavens were filled with brilliant stars. Carly just couldn't see them. "Just a little cloud coverage," he lied. "It'll pass over."

"Oh, I hope so. Today was so much fun. If it rains, it'll spoil everything."

"No rain, I promise." He drew her back into a walk. "Come on, pretty lady. It's time to get you to bed. Tomorrow will be a busy day."

He felt her hesitate as they left the asphalt and ventured onto uneven ground. Because they'd been dancing only minutes before, he didn't hesitate to slip an arm around her waist. "Careful through here. The ground's pretty rocky."

She leaned more of her weight against him. In the moonlight, Hank could see her staring intently ahead, her eyes wide. He knew she could see very little in the darkness. Tomorrow the sun would bathe the world with light again, and she'd be able to see once more. Perhaps not clearly, but she'd still be able to see. Soon, though—far too soon—not even the sunlight would help.

Once at the chalet, Carly stood at the center of the small living room, looking at him with questions in her eyes. If she'd been any other woman, Hank might have hoped she was issuing a silent invitation.

"What?" he asked.

She hugged her waist, smiled faintly, and shook her head. "Nothing."

She was so damned beautiful. Dressed in jeans and a simple white blouse, with her hair tousled from the night wind, she was, hands down, the prettiest thing he'd ever clapped eyes on.

"Can I tell you something?" he asked.

Her cheek dimpled in a smile. "That depends. If it's bad, I don't want to hear it. Why ruin a perfect day?"

He laughed and bent his head. When he looked up again, she was watching him expectantly. "You're beautiful. No lie, darlin', just fact."

She rolled her eyes and blushed.

"No, seriously." Hank slowly closed the distance between them. "You have to know I'm not just saying it." He caught her chin on the crook of his finger and lifted her face. "No hokey pick-up lines. We've got an agreement. I won't break it. I just need for you to know. You're so beautiful."

Her eyes went bright with tears. "Thank you. You're not bad, either."

He'd received more flattering assessments, but none of those counted now. All that mattered was what she thought. "Thank you," he said huskily.

She trailed her gaze over his face. "I'm no expert, mind you. But you're the handsomest man I've ever seen."

He laughed. He couldn't stop himself. "And how many have you seen?"

"Not many compared to most women. I am an expert on auras, though."

"On what?"

"*Auras.*" Her mouth curved into an impish smile. "It's the essence of a person. It creates a field around you."

"Really?" Normally, Hank might have discounted that as malarkey, but Carly had been blind all her life. It was entirely possible that she'd sharply honed all her other senses to make up for her lack of sight. "What's my aura like?"

She cupped a hand to his cheek. "Kind. Warm. I felt safe with you that very first night. Even while we were dancing, you put off really nice signals."

"Did I, now?"

She nodded. Then, lightly trailing her fingertips over his mouth, she whispered, "You still do."

Hank stood there, trying to decipher the meaning behind that, as she left the room. He stared after her, a part of him convinced she had just given him the proverbial green light, another part wondering if he

had lost his mind. If she'd meant it that way, she
wouldn't have skedaddled so fast.

He headed upstairs, stripping off his shirt as he
went. *Nice signals.* What the hell did that mean?

Carly listened to Hank go up the stairs. Then she
quickly slipped on her nightgown and dove under the
covers. The chalet was equipped with several beds.
He'd given her the downstairs bedroom, which sported
only one, a king-sized monstrosity that made her feel
horribly small and alone, like a postage stamp stuck
on one corner of a business envelope. She stretched
out a hand to skim the sheet beside her, acutely aware
of how cold the linen felt. Spending so much time with
Hank had weakened her resolve. She wished he were
there beside her—that she could smell his cologne and
the musky masculine scent that clung to his skin, that
she could feel his warmth all around her again.

Those thoughts made her wonder if she'd gone over
the edge. No, she decided. She was completely sane—
maybe saner than she'd ever been in her life. *Her
turn.* Finally, at long last, she'd found an honest-to-
goodness prince, and, like a blithering fool, she was
passing on the opportunity to be with him. *Now or
never,* a taunting little voice whispered in her mind.
*When you first make love, wouldn't it be nice to still
be able to see while you're doing it?*

Why, she wondered, did there have to be a future
in it? Grab hold of the magic, Hank had told her.
Well, it didn't get any more magical than this. Why
was she holding back? Over the last few days, he had
been trying almost frantically to fill her head with
memories, but he was neglecting to give her the most
wondrous memory of all.

What if she never found Mr. Right in the city? What

if the next surgical procedure didn't work, and no man
ever looked twice at her again because she was blind?
When she faced permanent blindness again, she
wanted to have at least a few memories to take with
her into old age, namely how it felt to lie in a man's
arms and experience ecstasy.

Was that so wrong? For this period of time, they were
married. She didn't even have to worry about getting
pregnant. Why not fling her arms wide and experience
it all? If both she and Hank went into it knowing that
they'd eventually dissolve the marriage, how could it
hurt for them to make the most of this time?

Carly flung away the covers, slipped from the bed,
and then stood there in the dark, shivering. *Coward.*
What could he say but no? She marched from the
bedroom. At the bottom of the stairs, she hesitated,
assailed once more with doubts. But then she found
her courage, closed her eyes so she wouldn't stumble,
and marched up to the second floor.

Almost sound asleep, Hank heard something and
rolled onto his side to peer through the moonlit
gloom. Carly stood in the center of the upstairs sleeping area, a large room with sloped ceilings and twin-
sized beds lining the walls. Her fists were knotted at
her sides. Her small chin was thrust out, as if she were
ready to do battle.

"Hank?"

He blinked to clear the sleep from his eyes. "Yo?"

She whirled to face him, one hand clamped over
the center of her chest. "Oh! There you are. You startled me out of ten years' growth."

He sat up, thinking she might be sick and thanking
God he'd kept his boxers on. "Is your stomach
upset, sweetheart?"

"No. I feel perfectly fine. I just can't sleep."

He rubbed a hand over his face. *Warm milk.* That might make her drowsy. "Let's go downstairs," he said, slurring his words slightly. "I'll fix you something."

"I don't want you to fix me anything."

"Oh." He blinked to see her more clearly. "What do you want, then?"

"Sex."

Hank didn't have any of that in the fridge. "Will you settle for chocolate milk?"

"*What?*"

"I didn't get any—" He almost said "sex" before his brain finally kicked into gear. He blinked again and stared at her. He was dreaming, he decided. A shy, wary, inexperienced female like Carly didn't invade a man's bedroom, demanding sex. It was like— well, one of those things that just didn't happen. He cleared his throat, scratched his temple. "What did you say?"

"Which time?"

"What was it you said you wanted?" he clarified.

"Sex."

He nodded. *Okay.* He tugged on his earlobe, wondering if he'd gotten water in his ears when he showered that morning. "Would you say that again?"

She made a slight sound of frustration, whirled, and marched toward the stairs. "Never mind. Bad idea. I don't know what I was thinking."

She stopped to firmly grasp the handrail before beginning the descent. Hank sat there, staring stupidly after her. Had she said sex? He tried to think of other words that came close. *Mex, Tex, hex, specks.* None of those made sense. *Shit.* She had said sex.

He was out of the bed and halfway down the stairs before he realized he was wearing only boxers. Back up the stairs. Where the hell were his pants? He tripped over his boots. Found his shirt. *Damn*. His hand finally landed on denim. He stuck one foot down a leg, then hopped around, stabbing with his unencumbered foot to find the other hole. To hell with it. He started down the stairs with his jeans only half on.

"Carly? Honey?"

Sex. She'd said she wanted sex. *Lord, help me*. He finally got his foot stuffed in the pant leg, then nearly did somersaults down the rest of the stairs. In the nick of time, he caught hold of the railing to balance himself until he got his jeans jerked on. He finished fastening them as he completed the descent. His balls and his boxers were bunched into a throbbing knot at one side of his fly.

When he reached her room, he stopped to jiggle one leg and jerk at his trousers. "Carly?"

"Just go away."

Not in this lifetime. Hank pushed open the door. She lay huddled under the covers. He cautiously entered the room. "I'm sorry. I can't think real straight when I first wake up." *Sex*. No mistake. She'd definitely said sex. She didn't move, didn't look at him. He inched closer. "Carly?"

"*What?*" Her brow pleated in a frown, then she sat up, clutching the covers to her chest.

"Did you say what I think you said?" he asked.

Her eyes were huge, luminous spheres in the shaft of moonlight coming through the window. "What if I did?"

Brace yourself, Bridget. Hank rubbed a hand over his face again, trying to choose his words carefully, which was no easy task when his brains felt like half-cooked scrambled eggs. "I, um—I'd say sure." He cringed. "I mean—well, *yeah.*"

"That's it? *'Well, yeah'?"*

He sat on the edge of her bed. Took a deep breath. His heart was still tapping out a sharp tattoo against his ribs from his close call with death on the stairs. "Can we back up and start over?"

"I'd rather not. It wasn't one of my better moments."

Hank felt like laughing. "It wasn't one of my better moments, either."

She combed trembling fingers through her hair. Then she sighed, and her shoulders slumped. "I don't know what I was thinking. I was just—you know—considering the possibilities, and the next thing I knew, I was upstairs."

"What possibilities, exactly?"

"You and me. We've had so much fun over the last few days. It seems such a waste not to fully enjoy this time we have together."

On a scale of one to ten, it was clear off the chart as far as sinful wastes went. She was so damned beautiful his teeth ached.

"Nothing permanent, of course," she quickly added. "We'll still be only friends. No muddying it all up with emotional stuff. Just—well—you know—sex."

Now that he understood exactly what she wanted, his heart sank. Somehow, with no emotional stuff to muddy it up, the offer didn't match very well with the lady making it. Carly wasn't a no-strings lady. She never had been. He wasn't making that mistake again.

"That's all you want?" he asked softly. "Just sex?"

She nodded. "I'd like it to be romantic, of course. Can you make it romantic?"

The very fact that she wanted it to be romantic told him more than she could possibly know. Studying her oval face, searching her beautiful eyes, Hank knew in that moment that he wasn't the only one who'd fallen in love. She never would have made this proposition, otherwise.

Oh, how he wanted to take her up on it. Instead he pushed to his feet, determined to do it right this time—or not at all. "I'm sorry. If all you want is a convenient body, go find one in town."

She flashed him an incredulous look. "What?"

"You heard me. I'm in love with you. Done deal, no turning back. If we take this relationship to a new level of intimacy, I'll just dig myself a deeper hole, and it'll break my heart when you leave me."

"Oh, Hank," she whispered. "Oh, *God.*"

"Sorry. I know falling in love wasn't part of our bargain, but my heart didn't agree to the terms. I'd dearly love to join you in that bed." He shoved his hands in his hip pockets to keep from touching her. "If you were offering me more—a shot at having a life with you—I'd jump at the chance. But that isn't in your game plan, is it?"

"No," she admitted faintly. "We could never make it work."

"In your opinion. I think you're wrong. If two people love each other, they can make almost anything work."

"It's a nice thought, but practically speaking, it's not very realistic in our situation."

He gazed sadly down at her for a long moment and then turned to leave.

"Where are you going?"

"Back to my room." He paused in the doorway to

look at her. He'd been brutally honest, except on one small point. His heart was already breaking. "I've said my piece. I'm an all-or-nothing deal."

When he turned to leave again, she cried, "Wait!"

He shoved his hands back in his pockets and pivoted to face her. "What more is there to say? We're poles apart on this. You're bent on going our separate ways. I want us to stay together forever. You see nothing but potential problems. I see nothing but solutions. I don't think we can meet halfway."

"I'll eventually go permanently blind." She lifted her hands. "When I do, have you any idea how much it would cost just to make the immediate area around the cabin safe for me? That isn't to mention that I'd be stranded out there on the ranch, unable to catch a bus to town, unable to go to work. The entire situation would be impossible."

"Difficult, not impossible," he corrected. "I could make it work if you'd give me half a chance. Transportation sure as hell wouldn't be a problem. If I couldn't drive you into town, we've always got hired hands available."

"I'd be dependent upon you or them for everything. Can you imagine how I'd feel, living that way?"

"In the city, you'd depend on a bus driver. What's the difference?" Hank leaned against the doorframe. "You don't like to depend on anyone, do you?"

"You make it sound like a crime."

"No, more a fixation, I think. You've struggled all your life to be totally self-sufficient. Now I'm asking you to enter into a situation where complete independence may be impossible."

"No maybe to it. I couldn't even go grocery shopping by myself."

"Is going by yourself that important to you?" He arched an eyebrow. "A lot of married people go shopping together."

"That's only one example. Don't twist everything around, trying to make me out to be the bad guy. I'm doing you a big favor. If we stayed together, I'd be an anchor around your neck after I went blind—a constant responsibility."

"A very sweet anchor," he replied, "and a responsibility I'd thank God for every day of my life."

"You say that now, but you'd come to resent me in time. It would cost you thousands upon thousands of dollars to make that ranch safe for a blind woman."

"We could improvise and make do until your surgery next summer. After that, if all goes well, we'll have years to save for all the necessary improvements."

"And if everything doesn't go well? What then?"

"If all doesn't go well, then we'll manage somehow," he assured her. "I'll take out a loan if I have to. Whatever it takes. I love you. I want you in my life."

"Even if it means going in debt up to your eyebrows? You could end up like your father, a struggling, middle-aged rancher with broken down equipment, old nags in the stable, and a son who resents you because he can't go off to college. Is that what you want, all your dreams turned to dust?"

"Being with you is my dream now. And being like my father wouldn't be so bad. He's a damned fine man."

"I didn't mean to imply he isn't. I just—oh, never mind! You're not being realistic about this. Have you ever even been around a blind person?"

"No, I haven't."

"I rest my case."

He straightened away from the doorway. "You're not giving me a whole lot of credit here." Anger seeped into his voice. "Do you honestly believe I'll just turn off my feelings if life gets difficult, that I'll stop loving you because it's not easy? That's not who I am. It's not how I'm made."

She covered her face with her hands. "I know that, Hank. That's the whole problem. Don't you see? You'd grin and bear it, and I'd feel guilty for messing up your life."

"Do you love me?" he asked quietly.

"No," she said, the denial muffled by her hands.

"Look at me when you say it, damn it."

She dropped her arms. Her expression had gone completely deadpan, every muscle in her face carefully held in check. Ah, but her eyes. They couldn't lie. Hank gazed into them and had his answer. He moved toward her.

"I'm not the only one who's fallen in love."

She flopped over onto her back and jerked the sheet up to her chin. "You're out of your mind."

"Maybe, but it's a good kind of crazy." The edge of the mattress bumped Hank's shins. He rested his hands at his hips and stared down at her. "This puts a whole new slant on things. If you love me and I love you, meaningless sex is an impossibility."

"I do *not* love you. I *can't* love you. You're completely wrong for me, and I'm completely wrong for you. I absolutely, unequivocally do *not* love you."

"Love isn't a decision, Carly. It's a feeling. You can't force it, and you sure as hell can't reject it. It just happens. Forget about the impact it may have on my life and answer my question. Do you love me?"

"Just go back to bed."

She turned onto her side, presenting him with her back, the sheet twisted around her like a shroud. Hank sat next to her, staring thoughtfully at the back of her head. Then he trailed a fingertip down her spine. She jumped as if he'd touched her with a high-voltage prod.

"Stop it!" she said waspishly.

He smiled slightly and did it again. Same reaction. He took that as an encouraging sign and promptly jerked the sheet away. That brought her around to face him. "What do you think you're doing?"

"Exploring the possibilities."

"We've just concluded that there are none." She slapped at his hand when he reached to touch her cheek. "Stop it, I said."

"Why?"

"Because!"

"Evasive answer. Give me a reason."

"There's no future in it. You want forever. I can't promise you that. End of conversation."

"Can you promise to give it your best shot?"

"Give what my best shot?"

"Forever," he said softly. He brushed at a tear on her cheek, loving her so much it was almost a physical ache. "No guarantees. If everything goes to hell, and we can't fix it, I won't hold you to the promise. But if it can be fixed, if we can figure out a way to make it work, the promise stands. How does that sound?"

Her eyes went bright with tears. "You have no idea what marriage to a blind person will be like."

Heaven. "Let me find out."

"You're crazy."

Clear over the edge and hanging on by my finger-nails. "Yeah, crazy about you."

"I'm afraid you'll come to hate me."

"*Never*. When you do go permanently blind, whether it happens in five years or thirty, I want to be the guy who holds your hand and takes you for evening walks. I want to be the guy who draws pictures with words so you can still see the sunsets—or the first light of dawn. I want to be the guy whose face you memorize with your fingertips. When our child graduates from college, I want to be the lucky bastard beside you, the one whispering in your ear so you can *see* it all in your mind. I'll look at you and think you're the best thing that ever happened to me. That's what I'll think. And I'll thank God you stayed with me." His throat went tight. "You know why? Because if you don't, something inside of me will die, Carly Jane. You seem to have the mistaken idea that I can simply *decide* not to love you, that I'll move on and find someone else. Well, let me tell you something. Coulter men aren't built that way. When we love, we love with everything we've got, and we don't change our minds, ever."

"Oh, Hank," she whispered tremulously.

"Give me a maybe," he pleaded. "Tell me you'll give forever your best shot. Is that so much to ask? Nothing written in stone. If everything goes to hell in a handbasket, you can still back out. Just say that you'll stay with me as long as you can. We'll take it one day at a time."

"You have no idea how much I want to say yes. You have no *idea*."

He was inches away from crawling into bed with the lady. Only some things couldn't be rushed. This was one of them. Until they reached some sort of resolution, she was too upset and worried to melt into his arms.

"If you want to say yes, what's holding you back?"

"You have to promise me that the 'no guarantees' thing will go both ways. I have to know you won't stay with me out of a sense of duty. Otherwise, no, Hank, I can't say I'll give it my best shot."

"I swear to you that I'll never stay with you out of a sense of duty," he promised her, and he meant it from the bottom of his heart. Love would be what bound him to her, nothing else. "You have my oath on it. If things ever reach that point, we'll cash in our chips and call it done."

She peered up at him through the gloom, clearly trying to read his expression and not succeeding. Hank grazed the backs of his knuckles along her fragile cheekbone, then smoothed her hair, waiting for her response.

"All right," she finally whispered. "I'll give it my best shot."

Relief flooded through him. He was shaking as he stretched out beside her. Looping his arm over her waist, he rolled her to face him. He wiped the tears from under her eyes, kissed the tip of her nose. Spiked with wetness, her lashes fluttered upward. Her eyes shimmered in the moonlight like quicksilver.

"I love you, Carly Jane," he whispered. "I think I lost my heart to you the first time I saw your sweet face, and I was just too damned drunk to realize it."

She wrapped her arms around his neck and clung to him. "You could have anyone you want. I never meant for this to happen."

He kissed her hair, nuzzled his way to her ear. "If

I can have anyone I want, I choose you. As for intending to fall in love, it doesn't happen that way. Love just runs up and bites you on the ass."

She laughed wetly. "What a romantic analogy."

He grinned and tightened his arm around her. "You did ask for romantic. Remember?" His smile slowly faded. Burying his face in her curls, he just held her for a time, savoring the feeling of her softness pressed against him. "Ah, Carly, I love you so much. Don't worry. Please? We can conquer anything."

She shivered when he touched the tip of his tongue to the edge of her ear. He smiled and dipped his chin to nibble on her earlobe, which sent another shudder coursing through her. He flattened his hand on her back, tracing her spine with his fingertips. She sighed and pressed closer.

"Oh, Hank. I love you, too," she murmured. "I love you, too."

He drew back to unfasten the buttons of her nightgown. When he'd dispensed with the fourth one, she said, "I may not be very good at this the first few times. I haven't had much practice."

He searched her face. "Are you nervous?"

"A little."

They couldn't have that. He wanted this time to be perfect for her. "What we need here is a lead-in."

"A what?"

"A lead-in. Instead of going at it like we're killing snakes, let's forget about having sex for the moment and just enjoy being together."

She looked relieved. "That sounds good." Her brow creased in another frown. "When will we have sex then?"

Within five minutes, if he had his way. "When it feels right."

In her prim, long-sleeved gown, she'd never looked more like an angel. Hank lightly touched her hair, then her arm, fully prepared to commit a sacrilege.

She smiled hesitantly. He grasped her chin. In the moonlight, she looked too lovely to be real. He lifted his head and lightly touched his mouth to hers. She tasted just as sweet as he remembered—hesitant but willing, her lips soft and warm and deliciously moist. He curled a hand over her hip and felt her shiver at the press of his fingers.

Carly's breath started to come in short, ragged bursts. She couldn't help but remember the last time with him and feel a little afraid. When Hank bent toward her again, she pressed a hand to his jaw, thinking to hold him away, only somehow, between thinking and doing, she felt the cool strands of his hair moving over her fingertips. It felt just as she remembered, thick and silky, yet coarser than her own, and she couldn't resist running her hand through it.

As lightly as a butterfly wing, he touched his lips to hers again. *Dream or reality?* His breath mingled with hers, warm and sweet from the soda he'd drunk at the resort bar. The taste of him worked on her senses like heady wine. She parted her lips, breathlessly expectant, but he still didn't deepen the kiss. His mouth grazed hers, the contact whisper soft. *Moist, silken heat.* Her lashes swept low over her eyes. Her blood began to slog in her veins, as thick as honey. Her lungs grabbed frantically for oxygen.

"Hank?"

He angled his head and tormented her lower lip with light nibbles of his teeth. "What?" he whispered.

Carly had no idea what she needed, only that he made her want. She smoothed her hands over his shoulders. Warm, slick skin. Thick, vibrant pads of muscle over bone. The leashed power she felt beneath her fingers made her heart trip and then stutter to regain its rhythm.

"You are so beautiful," he murmured. "So damned beautiful. I've never wanted anyone or anything the way I want you."

As though he meant to memorize every line of her face, he slowly began tracing her features with his lips, the arch of her brows, the bridge of her nose, the curve of her cheek, the angle of her jaw. With every caress of his mouth, he made her skin feel more electrified.

Carly squeaked in alarm when he suddenly caught her in his arms and rolled onto his back, drawing her up to sit astride his hips. The position drew the hem of her gown taut across her thighs. His white teeth gleamed in the moonlight as he gave her a slow grin. He reached to toy with a curl that lay over her breast, the light graze of his knuckles making her nipple grow instantly hard and sensitive.

"I love your hair," he told her. "Your hair and those fabulous eyes were the first things I noticed about you."

"Really?"

"You're still nervous." His grin broadened. "There's no need to be. Not with me. I'll never hurt you again. You know that, don't you?"

She gulped and nodded. "Yes, I know. I, um—hmm. I'm just sort of—"

"Nervous?"

She laughed and nodded.

He stopped toying with her hair to settle his big warm hands on her bare thighs. She leaped and grabbed for his wrists.

"Easy," he said softly.

He lightly caressed her skin with the pads of his fingers. His thumbs dipped to the sensitive inner part of her thighs, circling, tantalizing. Once again her heart began to pound like a piston, each labored beat a blow against her ribs.

He nudged her nightgown higher. With a feeling akin to horror, she realized that the hem wasn't under her rump. She was sitting on him, bare butt naked, her buttocks on the denim of his jeans, the rest of her pressed against his hard belly. She wondered if he realized, then decided he probably did, which made her blush all over.

"The second thing about you that caught my eye was your legs. No contest, lady. You've got the most gorgeous legs I've ever seen."

He continued his exploration of them as he spoke, his hands lightly skimming upward to trace the flare of her hips. Carly's breath snagged in her chest. Her grip on his wrists impeded him not at all as he cupped his hands over her bare bottom.

"And you feel even better than you look," he whispered throatily. "So soft and smooth and absolutely sweet." He twisted his wrists free of her grasp to make fists on her nightgown. "I want to see all of you."

"I thought—" She swallowed to steady her voice. "I thought we'd decided we needed a lead-in."

He smiled as he pushed her nightgown higher. The cotton snagged on her tight nipples. The sensation made her gasp. He sat up suddenly, startling her half out of her wits. The friction and sudden pressure of his hard belly against the sensitive apex of her thighs sent jolts coursing through her.

"Arms up," he whispered.

In one smooth movement, he peeled the gown off over her head. As he lay back down, he tossed the garment away. His eyes glittered in the moonlight as he trailed his gaze over her. Everywhere he looked, her skin burned, an exquisite torture that made heat build low in her belly.

"You are absolutely perfect."

With the backs of his knuckles, he explored the indentation of her waist, the ladder of her ribs. When he reached her breast, he lightly stroked the plump underside with his fingertips, the caress so fleeting she craved more. He didn't leave her to think about it overlong. The next instant, he'd settled his hands on her legs again. His fingers moved in titillating circles over her inner thighs, inching ever higher until his fingertips grazed the nest of curls at their juncture.

Anchoring her with one hand on her thigh, he parted the silken folds of feminine flesh and lightly touched an excruciatingly tender place. Carly gasped and jerked at the sensation. He smiled and continued to touch her there, teasing her with light flicks of his fingertip. She'd never felt anything like it. The heat within her intensified. Ribbons of electrical sensation curled through her belly.

When he suddenly stopped, her body had arched like a bow. He sat up and touched the tip of his tongue to each of her nipples. Then he caught her around the waist and rolled with her again, this time coming out on top, his torso forming a shadowy canopy of rippling strength over her. Dipping his head, he kissed her, deeply, thoroughly, tasting the tender inside of her lower lip, tracing the shape of her teeth, then pressing the tip of his tongue to hers in a teasing rhythm of advance and retreat.

Carly made fists in his hair, lost to the sensations and to him. *Hank.* This was how she'd felt the first time he kissed her—totally focused, wanting to melt into him. The mere brush of his hand over her skin sent lightning bolts shooting through her, and the heat within her became searing tendrils of fire.

"Hank," she whispered feverishly. "Oh, yes."

He grasped her wrists and drew her arms above her head. Then he moved back to look down at her, his eyes burning a trail from her face to her breasts.

"We're not going to rush this," he said in a raspy voice. "Not this time."

He pressed his hot mouth to the sensitive place just below her ear, then he drove her nearly crazy, nibbling his way down the column of her throat. Her collarbone received his attention next. He trailed his tongue from her shoulder to the V, where he settled in with warm draws of his mouth over the pulse point, as if he wanted to drink in the very essence of her.

Carly's spine arched when his hot mouth closed over her nipple. He pulled sharply on it, then gently grazed the throbbing tip with his teeth. She sobbed. He intertwined his large fingers with hers, keeping her arms above her head, while he teased and suckled her. When she tried to twist her hands free, wanting to touch him, he held them fast and continued the exquisite assault on her tender flesh until she quivered like a plucked bowstring.

Dimly she was aware that he shifted to one side of

her and finally released her hands. She immediately
made fists in his hair, holding on for dear life as he
continued to kiss her breasts. He ran his work-
roughened palm over her belly, kneading gently, his
fingertips finding every sensitive nerve ending with un-
erring accuracy. Then he curled his fingers over the
throbbing place between her legs. She jerked and cried
out when he found the sensitive flesh that he sought.

He dipped for the warm, slick wetness at her opening and then laid claim to that throbbing flange of
flesh again with the flat of his fingers, rubbing in a
slow, circular motion that brought her hips up from
the mattress. "There's my girl. Give it to me,
sweetheart."

Carly could have withheld nothing from him. She
arched against his hand. He pressed harder and quickened the strokes. Need consumed her. She felt as if
she were poised precariously at the edge of a preci-
pice. She tried to pull back, frightened by the sensations that burned out of control inside of her.

"Let it come, sweetheart. It's okay, I swear. Just let
it happen."

She sobbed, arching higher. And then it felt as if a
starburst went off inside of her—shards of sensation
ricocheting out from the place he stroked. Her muscles
quivered and then jerked with every pass of his fingers. She was vulnerable to him in a way she'd never
allowed herself to be with anyone, completely and totally helpless, her body manipulated by each electrical
pass of his hand.

Her skin damp with sweat, she collapsed in a puddle
of sated flesh beside him. She was grabbing for breath
as if she'd just run a dash. She pressed a hand over

her heart, scarcely able to believe it hadn't pounded from her chest.

Hank kissed her eyes closed, whispering nonsensically to her, the meaning of his words evading her. Slowly, reality moved in around her. The moon-touched darkness. The dark outline of the man who lay, still half-clothed, beside her. He soothed her with soft brushes of his hand over her moist skin.

When her breathing slowed, he claimed her mouth in another deep kiss that set her head to spinning again. Then he moved down to her breasts, rekindling the fire that he'd just extinguished.

Dimly, she was aware of his lips on her belly. Then, with a shock, she felt his warm, wet mouth close over the tuft of flesh he'd so expertly teased with his fingers. Appalled, she bucked and tried to push him away, but he was a solid wall of strong, determined male. He drew on her there and lightly flicked her with the tip of his tongue until she forgot why she'd been so bent on making him stop.

Soon she was quivering, her breath coming in shallow bursts, her body once again helplessly responding to every teasing pass. When he'd brought her to the edge again, he gentled the strokes, soothing her throbbing flesh until she quieted. Then he took her to the edge again.

When he finally allowed her to climax, he rode her out, rubbing her lightly throughout the first wave, then teasing her to arousal again before the orgasm completely expended itself. She peaked again—and then again.

Carly was spent when he finally rose over her. She didn't think she could move if he stuck her with a pin.

She realized that he'd shed his jeans. She blinked and tried to focus. He was a glorious blur of moon-kissed bronze, his shoulders and arms bunching with strength. She felt his shaft, hard yet silken, nudge at her opening, and she tensed, expecting to feel pain again.

"Don't tighten up, sweetheart. I swear to God, I won't hurt you."

He dipped his head to kiss her, and while their lips were joined, he inched into her. Carly gasped and clutched at his shoulders, shocked by the feeling. He was barely inside, and already she felt his hardness stretching her flesh. It didn't really hurt, though.

"You don't fit."

He laughed tautly. "Oh, I'll fit. Trust me. I just don't want to hurt you." He pushed a little deeper. "If you feel so much as a twinge, just say so, and I'll stop."

"Okay." The instant she spoke, he pressed farther in.

Watching her face for a reaction, he smiled and eased deeper. When she still said nothing, he seated himself with one smooth thrust.

Carly was afraid to move. The feeling of fullness was alarming. Hank, however, had no such compunction. He drew back and gently thrust forward again. The sensation that exploded inside her was startling and incredible, and she dug her nails into his shoulders.

"Hurt?" he asked as he gently executed a second thrust.

Carly could scarcely believe it didn't. "No," she said with a shaky laugh.

He increased the tempo, his thrusts gaining force.

Mindless. Carly gloried in the power of him, running her hands over his roped arms, testing the dips and hollows of his back, curling her fingers over the ridged pads of muscle on his buttocks. Then the sensations took over. She wrapped her legs around his hips to meet him, slowly learning the rhythm so she could move with him. It was the loveliest experience she'd ever had in her life.

He slipped an arm under her shoulders and drew her against him. "Come with me," he whispered. "I'll take you to paradise."

With that whispered invitation, he increased his speed with powerful surges of his hips. She gasped at the fiery spurts of sensation that streamed through her. She hadn't believed anything could feel better than what she'd already experienced.

Paradise. He'd promised her paradise. She could now testify with absolute conviction that Hank Coulter was a man of his word.

At the break of dawn, Carly awakened to find herself wrapped in Hank's strong arms. It was the loveliest feeling to have his big, warm body curled around her. She touched her fingertips to the dark, springy hair on his chest, explored his flat, penny-sized nipples, cupped her hand to a hard pad of breast muscle, and wished. Wished that he'd wake up. Wished that he'd tease her nipples with his hot, silky mouth—and then leisurely devour her.

He cracked open one blue eye. His firm mouth immediately tipped into a devastating grin. "You lookin' for trouble, lady?"

Carly nodded.

He chuckled and opened both eyes to regard her

with some surprise. "Where'd my shy little angel get off to?"

"She's seen the error of her ways." Carly pushed at his shoulder to put him flat on his back. Then she straddled his thighs. "It was excruciatingly boring, being an angel." She leaned back to look at his body, admiring the hard planes and padded contours as she trailed her fingertips over his striated belly to the thatch of dark hair nested around his manhood. "You're so pretty."

His eyes darkened with desire as he moved his gaze over her. "Do you realize you're stark-naked and sitting, bold as can be, in a stream of sunlight?"

Carly glanced down. Then she grinned. "That's a visual concept."

"Meaning?" he asked, his voice grating with desire.

"What's naked, exactly? Until last night, I'd never seen naked except in a mirror."

"Does that mean you could greet me at the door in an apron, spike heels, and nothing else without feeling self-conscious?"

"Spike heels? I'd break an ankle. Will you settle for low-heeled pumps?"

He came up off the bed so swiftly that Carly was caught in the circle of his arm, flipped onto her back, and pinned before she could even squeak in surprise. "You'll cook me dinner, wearing nothing but an apron?"

"If you want."

He bent to nibble her breasts. "I've died and gone to heaven."

Carly was halfway there herself. Her insides curled and tingled with every pull of his mouth. She tucked in her chin to watch. When he caught her at it, his eyes danced with mischief. "Making memories, Carly Jane?"

She nodded. "I want to remember all of it. Everything about you."

He reared back to lightly run a hand from her chest to her thighs. "Sunlight has never touched anything so beautiful as you. *Nothing*."

After making that heartfelt proclamation, he set himself to the task of giving her a treasure trove of visuals to store away in her mind.

Chapter Nineteen

All too soon to suit Carly, the trip to Portland was behind them, and the week of sight-seeing was over. True to his word, Hank had shown her zebras, giraffes, camels, monkeys, apes, tigers, and lions, and she'd seen some beautiful scenery as well, including Mount Hood, the Columbia Gorge, and Mount St. Helen's. She was glad of every memory because the news she'd received from the specialist wasn't good. The lattice dystrophy had gained a strong foothold in her already diseased corneas and was now cracking and hardening their surface at an alarming rate. Merrick couldn't predict how long it would be before she went blind, but without his saying a word, Carly knew it would happen soon.

She refused to feel depressed about it. Hank had filled her mind with so many beautiful memories. She hugged those close for comfort, knowing they'd be with her in the darkness, images in full color that not even the lattice could steal from her.

On Tuesday night, July 15, when they returned to the ranch, Carly expected Hank to hotfoot it to the stable. He'd been gone for a week, and she knew he had work to do. Instead, he returned to the cabin shortly after leaving, his arms laden with black boxes and dangling cords.

"Stereo. Had it in my room at the main house. May as well enjoy it here."

After setting it up, he put on a CD, caught Carly in his arms, and proceeded to waltz her around the house. When she grew dizzy from swirling, she laughed and said, "Don't you have something else to do?"

"Nothing as important as this."

He stopped dancing to kiss her. As always, the kiss ignited them both, and soon they were moving toward the bedroom, dropping articles of clothing as they went. Once on the bed, he pleasured her with his hands and mouth until she thought she could bear it no longer.

"Hank?" she whispered. "*Please.*"

He nibbled on the sensitive skin under her ear. "No mercy," he breathed. "I'm going to tease you until you beg me for it, and then I'll make you climax so many times you can't move, can't think—until you just lie there, all mine from the tips of your toes to the top of your head."

He followed through on the promise, expertly using his talents to push her to the very edge, only to soothe her throbbing flesh at the last second and bring her back down. It was heavenly torture, and soon Carly's body was quivering with frantic need, the urges within her molten and primal.

"Please, please, please," she sobbed.

With a low rumble of masculine satisfaction, he gave her release, only to tease her back to a fever pitch again and then draw on her until she pitched in the throes of orgasm, every muscle in her body beset with spasms of delight.

Much later, Carly couldn't move, couldn't think, and was entirely his. Only then did he come to her—and take her with him to paradise once more.

"Wake up, gorgeous."

Carly groaned and drew the blankets over her head. "What time is it?"

"Seven. The day's wasting." Hank jerked the covers off of her, playfully swatted her bare fanny, and said, "If you aren't up in two seconds flat, I'll stick you under a cold shower. I want to take you shopping."

All Carly wanted was to sleep. "I don't get up until eight."

She squeaked when he scooped her up in his arms. "I warned you."

She clung to his neck, laughing sleepily. "Don't you *dare* put me in a cold shower. I'm wicked when I get even."

He carried her to the bathroom, set her on her feet, and bent to adjust the water temperature. "How's about a warm one then?"

"Shopping for what?" She rubbed under her eyes. "I hate to shop."

"Baby stuff." He turned on the shower and dipped his dark head to kiss her, the glide of his mouth sweet and slow. "I want you to see everything. Little pajamas, T-shirts, blankets, a cradle, and a crib. Interested yet?"

"Do we have the money?"

"Money, money, money. Your needle's stuck in a groove." He grasped her elbow and steered her into the tub. She gasped when the warm water struck her body. He jerked the curtain closed. Then, just as quickly, he partly opened it again. "On second thought, can I watch?"

She laughed and flicked water in his face. "Go away. After last night, you can't possibly be thinking about *that*."

"Men think about *that* on an average of every three minutes."

She threw him a startled look. "You're kidding."

"God's truth, I swear. It's a statistic. We think about it while we work, while we eat, while we talk. Then we dream about it." He grinned and grabbed the bar of soap. "Do you know how sensuous it is to have someone wash your body with soap-slicked hands?"

"Later, cowboy. I'm all used up."

Hank grinned and soaped his hands anyway. Just a kiss heated her up. He leaned in to grab her arm. She squeaked and swayed toward him. Her lashes fluttered when he ran a hand over her rosy-pink nipples, which hardened and peaked at the brush of his palm. God, how he loved her. She responded to him so readily, each surrender so sweet that he couldn't get enough of her.

As he played with her nipples, rubbing and tweaking until they swelled, she moaned and let her head fall back. Every line of her slender body was perfectly formed, her skin a satiny alabaster that fascinated him. He wanted her with an insatiable need that couldn't be slaked, no matter how many times he took her.

Later, Hank was never quite sure how it happened, but somehow he ended up in the shower with her, fully clothed, boots and all.

It was the best sex he'd ever had in his life.

*   *   *

"We can't afford an eight-hundred dollar crib," Carly protested three hours later.

Hank signaled to the floor clerk. "We'll take it," he said.

"Hank!" Carly clutched his shirtsleeve. "That's way too much money."

"It makes down into a youth bed," he argued. "Two for the price of one."

"Two for the price of three, don't you mean? We can get something much less expensive."

"Where, at the Goodwill?"

Carly gave up and let him go. And to her horror, he went. They bought sheets, bumper pads, darling little unisex sleepers, blankets, and slippers. At the end of the shopping spree, Hank had spent almost four thousand dollars, and they were the proud owners of an oak crib, a hand-tooled cradle, a bath table, a baby bureau, a high chair, a playpen, a swing, a car seat, three mobiles, assorted baby toys, and more clothing and blankets than any one baby could ever possibly need.

On the way home, he flashed her a grin and said, "When we find out if it's a boy or a girl, we'll go back for more outfits."

Carly groaned. "I'm glad we've decided on taking a shot at forever. Paying you back for everything would take me into the next millennium."

He lowered his brows and scowled at her. "Are you under the mistaken impression that you no longer have to pay me back?"

He was always so generous that Carly could scarcely believe her ears.

"The financial arrangement stands," he said firmly. "You still have to pay me back." The corners of his mouth twitched. He sent her a twinkling, purely devilish look. "The way I see it, you can work off the debt—starting tonight."

She gave a startled laugh. "Your boots haven't even dried out yet, and already you're thinking about next time?"

"Yeah. You game?"

She was always game. The most wonderful thing about that was that the sex wasn't *just* sex. It was sweet, beautiful lovemaking.

The next morning, Hank was at the junction store and happened to see a baby magazine in the rack. He plucked it out and started leafing through. When he came upon several pictures of babies, he wondered if Carly had ever even seen one. All the kids at the Fourth of July barbecue had been older. If she had seen an infant, it had probably been from a distance, which meant that she couldn't have studied it and filed away the memories.

The thought that she might give birth to their child and have no clear idea of what it looked like bothered Hank. After leaving the store, instead of heading home, he drove into Crystal Falls to look around at the bookstore for baby publications. He wanted his wife to see all kinds of babies, fat ones, skinny ones, curly headed ones, and the funny-looking ones, with spikes of hair poking up. That way, when their child was born, he'd be better able to tell her how it looked.

When he left the store, Hank's arms were laden with books. He'd even found a prenatal tome with pictures of fetuses at different stages of pregnancy. When he presented his finds to Carly an hour later, she began to cry.

"Oh, Hank."

"What?" He bent over her where she sat at the table. "Sweetheart, I didn't mean to make you sad."

"I'm not sad," she blubbered. "I'm h-happy."

Could have fooled him.

Wiping away tears as she went through the collection, she came upon a magazine chock-full of baby pictures. "Oh, aren't they *sweet*?" She laughed wetly. "Just look at him. Isn't that the cutest little dimple you've ever seen?"

Hank sat with her to go through the books. They both became solemn as they perused the ultrasound photographs of fetuses in different stages of growth. "That's ours," she whispered, touching a fingertip to one picture. "And next month, he'll look like this."

"He?" Hank leaned around to steal a quick kiss. "I want a girl who looks like you."

"Too bad. I want a boy who looks like you."

"We've encountered a serious glitch then," he said with mock sternness. "And there's only one way to resolve the problem, having two kids, one for me, and one for you."

She smiled dreamily and went back to looking at babies. "Next time, we'll have to plan things much more carefully. The doctor will want me to get pregnant right before a transplant when my corneas are about shot so the lattice can do no real damage."

Hank hadn't thought of that. "Well, then." He caught her chin and made her look at him. "No more babies. We'll just have the one—or we'll adopt. I don't want you to be blind for nine months in order to have another child."

"I want it to be ours."

"An adopted child will be ours."

Her eyes went bright with tears. He could tell she wanted to argue, but something held her back.

Hank had always hoped to have a passel of kids—and he naturally wanted them to be his biological children, if possible. But at what cost?

As Carly's sight worsened over the next two weeks, Hank juggled his work schedule to take her on day trips. When they weren't off somewhere playing, he helped her reorganize all the cupboards. Coffee, third cupboard, second shelf, first can on the right.

"I can do this," he assured her. "If I have to, I'll label the edges of the shelves so I don't forget where things go."

Carly couldn't help but be touched by Hank's efforts. She went up on her tiptoes to hug his neck. "Most importantly, don't forget where I'm at," she said softly. "I want to enjoy being with you as much as I can while I can still see."

He kissed her deeply, and before Carly knew it, she was in his arms, the cupboards forgotten.

After their lovemaking, Carly stretched languidly and slipped out of bed, her destination the shower. She had taken only three steps when her foot landed on something that rocked sideways, and she almost went crashing to the floor. Hank leaped to his feet in a flash.

"Are you okay?" He grabbed her arm as if he still feared she might fall. "My boot, you stepped on my boot. I'm sorry, honey. I'll kick them under the bed from now on."

"I'm fine, Hank. It was only a little stumble."

Even as she reassured him, Carly knew she wasn't truly fine. She hadn't seen his boot. When, she wondered, had her eyesight become so poor? She glanced down, hoping against hope that she'd be able to see the floor planks. Instead, it looked as if a dense fog had gathered around her ankles. She turned her gaze to the wall at the opposite side of the room, and it, too, was obscured by fog.

Hank touched her shoulder. "Sweetheart, what's wrong?"

Carly groped for her robe on the foot of the bed and slipped it on. "Nothing. I'm fine." The return of her blindness shouldn't have come as a shock. She just couldn't quite believe it had sneaked up on her so quickly. Her throat went tight. "It's time to start being a neat freak, though." She forced a smile. "I can't see the floor anymore." She laughed and flapped her wrist. "How that happened without my noticing, I don't know."

He glanced down. "You can't see it at all?"

She shook her head. Then, needing to be alone with the discovery for a few minutes, she hurried into the bathroom.

From that moment forward, Hank became a neat freak, never kicking off his boots and leaving them lie, never moving furniture and not putting it back, and always, always making sure he left the cupboards exactly as they had arranged them. Occasionally, when he slipped up, Carly couldn't bring herself to say anything. He'd been so sweet, and he was trying so hard, how could she possibly complain?

A few days later, Hank was holding up flashcards for her when she realized he'd begun holding them much closer than in the past.

"How long have you been doing that?" she asked softly.

He didn't pretend not to know what she meant. "I'm not sure. A while." He returned the cards to the box. "I, um—" He cleared his throat and met her gaze. "Every time we use them, I have to hold them just a little closer."

Looking at his face, it struck Carly like a dash of ice water that his features weren't as clear as they'd once been. It was like looking at a photograph with brushed edges, the planes and lines indistinct.

She'd been so sure she was prepared for this—so sure she could deal with it when it happened. But it was much more difficult to accept than she'd expected. She knew what it was like to see now. She'd grown accustomed to it. Now, in too short a time, the shutters would be closed again.

In that moment, Carly knew that as much as she would miss seeing countless things, the one thing she would miss most was seeing Hank's face.

"You okay?" he asked.

She nodded and smiled. "I'm *fine*. No big deal."

Only it was a big deal. She didn't *want* to be blind again. The thought of it made her want to run, but it was darkness she couldn't escape.

As if he sensed her panic, Hank distracted her by carrying her to the bedroom and making passionate love to her. Afterward, Carly lay replete in his arms, loving him as she'd never loved anyone.

When he left a few minutes later, she stood at the window and peered out at the ranch, trying desperately to see the landscape. It was all a blur wherever she looked, but memory served her well. There were perils everywhere—unruly horses, uneven ground, irrigation ditches, ponds, and barbed wire. She could make her way safely right now if she exercised caution, but she knew that wouldn't last for long.

The next morning Carly was awakened at six by a searing pain in her eyes. At first, she tried to go back to sleep, but the discomfort was so acute she couldn't. Holding a hand cupped over her face to block out the light, she went to the medicine cabinet for her drops, but when she trailed her fingers over the shelf, she couldn't find the bottle. She or Hank had evidently moved them.

Pain lanced into Carly's eyes as she tried to read the labels on the containers in the cabinet. *Blurry shapes*. She could barely make out the containers, let alone the lettering.

Defeated, she closed the cabinet and rested her throbbing forehead against the cool mirror. The pain was too intense to ignore. Hank might not return to the house until lunchtime, and she couldn't wait that long for her drops, not with her eyes hurting like this.

She stumbled to the kitchen. Closing her eyes, she dialed him on his cell phone. No answer. She got his voice mail instead. "Hi, this is Hank. I'm sorry I can't take your call right now."

Carly realized that he'd probably left his cell phone in the truck. She tried to call the main house to ask if Molly could come down to help her, but there was no answer. She belatedly remembered that Jake and his wife had taken an unplanned trip to Portland last night, something about a problem at the investment firm that Molly now managed with admirable diligence.

There was no help for it, Carly decided. She'd have to get dressed and walk over to the stable. Hank had to come home and find her drops.

En route to the stable a few minutes later, Carly stepped off into a hole and wished for the first time in her life that she'd learned to use a cane. She'd always managed well in the city without one. Unfortunately, the ground surfaces weren't as even or predictable here. She staggered but managed to catch her balance before she fell.

The close call made her stop and take a long look around her. Her bubble, she realized, had shrunk to a diameter of about three feet. She couldn't see the ground at all. If she wandered from the beaten path, there were logs and stumps everywhere.

Fixing her gaze straight ahead, she moved cautiously toward the stable, feeling ahead of her with the toes of her shoes for obstacles in her path. *No problem.* She had skateboarded blind, she reminded herself. She could surely walk a hundred yards over slightly uneven ground without killing herself.

As she continued walking, she tried to listen for sounds, but all she heard was the whisper of the wind in the trees. She also counted her steps, straining to see the outline of the stable up ahead. She wasn't surprised when she saw nothing. Three feet of clearance didn't allow for much in terms of long distance vision. Feeling her way, she kept going, confident that she was headed in the right direction.

After a while, Carly's confidence abruptly faded. She didn't remember the stable being this far from the house.

"Hank?" she called.

No answer.

Growing frightened, she turned in a slow circle, squinting to see through the fog. Three feet in all directions, the world was blanketed in a gray blur. Overnight, her vision had grown much worse.

Calm. She had to stay calm.

"Hank!" she screamed, hoping he might hear her.

He didn't respond. She stood still and listened. She heard no sound to indicate which direction the stable was. Big problem. That meant she'd veered off course somehow, and she no longer knew for certain where she was.

She froze in her tracks and tried to remember exactly how many steps she'd taken. There'd been a time when she'd never taken a single step without automatically keeping count. How, in so short a time, had she come to depend so much on her eyes that she no longer did that?

Okay. Deep breaths. Stay calm. She couldn't have walked that far. She had to be standing out in the open where people working outside could probably see her. The smart thing to do was to stand fast and yell. Sooner or later, someone would hear her, and she'd be fine.

"Hank!" she screamed. "Hank!"

Carly soon lost track of how many times she yelled her husband's name. *Nothing.* Her voice went scratchy from the strain of screaming. Her eyes hurt. She needed her drops. She passed a trembling hand over her face, wondering how long she'd be left to stand there. An hour, two? She needed something for the pain in her eyes *now*. She'd struggled all her life to be self-sufficient. Now, in a twinkling, she'd become a needy, helpless person, someone who couldn't manage to do the simplest things without help. If she continued in this vein, Hank would detest being married to her within a month, and she would also hate herself.

From off to her left, Carly heard a horse whinny. Hope welled within her. She listened a moment longer and was rewarded by the sound of a hoof striking metal. *The stable*. She turned in that direction and cautiously set off again, toeing the way in front of her so she wouldn't stumble over something and fall. "Hank!" she yelled again. "Hank! Are you there?"

When she'd taken fifty steps, she stopped. *Too far*. Her heart was pounding. Her body had gone clammy with sweat. She listened for the horse again. Soon it chuffed. She corrected her direction and set off, walking more slowly now, her movements jerky with trepidation. Was there barbed wire ahead of her? Afraid of running into something, she began patting the air in front of her as well as feeling with her feet.

"Hank! Answer me!" she cried. "Hank!"

She stepped forward again, and nothing was there. She felt herself falling and started to scream. The cry was cut short. Icy water engulfed her. The shock of it made her gasp as she went under. Up her nose, down her windpipe. *Oh, God*. She flailed in a panic and shot back to the surface, choking. *The pond*. It was her worst nightmare, a page from the past. The blind girl no one really wanted, fighting frantically not to go under.

She had to swim toward the bank, but she'd lost all sense of direction. Her water-soaked clothes weighted her down. She paddled in a panic to stay afloat, first one way, then another. Where was the damned bank?

She remembered Hank saying that the pond was ten feet deep at the outer edges, twenty at the center. She swam one way, then another, clawing at the water and open air, hoping to close her hands over something solid. Cold talons of terror squeezed her heart. Water, the thing she feared most.

She had to keep her head, she thought. *Think*. She'd just stepped off into the pond. If she swam in an ever-widening circle, she'd surely find the bank. She couldn't be that far from shore. Dog-paddling, she struck off, praying she actually was swimming in a circle. In water, she grew disoriented when she couldn't see. It diminished her ability to hear, made her feel weightless.

Circling . . . circling. Soon, she grew exhausted. Her clothing clung to her arms and legs, making them feel leaden. She would go under soon.

"Hank!" she shrieked. Water got into her mouth, nearly strangling her. After coughing to clear her windpipe, she called his name again, hoping and praying that he would hear her. "Hank!"

Dimly she realized that she'd begun to sink. The waterline lapped at her mouth. She fought to keep her chin up, but she'd never been a strong swimmer, and exhaustion made her movements sluggish.

She slipped under and took in water. A tight, airless pounding began in her head. She struggled back to the surface, fighting to breathe. *Oh, God—oh, God.* Once again, she slipped under. Searing pain in her windpipe. A horrible burning shot up the back of her throat and into her nose.

Drowning. She was drowning.

Chapter Twenty

Hank turned off the faucet and cocked his head. Glancing at Shorty, sitting on a milk stool outside the stall, he said, "Did you hear something?"

The sixty-five-year-old wrangler glanced up from the bridle he was repairing and cupped a hand behind his ear. "Come again?"

Hank stepped out into the center aisle. "I thought I heard someone yelling."

"Could be. We got nigh onto twenty men workin' here."

Hank had an eerie feeling. He strode to the open doorway. Nothing, not even a hired hand. Even so, he felt uneasy. Glancing back at Shorty, he said, "I'm going over to the cabin to check on Carly."

"See ya this afternoon sometime," Shorty said with a toothless grin.

Hank snorted with disgust and headed for home. By the time he reached the house, he was smiling. Maybe, he thought lasciviously, he wouldn't return to the stable until afternoon. Let Shorty put that in his pipe and smoke it.

"Carly?" he called as he let himself in. "Yo, sweetheart. You awake?"

He covered the distance to the bedroom in four

long strides and peeked in the doorway. No Carly. He checked in the bathroom. Not there, either. That was strange. Normally she didn't venture from the house alone unless she came to the stable.

He stepped back out on the porch. "Carly! You out here, honey?"

No answer.

He stood there for a moment, searching the terrain with growing alarm. *Shit*. If she'd wandered off, could she still see well enough to find her way home? He rubbed the back of his neck, panning the landscape.

And then he saw it—something white in the pond. His heart damned near stuttered to a stop. He leaped off the porch and hit the dirt at a dead run. *Sweet Jesus*. Something white—in the pond. *No. Please God, no.*

His boots pounded the dirt, each impact jarring his body. As he ran, Hank kept his gaze fixed on the spot of white in the water, and he knew long before he finally reached the bank that it was his wife, floating facedown, her slender arms flung out from her body.

He didn't stop to take off his boots or hat when he reached the bank. He hit the water in a running dive, the momentum of his thrust carrying him halfway to her before he ever took a stroke. "Carly!" he cried as he covered the remaining distance. "Oh, Jesus!"

He caught her in his arms. She was limp. When he rolled her over, he saw that her lips were purple and her face had an awful, bluish cast to it. Frantic, he swam to shore with her caught in the circle of one arm.

Once on the bank, he went to work, shoving on her chest, breathing into her mouth, and praying mindlessly. *Please, God—please, God—please, God.* It seemed to him that hours passed. *Dead*. She'd tried to tell him. Oh, *God*. She'd tried to make him understand how dangerous it was for her here.

Hank sobbed and grabbed her shoulders. "Breathe!" He lifted her halfway to a sitting position, shouting her name. *Please, God*. He couldn't live without her. "Breathe, Carly. Don't you dare die on me! Breathe, damn it."

He lowered her back to the ground to share his breath with her again. Then he pumped her heart. *Nothing*. He hadn't checked his watch. He had no idea how long he'd been trying to resuscitate her. One minute, ten? It didn't matter. He couldn't stop.

To stop meant the unthinkable—that she was gone.

Suddenly, her body jerked, and a huge gush of water shot from her mouth. Hank reared back, expecting her to suddenly open her eyes and start breathing like drowning victims always did in the movies. Instead she went absolutely motionless again and still looked dead. He was about to resume resuscitation when water spewed from her lips again.

Then she choked and began struggling to breathe, her lungs making horrible, rasping sounds. Hank rolled her onto her side. "Thank God. Thank *God*."

Shorty appeared at Hank's side.

"Bring my truck around! I have to get her to the hospital. Hurry, Shorty!"

As the old man raced away, Carly drew her knees to her chest. One arm hugging her waist, she coughed up more water. Then she began breathing easier. Hank stroked her wet hair with shaking hands.

"Oh, God, Carly. Oh, God."

She stirred to look up at him. "Hank?" she croaked. He leaned closer, touching her sweet face, which was finally getting some color back. Her lips were still blue, but even as he watched, he saw pink rising to the surface.

"Don't try to talk, honey. I'll get you to the hospital. You'll be all right."

She closed her eyes. "My baby. Oh, Hank, my baby."

Until that moment, Hank hadn't even thought of the baby. "It'll be okay," he said. "The baby will be fine."

Even as he said the words, Hank wondered if it might be dead. He had no idea what a near drowning might do to a first-trimester fetus.

"Your wife and baby are fine," an ER physician told Hank a little over an hour later. "Carly's lungs are clear. She's lucid. And the baby's heartbeat is strong."

"Thank God," Mary Coulter whispered.

Hank was dimly aware of his parents sitting nearby. Everyone in his family, except for Jake and Molly, who were out of town, had rushed to the hospital to be with him, and they'd waited in an agony of suspense for word of his wife and child's condition.

"Thank God," Hank echoed. He dropped onto a waiting-room chair, his legs suddenly so weak they wouldn't hold him up. He sat forward, resting his head on the heels of his hands. "Thank God," he whispered raggedly. "My fault, all my fault." He realized he was talking to himself and glanced up. "Thank you, doctor."

The physician, a wiry little man in a white jacket, warm-up pants, and golf shoes, patted Hank's shoulder. "They're both ready to go home, Mr. Coulter.

and you can thank God and yourself for that, not me. You're the one who kept your head and did what needed doing."

"That's right," Hank's father seconded. "You kept your head and saved her life."

Hank didn't see it that way. If not for his stupidity, Carly never would have fallen in the pond to start with.

When Carly emerged from the ER, she smiled wanly at him. Her clothes were still slightly damp, and her hair hung in kinky ropes over her shoulders, reminding him of drizzled honey, but he'd never seen anyone on earth more beautiful.

"Hey," he said, pushing unsteadily to his feet.

She walked straight into his arms. Hank locked her in his embrace and buried his face in her hair. Chilling terror sluiced down his spine every time he thought of how she'd looked after he pulled her from the water. *Dead*. He'd come so close to losing her.

Hank was glad of the fact that his family had come. They all rushed forward to hug her and say how glad they were that she was all right. It gave him a chance to back away, collect himself, and paste on a smile. She'd felt so fragile when he held her in his arms.

All the way home, Hank kept remembering how she'd looked, her body so lifeless, her face so blue. Guilt squeezed his chest, making it difficult to breathe. "I'll fix things somehow. No worries. I'll build fences and stuff. I'll fix it so you never get lost out there again."

She just nodded and said nothing.

When they got back to the ranch, Hank needed some time by himself. After getting her into dry clothes and safely put to bed, he crept from the cabin

and went to the stable, where he sat on a hay bale
and agonized over how close he'd come to losing her.
Jake came out and sat with him.

"It wasn't your fault, Hank. Would you stop beating
up on yourself?"

"It *was* my fault. She tried to tell me she'd have
special needs. I was so cocksure I could handle everything and take care of her. Now I'm scared to death
I'll overlook something else, that she'll get hurt and
I'll lose her."

"Have you talked to her about this?"

"No," Hank said hollowly. "But I will."

When Hank got back to the house, he thought Carly
was asleep. She wasn't. She heard him sit down in the
living room. After several minutes of silence, he emitted a broken, masculine sob—the sound so soft she
might have imagined it. Then she heard him whisper
"Oh, *God,* oh, *God.* I had no idea. No *idea.* What if
I can't do this?"

Carly huddled on her side. Scalding tears filled her
eyes. She'd told Hank a dozen times that he had no
clue what he was getting into with her. Now reality
had finally been driven home.

He came to her later. After taking her into his arms,
he promised over and over that he'd make the ranch
safe for her. "I'll start on it first thing tomorrow, and I
won't rest until everything is absolutely safe, I swear."

Despite all his reassurances, he failed to do the one
thing that might have eased Carly's aching heart. He
didn't make love to her. When she tried to encourage
him, he caught her hand and drew it to his lips. "Not
tonight, sweetheart. I'm sorry. I just—can't."

It was the first time since the night at the lake that

he'd turned away from her. Carly huddled on her side, her heart splintering into a hundred lacerating pieces.

True to his word, Hank was at The Works, the Coulter ranch supply store, when Zeke opened the doors the next morning.

"Hey, little brother," Zeke said with a smile. "You're in town early today."

"I need wire and posts," Hank told him. "A shit load. Carly's scared to death. And who can blame her? I've got to make it safe for her out there, Zeke."

"Her vision is getting that bad already?"

Hank nodded. "Seems a little worse with each passing day. She can still see up close, but I think even that's getting blurry."

When Hank returned to the ranch an hour later, Levi met him just outside the stable. The older man scratched his head and shuffled his feet, clearly at a loss for words. When he finally found his voice, Hank could barely credit what he said.

"Carly left," Levi said flatly. "With that friend of hers. Bess, I think's her name. Looked to me like she took most of her things with her."

Hank rushed to the cabin. Irrational though he knew it was, he hoped to see Carly at the kitchen table, devouring her morning sickness cure. She wasn't there. As he closed the door, an eerie feeling of emptiness assailed him. The cabin never felt this way when she was there.

Not wanting to believe that Levi was correct about Carly leaving him, he moved quickly through the house. A glance into the front closet told him her clothes were missing. In the back bedroom, he discovered that most of the baby clothes and blankets had been removed from the bureau.

En route back to the kitchen, he saw a letter lying on the table. Feeling drained and strangely detached, he sank onto a chair to read it. Her lines were hopelessly crooked, but the writing was legible.

Dear Hank: It's difficult for me to write, so I'll make this short. I need to live in the city where there are sidewalks and crosswalks and public transportation systems. You need to live where you are, close to the land, working with your horses. I'll always remember you here, in your element, my handsome prince in riding boots with a Stetson tipped low to shade his eyes. For a while, you made all my dreams come true. Unfortunately, you were only on loan. Just know that for a time, I was happier than I ever thought I could be, and that I'll treasure my memories of you forever.

She had tried to draw a happy face, which was lopsided, with one eye outside the circle. *I'll be in touch. In time, when we've both distanced ourselves from this a bit, maybe we can see our way clear to being good friends. For the baby's sake, we should aim for that.*

She ended with a flourish. *Yours always, Carly.*

Hank tossed the letter onto the table and just sat there, staring through tears at nothing. *Gone.* She was gone. No matter how he tried, he couldn't wrap his mind around that. Even worse, he couldn't contemplate a future without her.

Late that afternoon, Bess answered her phone on the fourth ring. "Hello?"

Hank swallowed to steady his voice. "Hey, Bess. It's Hank."

Long silence. Then she finally said, "Hey, Hank. What a surprise."

He smiled sadly. "I know you came out and picked her up, Bess. She told me so in her letter."

"Okay. So you know. End of subject."

Hank sank onto a chair. "You have to tell me where she is."

"No," she replied. "I don't have to tell you that."

He sighed and closed his eyes. "Let me put it another way. I'll find her, one way or another. Be a friend. Save me a lot of trouble and money."

"I can't. I promised her. I betrayed her once. I won't again. I can't help but think that maybe she's right this time."

"How the hell can you say that? I love her, damn it, and she loves me. We belong together. I'll also remind you that she's carrying my child."

"Calm down, Hank."

"I won't calm down. My wife left me! She went to her father's, didn't she?"

Silence.

"I'll take that as a yes." Hank tightened his grip on the receiver. "Damn it, Bess. Don't play these games. Is she going to be happy away from me? Ask yourself that."

"No, she won't be happy," Bess admitted, "but at least she'll be safe, and so will you. Sometimes you have to love someone enough to walk away. Wouldn't you do whatever it took to stop her from throwing away everything that mattered to her?"

"She is what matters to me, Bess. She hasn't saved me, she's destroyed me."

"You know what I mean. We're talking thousands, maybe over a hundred grand to make that place safe for her. How in the hell can you cough that up?"

Hank laughed bitterly. "Oh, come on. It won't cost that much."

"Want to bet? You can't just drive some stakes and string some rope. You'll have to network the place with concrete paths, bordered with metal rails. There should be intercom systems everywhere so she can call the stable, the cabin, or the main house in case of an emergency. And you need hurricane fencing around the pastures, not barbed wire. I could go on and on, and that's just improvements to the land. She also needs handrails on all the porches, and the inside of the house has to be arranged just for her. A hundred grand isn't really a stretch. It could cost a hell of a lot more than that."

Hank hadn't realized so many things needed to be done. "I'll handle it."

"How? You tell me that, and maybe I'll give you her father's address."

Bingo. Hank relaxed on the chair. Now that he knew for sure where Carly had gone, he was that much closer to bringing her home. "Thanks, Bess."

"For what?"

"Telling me where she went."

"Shit."

He chuckled humorlessly. "You want to save me the trouble of sniffing out his phone number and address?"

"No. Oh, all right. But I'm warning you, Hank. She won't come back with you. Not unless you perform miracles out there. She and the baby almost died."

"It'll never happen again. I'll see to it. She wants

miracles, I'll give her miracles, I love her, bottom line. She belongs here with me."

"Then call in experts."

"Experts?"

"Yes, professionals—people who can look at the ranch, the house, and all the outbuildings, then draw up plans that will work for her."

"That *will* cost a bloody fortune."

"Exactly."

"Okay. Fine. Experts. I can do that."

Bess reluctantly gave him Carly's father's address and phone number. "Don't go get her until you're positive, absolutely positive, that you can make it work. Promise me. She's already bleeding, and so are you. If you bring her home, and things don't work out, you'll only be prolonging the inevitable."

Hank had seen Ryan and Bethany make their marriage work. Everything had been against them, but they'd somehow managed to beat all the odds and create a workable solution, a life that accommodated both of them. Love and a determination to overcome every obstacle had seen them through the difficulties.

Hank loved Carly, and he was damned sure determined.

Bethany and Ryan were eating dinner when Hank rapped on their door and let himself in. Bethany beamed a smile when she saw him. "Hey, big guy. How's Carly feeling today?"

Hank started to reply, but his nephew cut him short.

"Unko Hank!" Sly chortled as he squirmed to get out of his high chair. "Unko Hank!"

Forcing a smile, Hank circled the table to hug the

child. "Hey, partner." He pretended to snitch some of the child's food. "Yum! Green beans."

Sly clearly didn't share the sentiment. He promptly tried to shove a fistful of the beans into Hank's mouth. Bethany laughed as she wheeled into the kitchen for an extra place setting. "Have a seat!" she called over her shoulder.

Ryan stood to shake Hank's hand. "What brings you out this way?"

"I have a problem I need to discuss with you," Hank replied.

His sister returned to the table, arranged a place setting, and then patted the seat of a chair. "Problems are always easier to solve while breaking bread together. Sit down, you big lug."

Hank took the chair. "I'm really not hungry." He wasn't sure he'd ever feel hungry again. "Carly's left me."

Bethany froze. "Oh no," she whispered.

"I'm sorry to hear that," Ryan commiserated.

Both Ryan and Bethany stopped eating while Hank filled them in on Carly's flight that morning. Bethany's expression conveyed her understanding. "It had to have been pretty scary for her Hank," she said softly. "Carly almost died in that pond, and it's a miracle she didn't lose the baby."

Hank nodded, his throat so tight it was difficult to speak. "I need to make a lot of changes on the Lazy J, fix it so she'll never be in danger there again. Only I'm not sure how to start."

Bethany went into the kitchen for a bottle of wine and three goblets. En route back to the table, she said, "It'll be extremely expensive, especially if you bring in experts to draw up the plans. I have several blind friends from college. I'm sure I can hook you up with the right contacts. But they'll probably make a list of needed improvements longer than your arm. They usually do."

Hank rubbed the back of his neck to ease away the tension. "I'm not worried about the costs. The Lazy J is half mine. I'll borrow against my equity."

Ryan took the wine Bethany poured for him. Leaning back on his chair, he took a sip and said, "That won't be necessary. I'll float you a loan."

Hank knew Ryan was richer than Croesus, but it went against his grain to tap family. "I can't take your money, Ryan. I need to do this on my own."

"Bull hockey." Ryan set his glass on the table with a decisive click. "I know you're good for the money. And the truth is, Carly won't be the only one to benefit from the changes. Bethany has a hard time getting around out there. She worries about getting stuck if she goes very far from the house."

"That's true," Bethany inserted. "On the Fourth, I was afraid to take Sly down to play in the creek because the ground is soggy. Ryan had to go with him. I'd visit you guys a lot more if there were pathways for my wheelchair."

Hank shook his head. "I came for information and advice, not money."

"Yeah, well, what you came for and what you get may be two different things," Ryan said. "It doesn't make good business sense to borrow against the ranch, putting the family land, not to mention your source of income, at risk, when I've got more money than I know what to do with. I'll be royally pissed if you go that route. How can you turn down a pay-it-back-as-you-can, no-interest loan?"

Hank arched an eyebrow. "No interest? Who has no business sense?"

Ryan winked at his wife. "My interest return will be having that hell hole you call a ranch transformed so my wife can visit there without one wheel of her chair dropping off into a hole large enough to swallow a Volkswagen."

Hank laughed in spite of himself. "Hell hole? Excuse me. You're talking about the Coulter family heritage."

"Exactly." Ryan inclined his head at Bethany. "She's a Coulter by blood. I reckon if anyone has a right to go all over that ranch, it's her. Go all out, Hank. Turn that ranch into a dream come true for handicapped ladies. My reward will be watching your sister wheel all over the place with our kids, showing them all the things she used to do when she was growing up."

"Amen," Bethany said.

"You've got one kid." Hank motioned toward Sly, who was devouring his mashed potatoes without benefit of utensils. "Why are you using the plural?"

Bethany blushed and flicked a glance at Ryan.

"You're pregnant?" Hank laughed incredulously. "Wow! That's fabulous, Bethie. I'm happy for you guys."

Her blush deepened. "We're not sure yet. Maybe." She glanced at Ryan again. "Probably. I'm late."

"A *whole* lot late." Ryan grinned, his twinkling blue eyes warming with gentle affection as he regarded his wife. "She's been so busy this summer with the riding academy for handicapped kids that she's neglecting the important stuff—like letting me know I'm about to be a dad again."

Bethany wrinkled her nose. "I'm not *neglecting* anything. I just haven't had time to take a test, thank you very much. I either am or I'm not." She slanted her husband a sultry look. "If not, we'll just keep trying."

"I'm thrilled for you guys," Hank said. "Congratulations."

"About accepting that loan." Bethany gave Hank an accusing look that said, *"You owe me this."* "Ryan has an obscene amount of money. If you borrow against that land and put *my* family heritage at risk, I'll never forgive you."

Hank couldn't speak for a moment—couldn't even think what to say. He only knew he was the luckiest man alive to have such a wonderful family.

"I accept," he said huskily. "Thanks, Ryan. It might have taken me a month to secure a bank loan. Now I'll be able to start the work right away."

"And bring your wife back home where she belongs a whole lot sooner," Bethany inserted with a happy grin.

"I can't wait," Hank said hollowly. "I promised her friend Bess I'd wait to go get her until all the work is completed, but it won't be easy."

Ryan pushed up from his chair and went to get the portable phone. "Bethany, go find those contact numbers for Hank," he said as he punched out a number himself. A moment later, he said, "Hey, Rip. Ryan Kendrick here. How's business this summer? Do you happen to have a work crew available?" He listened for a moment. Then he gave Hank a thumbs up and said, "That's great. My brother-in-law needs some work done, ASAP, a major project similar to the one you did for me on the Rocking K." Ryan's grin broadened. "Two crews? Hey, buddy, that'd be fantastic.

He'll need a few days to get the plans drawn up. If you could book both crews for the first part of next week, I'd really appreciate it." Ryan paused. "You bet. Hank Coulter. He owns the Lazy J, east of town." He recited Hank's cell phone number. "That works. He'll be expecting you to call. Thanks, buddy."

After breaking the connection, Ryan grinned. "You're halfway there. Rip Tanner's top-notch. He runs a tight ship and hires the best men around. Things have been slow this summer, and he's got two crews that aren't booked right now. He can have them on site next Monday, ready to break ground."

Hank had seen the quality of Tanner's work on the Rocking K. As he recalled, the construction company had also gotten the project finished in record time. "That's fantastic. Thank you, Ryan."

For the first time since he'd walked into the cabin and found Carly gone, Hank was able to relax. He had the money to revamp the whole ranch, and paying off the loan wouldn't put him in a bind. He also had two crews lined up to get the work done. Bethany would get him in touch with other top-notch professionals to plan the project.

If all went well, Carly might be back home on the Lazy J in only a few weeks.

Chapter Twenty-one

Art Adams stood in the doorway of the shadowy guestroom, gazing solemnly at his daughter, who had finally fallen asleep in a fitful sprawl on the queen-sized bed. In the summer heat, even central air couldn't keep the rooms comfortable without costing him a fortune, so he kept the thermostat at eighty. As a result, Carly was covered only with a sheet, the sharp projection of her hipbone and the pointed thrust of her shoulder clearly visible through the limp drape of linen.

In the three weeks since she'd shown up on his doorstep, she'd done nothing but spin her wheels, enlisting him to spend hours on the Internet to try to help her find a teaching job, either here in Arizona or in Oregon. When that endeavor had failed, she'd asked him to read her the Help Wanted section of the classified ads each evening, her eyes fixed almost feverishly on nothing, her face taut. There were no jobs in the immediate area that she could perform. Each night as he'd opened the paper, Art had prayed that they might happen across something. Even a position as a phone solicitor would have given her some sense of purpose, but so far, they'd found nothing.

Without a specially equipped computer, Carly couldn't even write a letter of introduction by herself.

It hurt to watch his daughter, who'd always taken such pride in being self-sufficient, being brought to her knees. In trying circumstances, other women could wait tables, take care of other people's children, or sling hamburgers to make an income. None of those options were open to a blind woman.

In the interim, Carly had lost an alarming amount of weight. It was like watching someone be bled dry. With each passing day, her dauntless spirit had weakened and she'd become more pale and listless. Now she spent most of her waking hours sitting by the window, listening to country-and-western songs on the radio while staring blindly at the desert, her once expressive eyes gone empty except for an awful hopelessness that Art couldn't dispel.

Watching her suffer this way, Art had come to hate Hank Coulter with a virulence that frightened him. His child's heart was breaking, and the man she mourned didn't care enough to pick up a phone and call her. Never in his life had Art felt so frustrated, angry, or horribly helpless.

Over the last few days, he'd tried to distance himself and regain his emotional equilibrium, but it was impossible. How could a father pull away from his only child? Her joy was his joy. Her pain was his pain. Right now her world was falling apart, so his own was in a shambles as well.

The phone rang just then, jerking Art from his musings. With one last look at his girl, he carefully closed the door and limped into the living room to grab the portable. "Hello?"

"Hello, Mr. Adams?" a deep, masculine voice said. "This is Hank Coulter, Carly's husband."

For an instant, Art was so taken aback he couldn't think what to say. Then anger surged through his body, so sudden and searing he began to shake. For days, he had fantasized about all that he would say to this worthless excuse for a human being if he ever got the chance. He headed for his bedroom where he could speak his mind without waking Carly.

The moment the door was closed behind him, Art said in a voice several decibels above normal, "You rotten, good-for-nothing son of a *bitch*!" That wasn't exactly the delivery he'd planned, but it sufficed—for starters. He wondered if Coulter had hung up and hoped he had. Carly was better off without him in her life. "Are you still there?"

Another brief silence ensued. Then Coulter cleared his throat and said, "Yes, sir, I'm still here."

The "sir" caught Art totally by surprise, making him wonder for a fleeting instant if he had made all the wrong assumptions about this man. *Nah*. The polite response was undoubtedly just for show. Well, Art wasn't that easily fooled. Coulter's actions spoke for themselves, and they weren't those of a man who loved his wife.

"How dare you call this house after three weeks of silence?" Art cried. "If you think I'll let you talk to my daughter, think again. You got her pregnant, robbed her of her sight, derailed her education, and then broke her heart. I think you've done quite enough damage."

Art expected Coulter to cuss him out and hang up— or demand to speak with Carly. Instead, the younger man said nothing for a long moment. His voice had gone husky with what could only be regret when he finally responded with, "You're absolutely right. Guilty as charged on all counts—except the last one."

"Meaning?" Art asked incredulously. "My daughter's emotionally devastated. If you're not responsible for that, who the hell is?"

"Circumstances."

"Circumstances?"

"Yes, sir, and I've been working to remedy the problems ever since she left me. Now that I've accomplished that, I'd like to talk with you about how I should proceed, hopefully with your blessing."

"Proceed? With my daughter, you mean? Think again."

"I don't blame you for feeling afraid for her, Mr. Adams. I had my head up my ass. I admit it."

Again, Art was surprised. An admission of guilt was not what he expected.

Coulter dragged in a shaky breath, then rushed to add, "In my own defense, I have to remind you that I'd never been around a blind person. I knew Carly's sight was failing, but I had no idea she was in any physical danger. We'd talked about making improvements to the ranch. I figured we could make do until next summer when she had her second surgery. The pond incident drove home to me what danger she was in, and I swear to you, I've barely slept since, trying to get everything fixed."

Art still wasn't following, but before he could demand clarification, Coulter continued. "She'll be absolutely safe with me now. I know you're probably thinking I couldn't possibly transform an entire ranch in only three weeks, but I promise you I have. I brought in professional analysts, they drew up the plans, and I hired two full-time work crews to get everything done."

Art held up a staying hand, then realized Coulter couldn't see him. "What's this about a pond incident?"

"It'll never happen again," Coulter assured him. "I know it terrified her. She almost died. I'd be terrified, too. I've built walkways with guide rails all over the ranch, complete with intercoms at every intersection so she can call for help if she grows disoriented. Staff from our local Blind and Low Vision Services came out to lend a hand as well. In addition to organizing the house, they ordered metal tags, imprinted in braille, for every intercom station so Carly will know where she is at all times. I also got a pager to wear on my belt so she can beep me no matter where I am on the property. The digital readout will tell me exactly where she is whenever she pages me."

All the anger drained out of Art, and he sank onto the bed like a slowly deflating helium balloon. "My daughter fell in a pond?" It wasn't really a question. Suddenly, all the pieces were beginning to fit together for him.

"She didn't tell you about that?" Coulter sounded as bewildered as Art felt. "What reason did she give for leaving me, then?"

For twenty-one miserable days, Art's hatred of this young man had been mounting to mammoth proportions. It took a considerable rearrangement of his thoughts to accept that his daughter had been the one to leave her husband, not the other way around. "She didn't actually give me a reason," Art admitted. "I assumed you took her for a ride and dumped her when you got bored."

"When I got *bored*?"

For the first time in three long weeks, Art found himself smiling. This young fellow clearly loved his daughter, and Art realized now that he'd been way out of line, saying the things he had at the beginning of the conversation. He almost apologized but then thought better of it, choosing instead to find out, once and for all, what Hank Coulter was made of.

Putting a gruff edge on his voice, Art said, "Talk is cheap. My daughter has been here for three weeks, and you haven't picked up a phone to call her. That tells me all I need to know, namely that she's better off without you."

"I waited to call until all the work was finished," Coulter protested. "That's why she left me, not because of anything I said or did, but because of all the dangers here on the ranch. She had it in her head that I'd be financially devastated if I made all the necessary improvements, that I'd be better off without her in my life. *Wrong*. To have her with me, I'd kiss this ranch good-bye in a heartbeat."

Carly had always been afraid her blindness was a burden to the people she loved. Art's smile deepened. "That's your story," he said, injecting just enough disbelief into his voice to spur Coulter on.

"It's the *truth*! I love that girl with all my heart."

Art greeted that with a sarcastic huff. "You have a strange way of showing your love. Thanks to you, my daughter looks like death warmed over. She's dropped so much weight, it frightens me."

"Oh, God," Coulter whispered raggedly.

Art continued relentlessly. "I'm deeply concerned, not only about her health, but also the baby's." That was absolutely true. "Now, out of the blue, you call here, expecting to reestablish communication? I don't think so."

A loud clacking sound came over the line. When Coulter spoke again, his voice throbbed with anger. "Okay. I understand your position. Now try to understand mine. With all due respect, sir, that's my *wife* you're talking about. I'm coming to get her tomorrow. If you plan to stop me, you'd best be standing on the porch with a loaded shotgun and be prepared to use it."

"Calling the police would be a much simpler solution."

"Do what you have to do. A night in jail won't kill me. Understand something. I love your daughter, and she loves me. No matter how many nights I spend in jail, sooner or later, I *will* bring her home where she belongs. When that day arrives, won't it be more convenient for you to be on speaking terms with your son-in-law?"

Art admired this young man's grit. Strength emanated from him, even over the phone line, and he obviously wasn't one to be easily buffaloed. He was exactly what Carly needed in a husband, someone who would stand beside her through thick and thin. "Excellent point."

"I hoped to get your blessing before I—" Coulter broke off, his silence filled with question. "Pardon me?"

"I said that's an excellent point. I'll definitely want to be on speaking terms with my daughter's husband and the father of my grandchild. What time should I expect you tomorrow?"

"Shortly before noon," Coulter replied, his tone cautious and hesitant. "I, um—did I miss something?"

Art finally allowed himself to chuckle. "No, son. I think it would be more accurate to say that I've over-looked a few things. When Carly arrived here three weeks ago, her eyes all red from crying, I couldn't think past my anger. Someday soon, you'll understand what I mean. I didn't think; I just reacted. My little girl was hurting, and in my mind, you were respon-sible."

"And she didn't set you straight?"

Art laughed again. "No. Every time I asked what happened, her stock response was, 'It just didn't work out.' Since it was obvious as hell that she still loved you, I jumped to the wrong conclusions. In short, I owe you an apology for the things I said at the start of our conversation."

"No apology is necessary. It's enough to know that you won't shoot me when I ring your doorbell. I love her, Mr. Adams. All I want is to build a life with her and make her happy."

Art had already deduced that. "Would you resent some well-intended advice from a tired old man?"

"No, sir. I'm always open to good advice."

Art shifted on the bed to brace his back against the headboard. "I hope you're comfortable. I have a long story to tell you about my daughter."

The following morning at precisely eleven forty, Ryan Kendrick pulled the rented SUV to a stop be-fore Art Adams's prefabricated home. Hank gazed out the rear passenger window at the house, taking in the green aluminum siding, sparkling white trim, and twin bay windows that flanked the covered front porch. Typical of retirement homes in Arizona, the yard had been landscaped with cactus, other hardy plants, and decorative rock. A multistriped windsock, attached to a porch post, fluttered in the errant breeze. Colorful pots of flowers decorated the railings.

"Well?" Ryan turned to look at Hank. "You going to sit there all day, thinking about it, or go in and get her?"

Hank took a bracing breath. "I'm so nervous, I couldn't spit if you yelled 'Fire.' Should I try to reason with her first? Or should I just scoop her up and carry her out?"

Bethany twisted on the seat. "Hank, for heaven's sake. She's not going to listen to reason until she sees all the improvements you've made to the ranch. You can talk yourself blue, promise the moon, and she'll still never believe the two of you can have a life together. You have to show her first."

His blue eyes dancing with laughter, Ryan shrugged and lifted his hands. "She's the expert, not me. It's a woman thing."

"It is *not* a woman thing," Bethany retorted. "Handicapped men feel exactly the same way. Hooking up with an able-bodied person is frightening enough. When that person lives miles from town on a ranch, the prospect is downright terrifying."

"That must be her dad," Ryan said, inclining his head at the house.

Hank turned to see a frail, stoop-shouldered man standing at the screen door. He looked much older than Hank had envisioned. Most people Carly's age had parents in their late forties or early fifties.

"He's motioning you to come in," Bethany said, flashing Hank a bright smile. "A friend in the enemy camp! Go for it, Hank. Carly might be miffed at first but once she settles down, she'll think it's wonderfully romantic."

Somehow, Hank doubted that. Carly was the stubbornly independent type. She wasn't likely to appreciate being bodily removed from her father's house Sweat trickled down his spine as he pushed open the rear door.

"Here goes nothing." After gaining his feet, he leaned back into the vehicle to say, "Be ready to roll Ryan. If this turns nasty, I want to be halfway back to the airport before any neighbors call the cops."

Ryan gave him a mock salute. "All systems ready. I've been cuffed and stuffed once." He slanted Bethany a teasing glare. "I don't want to repeat the experience."

Hank's sister playfully socked her husband's shoulder. "You'll never let me live that down. Will you?"

"Absolutely not. It was entirely your—"

Hank slammed the door and missed the rest of Ryan's response. It helped calm his misgivings to hear Bethany's muffled giggles coming through the window glass. No one could argue that she and Ryan were the perfect couple or that theirs was a match made in heaven. Against all the odds and despite Bethany's paraplegia, they'd built a fabulous life together.

If they could do it, Hank and Carly could, too.

Hank started up the pathway, his boots crunching on the white pebbles that covered the parched desert sand. Art Adams splayed a hand on the screen door to push it open and nodded a greeting as Hank ascended the steps.

"Who is it, Daddy?" a feminine voice called from inside.

Hank inclined his head at Art, crossed the porch, and stepped inside the house, his boots making hollow thumping sounds on a small square of marbled entry tile, bordered on three sides by ivory carpet. Hank took in the living room and adjoining dining area that opened onto a kitchen at the rear. The place was tidy, modestly furnished, and had that acrylic odor common to new homes with carpeting and molded countertops.

Hank no sooner registered the smell than another drifted to him, the unmistakable, never-to-be-forgotten scent that he'd come to associate with only Carly, a light but heady blend of baby powder and roses. As though his eyes were metal shavings and she was a magnet, his gaze jerked to where she sat in a rocker by the living room bay window. Sunlight slanted through the glass, limning the cloud of curly blond hair that lay around her shoulders and delineating the gauntness of her small, pinched face.

Hank felt as if a horse had kicked him in the chest. The air rushed from his lungs. His knees threatened to fold. *Dear God.* Dark circles of exhaustion underscored her wide, blue eyes. The once delicate hollows beneath her cheekbones were now prominent and sunken, making her look almost skeletal. Art had told him what to expect, but nothing could have prepared Hank for this.

He took three halting steps toward her. She tipped her head to listen, her expression growing bewildered. Her gaze was trained directly on him. He kept waiting for some sign of recognition, but none came, and he finally realized she couldn't see him—not even in blurry silhouette. In the last three weeks, she'd gone almost totally blind.

"Hank?" she whispered incredulously.

Bracing his hands on the arms of the rocker, he leaned down to get nose to nose with her so she could see his face. "Hell, no. It's the UPS man, here to collect a parcel bound for Oregon."

"What are you—?" Her question was cut short by a startled gasp when he scooped her out of the chair, one arm angled to support her back, the other behind her knees.

Hank thought he glimpsed a shimmer of joy in her beautiful eyes. Then, with an outraged little huff, she cried, "Put me down this *instant*. What on earth do you think you're doing?"

"I'm collecting my wife."

Hank jostled her in his arms to get a better hold, which had the pleasurable effect of making her grab for his neck.

"Oh, God, don't drop me!"

Not a chance. A down quilt had more substance than she did. Hank turned to leave the house and was surprised to see Art standing at the door, one arm angled out from his body to hold open the screen, his hands gripping four white plastic bags, filled to bursting with what looked like clothing.

"If I've missed anything, I'll stick it in the mail," he told Hank. "You carry her. I'll manage these."

"Daddy?" Carly's voice was shrill with disbelief. "*Do* something!"

"Like what?" Art asked.

"*Stop* him!"

His blue eyes very like Carly's, Art grinned and winked at Hank. "He's forty years younger than I am, sweetheart. I can't possibly stop him."

Hank turned sideways to maneuver out the doorway, Carly's flailing feet catching on the doorframe.

"Unless you want to be tossed over my shoulder like a sack of grain," he warned, "you'll stop that kicking."

She went suddenly still in his arms. Then she stiffened. "You wouldn't *dare*."

"Don't try me."

Hank hurried across the porch and down the steps. As he marked off the distance to the SUV with long, sure strides, Ryan jumped out, circled the vehicle, and opened the rear passenger door.

"Hi, Carly. Ryan Kendrick, here. Good to see you again."

"Hi, Carly!" Bethany called gaily from the front seat. "I came along as Ryan's copilot. We flew down in the Kendricks' old rattletrap jet."

"That's a joke," Hank inserted quickly. "It's a very nice, comfortable plane, and Ryan's an experienced pilot."

"Well, of course, it was a joke," Bethany retorted. "Ryan would never take his pregnant wife up in anything less than an airworthy plane." Bethany winced, touched her lips, and said, "Oops. I meant to save that news for later." She beamed a smile. "We're pregnant together, Carly. Isn't that totally cool?"

Carly didn't seem to register anything Bethany said. She twisted in Hank's arms, searching blindly for her father. "I'm not going with you, Hank," she insisted frantically. "Daddy? You have to do something. You can't just let him take me!"

Art swung open the rear cargo door to stuff in Carly's things. "I can and I will," he said gruffly. "A wife's place is with her husband. Go back to Oregon, sweetheart. Build a wonderful life, have a beautiful baby, and send me lots of pictures. I'm seventy-three and retired, remember. I raised my child. I want to enjoy myself from here on out. You made your bed, as the old saying goes. Don't ask me to sleep in it with you."

Hank felt Carly wince at the words and knew they'd pierced her to the quick. He gently deposited her on the back seat, half expecting her to bolt for the opposite door the instant he turned loose of her. Instead she just sat there, looking lost, forlorn, and wounded. Hank's heart gave a painful twist. The one person she'd always been able to count on had just jerked up the welcome mat and implied that he didn't want her in his life.

Hank almost closed the passenger door to tell Art he had overplayed his hand. But, no. No one knew Carly better than her father, and Hank had to trust that Art knew what he was doing. By cutting the familial ties, he'd cast Carly adrift, leaving Hank as her only anchor. As deeply as that might hurt Carly now, it might be best for her in the end. This way, she would be forced to depend on Hank, and in the doing, she'd learn that she could count on his love.

As Hank turned to shake his father-in-law's hand, he couldn't help but marvel at how far they'd come since the beginning of their phone conversation last night. Then again, maybe it wasn't so strange. They both loved the same woman.

Art's eyes swam with tears and his mouth trembled as he gripped Hank's hand. "Take good care of her," he whispered.

Normally Hank gave another man a firm handshake and quickly loosened his hold. This time, he maintained contact, trying to convey without words how deeply he loved Art's daughter and that the request was totally unnecessary. Somehow, though, with Art

struggling against tears, a mere handshake didn't
seem enough.

To hell with it, Hank thought, and hooked his left
arm around Art's thin shoulders to give him a hug.
"I'll make her happy," he whispered. "You've got my
solemn oath on it."

His thin body trembling, Art fiercely returned
Hank's embrace and whacked him on the back. "I
know you will, son. If I didn't, you'd play hell taking
her away."

"Phone collect. We get business rates, and I'll happily cover the charges. She'll need to hear from you
regularly."

As they drew apart, Art nodded and murmured,
"I'll wait a few days, give her some time to settle in."
He swallowed and brushed tears from his weathered
cheeks. "Make the most of it. I can't leave things like
this for long."

Hank nodded and turned to climb into the SUV.
Hands lying limply in her lap, shoulders slumped,
Carly stared straight ahead as he slid in beside her.
Her pale face had gone absolutely expressionless. He
considered giving her some space for a while, but then
he recalled the story Art had told him last night and
decided that was the worst mistake he could possibly
make. Instead, he looped an arm around her, drew
her snugly against his side, and didn't resist the urge
to press his face against her hair.

"I love you, Carly Jane," he whispered gruffly. "I'll
always love you. You can't distance yourself from that.
You can't run from it. You may as well stop trying."

Her painfully thin shoulders jerked as he curled his
hand over her arm.

Bethany turned and reached over the seat to pat Carly's knee. "I'm so excited to see you again, Carly. I know you and Hank have some wrinkles to iron out and need to talk. I just want to say that everyone in our family will be there to support you." She shoved some folded papers into Carly's limp hands. "Those are letters from Jake, Zeke, and the twins. They've each committed to a weekday when they will chauffeur you into town if something happens and Hank isn't available. Isn't that great? You'll never have to worry about being stranded. In addition to that, Mom and Dad have volunteered to babysit. If you go to work and Hank is busy on the ranch, daycare won't be necessary."

Carly smiled wanly but said nothing. Bethany shot Hank a worried look. He lifted his eyebrows, hoping his sister might take the hint and shut up so he could get a word in edgewise. Bethany fell quiet and turned to face forward again. It wasn't much by way of privacy, but for the moment, it was the best Hank could hope for.

He ran his hand lightly over Carly's sleeve. She wore the same white blouse that she'd been wearing that wonderful evening at Lake Lemolo before they'd first made love.

He took a deep breath and began his spiel, which he'd rehearsed a fair hundred times so he wouldn't mess it up.

"Now that I know how poor your eyesight actually was the day you fell in the pond," he began, "I completely understand how frightening a place the Lazy J must have seemed to you. I want you to know up front that I'm not angry with you for leaving me. I never was." He dragged in another quick breath.

"That's all behind us now. The condition of the ranch is no longer an issue. It's totally safe for you now. I won't go into all the details. You'll see the improvements for yourself soon enough."

"No," she said tautly. "I will not see the improvements. I'm almost totally blind again, Hank. The word *see* isn't in my vocabulary."

It was telling to Hank that she had focused on her failing eyesight and hadn't asked how he'd managed to afford the improvements. That was, after all, the reason she'd given for leaving him in the first place, a deep concern about him going into debt. Art was right. This wasn't so much about their ability to overcome the obstacles, but more about Carly's fear that he'd want out of the relationship once the excitement wore off.

The fact that she didn't know how much he loved her made him want to shake some sense into her. He wasn't an untried kid with raging hormones, no depth, and a complete lack of honorable intent. He was a grown man who knew his own mind. When he gave his heart to a woman, it was forever.

But that was a discussion for later, something they needed to address in private. For now, he could only say he loved her and assure her that he hadn't taken a huge financial risk by doing the necessary improvements to the Lazy J. To that end, he launched into an explanation, telling her how Ryan had floated him a sizable, no-interest loan, which they could repay over time.

"Whatever you do, don't say thank you," Bethany inserted. "The truth is, Ryan backed the project as much for my benefit as yours." Hank's sister went on to describe how trapped she'd always felt on the Lazy

J. "It's so wonderful now, Carly! There are cement paths going all over the place. I took Sly down to the creek yesterday all by myself. It's only ankle deep in most places, a perfectly safe place for him to play, but before, my chair always got bogged down in the swampy earth. Now I can wheel along, no problem, and keep an eye on him while he chases salamanders."

Carly flashed a brittle smile. "That's great, Bethany."

Listening to Carly's stilted half of the exchange, Hank could only wonder how long it might be before she let down her guard and dared to feel happy for herself.

The return flight to Oregon in the Kendrick family jet seemed interminably long to Hank, even though they landed on the Rocking K airstrip less than four hours later. His nerves were shot by the time he got Carly and her belongings transferred from the plane to his truck. The tension only increased during the forty-minute drive to the Lazy J.

After parking his truck near the main house, Hank drew the keys from the ignition, cupped them loosely in his hand, and stared sadly across the ranch. Everywhere he looked, there were cement walkways, bordered on both sides by metal railings. It had been no easy task to plan the layout so large trucks and heavy equipment could pass through the fencing to reach the vast expanses of Lazy J land beyond the creek. Hank and Jake had spent hours going over the blueprints and requesting changes so the ranch would be a friendly place for the handicapped, yet still fully operational.

Over the last three weeks, Hank had imagined this

moment a hundred times, picturing the glow of happiness on Carly's face as he took her for a tour. Now, after talking to her father about her past, he knew it wasn't going to play out that way. Before Carly could experience joy, real joy, she had to revisit one of her greatest heartbreaks, and he was the unlucky bastard who had to force her to take that final walk down memory lane.

"Well," he pushed out, "we're finally home." He leaned across the cab to unfasten her seat belt. "Go have a look."

"I can't look," she reminded him stonily.

"Okay," he replied with exaggerated patience, "go have a *feel*."

Her lips thinned to a grim line. "You're joking, right? Been there, done that. I'm not going anywhere on this ranch by myself."

After five hours of trying to coax a smile from her, Hank's patience really had worn thin. He guessed maybe that was a good thing. If he could get his temper up just a little, it would make what he had to do a whole lot easier.

He deliberately thought of how unfair she was being to him. That inched his blood pressure up a notch. How dare she compare him to an eighteen-year-old kid? He could get really pissed when he thought about the injustice of that. To add insult to injury, she actually believed he'd love her only as long as it was fun, that when the going got tough, he'd bail. That raised his blood pressure several more notches.

He could do this. All he needed to do was focus on his side of it, and he'd be well on his way to seeing red. He stared for a moment at the ranch again, thinking of the fortune he'd spent on all the changes. Had he gotten a thank-you? No. So far, she hadn't even given him an attaboy.

He threw open his door, swung out, slammed it closed with enough force to shatter window glass, and circled around to her side of the vehicle with angry strides. She had huddled in her corner the entire trip, so she nearly pitched out of the truck when he jerked open her door. He caught her from falling, then grabbed her at the waist and swung her unceremoniously to the ground. She flinched when he drew back and booted the door closed.

"Are you wanting to fight with me, Carly Jane?" he asked, his voice several decibels louder and a whole lot angrier than he intended. "Because if you are, let me give you fair warning. I've busted my ass for three weeks with very little sleep, trying to perform miracles here. I'd appreciate just a little cooperation and gratitude."

"I asked you for nothing."

"I did it anyway. You promised me. Your best shot at forever. That was the bargain! Don't renege on the deal."

"I gave it my best shot!"

"You did not. You ran at the first sign of trouble."

"I almost died."

"But you didn't die. And now that all the problems are fixed, you won't turn loose of what happened."

She set her jaw, lifted her chin, and clamped her arms around her waist. "Would you stop yelling?"

"No, I won't. Not until you see reason."

"You're the one being unreasonable. You want me to live out here and give up all semblance of an ordinary life."

"That is *not* true!"

"Stop yelling! You can't intimidate me. I'm not the least bit afraid of you."

"Liar." He leaned down so their noses were scant inches apart, making her rear back with a start. Jabbing a finger at her chest, he said, "Body language 101. I got straight A's. Yours screams, 'Don't touch me!' Well, news flash, darlin'. I'll touch you any damned time I want. You're my wife!"

"That's a situation that can be easily rectified in a court of law any damned time *I* want!" she flung back.

Hank heard the front door of the main house open. He glanced around to see his brother Zeke start to step out onto the veranda. Zeke took one look at Hank's face and eased the door closed again. Good thing. This was going to get worse before it got better, possibly a hell of a lot worse.

Hank turned back to his wife. "You'll divorce me over my dead body. I'll chain you to the bedstead before I allow that to happen."

"Don't threaten me. It worked once. Never again. You talk a mean game, but you're a big old teddy bear when it comes to carrying through on it."

A big old teddy bear? Until she said that, Hank had mostly been pretending to be mad. Now he actually felt pissed. He'd been called every filthy name in the book at one time or another. But a teddy bear? *That* was an attack on his manhood.

If she wanted mean, by God he'd show her mean. He dipped, caught her behind the knees, and slung her over his shoulder, taking care to make her landing soft. She shrieked like a banshee, curled her hands over the back of his belt, and stiffened her arms to shove upward. "*What* in God's *name* are you *doing*?"

Hank wasn't sure what the hell he was doing, only

that it felt good to finally do something. *Three long
weeks*. He'd missed her so bad that he'd cried like a
baby a couple of times, terrified at the thought of
living the rest of his life without her. Now she was
acting like he had fleas.

He knew she loved him, damn it. She'd shown him
her love in a hundred different ways. He'd seen it in
her eyes, felt it in her touch. A woman like Carly
didn't give herself so completely to a man unless her
heart was part of the package. He'd never kissed her
yet without her melting into his arms, as pliant and
sweet and warm to his touch as melted taffy.

With that thought in mind, Hank headed for the
cabin. If she was still threatening to divorce him when
he got through with her, his name wasn't Hank
Coulter.

"Put me *down*!" she yelled.

"Sorry. It ain't happenin'. I'm chaining you to the
bed and making love to you a dozen times a day until
you admit how much you love me."

"Oh, for Pete's sake." She relaxed her arms to let
herself dangle. "This is absurd, Hank. You know you
don't mean it. What can you possibly hope to prove?"

Good question. What was he thinking? He'd gotten
way off track. Making love wasn't part of his strategy.
At least not yet. The woman made him weak in the
head.

Hank veered right, which made her squeak in alarm
again. "Where are you taking me?"

He didn't answer. Never breaking stride, he covered
the distance to the new walkway that led to the cabin.
Once at the railing, he stooped to set her down,
opened the gate, and pushed her through.

"Where am I?" she asked in a thin voice, patting

the air around her with open hands. "Hank?" A thread of panic wove through her tone as she said his name. "Don't leave me out here!"

He curled his hands over the top rail, straightened his arms, and bent his head, struggling to collect his thoughts. It was a no go. He loved her too much to calmly accept her indifference, even when he knew what caused it.

"Hank, please!" she cried, her panic growing more pronounced.

He raised his head to look at her. She was reacting just as he'd hoped. On all counts, his plan was playing out perfectly. She believed he was angry with her. She was blind and had no idea where she was, only that she was surrounded by death traps. He saw the terror in her eyes, the apprehension in every line of her body. She honestly believed that he might turn his back and leave her there.

"I'll never leave you, Carly," he rasped out. "Not today, not tomorrow, *never*. I'm not Michael."

She flinched at the name. Her eyes quickened with tears, and her already pale face lost even more color. "Who told you about Michael?"

"Imagine my surprise when I found out I wasn't the first prince who came along and swept you off your feet. It seems you omitted a few details about your teens. There was one boy who gave you a second look. Why didn't you tell me about him?"

She knotted her hands into fists at her sides. "It was none of your business," she said fiercely.

"Bullshit! If ever it was anyone's business, it was mine. When your father told me the story last night, it was like a light came on in my brain. The mystery surrounding Carly, suddenly solved. It explained ev-

erything—your shyness the first time we met, your re-
luctance to even speak to me afterward, your absolute
refusal to accept my financial help, let alone marry
me. I was prince number two, and even worse, I was
true to form, a worthless bastard who only wanted
you for sex."

"Stop it!"

Hank fell back a step, then vaulted over the railing
to join her on the walkway. "I can't stop, Carly. Some
things have to be said. You've been afraid I was another Michael ever since we met. He pretended to
love you, he pretended not to care that you were
blind, and you were too young and naive to realize
he had an ulterior motive, namely to get in your pants.
Isn't that right?"

"I'm not going to discuss this!"

"Fine. Don't. I'm doing okay on my own, thanks to
your dad."

She gulped and shook her head. "I can't believe he
told you."

"Why wouldn't he when he saw you throwing away
a chance to be happy? I thank God he talked to me.
At least now I know what I'm really up against. It
isn't about improvements to the ranch so you can be
independent. It's about your terror of needing someone—of believing in someone. For a time, you set
your fears aside and dared to believe I really loved
you. But then you fell in the pond, and all the fears
came rushing back. It was only a matter of time before
you'd completely lose your sight, and then you'd be
the reject no one wanted again, not to mention a big
pain to anyone who loved you. Rather than face that,
you ran, feeding me a line about not wanting to de-
stroy my life. Better to dump me first. Right? Better

to cut your losses and get out with your pride intact than to stay with me and get hurt again."

"*Stop* it!" She swung away to escape him and bumped into the railing. Using it to guide her, she fled the way they'd come, moving back toward the main house. She went several feet before she came to an intercom station. When her hand bumped into the metal box, she stopped and traced its shape. "Wh- what is this?" she asked in a panicked voice. "Where am I?"

"You tell me," he challenged.

She found a braille tag and trailed trembling finger- tips over the bumps. "The stable?" She ran her thumb over the raised arrow that pointed the way. Then she found the tags that directed her to the cabin and main house. "Oh, Hank," she whispered, her voice raw with pain.

"Directly to your left are perpendicular gates," he said hoarsely. "One leads to the stable, the other to the main house. They swing either way and close by themselves. You'll always know when you reach a gate that you've come to an intersection. Not that you care. You want no part of this world I've created here for you because loving me and trusting me and counting on me is too scary a proposition."

She cupped a hand over her mouth and just stood there, trembling.

"I did all this to have a life with you, Carly. Because I love you and can't stand to be away from you."

She sent him an imploring look, a wealth of pain shadowing her eyes. "I'm going blind!"

Hank's heart broke a little as he studied her. Direct eye contact, head held high. She'd been perfecting the act all her life, and she was damned good at it. No one would guess, just by looking at her, that she couldn't see. "You're already blind," he said softly.

"Not completely."

"Close enough. You can only see my face when I'm almost nose to nose with you." He moved a step closer. "Where am I, Carly?" He took another step. "Right beside you! That's where I am. You're blind, and I'm still here. Get used to it. There are a lot of Michaels in the world, but, God damn it, I'm not one of them."

Her face twisted, and a ragged sob tore up from her chest.

"Remember him for what he was!" he cried. "He was a spoiled, selfish little jerk who didn't give a shit about anybody. He thought you'd be an easy mark, that you'd give him sex if he paid you a little attention. He dated you for a few weeks, gained your trust. Then the night of the bonfire party out by the lake, he took you for a walk in the woods, demanded more than just kisses, and you told him no."

"Oh, Hank, *don't*. You already know the story. Why go over it, blow by blow?"

"I'm trying to make a point."

"What point?" she cried. "Just make it and be done with it then!"

"I'm nothing like Michael."

"I know that."

"Do you? From where I'm standing, that's not real clear, Carly. So we're going over the story, count by count, to establish, once and for all, that I'm nothing like him. The little shit left you out there, for God's sake, never sparing a thought for what might happen to you."

"*Don't*," she whispered.

Hank had gone too far to turn back now. "While trying to find your way back to the fire, you ran into trees, fell over logs, tripped in the rocks. Your father says there wasn't a spot on you that wasn't bruised and scratched. And the crowning glory was that you fell in the lake. Isn't that right?"

She nodded, her shoulders jerking violently as she struggled to hold back tears.

"That's why you're so terrified of water—because you damned near drowned that night. More importantly, it's why you're afraid to believe I love you. Deep down inside, where reason holds no sway, you're afraid that sooner or later, I'll get tired of having a chain around my neck and walk away. Maybe I won't leave you alone in the woods, but I'll leave you, sure as rain, and there you'll be, alone, helpless, and scared to death because you were dumb enough to trust in some bastard's promises again."

She finally lost the battle and started to weep, her sobs ragged and dry, the sounds tearing up from deep within her. Hank hooked a hand over the back of her head and drew her against him. He was foolish enough to hope it was over, that she'd be able to turn loose of it now and see it for what it was, an awful memory that had nothing to do with them or their future.

Not. She balled her fists and pummeled his shoulders. "I *heard* you! That night, after I fell in the pond. I *heard* you, Hank!"

He had no clue what she was talking about.

"You were in the living room," she cried. "I heard you sobbing. And then you said, 'Oh, God, what if I can't do this?' "

His stomach dropped. The pain he saw in her eyes almost took him to his knees.

She gulped and held her breath, no longer hitting him, just standing there, rigid with pain, her back arched to put distance between their bodies. In a thin voice, she said, "Afterward, you didn't want me. I tried to make love with you, and you pushed me away. You were the one who broke our agreement. You *promised* me. No staying with me out of a sense of duty. You promised!"

"Oh, God." Hank remembered that night vividly. He'd relived those last hours with her a dozen times over the last three weeks. And she was right; she'd tried to arouse him, and he'd turned her away. "Sweetheart, *no*. You misunderstood."

She averted her face, clearly not believing him.

"I couldn't make love to you. I was too upset. You'd almost died that day. I blamed myself. You'd told me, over and over, that I had no idea of your special needs, and I didn't listen. My stupidity almost killed you. I felt so guilty—and I was terrified I couldn't make the ranch safe. It wasn't that I didn't want to be with you. I wanted that more than anything. I hadn't stopped loving you. How could you think that?"

The moment he asked, he knew it was a stupid question. With her past to muddy the water, of course she'd thought that. He grabbed her arm and drew her back to the intercom station. Like a crazed man, he grabbed her finger and started punching buttons. "That's a direct line to the main house. That's connected to the stable."

After taking her through the sequence of buttons, which called every building on the ranch; he pushed her finger against the panic button. The shriek of the outside alarms pierced the silence, and she nearly jumped out of her skin. Hank quickly depressed the button again to turn it off.

"The emergency alarm!" he cried. "Just in case the pager and intercom lines aren't enough. Would a man who doesn't love you go to these lengths? Damn it, Carly! I love you with every fiber of my being! If I didn't, I would have left you in Arizona."

Violent sobs racked her body. Hank drew her back into his arms. At first he just let her cry. When her sobs finally began to abate, he began to rock her, stroking her hair, kissing her brow, loving her as he'd never loved anyone.

"You're blind, Carly. And I'm still here. If something happens and the next surgery fails, I'll still be right here, holding you, loving you, unable to draw an easy breath without you. I won't ever decide I don't want you because you can't see. I'll love you with every beat of my heart for the rest of my life."

Carly pressed her face against his shirt, so exhausted she could barely think, let alone guard what she said. She was running on pure emotion now. "I thought Michael loved me," she whispered.

"I know," he murmured. "Damn it, you were only eighteen. I know, sweetheart."

"No, you don't understand." She made fists on his shirt. "I really, *really* believed him. I swore I'd never be that stupid again."

"And then I came along, a cowboy with a well-rehearsed line of bull, and you fell for it all over again." He tightened his arms around her, making Carly wish she could melt and simply be absorbed by him. "I understand how that must have hurt. And I also finally understand why you were so wary of me after that. There's just one flaw in your reasoning. I really do love you, Carly Jane, not just because you're beautiful, not just because we have fun together, not just because the sex is great. I love the whole package, every single thing about you. You can take half of those things away, and I'll still love you with all my heart."

Carly tipped her head back to see his face. "I want to believe that. But there's this place inside of me that's terrified."

"We make a great pair, then. I'm terrified, too."

"You?" She peered incredulously at his dark face, which swam in and out of a gray blur. "You're terrified?"

"Damn straight. Terrified that you won't believe I love you. Terrified that I may lose you. I'll do anything, Carly. Just name it. I'll go to counseling with you. I'll rip up every damned walkway on the ranch and redo them to suit you. Just, please, don't ask me to live without you. That's the one thing I can't give you, sweetheart, your freedom."

The husky sincerity in his voice went a long way toward convincing Carly that he truly did love her. The tension she felt in his big body took her the rest of the way. He honestly was afraid that she might leave him. Knowing that gave her the courage she needed to stay.

Cupping his face in her hands, she went up on her tiptoes to touch her mouth to his. He groaned and ran his hands into her hair, then tipped his head to gain control of the kiss, his lips claiming hers in a moist, white-hot joining of tongues that robbed her of breath and made her head swim. *Hank.* She ran her hands down his neck, curled her fingers over his shoulders, trailed her palms down his arms to trace the bunched muscle and steely tendons under his shirtsleeves.

When she reached his wrists, he turned his hands palm up and ended the kiss to grab for breath. "These hands will always be there," he whispered. "Your strength when your own is flagging, your support when you can't stand alone. I meant those vows when I said them, I stand behind them now, and I'll still do my damnedest to honor them when I'm an old man. There's just one more vow I'd like to make."

"What's that?" she asked.

"That my eyes are yours as well. When you go blind, I'll draw pictures with words so you can still see all the beautiful things. You told me once that the most gorgeous thing you first saw was the Central Oregon blue sky. That's my vow to you, Carly—nothing but blue skies for the rest of our lives, even after you go permanently blind."

Carly hugged his neck. "Take me home, Hank."

He bent at the knees to catch her up in his arms. As he carried her toward the cabin, she gazed up at his beautiful face, drinking in every hard line and chiseled plane so she could remember it later. If she were given a choice of one thing she could remember and take with her into total grayness, it wouldn't be a sunset or a gorgeous blue sky.

It would be her memory of the love she saw shining in Hank Coulter's eyes.

Epilogue

When the newest Coulter male finally made his debut, Art Adams, Bess, Cricket, the entire Coulter clan, and all the Kendricks were gathered in the hospital hallway outside the birthing room. Hank was inside with his wife, vacillating between roles of coach and worried husband. He had delivered countless foals and honestly hadn't believed childbirth would faze him, but he was badly shaken every time Carly cried out in pain.

Instead of telling her to breathe, all he could say was, "Sweet Christ," or, "I'd give my right arm to go through this for you," or, "Why did God decide it should be women who bear the children?" Each prayer, proclamation, and question was followed with, "Never again. You hear me, Carly? I'm getting cut."

In between bouts of labor, Carly smiled weakly. "You'll get a vasectomy over my dead body, Hank Coulter. I want at least one more baby, and maybe even more than that."

"Later. I can't even contemplate it now."

Carly had no such problem. "I can get pregnant between transplants without causing serious complications."

"Does the father dying of a massive coronary qualify as a complication? I can't watch you go through this again."

When Hank Jr. was born and swaddled in birthing room blue, Hank collapsed onto a chair, his sigh so exhausted that he might have delivered the child himself. He clung to Carly's hand, the baby cradled in his other arm. Carly could see only a thick gray gloom. Just as her corneal specialist had predicted, she'd gone completely blind only a few days after Hank had collected her in Arizona, and she'd lived in grayness ever since.

Carly consoled herself with the thought that it would be only temporary. As soon as her specialist felt it was safe, he'd perform a second SK to restore her sight, and when that procedure began to fail, she could have her first corneal transplant. If all went well, and she had to believe it would, she had many years of sightedness to look forward to.

Maybe, with a little luck in her corner, Hank Jr. would be married with children of his own before her sight failed permanently. Carly could hope. Seeing her children grow to adulthood would be so wonderful. Seeing her grandchildren would be a fabulous bonus.

She just wished with all her heart that she had her sight right now so she might see her little boy.

As if Hank guessed her thoughts, he began describing their child to her. "He's so perfect, Carly Jane," he whispered huskily. "His hair is dark brown, just like mine, and his skin is dark as well. He's got chubby red cheeks and a mouth just like yours."

Tears filled Carly's eyes, for now that she had been sighted, she actually knew what the color red was and what color brown was and what her own mouth looked like.

"He's wearing a funny little blue stocking cap," Hank murmured. "It makes him look like a wizened little cone head."

Carly laughed, seeing their baby in her mind.

"His fingers and toes are so tiny, and they're the prettiest pink you ever saw."

Hank suddenly went quiet. Carly could almost feel his reverent awe. "Oh, *God*," he whispered.

"What?" she whispered.

"The first light of morning," he replied.

Carly could tell that the room had grown brighter. The grayness around her wasn't quite as dark.

"I wish you could see it," Hank whispered. "Pearly white, coming through the window blinds, touching the room with stripes of wispy rose and gold. It's as if angels are here and filling the room with soft light."

Carly clung to her husband's big hand, seeing it all in her mind so clearly. It was almost as good as seeing it herself. And maybe angels were there. Angels were created from love, weren't they? This room was brimming with love.

Hank bent to kiss her and slipped the tiny bundle of new life into her arms. Guiding her hands, he showed her their son's fingers and toes, whispering, "Have you ever seen anything so tiny and perfect?"

As they stripped their baby naked, Hank painted pictures with words so Carly could see everything in her mind's eye. There was such love in his voice as he described their son's bowed legs, his swollen belly, the umbilical cord, and his wrinkled little face. He said each word with such heartfelt devotion and tenderness. Carly wondered now how she ever could have believed this man might not want her because she was less than perfect.

A lovely warmth filled her, and with an exhausted sigh, she let her eyes fall closed. She had known all her life that she would see only for a time and then go blind again in her later years. Never, though, had she imagined that she would be able to face the eventual return of blindness with such peace.

With Hank at her side, she would never really be blind again. His eyes were hers, just as he'd vowed. When they grew old, they would take walks at sunset, and she'd be able to see everything. His gift to her—pictures painted with words. Love wasn't about easy, according to Hank. It was about sticking through thick and thin. He would always be with her, unless death took him first, and even then, Carly knew she'd never be left in complete darkness again.

She would have the love of this man to light her way.

Dear Readers:

I am often asked how I come up with a story idea, so I'd like to take this opportunity to answer that question before it's asked. When I wrote *Phantom Waltz,* I received hundreds of letters from readers who loved the story and said it was unforgettable. A small percentage of those letters were from women with physical handicaps. They waned to thank me for giving them a romance about a young woman in a wheelchair. Finally, they said, a story about someone like them! Even better, with the publication of *Phantom Waltz,* it was proven, once and for all, that a romance featuring a disabled heroine could be just as magical and fun to read as any other romance, have mass-market appeal, and hit the bestseller lists.

Some of the women who wrote to me were paralyzed, like the heroine in *Phantom Waltz,* but just as many had other afflictions, such as MS, deafness, and blindness. *Phantom Waltz* was a break-out book of sorts for them, and they were excited because it was so enthusiastically accepted by such a broad audience. It gave them hope that other authors would follow my lead and give them more love stories about women who are physically challenged.

One of these young women who wrote to me, Melissa Lopez, particularly captured my interest because she'd been born blind, had recovered her sight in her early twenties, and would be able to see for only a period of time before her eye disease once again robbed her of sight. Never have I known anyone with such a positive, upbeat attitude or such courage as Melissa Lopez. After hearing her life story, I was hooked, and I knew I had to write a book about lattice dystrophy, a disease that was first discovered in 1967 and was not diagnosed in Melissa until she was twelve years old. Hearing about how her parents and grandmother supported her in her blindness, even when doctors claimed that she could see, brought tears to my eyes. Learning that Melissa's sister and friends were her guides throughout childhood also touched me deeply. Such love and unfailing devotion deserved a tribute!

Melissa was very excited to learn that I wanted to write a book about someone with lattice dystrophy. It was a big undertaking for me, and I might have lost courage if not for her steadfast interest and frequent input about the disease, how it affects the eyes, and the many ways in which it makes everyday life a challenge. Melissa was on the phone several times with her doctor, William E. Whitson, to ask him questions so this story would be accurate. As a result, I'm indebted to both her and her physician for providing me with the information I needed to accurately depict the disease in *Blue Skies*.

Blue Skies is entirely a work of fiction and in no way reflects the story of Melissa's life. I hope all of you enjoyed reading it. It is my hope that, in the tradition of *Phantom Waltz,* it will touch your heart and become a keeper on your bookshelf.

Sincerely,
Catherine

Zeke saw a boy, who looked to be about twelve, racing from behind the house. Just the way the kid ran, shoulders hunched and body low to the ground, told Zeke that trouble was afoot. Cursing under his breath, he swung out of the vehicle.

"Hey!" he yelled.

T-shirt flapping and sneakers flying, the kid never broke stride. Zeke watched him cut across the field that lay between his forty acres and the neighboring farm. *Fantastic.* He could well remember being that age. Summers in the country could be long and boring for a boy who wasn't kept busy, and boredom often led to mischief.

The late afternoon sunlight burned through Zeke's blue shirt as he strode along the west end of the house to see what the kid had been up to. When he reached the side porch, he saw a splash of red on the cream-colored siding just below the kitchen window. He snapped to a halt and then circled the flagstone steps to get a better look. The pulp of a ripe tomato had been splattered on the new paint.

"Damn it!" Swearing enough to turn the air blue, Zeke rounded the corner of the house to find countless more splotches of red on the siding. And that wasn't all. The family room slider and bathroom window were shattered, and the door of the storage shed hung from one hinge, the cross bucks broken clean in two.

When Zeke turned to survey his garden, a wave of regret washed over him. His tomato plants and corn looked as if a tornado had flattened them. Fury, sudden and searing, fired his blood. This wasn't mere mischief, but malicious vandalism. The tomato stains would never wash off his house. He'd have to repaint. And that wasn't to mention the cost of replacing the windows and storage shed door.

Spurred by rage, Zeke set off across the field, following the boy's footprints. *What the hell is the world coming to?* he asked himself as he marked off the distance with angry strides. Just as he suspected, the kid's tracks led directly to the old farmhouse, a white, two-story monstrosity with a wraparound veranda, peeling paint, and a green shingle roof sorely in need of repair. As Zeke entered the patchy side yard, which was peppered with shady elms and oaks, he saw movement on the front lawn. His steps long and purposeful, he circled the house, hoping to collar the child before he escaped inside.

Instead of finding the boy, Zeke came upon a woman. No question about her gender. She was bent over a long plank table, struggling to cover an assortment of odds and ends with a blue plastic tarp that kept catching in the breeze. Her skimpy black dress rode high on her bare thighs, revealing long, shapely legs the color of coffee generously laced with cream. When she stretched farther forward to catch the tarp, her hemline inched higher. *Sweet Lord.* If he had known someone like this lived next door, he'd have come over to borrow a cup of sugar.

"Excuse me," he said to her attractive backside.

"Oh!" Startled by his voice, she jerked erect and spun around.

The front of her was just as delightful to look at as the back. Normally Zeke preferred fashionably slender women, but he quickly decided there was something to be said for females who were generously round in all the right places, especially when the roundness was showcased in clingy black stuff that revealed every dip and swell.

"I'm sorry. I didn't hear you drive up." She tugged her skirt down and fluttered a hand at the collection of stuff on the table. "I was just closing up shop until morning, but if you'd like to take a quick look, feel free. This is the third day, and I just marked everything down."

Zeke decided she was having a yard sale. Unfortunately, the only item of interest didn't sport a price tag. Despite the heavy layer of makeup, she was beautiful. A mane of curly black hair cascaded past her slender shoulders, which were bare except for black straps no wider than spaghetti strings. Her mouth was lush, soft, and defined with deep burgundy gloss, the lower lip pouted and glistening in the sunlight, the upper shaped in a tempting bow. Above the bodice of the dress, full, creamy breasts plumped up, displaying a dusky cleavage that invited him to stare. Raised to be a gentleman, Zeke resisted the urge, dropped his gaze, and found himself staring at her legs, instead. *Not good.*

He caught the scent of vanilla, which rattled him even more. His most pleasurable moments were spent in the kitchen. "I, um—I'm not interested in buying anything," he finally found the presence of mind to say.

Smoothing her short skirt again, she gave him a questioning look, her sherry-brown eyes warming as she smiled. "Are you here to see my father then?"

For an awful moment, Zeke couldn't recall why the hell he was there. Then he glanced at his feet, saw a chunk of tomato clinging to the toe of his western-style boot, and remembered in a rush. Before he could launch into an explanation, she dimpled a cheek at him and said, "Are you *sure* I can't sell you something? I have a set of Ping golf clubs that are like brand new."

You could sell me almost anything. Zeke shook his head. "I'm not into golf."

Her eyes fairly danced with mischief. "I've also got every issue of *Playboy* dating back to March 1970. You can have the entire lot for a dollar."

"That's quite a collection."

"Yes, well, Robert is—" She broke off and shrugged. Something dark flashed in her eyes, momentarily veiling the shimmers of brightness. "He's an enthusiast, I guess you might say."

Zeke wondered how any man in his right mind could ogle other women when he had something like this at home. With a soft sigh, she regained her composure, and the shadows left her eyes. Her mischievous smile was infectious, and Zeke found himself grinning.

"You aren't, by any chance, getting a divorce?" he asked.

"Done deal. Now I'm just trying to recoup some of my losses and exact a little revenge while I'm at it. I don't mean to be rude, but I'm running late for work. If you're here for eggs or milk, you'll find my dad in the house."

Zeke wondered what kind of work she did, to be dressed like that. *Don't even go there, son.* She looked to be in her late twenties or early thirties, which, if she had married young, put her at about the right age to be the tomato thrower's mother. Zeke looked into her pretty eyes and regretted his reason for being there.

"I'm Zeke Coulter. I live next door."

"Ah, Pop's new neighbor." She finished drawing the tarp over the table and stepped forward to offer him her hand. "It's good to finally meet you. Right after you moved in, I baked you a cake, but it met with disaster before I got it out of the oven. My daughter Rosie jumped rope in the kitchen."

"Uh-oh. Rope jumpers and rising cakes don't mix." Taking care not to squeeze too hard, Zeke shook hands with her. Her fingers felt slim and soft against his callused palm. "That's a shame. I love a good cake."

"I didn't say it was a good cake." She wrinkled her nose. "I'm not much of a cook, I'm afraid. It probably would have fallen, regardless. Rosie just gave me a good excuse."

With those looks, who needed culinary skill? Zeke hated to let go of her hand. "And your name is?"

"Oh!" She laughed again and rolled her eyes. "I'm sorry. Natalie Patterson." She tugged her fingers free and glanced at her watch. "I'm sure you'd like to meet my father."

"Actually, meeting your father isn't what brought me over." Zeke wished he knew a gentle way to say this, but straight and to the point was more his style. "When I got home from work a few minutes ago, I saw a boy running from my backyard. I followed him here."

Her smile slowly faded. "That would be my son, Chad. Is there some sort of problem?"

"You could say so, yes." Zeke told her about the vandalism to his property. "At a quick guess, if I do the repairs myself, I'd say about a thousand dollars worth of damage has been done. That isn't to mention all my hard work on the garden, down the drain. I've been babying those tomato plants since early June, and the fruit was just getting ripe enough to pick."

Her finely arched brows drew together in a frown. "Oh, Mr. Coulter, I'm so sorry."

Zeke had expected her to jump to the defense of her son, not immediately conclude that the boy was guilty. "No sorrier than I am."

Natalie's slender throat convulsed as she swallowed. "Look, Mr. Coulter." Her gaze chased off to the fields. "I'm sure you're not interested in our family dynamics. Suffice it to say that I know Chad did the damage to your house and garden. No contest." She looked him straight in the eye again. "It's just—well, I'm not in the best position right now to make restitution. Things have been tight." She swung her hand at the table behind her, which told him the yard sale had been prompted more by sheer necessity than a need for revenge. "I'd like to say I could pay you next month—or the month after that." She straightened her shoulders. "But the truth is, I honestly don't know when I'll be a thousand dollars ahead. Would you let me make installments?"

Zeke understood that this must be a difficult time for her. On the other hand, though, her son had damaged Zeke's property. Zeke didn't want to be a hard ass and call the cops, but there was no way he could let it slide, either. When a boy inflicted costly damages, he had to be held accountable.

Zeke rubbed his jaw. He didn't want this prank, if it could be called that, to go on Chad's record. "How about if we strike a deal?"

Her eyes filled with suspicion. "What kind of deal?"

"I was thinking that Chad could work off the debt. It'll be cheaper if I do the repairs myself. Why can't he come over and help me?"

"I'm not sure that's a good idea."

The more Zeke considered the solution, the more he thought it was a great idea. Inspired, even. The kid had a problem. A little hard work might be good for him. "The way I figure, if I pay minimum wage, he owes me"—he broke off to do some quick calculations—"about a hundred and forty hours. Calculating on a forty-hour week, that works out to be"—he paused again—"three and a half weeks."

She looked distressed. "But he has *camp.*"

"Camp?"

"At the Lake of the Woods the last of August. He goes every year."

Zeke arched an eyebrow. "Isn't camp expensive?"

"It's church camp. The kids raise the money themselves with bake sales and car washes. So much else has been turned upside down in his life. I can't take that away, too."

"This is the boy's mess to clean up." It seemed simple enough to Zeke. If you screwed up, you had to pay. "He'll work off the debt himself, or I'll call the law, your choice."

"But—"

Zeke had been raised by his father's iron hand. Right was right. If he'd been in Chad's shoes, he'd have gotten a whipping and still been made to work off the debt. "Let me make myself clear, Mrs. Patterson. I'm bending as far as I intend to bend."

"Chad is very—" She broke off to fix him with an imploring look. "He's been through so much, Mr. Coulter. Things you don't understand. He's very delicate right now."

Delicate? The kid was a bank robbery waiting to happen. "That's my offer. Take it or leave it."

"I understand that you're angry. That's one of my concerns. I don't want my son indentured to an unreasonable taskmaster for three and a half weeks. He needs to go to camp. He needs the interaction with other kids and some time with the counselors."

He needed a swift kick in the ass. But Zeke was through arguing. "I'll expect to see your son at my door at eight tomorrow morning," he said in his "boss" voice. "If he doesn't show, I'll turn this matter over to the police."

Zeke didn't trust himself to stand there, looking into those pleading brown eyes, so he pivoted and took off. He'd gone about three paces when he heard a malevolent hissing sound. Before he could whip around, something bit him on the ass. He whirled to confront a flapping, maniacal gander, bent on doing him physical injury.

"Chester! Stop it!" Natalie cried. "Oh, God, Mr.

Coulter, I'm sorry! Rosie must have let him out. I've had him in the pen all day because of the yard sale. He hates strangers."

Trying to maintain his dignity, Zeke swatted at the gander as it flapped its way airborne to nip at his chest. *Problem.* There was nothing meaner or more viciously effective than a gander protecting its territory. Not even the sight of a rottweiler was as ominous.

Zeke did the only thing any self-respecting cowboy could do.

He ran.

Join top authors for the ultimate cruise experience. Spend 7 days in the Western Caribbean aboard the luxurious Carnival Elation. Start in Galveston, TX and visit Progreso, Cozumel and Belize. Enjoy all this with a ship full of authors, entertainers and book lovers on the **"Get Caught Reading at Sea Cruise"** October 17 - 24, 2004.

PRICES STARTING AT $749 PER PERSON WITH COUPON!

Mail in this coupon with proof of purchase* to receive $250 per person off the regular **"Get Caught Reading at Sea Cruise"** price. One coupon per person required to receive $250 discount. For further details call **1-877-ADV-NTGE** or visit **www.GetCaughtReadingatSea.com**

*proof of purchase is original sales receipt with the book purchased circled.

Carnival.
The Most Popular Cruise Line in the World.

- -

GET $250 OFF

Name (Please Print)

Address   Apt. No.

City   State   Zip

E-Mail Address

See Following Page For Terms & Conditions.

For booking form and complete information go to www.getcaughtreadingatsea.com or call 1-877-ADV-NTGE

Carnival Elation

7 Day Exotic Western Caribbean Itinerary

DAY	PORT	ARRIVE	DEPART
Sun	Galveston		4:00 P.M.
Mon	"Fun Day" at Sea		
Tue	Progreso/Merida	8:00 A.M.	4:00 P.M.
Wed	Cozumel	9:00 A.M.	5:00 P.M.
Thu	Belize	8:00 A.M.	6:00 P.M.
Fri	"Fun Day" at Sea		
Sat	"Fun Day" at Sea		
Sun	Galveston	8:00 A.M.	

TERMS AND CONDITIONS

PAYMENT SCHEDULE:
50% due upon booking
Full and final payment due by July 26, 2004

Acceptable forms of payment are Visa, MasterCard, American Express, Discover and checks. The cardholder must be one of the passengers traveling. A fee of $25 will apply for all returned checks. Check payments must be made payable to **Advantage International, LLC** and sent to: Advantage International, LLC, 195 North Harbor Drive, Suite 4206, Chicago, IL 60601

CHANGE/CANCELLATION:
Notice of change/cancellation must be made in writing to Advantage International, LLC.

Change:
Changes in cabin category may be requested and can result in increased rate and penalties. A name change is permitted 60 days or more prior to departure and will incur a penalty of $50 per name change. Deviation from the group schedule and package is a cancellation.

Cancellation:

181 days or more prior to departure	$250 per person
121 - 180 days or more prior to departure	50% of the package price
120 - 61 days prior to departure	75% of the package price
60 days or less prior to departure	100% of the package price (nonrefundable)

US and Canadian citizens are required to present a valid passport or the original birth certificate and state issued photo ID (drivers license). All other nationalities must contact the consulate of the various ports that are visited for verification of documentation.

<u>We strongly recommend trip cancellation insurance!</u>

For further details call 1-877-ADV-NTGE or visit www.GetCaughtReadingatSea.com

- -

For booking form and complete information
go to <u>www.getcaughtreadingatsea.com</u> or call **1-877-ADV-NTGE**

Complete coupon and booking form and mail both to:
Advantage International, LLC,
195 North Harbor Drive, Suite 4206, Chicago, IL 60601